Praise for
KAIKEYI

"Like the best stories, this engaging portrait will move you to take another look at the things you think you already know."
—*New York Times*

"A powerful, feminist retelling of the epic....Patel resets the balance of power, creating an unforgettable heroine who understands that it isn't necessarily kings or gods who change history." —*Washington Post*

"Patel's mesmerizing debut shines a brilliant light on the vilified queen from the *Ramayana*....This easily earns its place on shelves alongside Madeline Miller's *Circe*."
—*Publishers Weekly* (starred review)

"[A] bold reimagining....Even readers unfamiliar with the ancient Indian epic will find a lot to love in Patel's spellbinding details." —*BookPage* (starred review)

"Mythic retelling at its best: entrancing, troubling, and complicated. *Kaikeyi* is marvelous." —R. F. Kuang, author of *Babel*

"A powerful examination of a woman maligned by myth and men. Patel's imagination takes a hammer to the image of a stone-hearted villainess and reveals the woman within, whose choices sparked immortal legends. Compulsively readable and infinitely compassionate, this is the story I've been yearning for all my life."
—Roshani Chokshi, author of
The Last Tale of the Flower Bride

"The novel is compelling and rich, drawing on the source material while furnishing its characters with new complexity and motivations." —*Booklist* (starred review)

"With spellbinding twists and turns, this is a political novel and very much a feminist one." —*Kirkus*

"Patel's brilliant debut novel humanizes Kaikeyi." —*BuzzFeed News*

"A rich and engrossing debut." —*Ms.*

"Utterly captivating from start to finish. I was immersed in Kaikeyi's world from the moment I opened Vaishnavi Patel's stunning debut. *Kaikeyi* truly shines." —Genevieve Gornichec, author of *The Witch's Heart*

"Patel shines an elegant, incisive lens on an ancient epic and the vilified queen tangled within it. Brave, compassionate, and powerful, *Kaikeyi* is a novel that will live in my head and my heart for a long time to come." —Tasha Suri, author of *The Jasmine Throne*

"A lyrical and evocative retelling, full of power and grace. Kaikeyi's life is rendered with richness and nuance, yielding a story that feels both novel and classic. A spellbinding debut." —Ava Reid, author *The Wolf and the Woodsman*

"A thought-provoking, nuanced new look at one of humanity's most foundational stories." —S. A. Chakraborty, author of *The City of Brass*

"If you liked *Circe*, *Ariadne* or *The Witch's Heart*, you'll love this stunning debut." —Jenny Lawson, *The Bloggess*

VAISHNAVI PATEL

KAIKEYI

A NOVEL

REDHOOK

Copyright © 2022 by Vaishnavi Patel
Reading group guide copyright © 2023 by Hachette Book Group, Inc.
Excerpt from *Ithaca* copyright © 2022 by Claire North

Cover design by Lisa Marie Pompilio
Cover illustrations by Shuttershock
Cover copyright © 2022 by Hachette Book Group, Inc.

Redhook Books/Orbit
Hachette Book Group
1290 Avenue of the Americas
New York, NY 10104
hachettebookgroup.com

First Paperback Edition: March 2023
Originally published in hardcover and ebook in Great Britain by Orbit and in the U.S. by Redhook in April 2022

Redhook is an imprint of Orbit, a division of Hachette Book Group.
The Redhook name and logo are trademarks of Hachette Book Group, Inc.

The publisher is not responsible for websites (or their content) that are not owned by the publisher.

The Hachette Speakers Bureau provides a wide range of authors for speaking events. To find out more, go to hachettespeakersbureau.com or email HachetteSpeakers@hbgusa.com.

Redhook books may be purchased in bulk for business, educational, or promotional use. For information, please contact your local bookseller or the Hachette Book Group Special Markets Department at special.markets@hbgusa.com.

The Library of Congress has cataloged the hardcover edition as follows:
Names: Patel, Vaishnavi, author.
Title: Kaikeyi : a novel / Vaishnavi Patel.
Description: First edition. | New York, NY : Redhook, 2022.
Identifiers: LCCN 2021039925 | ISBN 9780759557338 (hardcover) |
    ISBN 9780759557321
Subjects: LCGFT: Fiction.
Classification: LCC PS3616.A86673 K35 2022 | DDC 813/.6—dc23
LC record available at https://lccn.loc.gov/2021039925

ISBNs: 9780759557307 (trade paperback), 9780759557314 (ebook)

Printed in the United States of America

LSC-C

Printing 1, 2022

To Ajji, Aai, and Ananya, three generations
of strong women

AUTHOR'S NOTE

The seeds of *Kaikeyi* were planted seventeen years ago in a discussion between my mother and my grandmother. Each summer, my grandmother would tell my sister and me stories, passing down myths and legends centered around Hindu gods and heroes that she herself had grown up hearing. One particular summer, she told us the story of how the noble prince Rama was exiled by his jealous stepmother Kaikeyi, who was convinced to banish him by her wicked servant Manthara. At this, my mother stepped in to add that Kaikeyi had actually *helped* Rama. Without Kaikeyi, my mother pointed out, Rama would have never achieved his destiny by slaying the demon king Ravana, his main adversary in the *Ramayana*. My grandmother disagreed, arguing that it was cruel to exile your child, no matter the circumstance.

And then we moved on. But their minor dispute stuck with me for years, and I would periodically search for stories told from or studying Kaikeyi's perspective to make sense of the contradiction. I never found them. Eventually, I decided to write my own. I wanted to give Kaikeyi a chance to explain her actions and explore what might have caused a celebrated warrior and beloved queen to tear her family apart. I hope that *Kaikeyi* gives voice not just to its titular character but to the many women who populate the world of the *Ramayana* and have rich and worthy lives of their own.

As a primary text, I used the Ralph T. H. Griffith English translation of Valmiki's *Ramayana*, available online through Project Gutenberg. Although there are many Sanskrit versions of the *Ramayana*, Valmiki's *Ramayana* is considered the original text—but even Valmiki's epic was born of several antecedent stories. Beyond the Sanskrit epics, there exist many other versions in a multitude of languages across South, Southeast, and East Asia.

Each of the surviving iterations of the *Ramayana* has a slightly different focus or purported author. Readers familiar with Valmiki's *Ramayana* may notice in *Kaikeyi* unfamiliar variations of the story, some of which have been inspired by these alternate tellings. For example, in some versions, including the Adbhuta *Ramayana* and the Jain *Ramayana*, Ravana is in fact Sita's birth father. The idea of Ravana as a tragic or misunderstood figure who may not be purely evil is present in many Southeast Asian tellings. And some elements that may feel new, such as Dasharath's promise that Kaikeyi's son will become king, are in fact present in Valmiki's *Ramayana*—but they are not often included in popular adaptations or dinner table recitations.

Of course, there are deviations from the *Ramayana* that are my own invention for *Kaikeyi*. There are too many to concisely name, but among the more important ones stand the presence of Ahalya's husband as Rama's tutor and Bharata agreeing to take the throne during Rama's exile. And Kaikeyi's magic and aspects of her story, including her journey to Janasthana and confrontation with Bhandasura, are my own imaginings, as much of her life is simply a blank space in the original epic. This book does not strive to be an exact retelling of any version of the *Ramayana*—it is Kaikeyi's story, and thus it is its own story.

Kaikeyi also does not seek to replicate the world, technology, or customs of any exact time period or civilization in South Asia. Instead, it draws on aspects of culture and science from across thousands of years of ancient Indian history, primarily before 1 BCE. As but one example, it borrows elements of political structure and governance from Patrick Olivelle's translation of Kautilya's *Arthashastra*, an ancient political science text purportedly written by the teacher of Chandragupta Maurya. While it would be impossible to name here every source consulted to determine, for example, the build of chariots or the type of windows or the varieties of court entertainment in ancient India, I owe a great debt to scholars of ancient civilization. Of course, creative choices have also been made in fashioning Kaikeyi's world—for example, paper was not in common use in ancient India, but is present in the narrative.

For those interested in learning more about the *Ramayana*'s evolution and breadth across its many tellings, I found A. K. Ramanujan's "Three Hundred Rāmāyaṇas: Five Examples and Three Thoughts on Translation," an essay in *The Collected Essays of A. K. Ramanujan* edited by Vinay Dharwadker, absolutely invaluable. Ramanujan's essay can also be found in *Many Rāmāyaṇas: The Diversity of a Narrative Tradition in South Asia*, a collection of essays edited by Paula Richman. I highly recommend this collection as a whole—in particular, I drew inspiration from stories recounted in Velcheru Narayana Rao's essay, *A Ramayana of Their Own: Women's Oral Tradition in Telugu*. *The Rāmāyaṇa Revisited*, a collection of essays edited by Mandakranta Bose, was also of particular use to me in thinking about the portrayal of gender and ethics in the *Ramayana*.

The *Ramayana* is not a static story. Like any myth, it evolves and changes with each telling. Even today, the Ramayana exists as a Sanskrit epic and as hundreds of different translations, as stories told around dinner tables and episodes of television shows, as movies and plays, as comics and books. Each version says something slightly different and new about these familiar characters. With *Kaikeyi*, I add my own voice to this long tradition. Thank you for reading.

MAJOR CHARACTERS

AGNI: God of fire; carries offerings to the gods

ASHA: Servant of Kaushalya and Kaikeyi

ASHVIN: Prince of Kekaya, younger brother of Kaikeyi

ASHWAPATI: King of Kekaya, father of Kaikeyi

BHANDASURA: A fire demon

BHARATA: Prince of Kosala, son of Kaikeyi and Dasharath

DASHARATH: King of Kosala, husband of Kaikeyi, Kaushalya, and Sumitra, and father of Rama, Bharata, Lakshmana, and Shatrugna

DHANTERI: Servant of Kekaya

KAIKEYI: Princess of Kekaya, Queen of Kosala, wife of Dasharath, and mother of Bharata

KAUSHALYA: Queen of Kosala, mother of Rama

KEKAYA: Queen of Kekaya, wife of Ashwapati, and mother of Kaikeyi

LAKSHMANA: Prince of Kosala, son of Sumitra and Dasharath

MANTHARA: Trusted servant of Kaikeyi

NIDRA: Goddess of sleep

RAMA: Prince of Kosala, son of Kaushalya and Dasharath

RAVANA: King of Lanka

SARASVATI: Goddess of wisdom and learning

SHATRUGNA: Prince of Kosala, son of Sumitra and Dasharath

SITA: Princess of Videha, wife of Rama

SUMITRA: Queen of Kosala, mother of Lakshmana and Shatrugna

VAMADEVA: Sage blessed by the gods, learned tutor of the princes of Kosala

VIRENDRA: Minister of War of Kosala, advisor to Dasharath

YUDHAJIT: Prince of Kekaya, son of Ashwapati and Kekaya, and twin brother of Kaikeyi

PART ONE

CHAPTER ONE

I WAS BORN ON the full moon under an auspicious constellation, the holiest of positions—much good it did me.

In Bharat, where the gods regularly responded to prayers and meddled in mortal affairs, the circumstances of my birth held great promise. This did not matter to my father, who cared only that my brother Yudhajit followed me into the world minutes later under the same lucky stars. Regardless of birth position, Yudhajit, being a boy, was the heir to the Kekaya kingdom. I was but a dowry of fifty fine horses waiting to happen. For each of my mother's subsequent pregnancies, my father made sacrifices to the gods, requesting sons. In return, he was blessed with six more healthy boys, portents of future prosperity.

The people of Bharat have often blamed my father for my sins, as if a woman cannot own her actions. He was not a perfect man, that I freely admit, but for all his faults he loved each of his sons fiercely, playing with them in his throne room, bringing them the finest tutors in all the kingdom, and gifting them ponies so they would grow into brilliant cavalrymen.

If he bears any fault for my actions, it is through his inaction.

I remember few occasions when we exchanged words, and fewer still when he sought to speak with me—save one.

My brothers and I were playing hide and catch in the sweeping field behind the palace and it was my turn to find them. I kept my eyes shut as their laughter faded into wind, opening them only after counting to twenty. I immediately saw a glimmer of movement by the stables.

I crept slowly toward whichever brother was hiding there, knowing that they would get more nervous by the second, and planning how best to catch them. I doubted it was Mohan, who was three years younger than me. He was short and slow and knew I could easily grab him. Shantanu was a bit older and was fast as a deer, but I could try to trap him by chasing him toward the palace wall. If it was Yudhajit, he would be almost impossible to catch, though maybe—

Shantanu stumbled out from behind the stable. With a whoop, I began sprinting toward him, my blood racing through my veins. But as I followed him past the side of the building, I stopped short. Had I just seen movement? I whirled around to find Yudhajit pressed against the wood, and my face split into a wild grin. He must have shoved Shantanu out of their mutual hiding spot to distract me.

I spun, chasing Yudhajit around the stable, knowing as I did that I could never beat him in an outright footrace. He rounded the corner out of sight, and from just beyond the wall came a strangled shout. A second later, my shin collided with bony flesh, and I fell onto a tangled heap of bodies, Yudhajit right below me.

"I got you!" I shouted breathlessly. Someone, probably Shantanu, groaned. I rolled off the pile and onto the hard ground, laughing, asking if they knew where Mohan was, when I saw legs coming toward me.

I sat up, squinting at the guard, aware my white kurta was smeared liberally with dirt and grass and my hair was falling from its braids, but only half-embarrassed. "Yudhajit, get up," I hissed.

"You two," the guard said, nodding his chin toward the group of us. "The raja would like to speak with you immediately."

I rose to my feet. "We can play later," I said to my brothers. "You two go, I'll find Mohan." I had started to walk away when the guard called.

"Yuvradnyi Kaikeyi, the raja wants you *now*."

I turned to look at Yudhajit, shocked. He only shrugged at me.

We trailed behind the guard back to the palace, and each of my steps felt heavier than the last. Something had to be amiss for my father to summon me. But if I had done something to anger him, why would he want Yudhajit too?

As we approached the throne room, I dragged my feet against the stone, letting the guard and Yudhajit get farther and farther ahead. At the end of the hall the guard turned and glared, waiting by the closed door until I reached him, then swinging it open in a precise movement.

Yudhajit went in first, and I lingered a few seconds longer before following him into the flickering light of the hall. He half turned his head as I approached, and the light cast strange shadows on his wide forehead and narrow nose. His dark brown eyes held a flicker of apprehension and his lips were pressed into a thin line, in what I was sure was an eerie rendering of my own face.

I took my place a pace behind him and glanced surreptitiously around the room, afraid of attracting attention. During feasts, the high-ceilinged room was filled with rows of tables and throngs of people, and its cavernous depths did not seem large at all. Absent these preparations, the wooden pillars cast long shadows, the carvings of bulls and snakes and long-plumed birds that so entertained my younger brothers fading into the gloom. The huge crackling firepits, built partially to warm the entire hall when the weather turned in the winter and partially—I suspected—to intimidate visitors, made me feel even smaller than I usually did.

My father's throne was carved out of dark wood into stark, undecorated lines, much like the man who sat upon it. One hand stroked his beard as he stared unwaveringly into the nearest pit, his thick eyebrows deeply furrowed. Despite the warmth of the flames, gooseflesh crawled up my skin, and I tried not to shiver.

After several minutes, Yudhajit, with all the patience of a twelve-year-old boy, blurted out, "Why did you call us here if you wanted to sit there and say nothing?"

Raja Ashwapati looked up at him as if he had not realized we were there. He did not spare so much as a glance for me, hidden behind my brother.

"Your mother—" he began. I glanced around the room, look-ing for her, but she was nowhere to be found. She would not have added much warmth to the room, but she was rarely cold the way Father was. Father opened his mouth, closed it, opened it again, then said, "Your mother had to leave. She will not return."

At that, Yudhajit laughed, and I winced. I wished we had learned this news from the guards, without Father present, so I could tell him it was not a prank. Had he not seen how distant our parents were toward each other, how quick to snap they were, how the edges of their relationship were fraying? But my brother, the brilliant heir, said, "We're too old for you to joke with us this way, Father. Mother is radnyi. A queen wouldn't just leave."

"Kekaya is no longer radnyi," Father said, and his eyes sought me out for the first time.

"Why—what—" Yudhajit's shoulders drooped. "Who will...?" He trailed off, apparently unable to describe what our mother actually did.

Our father sighed. "As the yuvradnyi, Kaikeyi will slowly assume some of the duties of the queenship, until you are old enough to wed."

I bit down on my tongue. The metallic taste of blood filled my mouth and I swallowed before it could stain my teeth. I had no idea how to take on any of my mother's responsibilities, nor did I have any desire to.

Yudhajit took my hand and squeezed it. "Surely Mother will come back," he said. "She would not just leave us like that."

The raja shook his head. "She told me she would never return. Kekaya is no longer welcome here."

And just like that, we were dismissed.

In the hall, Yudhajit tried to speak to me, but I brushed him aside and raced back to my room, slamming the door behind me and falling to my knees. I knew what I needed to do.

Please, I prayed to the gods, those who watched over the land of Bharat. *Please help me.*

I invoked Chandra, the god of the moon, Nasatya, the god of twins, and Kubera, the god of the north. *Please, bring my mother back. Please, grant me the knowledge I need in her absence.*

There was no reply.

The gods always answered the prayers of princesses, my tutors liked to tell me, for princesses were the most devout and holiest of all. But whether it be for rains or sunshine, for strength or knowledge, for new toys or clothes, they had never answered a single prayer of mine. Yudhajit, it seemed, had stolen all the good fortune of our birth for himself, leaving me bereft of any assistance at all.

But now, surely, they would answer. They would understand that a girl needed her mother. Who else could show me how to make my way through this world? Without her I was alone.

Kekaya did not act toward her children the way other noblewomen at court did. She never kissed my scrapes or held me when I cried after fighting with Yudhajit, never cuddled me before I went to bed at night. Instead, she taught me how to read, drawing the characters in a pan of sand and repeating them with me ten times, and ten more times, until I knew them by heart. And even then, she did not praise me. But she gave me scrolls and listened as I picked out stories.

My favorite was the churning of the ocean, that wondrous tale of the gods and the asuras together churning the Ocean of Milk, seeking in its depths the nectar of immortality. The nectar must have been unimaginably delicious for them to form such an alliance—I could understand, for I loved sweets too. As they churned, they split between them the spoils that emerged from the Ocean: a tree twisted like the claws of a tiger, with sharp red flowers that could draw blood and grant boons. Wise and powerful goddesses including Lakshmi, seated on a pale pink lotus, her hair dripping gold. Even the moon itself, a luminescent pearl caught among the waves. And at last, they found the treasure they sought.

But the gods did not wish to share the nectar with the asuras, for this demonic race had long terrorized the earth and heavens with their lust for power. They were the only beings with the power to rival the gods, and the two were often at war. And so, the great Vishnu tricked the asuras out of the share they had been promised.

"But how could the gods lie when they are good?" I asked my mother, puzzled.

"The gods do what they must," she said, but she gave me a smile and I felt clever.

When I had finished the legends, she took me alone through the maze of palace corridors and through a polished door of teak, set into the floor with a great, glinting silver handle. Together, we descended into the library cellar filled floor to ceiling with precious texts and dusty scrolls. And this felt like the greatest compliment of all. It was because of her I loved reading, consuming even the dullest treatise in my quest to learn all I could.

I had often doubted whether she even liked me, her only daughter. But now, my heart clenched oddly at the thought of losing her presence. I felt as though I could not breathe deeply enough.

I did not cry. But I continued to beseech the gods, even as the chamber grew dark around me, my knees stiff and aching from my seated position on the floor.

Finally, Manthara came to comb my hair and put me to bed. I was relieved to see her. At least I would not lose her too.

"Would you like to hear a story?" she asked, smiling at me in the mirror. "I have a new one for you."

I shook my head, crossing my arms. Normally, I would beg her for songs or tales, and she would comply until my eyes grew heavy and images of splendid feats danced beneath my eyelids. But tonight, I said nothing at all. "Kaikeyi, I know you must be upset, but—" I slipped out of the chair, my hair half-braided, and flung myself onto the bed. Manthara could not bring my mother back. She did not understand how this felt. I had been relieved to see her, but now all I wanted was to be left alone until I could go find Yudhajit. I could not take her sympathy, and I hoped if I was rude to her, she might leave. But Manthara simply stood and came to sit at my bedside. I turned away from her, and still she only clucked her tongue, one hand rubbing gentle circles into my back.

"All will be well," she said, before bending down to press a kiss on the back of my head. My eyes filled with tears, so I clenched them shut, refusing to turn my head. Eventually, she rose and blew out the candle, closing the door very quietly behind her.

Seconds passed into minutes and I continued to lie there,

waiting until the quiet of night had fully descended and I could safely leave.

Finally, breathlessly, I opened my door slowly and checked both ways, then padded down the hallway on bare feet. There were no torches, and the dark gray stone turned nearly black at this hour, the moonlight barely filtering in through the few windows lining the corridor. The low ceiling seemed to bear down on me with every step, but I was intent on my task.

"Kaikeyi?"

My heart stopped for one agonizing moment. I pressed myself against the wall as it restarted at double speed. It was only my brother, whom I had ventured out to find in the first place. "Yudhajit?"

He was a few steps away now, clad in crisp white cotton sleep clothes that had clearly not yet been slept in. His eyes shone brightly in the darkness. He too must have been waiting for this still hour to leave his room. "What are you doing up?" he asked.

"What are *you* doing up?" I retorted, not wanting to admit I had been coming to get him.

He made a face. "I asked you first."

I shrugged and started walking away, trying to feign indifference. The court had taught me patience, but it had taught Yudhajit impulsivity. Only one of us knew how to hold their tongue.

"I couldn't sleep. I miss Mother. She did not even say goodbye to us. I—I don't understand." His voice twisted and broke, and I found myself fighting back tears as well.

Unwilling to face my own grief, I kept walking, and he easily caught up to me, filling the space by my side as he always did.

We slipped like ghosts through the hallways, not wanting to return to bed just yet. In unspoken agreement, we found ourselves heading toward the door to the kitchens, our stomachs growling in unison.

Yudhajit moved ahead to open the door. I had grown distracted thinking of what sweets I might find to snack on and did not realize he had stopped until I walked right into him. He stumbled slightly but did not make a sound, pointing his chin toward the entrance. After a moment, I heard what he did—the faintest murmur of voices. We tiptoed closer, closer, closer, until the murmurs became words.

"So long as nobody learns the truth, it does not matter." I could not recognize the deep voice, resonating through the small space like the beat of an animal-hide drum.

Yudhajit, more familiar with the men of the palace, mouthed *Prasad* at me. An advisor who I had seen at formal court occasions, but never interacted with. He sat near the king, so my father likely valued him.

The second voice I recognized immediately. It belonged to my mother's former lady-in-waiting, Dhanteri. "It matters to me," she said sharply.

"It shouldn't," Prasad replied.

"I know. Manthara knows. Why keep it a secret? The children deserve to know."

"Neither of you can tell another soul, or both of you will find yourself unable to work."

Dhanteri laughed, a sound without any happiness at all. "I am already without work. The raja saw to that when he banished Radnyi Kekaya."

If our bodies had not been nearly occupying the same space, I would not have noticed Yudhajit's quiet gasp.

Banished.

I was listening, straining for answers, as though by will alone I could force these adults to tell me what I craved to know.

"Woman, she is not your radnyi anymore. You will not speak another word, or I will ensure that you are the last of your name," Prasad hissed. His tone frightened me.

I snuck a glance at Yudhajit to see if perhaps he understood what that threat meant, but he looked as confused as I did.

"If you keep your mouth shut," Prasad added, "I will see to it that you are kept on, to manage the women's work in the court."

There was silence for a moment. "As you say, Arya Prasad." The faintest rustle of cloth came from behind the door. "I will speak to Manthara."

"See that you do. So long as everyone believes Radnyi Kekaya left of her own accord, it will not matter what really happened."

Yudhajit and I backed away from the door as one, rounding the corner slowly, carefully. But when we were sure we would not be heard, we darted fast, bare feet leaving brief impressions of dampness against the cool stone. Only when we reached our rooms did we stop, facing each other and panting.

"What do we do?" Yudhajit asked. "Surely they could not have been telling the truth."

"There's nothing we can do," I said.

"We can talk to Father—"

"No!" I cut him off. "Please, we cannot tell anyone. You heard what Prasad said. If you tell anyone, Manthara will have to leave." I couldn't stomach the thought.

"You shouldn't need your nurse anymore, Kaikeyi. We're twelve, almost adults." Yudhajit scoffed. He had only recently become taller than me. I hated his new height and the way he could look down upon me now, but I hated even more that he was right. Still, I would not give up Manthara.

"Please?" I asked.

He held my gaze for a moment, then sighed and nodded. "Perhaps we can pray to the gods to change Father's mind," he said.

I shook my head at him. "The gods cannot force someone to change their mind. You know how Father is. He has made this decision, and it will be final."

Yudhajit's shoulders slumped. "I suppose."

We stood there together in silence for several moments more, until I yawned, the energy that had pushed me out of bed and through the halls finally draining out of me. Yudhajit caught my yawn, and we both grinned at each other.

Even so, when I went back into my room and climbed into bed, sleep evaded me. I stared up at the ceiling, wondering what gods my family might have displeased to have such misfortune.

CHAPTER TWO

THE NEXT MORNING, I woke with the realization that I had not tried everything to bring my mother back. I had prayed to the important gods, to the ones I knew, but she always told me I had more to learn. She had showed me the cellar full of scrolls, and what better place than that to find a minor god? Perhaps one less busy answering the prayers of others would find time for me. They might not change my father's decision, but perhaps the gods could spirit her to me in secret. Or alter her face so my father could not recognize her. I had heard of such things in stories, at least.

I had no obligations that morning, and so I set out alone for the cellar, located in a far corner of the palace. The golden light of the morning sun filtering in through the small windows did little to make the narrow corridors feel less unwelcoming. The palace was laid out in a tight, intricate maze, and without my mother to guide me, I got lost twice on the way to the library. The wooden door embedded in the floor was heavier than I remembered without my mother's help, but eventually I heaved it open, then stood on my toes to fumble a torch from the wall so I could set off down the steps.

Immediately, the earthy scent of the room filled my nose. I breathed deeply, remembering how not so long ago, my mother had explained to me where I could find whatever I might want to read.

"Here, Kaikeyi, there are old stories," she said. "And here are histories of old kings. On this shelf are scrolls of prayers and rituals, and there some older religious texts. They are not much good to read, but if you want to, you may. Anything in this room is yours to know."

At the time, I had barely paid attention to her, opening and closing scrolls like a young child at a feast, unable to believe the sight that lay before me. She simply laughed and let me explore until I settled on a geography of Kekaya and its surrounding lands. I picked it simply because I knew Yudhajit was currently studying the same geography and I wished to impress him—but my mother did not care to know such information.

She picked a scroll of her own and beckoned me over to a corner. We sat and read together for some time, and although I quickly regretted the boring treatise I had picked, I basked in the closeness to my mother.

I picked my way through painstaking details about the swirling waters of the Chandrabagha River at the northern border of Kekaya, which sprang from the high peaks of the Indra Mountains, where stone pierced the clouds, and ran until it met the gentler waves of the tumbling Sarasvati River. That river marked the southeastern border of Kekaya and was the holiest place in the kingdom. I recalled few other lessons from that scroll, but I still held within me the memory of the steady presence of my mother, the feeling that we shared something.

Now I tried to remember her explanations, walking among the shelves until I found one devoted to prayers and rituals. I could tell after only a few minutes that these would not help me—they contained nothing I didn't already know. So, I moved on to the older scrolls.

The first one I opened referenced a goddess I had never heard of. The second was a prayer to a god whose name I could not decipher. This was what I needed. I grabbed as many as I could fit under one arm and then clambered back up the stairs, closing the door with a thud and returning the torch. I crept back to my rooms, hoping to avoid attention, for I did not want to answer any questions about why I had taken these scrolls or who had shown me where to find them.

I spent all day reading. I learned about the goddess of elephants, a lesser known avatar of Lord Ganesh, and sent a fervent prayer to her, although I did not expect she could help me much. I prayed to the god of travelers, Lord Pushana, thinking this more apt, for he was one of many brothers, overshadowed by Lord Surya, whose fiery red chariot pulled the sun through the sky, and Lord Indra, who wielded a five-pronged spear of thunderbolts and ruled the gods. If anyone might be sympathetic to my plight, surely it would be him.

There were other scrolls too, about which penances would help someone obtain boons from the gods. Except these were no use, as they all required the gods to answer in the first place.

Finally, I gently unfurled a scroll that was so thin and worn it seemed to have been written over one hundred years ago. Its edges were frayed, and the patterns of the language hard to decipher. I turned my attention to the neat rows of text and tried to remember my tutors' lessons as I used my finger to trace each word.

About halfway through, I realized this text made no mention at all of gods. It was simply a meditation exercise.

I threw it aside, frustrated. After a moment, I pulled a small box of sweets from under my bed and ate one, then another and another. Slowly my anger dissipated, the sugar softening the hard knot within me. I licked my fingers clean.

Calmer, I reread the title of the scroll: "Summoning the Power of the Gods by Concentration Alone." Perhaps it was a meditation ritual that would bring general godly attention? I laid the paper down in front of me and performed each of the steps in turn: I slowed my breath, fixed my gaze at a point one hand's length from my solar plexus, concentrated my energy, and—

I must have mistranslated, for the next step, to my best estimation, read, "Let your gaze slip into the Binding Plane. If you have trouble locating such a place, seek out the threads that connect you and use the words of focus given below."

This sounded like nonsense. But still, I had nothing else to try. I committed them to memory.

My breathing slowed and I stared ahead of me, focusing as hard as I could, then recited the syllables.

Nothing happened.

I tried again, and again. Nothing. The scroll provided no further insight, for the last few lines merely stated that this art was impossible to master by all but a select few.

I set the scroll down, tears stinging my eyes. Another day, another failure. I could not bring my mother back. I remembered what Prasad had said last night about why my mother left, and anger welled up in me at the idea that my father was responsible. It did not matter what my mother had done. How could he do this to me? My brothers needed her too, but what was I to do without her guidance? A tear slipped down my cheek, then another and another, as I gathered all the scrolls in a haphazard pile and pushed them under my bed. I curled up on top of the covers until dinnertime. Then I washed my face and joined my brothers, all of us silent and pale-faced.

The kitchens must have been trying to cheer us up—the table was laden with trays of hot roti glistening with ghee, delicately spiced vegetables sending a delicious fragrance into the air, and fresh yogurt dotted with bright pomegranate. Ordinarily such a feast would've been a treat, all of us negotiating for the largest portions—but today all it did was reinforce the fact that we were to be pitied, for our mother was gone.

That night, as Manthara combed out my hair in long, gentle strokes, I asked, "What did my mother do?" If anyone knew, it would be Manthara. She was my mother's age and had been my servant as long as I could remember, attending my mother before that. She was my favorite person in the world besides Yudhajit, the one who nursed me when I was ill, sat by my side if I was afraid of monsters at night, or wiped my tears away when my brothers pushed me down.

Manthara started. "Why do you think she did something?"

"I—" I knew I could not lie to Manthara, and so after a half-hearted second of considering it, I told her the truth. "I overheard someone talking."

She sighed, her movement pausing. I turned to look at her. Her nearly black eyes were soft, sad, and the dupatta she usually wore over her head had slipped down to her bun. "Kekaya would never willingly leave you, child."

"Then why did she make Father—"

"She did not force the raja to do anything," Manthara said. "I doubt anyone could."

She returned to combing out my hair, cool fingers brushing against my neck and providing some small relief from the pressing heat. I remained quiet. I knew her well enough to suspect she had more to say.

Some time passed before Manthara asked, "Do you know about your father's boon?"

This question surprised me. Boons were powerful gifts, granted by the gods to those mortals who had won their favor through their piety or goodness or courage, after they prayed and fasted and performed intricate rituals. People who received boons rarely discussed them, as they did not wish to lose their gifts through arrogance or carelessness.

But I was aware of my father's gift—it had been granted many years ago, for his steadfast devotion to Lord Vishnu. It was a boon I found oddly whimsical, when I considered my distant and pragmatic father. I nodded, then hissed in pain as the motion caused the comb to catch on a particularly nasty tangle. "Yes. He can understand the language of birds."

I hoped to earn a boon one day, but I intended to ask for something better, wiser than the gift to comprehend the chatter of the silly myna birds or ill-tempered peacocks that frequented our gardens. I would ask to be the ruler of a great kingdom. Or for the power to heal all the sick. Perhaps I would wish for the ability to find whomever I wished, or better yet to keep the ones I loved close to me.

Manthara's voice pulled me back. "That is correct. But there is a cost to his boon. He may never divulge what he hears, on pain of death. Not to anyone." Manthara worked through the knot with her fingers, slowly separating the strands of wayward hair. "He claims that while on a walk, he was privy to a conversation between two swans, and your mother begged him to tell her what the pair had said."

I twisted around, yanking my hair out of Manthara's grasp. "Why would she do such a thing? Surely she doesn't want Father to die!"

"Who knows?" Manthara replied, pushing my head forward again. She acted very familiar with me for a servant, but I loved her and did not care. "Kekaya told me a different story, but I do not wish to contradict our king."

We were both silent as she moved in front of me to rub oil into my scalp. Her fingers pressed into my skin, relaxing me. I thought of leaning against my mother in the quiet library, the scent of scrolls and the hidden mysteries they contained all around us. I thought of the texts filled with descriptions of the gods and their boons, how none of them had warned of the path that my family had traveled down. Suddenly, the words of the meditation mantra I had read earlier leapt unbidden into my mind.

I recited them silently, sleepily, leaning into Manthara's deft hands.

All at once, a red rope shimmered into existence, starting just above my stomach and ending at Manthara's. I almost cried out. I blinked hard, sure I was imagining it—but it didn't vanish. My mouth dropped open, and slowly I lifted my hand to touch it. But my fingers passed straight through.

"Kaikeyi? Did you see a fly?" Manthara asked, her hands stilling as she glanced around the room. The rope dissolved into the air. Bewildered, I continued to stare at the area where it had been. "Kaikeyi!"

"Y-yes." I stammered the lie. "But it's gone now." I rubbed at my eyes and saw the imprint of the rope dancing behind them.

"Hmm." She went back to her ministrations.

Cautiously, I repeated the words to myself again.

The rope reappeared. I nearly toppled out of my chair, Manthara accidentally yanking my hair as I started.

"What is it?" she asked, alarmed. "Are you well?"

"I—" The rope did not change but simply vibrated in a slow pulse. There was no way to explain what I was seeing. I righted myself. "I think I am just tired." I kept my eyes fixed on the rope.

Manthara sighed. "You are a child," she said. "I am sure this must be very difficult for you. I want you to know that I spoke to your mother before her departure. She was distraught. She did not want to leave you."

I had never seen my mother express any emotion on my behalf, and this absurdity was enough to distract me briefly from the rope. "Why would my father not tell us he banished her?" I asked. As I spoke, a small current seemed to shimmer down the rope, starting at my chest and going to Manthara's.

"I do not know what goes through the mind of the raja," Manthara said. "And it is not my place to guess." She bound the end of my braid and pressed a kiss to my head. "You're ready for bed. Be a good girl and go straight to sleep."

She left, the glimmering cord between us lengthening but not thinning as the door closed behind her. I climbed into my bed and stared at the place where the rope seemed to pass through the wood. Was this even real? My heart raced with the possibilities.

As I studied the red rope, an even stranger thing happened. I noticed other glimmerings in the air. When I shifted my concentration toward them, more cords materialized, all leading back to my solar plexus and extending out through the door. There were threads of gold, broad strands of varying thickness and color, mottled woolen strings, and floss so fine I could barely see it. It seemed impossible that I could have somehow imagined such a rich tapestry—but what other explanation was there?

Or perhaps my mother's departure had driven me to madness. I shut my eyes against the onslaught of color.

When I opened them again, the web of light was gone. I breathed a sigh of relief. I wanted the gods' approval so badly that I had convinced myself that some silly meditation on an old scroll had power in it. That was all. That had to be all.

Yet still I lay in bed, once again unable to sleep, reality as I knew it warring with curiosity over this strange world, even if it was of my own creation. I turned from one side to the other, trying to find a position that would allow me to relax, but I could not remove from my mind the possibility that this was real. My skin itched, and my limbs felt restless.

Finally, I decided, I would test it out just once more. I whispered the mantra all in a rush, almost hoping that it wouldn't work. But there the strings appeared again. I could find the red one I had originally associated with Manthara, more vivid and glowing than the others.

Breathlessly, I waved my shaking fingers through the strings, but once again, they shimmered around my skin, allowing my hand to pass through.

I focused instead on Manthara's strand and imagined plucking it like the string on a veena. It leapt up, vibrating as though I had touched it.

Excitement thrummed through me. I got out of bed, lit a small lamp, and pulled the Binding Plane scroll from beneath my cot. "Seek out the threads that connect you," it said. I pondered this. Perhaps from those words, *thread* and *connect*, I had convinced myself that this mantra showed me the connections between myself and others?

Suddenly, the door swung open. The strings disappeared and I dropped the scroll, nudging it behind me as Manthara hurried in. "Are you okay?" she asked.

I hastily snuffed the candle. "Yes?" I ventured after a moment. "Are you?"

Manthara had never come into my room this late at night before, but now she stood before me in a simple shift, her hair in a long braid down her back, breathing hard. "I'm sorry to disturb you. I was lying in my room when suddenly I grew so worried about you. I just had to check—" She seemed to notice then that I was out of bed with a lamp in my hand. "What were you doing up?" she asked suspiciously.

I stayed silent for a moment, considering her words. A few minutes ago, I had pulled on the rope that I imagined connected me to Manthara, and now she was here before me. Could it be that these threads were not made up at all—that I had somehow summoned her here?

I thought the mantra to myself and gave the red rope a light brush with my mind.

Manthara took two steps forward and wrapped her arms around me. "Are you sure you're all right?" she whispered in my hair. She smelled of mint leaves and crisp cotton, warm and comforting.

I hugged her back. "Yes, of course," I said. But my mind was reeling. My hands were shaking, so I clasped them together, pulling back from her. "I was only looking for some sweets," I lied. I resolved in that moment to never tell Manthara the truth of whatever I had discovered. She would think me mad, and I could not lose her.

Even in the darkness, Manthara's squint was evident. "You had the lamp lit. Were you trying to sneak out?"

"No!" I protested, casting about for some explanation that wouldn't involve admitting to the stolen scrolls. Nothing came to mind. "I really was just hungry."

In the Binding Plane, the thread between us jumped of its own accord. Did it know I was lying? Or was this due to Manthara's skepticism? I reached out with my mind to calm it. *Please let her believe me.* And somehow, as if by magic, the thread quieted.

Why had I done that? Had I harmed her? It had happened so instinctively.

I studied her anxiously, but she appeared to be fine. She merely sighed and said, "I suppose you must not have had an appetite at dinner, with all that has happened. But you need to rest. I will sit here until you fall asleep."

I did not think I could possibly sleep, knowing these threads existed—that I had somehow brought them into existence with my words and my mind. But I hadn't anticipated the power of Manthara's hand stroking my hair, smoothing away the emotional turmoil of the day, and the heartsick ache that filled me when I thought of my mother. Sleep pulled me under before I could stop it.

CHAPTER THREE

YUDHAJIT CAME EARLY TO my room the next morning, hoping to pull me into a rematch of hide and catch. But I was tired and irritable, and by the time I joined him outside, I didn't want to run around. The day was beautiful, the sky cloudless and a vivid blue. I settled myself on the grass and grabbed a pebble instead, hoping to play a contest where we threw it up into the air and tried to clap as many times as possible instead.

Yudhajit groaned. "No, Kaikeyi. That is such a boring game."

"Well, I think your game is boring," I argued. He remained standing stubbornly before me, arms crossed.

I frowned in return. Normally, he would complain until he got his way. But today, I thought of the previous night and how I had summoned Manthara.

I silently repeated the words from the scroll and found myself gazing at a deep sapphire bond, thicker even than my connection to Manthara.

"Come on," he whined. "Let's go." As he spoke, I poked at the bond with my mind, thinking, *Can we play my game instead?*

Out loud, I said, "Please, Yudhajit?" The ripple from my touch moved down the bond until it reached my brother's chest.

He groaned again. But to my astonishment, he sat down, reaching for the pebble. "Fine, fine. We will play your game first."

I beamed at him as he threw the stone into the air.

Once might have been random, but twice? I knew better than to think so.

I watched him carefully for any sign that he knew what I had done, but he clapped his hands happily enough and then tossed the stone to me, a smile on his face. "Six! I bet you can't get seven."

I could get seven, and in fact, I had practiced this game alone just so I could beat Yudhajit. But now, watching him, and distracted by the feeling inside of me—magic! I had *power*—I only managed four claps before fumbling the stone and nearly dropping it. Yudhajit laughed at me, and after a few seconds I laughed with him. I had lost, but by making him play the game I had won. I could hardly believe it.

When we were done playing and Yudhajit had gone to his archery lessons, I spent hours wandering the palace, following different strings to discover my ties with others.

My bonds with my brothers stood out, bold and strong, while other servants and people in the palace had varying degrees of connection to me. I had so many bonds tying me to others, and seeing them all laid out this way caused tears to prick at my eyes. I often felt lonely, with only my mother's quiet coolness and brothers who could not fully understand me for company. But here was proof that I was not alone. I tried, at one point, to figure out which one was my mother's. Perhaps I could send her a message. After all, I had been trying to bring her back when I had discovered this magic. But among the tangle of strings, I could not ascertain which would lead me to her.

By the time the sun set, my muscles were aching, and I limped on trembling legs back to my room, the strain of using the Binding Plane taking its toll on my body. But my mind still thrummed, even after I lay in bed.

On ordinary nights, I would pray to Nidra, goddess of sleep, for restful slumber and pleasant dreams. She was one of my favorite gods—Manthara had told me her story on many nights when I wished to stay up instead of sleep. Once, Vishnu fell into a deep, mysterious sleep and could not be roused by any of the gods. While he slept, two asuras were born from Vishnu's own ears, and they found Brahma defenseless. They conspired to steal Brahma's powers, and Brahma was unable to withstand their might. He tried with all his power to wake Vishnu, but Vishnu would not wake. Desperate, Brahma called upon Nidra, the goddess of sleep. She slipped into Vishnu's conscience and roused him from within. And so Nidra saved the gods from the asuras.

But despite this, I knew of no rites for Nidra, no prayers or festivals for her. She was forgotten, as I was. And she was my favorite for another reason—sometimes, if my dreams were soothing or my sleep deep and restful, I could wake pretending that she had favored me.

The thought struck me then—perhaps I *was* favored. The gods had ignored me for years, but was this not a great gift indeed? Could this power be from the gods? They may have bestowed this upon me for my patience. My cheeks flushed with excitement at the possibility. I would have to search in the cellar to see if any scrolls said more about this strange magic. But for now, I clasped my hands together and whispered a prayer for Nidra.

The next evening, my father had a guest of honor for the meal, some warlord who he could not put off, even with my mother's departure. Manthara was busy with preparations, so

Neeti had been sent to help ready me. Aside from Manthara, Neeti was my favorite among our servants. She was only two years older than me and had been in the palace since we were small. We had played dolls together when we were younger, using scraps of cloth given to us by Manthara to dress them in colorful saris we were too young to wear and finding small stones and ribbons to build them gilded thrones. Even now, on the occasions she would come to ready me, we would rush through the preparations so that we could steal a few moments sitting on my floor and sharing sweets as she told me tales of her life outside the palace.

"You will never believe what my neighbor did," Neeti said, straightening out the front of my stiff silken skirt. "He has a goat now. Can you imagine it!"

But today I did not want to hear her stories, for I did not intend to go to the feast. I could not bear to see my father, pretending as though nothing had happened. Pretending as though he hadn't exiled my mother. Just thinking of him caused my fists to clench.

"Neeti." I clasped her wrist, stopping her from pinning my blouse. "Will you tell my father I am ill and cannot attend?"

"Are you ill?" Neeti asked, her thick eyebrows furrowing in concern. She was shorter than me, and one hand worried her braid as she reached up for my forehead with the other. I ducked out of her grip.

"No," I said. "But please, can you do this for me?"

She looked uncertain. "I could get in a lot of trouble," she said. "Please, Yuvradnyi, can you not just go?"

I entered the Binding Plane, the mantra racing through my mind. It was becoming easier each time. *It's a small lie; you can do it*, I told the dark orange bond between us. "You know everything that has happened," I said to her, trying to make myself look as small as possible. "I only want a bit of time."

At this, her wide mouth softened in sympathy. "It must be

very hard," she said. "I am so sorry. I suppose this is a small thing. Yes, I will do it, Yuvradnyi. Do not worry."

My heart warmed at her affection, and I wondered if I had even needed to use the Binding Plane. Neeti was my friend, after all.

Neeti turned to go, and only when she reached the door did I realize I had not even thanked her. "Wait!" I called. I reached into my secret stash of sweets and offered a handful to her. "Thank you," I said. "Perhaps you can tell me about the goat next time?"

She popped one in her mouth immediately, the dimple in her cheek flashing in delight. "Of course, Yuvradnyi." She took a small step toward me. "You...you can come and find me if you would like," she said. "If you are ever lonely." She bowed and took her leave.

I stood where she had left me, my eyes feeling hot. Nobody else had thought about whether I might be lonely, a girl in a family of men.

I scrubbed at my eyes with my hands. I had a task to do.

The corridors were deserted and dim with shadows. I made my way to the library quickly and tore through scroll after scroll, searching the shelves for any mention of the Binding Plane or the strange, shimmering threads.

I found all sorts of stories, tales of the gods granting wondrous powers and even bringing mortals to the brink of immortality—but always in exchange for great penance. The more I read, the more my heart sank; it seemed unlikely the gods had chosen to grant me a boon when I had done no such thing. But I could find no example of my own experience either, of anyone discovering such magic in meditation, and unaided.

In the end, I took with me several more guides on the practice of meditation, hoping that the exercises in them might contain more hidden secrets.

* * *

I was to be disappointed as far as further secrets, but the meditation instructions helped me in another way: They taught me to focus my mind. It became easier and easier to use the Binding Plane to get what I wanted. Not only could I enter the Plane more smoothly as I practiced, but I could stay there for longer spans of time.

All of us children spent our mornings seated in a small chamber on flat cushions before low wooden desks, where tutors instructed us in reading, writing, and basic mathematics, which I enjoyed well enough. But only I was forced to endure weekly instruction in the arts, for princes were not expected to learn such gentle crafts—embroidery and weaving, painting and so on. My instruction was overseen by a number of minor noblewomen, women who had attended to my mother and would one day attend to the new radnyi. I never felt they much liked me, and now, with my mother gone, I was even more uncomfortable among them. I was useless to them, too young and unimportant to have attendants of their status, and they barely tolerated my clumsy efforts at the arts I cared little for.

Could the Binding Plane be put to use in my favor here as well? If my mother had been here, I never would have attempted it, knowing how important she deemed these skills. She was an excellent painter, her renderings joyful and unrestrained, marked with bright splashes of color that delighted even my untrained eye. While I thought her work beautiful, I had no desire to follow in her footsteps, though I doubted any magical manipulation would have altered her resolve.

But had she still been here, I would not have found the Plane at all. Now I had to move myself through a world that did not contain her.

"I do not wish to do this today," I said, putting down my brush.

The woman—Medha, or Megha, I could never remember her name—did not even look up from her sewing. "Your father says you must, so you will."

"My father does not know if I come here or not," I said, finding a thin gray cord between us in the Binding Plane and sending the same sentiment to her.

She looked up at me, her needle still moving. "Regardless, I know, and I care. Now sit down. If you don't wish to paint, pick up your stitching."

As I was only a young princess, the nobility could speak to me like this. But it made me hate this particular woman more. "Why should it matter to you if I can paint a tree or stitch in a straight line? There are others who can do such work." In the Binding Plane I tried again. *You dislike this task. Would it not be easier to leave?*

"That is true," she said. "But do you not think this is an important skill? It will aid in bringing you a good husband."

"Do you not think my father can bring me a good husband?" I retorted, a bit rudely. She gave a long exhale, then lifted her shoulders in a very ladylike shrug.

"If you do not think it is valuable, then I suppose you will not bother to learn whether I keep you here or not."

"I can go?" I blurted out, surprised at her acquiescence.

"If you insist." She did not look up from her work, and I backed out of the room, hardly believing it had worked.

I intended to spend my newly free afternoons wandering and playing in the Binding Plane. I managed to do this for about three days before Manthara came to my room one evening, looking rather cross with me. "You must think yourself very clever. But I know you snuck away from your lessons. So tomorrow afternoon, you can take lessons with me instead."

I could tell Manthara would brook no argument, and likely no manipulations either. And I was curious to see what her lessons would be, confident she would not let me languish with a paintbrush or a needle.

The next day, she brought me to meet the other servants and observe what they did. I learned their names and the names of their children and watched as our bonds in the Binding Plane slowly thickened.

Manthara also bid me accompany her when she attended to the highest-ranking noblewomen during their weekly gatherings. They were all wives to the men of the Mantri Parishad, my father's council of advisors. They had rarely spoken to me when my mother was around. The pleats of their saris fell just so, even when they were seated in chairs, and not a hair was out of place in their high buns. I found their effortless perfection intimidating. But Manthara simply deposited me at the table as though I belonged there.

The first time I attended, the ladies fawned over me, complimenting my hair and dress and asking after my studies. I sat there scowling, plucking at the bonds in the Binding Plane to *leave me alone* until they finally did.

Afterward, in the privacy of my room, Manthara chastised me. "Why did you behave like that?" she demanded, aggressively straightening my things so that I would know she was angry. "You had a chance to win them over. Think of what you could learn from them."

I could not think of anything to say, overwhelmed by shame at having disappointed Manthara.

The next afternoon, when they again asked about my studies, I told them the truth, explaining how I found most of the arts extremely boring. At the back of the room, Manthara pressed her lips together. So honesty too was wrong?

I gave a quick, awkward laugh, and said, "I am joking, of course." What did they want to hear? "I am enjoying my lessons," and "I hope my father will be pleased with my progress." I forced a smile onto my face as I added, "I hope to one day be as accomplished as my mother." At this I received a few sympathetic clucks.

But soon I grew bored of their discussions, of their veiled manner of speaking and of giving polite, forced responses. My mother had not seemed like the type to put up with such chattering—but then again, I had never seen her in such situations. I took Manthara's advice and decided to see what I could learn, not of the noblewomen themselves, but of the Binding Plane.

So at first, I simply told them, *Kaikeyi is so kind and clever*, and watched them warm to me, giving me praise for my maturity and intelligence. After a few meetings, when our bonds were better established, I began to ask other questions, things I was curious about. *Why is my father displeased with your husband?* I would ask, plucking the string, and the woman would sigh and start talking of how her husband had made a small error in his tribute and she was worried about him. Her kohl-lined eyes darted to me as she spoke, as though she was worried about me hearing too, but I gave her an innocent smile and told her, *Kaikeyi is too young to understand.*

At the end of each gathering, I was weary and drowsy with using the Binding Plane. But our bonds grew stronger, and so did I. With each passing week, my confidence grew. I could be good at this with time. I could take my mother's place.

Although mornings and afternoons were devoted to my improvement, some evenings I would hitch up my skirt, race to meet Yudhajit at the stables, and ride with him across the great fields behind the palace. In the dusk light, the tall grasses seemed to sparkle, and when the wind whipped around us I imagined we were flying through stars. We would travel for miles, until the palace was a toy house in the distance. In a soft valley between two hills, we would sit on a rough quilt Manthara had given me and feast on foods stolen from the kitchens, laughing freely without the watchful eyes of the court censuring us.

Sometimes, I could even convince Yudhajit to train me in the arts of war.

"Why do you want to learn?" he asked, the first time I made such a request of him.

"You never question why you are taught such things," I countered.

"I will have to lead Kekaya's armies one day," he said. "But women are not allowed on the battlefield."

There was little I could say to that. The sages had made it very clear: It was the gods' will that women should be left to tasks more suited to them, to keep our fragile bodies and delicate minds safe. The sages supposedly stayed apart from the governance of kingdoms, living in their temples and devoting their lives to interpreting the will of the gods. They performed penances and studied texts, and in return received visions and guidance. And while some wandered the lands, moving from kingdom to kingdom and sharing what they had learned, others lived and worked in one kingdom alone.

But despite being separate from my father's council, the proclamations of Kekaya's sages often became the law of our kingdom—for my father's council would take their words and turn them into decrees. I could not imagine that other kingdoms did differently. Nobody was so foolish as to risk failing to take advantage of assistance from the gods, or worse, drawing their wrath by ignoring their wishes.

From the time we were small children, it had been instilled in us that the gods required prayer and sacrifice, a life lived according to dharma and moral virtue. The rulers were to care for their subjects. The wealthy were to care for the poor. Parents were to care for their children. And men were to care for women. The sages went beyond this, divining specifics of how the gods wished us to behave to comport with this order. To hear it told by my tutors, the sages protected all of humanity from ruin with their rules upholding these virtues.

And so if I questioned why women could not be unaccompanied in public, or why they should allow their male relatives to speak for them, I was met with sharp admonitions from my instructors to bend my head in prayer and apologize for my audacity. Even the sages, however, could not account for a combination of sisterly annoyance and clumsy tugs in the Binding Plane, and my shameless exploitation of Yudhajit's vast affection for me.

He showed me how to shoot an arrow and hold a sword. But after my first mistake, he would flop onto the ground and complain about the difficulty in teaching a girl such things, and I would give up, tired by my brief lesson and the strain of using the Plane to convince him to do something he did not want to do.

At least as a princess of Kekaya, I was allowed freedom to practice my riding.

It was a point of pride that even many of the common people of Kekaya knew how to ride. Our horses were sought by other kingdoms, for they were without compare. It was said that they were relatives of the winged steeds that graced the heavens. That long ago, in the time before men rode, Indra clipped the wings of a few of his prized creatures so that they could bear his chariot in a war against the asuras. But when the battles were won, the horses could no longer return to their immortal home. Humans watched them with confusion and fear, for they had never seen horses before. These proud creatures wandered the plains, until they were found by a young man who built a stable for their shelter, cleaned their coats, and kept them warm. In return for this kindness, the gods granted him their blessing. Nobody could stand against his speed and prowess on horseback. Before long, he had united the neighboring tribes and founded the kingdom of Kekaya.

I often wondered, as our horses flew across the fields, as their hooves kicked up dust from sun-warmed earth and their breath dissipated into the cooling air, if they remembered where they came from. If they longed for more, for the vast expanse of the skies. Perhaps we were kin, they and I, yearning for something unnameable, a place where we could stretch our wings and belong.

CHAPTER FOUR

YUDHAJIT AND I PASSED the first months of our mother's departure in this way, straddling that strange space that precedes adulthood. I was trying to prove to the women of the court that I was a woman myself, even though I did not feel or act like one, and Yudhajit was trying to earn his way into our father's confidence, although he had little idea what the men of the palace really did when they were not out fighting.

One evening, about a year after my mother left, my father announced to us that a week hence we would travel to the Sarasvati River to pay tribute. There had been rumors of a rakshasa hiding in the northern foothills, where sparse herding villages dotted the rocky outcroppings. Each tale brought to our court was more fanciful than the last—that the rakshasa lived in a village and raided their neighbors, that the villagers worshipped the rakshasa for his protection, that some of the humans had begun drinking the blood of the rakshasa's victims just as the rakshasa did. But it was indisputable that one of my father's own scouts had seen the demonic ugliness of the rakshasa, and that any rakshasa walking our land was a threat.

Rakshasas were demons, though not as powerful as asuras. They satisfied the evil in their hearts by stalking humans rather than gods. I had only heard about them from scrolls and in Manthara's tales—rakshasas ate misbehaving children, slaughtered those abandoned by the gods—but we all knew they still walked the outskirts of civilization. And so, my father thought it best to obtain the blessing of a goddess before facing the monster.

The Sarasvati was the source of many blessings for our people—women went there to pray and nine months later were gifted with sons. Warriors who stood in the Sarasvati and asked for strength returned from battles where greater men died. But most of all, the river was known for granting visions to the most learned of sages, who used their knowledge of things to come to avert disasters. They would see a rising flood and pray to the gods to change its course or foretell a poor crop and pray for better harvest. When their visions did not come to pass, the kingdom was grateful for their work.

Sarasvati prized intelligence above all else, and for this reason I had prayed to her daily as a young girl. It was due to this river that Kekaya was the powerful kingdom it was. Our sages had used the knowledge granted by the goddess to ensure our people remained holy—and in return we had her favor.

It had been some years since we had last visited the river, for with a royal retinue the trip could take several weeks there and back. My brothers and I greeted the announcement with great enthusiasm—while traveling, we all got to ride and play and sleep together in tents with no lessons or other responsibilities.

But the last time we had visited the Sarasvati, my mother had still been with us, and as I thought of traveling without her, a strange loneliness came over me. Manthara would not be attending, for she did not like to ride, and so one evening when Neeti came to my quarters, a small silver platter of sugared almonds and pistachios in her hands and a story ready on her lips, I asked her, "Will you come with me to the river?"

Her face fell instantly. "I'm sorry, Yuvradnyi. I have not been asked to go."

"That is quite all right. I could arrange for it," I said confidently.

She shook her head. "Even if you could, I would not wish to go."

"It will be fun," I wheedled, slipping into the Binding Plane as I did. Our orange cord had about the thickness of a thumb, and I sent the simple message through it in a slow, steady pulse. "We will travel with a whole retinue."

Despite my work in the Binding Plane, though, Neeti shook her head. "I really am sorry, Yuvradnyi. Perhaps someone else can accompany you? I know a girl, Shruti, in the kitchens. You would like her."

Frustrated, I gave another tug on the cord. It started to move up and down more quickly, gathering speed as I said, "Neeti, I am asking you for this. Please." Now that I had the idea in my head, I would not be so easily dissuaded.

"I really do want to come," she said quietly, and I assumed victory was near. After all, with the Binding Plane on my side, I could not fail. Then Neeti shook her head. "But I can't."

In the Binding Plane, the cord between us was just a blur of orange movement. I was sure that soon she would acquiesce. "I am asking as your yuvradnyi that you attend to me."

Neeti's expression hardened from regret into anger.

And then, in an instant, the cord reached its highest peak and snapped.

I stumbled back, forgetting for a moment that the bond was not in the real world. Around us, the shattered remnants of the cord drifted like orange ash, and my heart hammered in my throat. What had just happened? Neeti took a step toward me and hissed, "My mother is very sick. Just because your mother left you does not mean everyone else's world is the same." And then she upturned the plate of sweets onto me, her kind eyes sharp with fury, and disappeared out the door.

I stood there unable to believe what had happened, repeating the events in my head over and over. I had seen hatred in her eyes as she left. In my mind's eye, I could see her face clouding over with ugly anger, directed at me. My stomach churned, and I reentered the Binding Plane, hoping to find this had all been a silly nightmare. But our orange bond was nowhere to be seen. A tear slipped down my face, my vision blurring as the Plane disappeared, but I brushed it away. It was stupid to cry over a servant who would turn on me so readily. But she had been more than that. She had been my friend, one of the few I'd had. And this was my own fault.

For it had been a normal enough request, and even if she had not wished to listen, that would not have ordinarily warranted such a reaction. The only thing out of the ordinary was that I had used the Binding Plane. Rather than merely annoying her, it appeared as though I had broken our connection. Did this mean, then, that my friendship with Neeti was over forever? That there was nothing connecting us anymore? Surely the effects of overusing the Plane would not be so severe—and yet, at potentially great consequence to herself, she had whispered those hateful words to me. Years of friendship gone in an instant, and over something so unimportant.

I had to be exceedingly careful about using the Plane on those I cared about. What if I had accidentally done this with my father...or Manthara, or *Yudhajit*? Just the idea brought the taste of acid to my mouth. My hands shook.

How could I have been so foolish? I should have known better than to use this power without thought, without knowing its full extent.

I would have to go to the Sarasvati alone. It was what I deserved.

*   *   *

For the first few days of our ride, I was subdued. Yudhajit tried to pull me into mischief, but all I could think about was Neeti. Every day I checked for our bond, but found nothing. But eventually the shock of it faded, and I joined Yudhajit, Shantanu, and Mohan racing through the camp in the evenings, chasing one another and shrieking with laughter. I reveled in the freedom I was afforded, for my opportunities to play with my brothers were becoming more and more scarce. We ran in and out of the forests near our camps, the air under the leaves cool and refreshing after a sweaty day of riding. We tried to catch small creatures, squirrels and little gray rabbits, and climbed up the branches of the smaller trees.

The day before we were due to arrive at the river, Yudhajit snuck into my tent and shook me awake. As the only royal girl, I slept alone with a guard posted outside the front of my tent—but clearly nobody had thought to protect the back flap. I had been in the throes of a nightmare that was already slipping away, and perhaps it was the adrenaline already coursing through me that made me hear him out instead of going back to sleep.

"The soldiers said that an elephant was seen in these forests not too long ago," he whispered. "I want to go find it. Come with me?"

Yudhajit knew as well as I that elephants did not live in our kingdom. They lived in the south of Bharat, far from our cooler climates. "They must have been joking."

"No, they said it was one of the elephants of the gods." His voice grew more excited as he spoke. "A *white* elephant."

My eyes widened. White elephants were incredibly rare, and even seeing one at a distance was considered a great blessing. The stories said that the first white elephant had risen out of the churning of the ocean.

But it was the middle of the night, and we were in unfamiliar forests.

40

"Come on, Kaikeyi," he cajoled. "Nobody will know."

I could never resist Yudhajit for long. I shooed him out and quietly pulled on a dark kurta before joining him outside. It was a few days before the full moon, so there was ample light to navigate by, but the cold silver glow gave the forest an eerie cast. I suppressed a shiver and followed Yudhajit as he confidently plunged into the woods.

"How do you know where to go?"

"Elephants need water, right? We have to find a pool."

As far as I knew, Yudhajit had no interest in geography. "This is a huge forest. We're searching for one animal within it." I turned and looked back toward the camp, which was nearly obscured by the tall trees, their branches swaying slightly in the wind. "Are you certain about this?"

"I'm praying to find it," Yudhajit said. "You should be praying to Lord Ganesha too. With his guidance, I am sure we will be blessed to see it."

I stared at Yudhajit's back for a moment, envious of his easy confidence. Then I followed him once more.

We remained silent as we marched, wary of garnering the attention of any passing predators. At some point, we twined our fingers together, not wanting to get lost in the darkness caused by the thick canopy. Just when my feet were beginning to tire, and I was going to suggest we turn back, Yudhajit gave a soft gasp. "Do you hear that?"

I strained my ears and, after a moment, heard the soft murmur of water. "A stream!" We rushed forward with new energy.

Soon we could see light glinting off running water. "Slow down," he whispered. "If it's there, we don't want to scare it."

But as we stepped cautiously toward the tree line, my spine tingled and a chill ran through me. Something was very wrong. I moved in front of Yudhajit, trying to tell myself I was being irrational, and peered between two thick trunks.

I stuffed my thumb in my mouth and bit down on it to

keep myself from shouting, flinging out my other hand to hold Yudhajit back. "We have to go," I whispered.

"What is it?" he asked, jostling me slightly to see. I clapped a hand over his mouth so he wouldn't make any noise and felt his body stiffen against me.

On the other side of the stream stood a rakshasa.

It could not have been anything else. It was tall, taller even than some of the young trees that lined the water, with orange-red skin that gleamed, unnaturally slick in the moonlight. Its skin matched its eyes, orange pupils and yellow where there should have been white. It had horns breaking through its skull, like some fiendish ram, and from here I could see the sharp curve of two wicked white fangs protruding from its lips. It had four arms, each hand gripping a different weapon, casting twisted reflections in the water. And where it should have had feet, it instead had clawed paws, hairy and grotesque with sharp talons.

Even many years later, it would have been impossible for me to describe the naked fear that filled me at the sight. This monster could rip me limb from limb and drink my blood without a second thought. The frightening stories had not been frightening enough.

But just as suddenly as the fear came, it was replaced by clear thought. We needed to get away. I took a careful step backward, then another. Yudhajit remained standing, paralyzed. I tugged at his hand.

"It's crossing the stream," he whispered.

There was no time to spare on words. I pulled him this time, hard enough that he fell into me, though I maintained both our balances. This seemed to be enough to wake him from his trance, for his hand clasped mine more tightly as we backed away, one step after another.

Behind us came a mighty roar, and we broke into a run. I imagined the earth itself was shaking. I did not know if it heard us running, but we did not dare turn around for anything. My chest ached and my lungs screamed for air. When I felt as though I would falter, Yudhajit pulled me on. At last, at long last, we burst into the clearing where we had made camp, behind my tent once more. We stood there panting for several seconds, gulping in the air, before I could gasp out, "We must tell our father. If it comes to the camp—" I could not finish the sentence.

"We have plenty of soldiers," Yudhajit said. "If they are prepared, they could slay it."

"But they are not prepared."

Yudhajit's mouth twisted into a grim expression, and then he set off without a word toward the center of camp. "We must see the raja immediately," Yudhajit said, drawing himself up as tall as he could get outside of our father's tent.

The soldier guarding his tent seemed unimpressed. "It is the middle of the night, Yuvraja. You can speak with him in the morning."

"We must speak to him now," Yudhajit said. Before, I would have ordered the soldier to do so in the Binding Plane. But now I simply waited with Yudhajit, afraid of using the Plane after what I had done to my bond with Neeti.

The soldier held Yudhajit's gaze for another moment, then nodded sharply and entered the tent. Yudhajit turned to me, reaching for my hair and pulling a leaf from it. I gave him a small smile, just as the soldier returned to beckon us in.

Our father was standing, still in his sleeping clothes, looking quite annoyed. "What is it, at this hour?"

"There is a rakshasa coming toward the camp," Yudhajit said confidently.

My father raised his eyebrows. "And how would you know this?" To my ears, his tone sounded slightly mocking.

Yudhajit turned toward me, the panic evident. We could not admit to sneaking out of camp, but we had to give our father proof. "I had a dream about it," I blurted out.

"You woke me about a bad dream?" Anger was seeping into my father's tone.

"I had it too," Yudhajit said quickly. "We both had the exact same dream about a rakshasa with orange-red skin and four arms. Headed toward us. That could only be a message from the gods."

My father rubbed his chin, thoughtful. I clenched my hands at my sides. Of course my father believed Yudhajit's identical story, without so much as considering what I had to say. "There have been reports of some horrible monster terrorizing nearby villages. I thought it a wild animal, but—" He broke off and strode toward the front of the tent to have a hushed conversation with the soldier there. Then he came and clapped Yudhajit on the shoulder. "You have done well to come to me about this. Did the gods see fit to show you where it was?"

"There's a stream in the forest," Yudhajit said. "To the south. It comes from there."

"Good boy," my father said. "Stay here. I will lead a party to put an end to this monster."

At that moment, a servant came in and wordlessly began helping my father into his armor. Outside, we could hear the sounds of others conversing despite the dark hour. The whispers were growing, and I imagined the news spreading like wildfire from tent to tent, the camp rousing to the sound of weapons being prepared.

Once our father had departed, I sank to the earth floor of the tent, suddenly exhausted. Even the anger at my father was gone, for now he was marching to fight a rakshasa. My eyes pricked, thinking of the danger we had been in and the danger our father would soon be in. Yudhajit sat next to me, looking equally afraid. We sat for what seemed like an eternity and must have drifted off, because the next thing I knew a clamor was echoing all through the camp. Yudhajit sprang to his feet, racing for the tent entrance. He ran straight into our father.

"You were right, Yudhajit," he said. His face was frightening in his grimness. "There was a rakshasa in that forest, and he looked to be coming for our camp. We were able to slay him, but not without a cost."

"What cost?" Yudhajit looked stricken.

"We lost three men." My father's voice was weary. "We will cremate them at the Sarasvati River. We were lucky this was a weak rakshasa, barely capable of intelligent thought. The gods smiled upon us to give warning—we would have lost more than three had the demon made it here. You have done well, my son. I will think on how to reward you."

I glanced at Yudhajit, wondering if he would mention me at all, but he just inclined his head and said, "Thank you, Father."

Father gave him a genuine smile, the kind that transformed his whole face. "You are quite welcome. Now make preparations to leave. We will still ride this day."

We left together.

Outside, I spun to face Yudhajit, unsure what to say. He smiled, tired but relieved. "I am so glad you were with me."

He walked away, not even waiting for me as I stood there dumbfounded. No thanks for saving him at the stream or covering our disobedience, not even an apology for Father's oversight.

But then, this was the way of the world to Yudhajit. And standing there, I knew that I would never truly grow accustomed to it.

The next day, our somber party reached the banks of the river. As relieved as we were to have survived, the deaths of the men weighed heavily on us all.

As we approached the water, silence fell over our group, a sort of mounting anticipation.

Even though I had seen it before, the sight of it took my

breath away, a clear white and blue ribbon weaving through the hills, its current dancing in the wind, seemingly playful but swift enough to carry unsuspecting travelers to their doom.

Standing barefoot, my toes pressing into the damp earth and the sound of the water surrounding me, I was gripped once again by the urge to pray. Around me, people were kneeling next to the water, cupping it in their hands and pouring it on their heads, each absorbed in their own rituals. The sages were preparing to perform the funeral rites, to ask for the river to bless my father.

I stepped forward, feeling uncertain, until I reached the edge of the water. For once, I knew nobody would scold me for getting my dress muddy.

"Sri Sarasvati, I pray to you for wisdom," I whispered. I glanced around, but nobody was near enough to hear me speak so softly. "I ask you for knowledge of my gift. Why do I have it? What am I meant to do with it?"

I shut my eyes so tightly that I could not even see the redness of sunlight behind my eyelids. There was some small hope still inside me that now, after helping to save our camp, the goddess might see fit to bless me. I waited for a vision, for a spark, but nothing came. "Please," I begged. "I have always prayed and tried my hardest to be good. Please give me a sign. Help me to understand how to use it." Even then I thought of Neeti, of her face and what I had done.

But Sarasvati did not seem inclined to help me fix what I had broken. There was silence, save for the rustling and murmuring of those around me. A breeze blew down the river, pricking my skin. I unclasped my hands and rubbed my arms, abandoning the last bit of hope that the goddess might listen to me. The sages began ringing their bells and I rose to my feet, rubbing at my stinging eyes. Slowly, I walked back toward the horses, knowing Father would not notice.

"Are you okay?" Yudhajit asked from behind me.

I whirled around. "I'm fine." Where had he come from? He should have been with Father. "You should go back."

"You looked sad," he said instead. "I wanted to check on you. Is it what happened with the rakshasa?"

"No, I said I'm fine." There was no way for me to explain to Yudhajit what was truly wrong. How could he understand what it was like to be ignored?

But Yudhajit wouldn't leave. I felt a flicker of annoyance that he would not let me have this solitude until he said, "Do you miss her? Mother? Last time we came here, she was with us. I miss her too."

I blinked at him, surprised at the sudden show of emotion. "I suppose," I said, though I hadn't been thinking of my mother at all.

He put a hand on my shoulder, his warm touch chasing away some of the abandonment I felt. "It will be all right."

"I know that," I said, pulling away and swatting at him.

He laughed for a moment, then grew serious. "Do you want to rejoin the others?"

I shook my head. "You go on, though."

"Is there anything I can do?" he asked. He seemed sincere, and all of a sudden I remembered there was something I wanted from him.

"There is," I said.

"Whatever it is, I'll do it," he said immediately.

I looked behind him, to where the ceremony was well underway. "You need to go now. But when we return to the palace, if you remember your promise, I'll tell you."

CHAPTER
FIVE

THE DAY AFTER WE returned to Kekaya, I made my request
to Yudhajit.

"Why are you so intent on this anyway?" he asked, but I
noticed he did not say *no*. "You will never have need of it."

"Father and the soldiers were able to bring down a rakshasa
with their training," I said. "If it had caught us, you would
have stood more of a chance than I. I want to be able to protect myself."

He stayed silent, observing my face, so I added, "It won't
hurt you at all to train me. Haven't you heard the masters say
that teaching a skill helps perfect it? So in that regard, you will
be improving too."

And that was all it took. The rakshasa had left us both
shaken, and perhaps Yudhajit felt the need to protect me. It
seemed I didn't need the Binding Plane all the time.

He refused to do it anywhere we might be found out, so we
took our horses into the fields, riding beyond the view of pry-
ing eyes.

As soon as we dismounted, I went immediately to his saddlebag, eager to see what weapons he had chosen for our first

lesson. My hands itched to hold a bow, for I found archery most elegant, but perhaps wooden staffs would be more practical—more like what might be found in a forest.

It was empty.

"What—"

"The instructors at the palace do not give us weapons for years," he said.

"Years?" I asked, incredulity coloring my voice.

He laughed. "I will not make you wait that long. But I think maybe it would be helpful to show you some forms first. Without that, you may as well ride home and ask Manthara to help you practice your embroidery."

I scowled at that but watched him intently as he moved slowly through a series of stretches and exercises. As he repeated the motions, I began to follow along, relishing the stretch and pull of my muscles, the solid ground beneath my feet, the brush of wind against my braids.

I had always thought myself fit, racing around with my brothers and riding as I did. But by the end of it, I could barely mount my horse. My whole body trembled.

"Does it always feel this way?" I asked him.

"What way?" he said. I did not answer, too tired and frustrated with my own abilities. "What way?" he asked again.

"Nothing," I muttered. But I vowed that my weakness would not last. I would master these forms and prove to Yudhajit I could handle weapons.

Every day I practiced the forms alone in my room. Each time left me drenched in sticky sweat, but I pushed through, celebrating every small victory.

Only Manthara knew of my determination to succeed in this—even with Yudhajit, I feigned a certain amount of casualness, for I sensed that there was a danger in letting him know the depth of my longing to prove myself worthy. But Manthara sometimes observed me struggling to balance on my hands or hold a lunge as she tidied my room. Once, she asked, "Why do you do this, when you have so many other things to spend your time on?"

"Why shouldn't I?" I responded, panting with the effort. I dropped to the ground, brushed stray hair from my eyes, and turned to face Manthara, whose expression was pinched. I had been rather rude. "I'm sorry," I added. "I just..." I could not articulate it, this need to learn. Manthara eyed me intently.

"You do not need to be able to fight," she said. "You will be radnyi of a kingdom one day. That will be all the power you need."

In a way, she was right.

I was learning my own power more and more each day as I took over duties of the court. This had recently come to a head with Dhanteri, my mother's former chief lady-in-waiting. I would never forget her whispered conversation with Prasad the night my mother had vanished, where she held her tongue in exchange for control of the palace's workings. In the week before Holi, Manthara had taken me to the kitchens to hear the plans for the celebration that would follow the great bonfire. Each year, we burned an effigy of the Holika, a wicked asura who had tried to immolate her devout nephew alive. Burning the effigy would cleanse our kingdom and bring a good harvest.

The supplies were limited for the feast; the usual caravans that would bring grain and rice had been delayed, and only after the harvest would our kitchens be replenished.

I listened carefully to our cook and, when Manthara nodded, encouraged him to use our flour stores to prepare vadas, delicious balls of dough mixed with fragrant herbs, then fried until they were golden and sizzling before being dipped in tangy yogurt. Our bins of dried chickpeas were plentiful, which meant we would be able to prepare my father's favorite spiced stew, and it was decided that we would slaughter several chickens besides—those who had become too old to lay. I felt a pang for the chickens but overall was quite pleased with myself, until the next day when Dhanteri came to confront Manthara.

"I heard you spoke to the cook," Dhanteri said without any pleasantries.

"I did—" Manthara began.

"It is my place to make such decisions until the yuvradnyi is able," Dhanteri continued. "I will ensure that Prasad hears about this. I cannot imagine he would want to keep you around after—"

"It was me," I blurted, not wanting Manthara to get in trouble for my actions. "I spoke to the cook."

Dhanteri stopped. Her expression fell slightly, before she marshaled a thin-lipped smile. "I see, Yuvradnyi. But you are still so young. You should not concern yourself with such matters."

"I want to," I said, stepping forward. "It is my role, is it not?" Manthara coughed behind me, or perhaps it was a laugh. Dhanteri's eyes flashed up to Manthara, then back down to me.

"Perhaps the raja would want a more capable—"

"I hope you are not saying that Kaikeyi is not *capable*," Manthara said behind me. There was an unpleasant note to her voice, one I had never heard before.

"I have been doing this for some time," Dhanteri said. "It is simply that I am more experienced. It is laudable that you want to help. In that case, it is my place to assist you."

"I appreciate your help," I said, for Manthara had always taught me to be generous. "But I do not believe I need your assistance."

"You don't need it?" Dhanteri asked, and now she looked a bit afraid, although I did not know why.

I looked to Manthara, confused, but she gave me a small

smile and a nod. "No, I do not. If these responsibilities are mine, I should be the one to handle them."

Dhanteri looked at Manthara. She seemed sad now, only moments after looking so angry, and I did not understand.

She pivoted on her heel and walked away so briskly she might have been running.

It was only after the feast, at which Dhanteri did not appear, that I realized what I had done. I had all but dismissed her. Of course, she might have stayed, but her place would have fallen, and she was unwilling to bear that. Once I had fully claimed my role, she had no reason to stay.

This was a different sort of power than the Binding Plane, and it didn't feel good, even when Manthara assured me that Dhanteri's departure was inevitable, and I was simply doing my duty. I remembered how I had felt when my father disbelieved me, dismissed my dream, and then trusted Yudhajit in the same breath. The despair that had rocked me the first evening after he sent my mother away. Even a radnyi did not have the power to stay with her children, or a yuvradnyi to gain the trust of her father. That could not—would not—be my whole life. I wanted to have power over *myself*, and I did not have that. In that regard, I was no different than Dhanteri.

This discomfort was still on my mind when I explained to Manthara why I wanted to fight. She must have observed something in the set of my jaw and the clench of my fists that gave her pause. "If it makes you feel strong, then by all means do it. But you do not need to prove yourself to anyone. If Yudhajit has put you up to anything—"

"No," I interrupted. "He thinks I am foolish as well."

"I do not think you are foolish," Manthara said gently. She moved in front of me and secured a strand of runaway hair with a pin, giving me a small smile. "It is admirable that you want to improve yourself. I just fear you will have little use for such things. I am sure it is hard to live here, surrounded by men, but there are other ways to be strong. You are already learning—see how the palace staff admire you."

"Can I not be strong in many ways?" I asked her. "I want to learn this for myself."

"Of course." Manthara picked up my dirty clothes, her expression grave. "You are your own mistress."

Yudhajit stayed true to his word and his teachings. As time passed, he began bringing weapons to our lessons. First, a simple bow. He stood behind me as I drew the string, lifting my elbow, correcting my stance, giving encouragement. It was hard work that left my arms numb, and so between lessons I began lifting objects around my room to gain strength.

After several months, Yudhajit set up a range of targets for me throughout the hills. I ran across the grass, and each time I spotted a target, I planted my feet, pulled the bowstring back, and let loose. Yudhajit followed behind me, shouting with joy at each hit. Some targets were far away, but when I pulled the string back as far as it would stretch, my arm did not tremble. Others required me to crest an incline, and yet my thighs did not burn. For almost an hour, I practiced. And when we studied the targets at the end, nearly every arrow had hit the center.

We flopped onto the grass afterward, tired from the exertion. I closed my eyes for a moment. With both of us lying sweaty in the dirt, I could imagine that I had been a warrior my whole life.

After that, Yudhajit insisted that I learn how to drive a war chariot, even though what I really wanted was to learn how to use a sword.

I had cautiously begun reentering the Binding Plane, using only the gentlest of touches on the strings and threads around me, and withdrawing at even the smallest tremor. So I sent a suggestion, just a tiny push, across our blue cord. *Would swordfighting not be more fun?*

"Our kingdom is known far and wide for its horsemanship," he insisted. "You know how to ride. Driving is what you need to master next." And, reluctant to test him or our bond, I complied.

At our next meeting, I arrived at our usual spot and found him waiting there with two matched horses and a chariot he had clearly stolen from the palace grounds. The horses tossed their heads, nickering, and I rubbed their noses in affection before examining the chariot itself.

It was large, designed to be swift and easily maneuvered. I ran a hand against the wood, marveling that something so vicious could feel so smooth.

"You can observe while I drive them in a simple circle," he said.

The day was a beautiful one, so I settled on a rock on the side of the hill to watch.

It went well at first, but after a few minutes, the horses seemed to decide they preferred to run in a straight line. He struggled to get them back in control, eventually pulling them to a halt and dropping the reins in disgust. He hopped down from the chariot, face red, and any jibing remark I was considering slipped from my mind. "You did very well," I told him sincerely.

"I don't know what happened," he growled.

"Shall I try?"

He shrugged half-heartedly, and so I climbed into the box of the chariot and took the reins in my hands. As I stood behind the team of horses, adrenaline rushed through me. I flicked the reins and the horses began moving forward, slowly at first, then faster. The box was steady beneath me, and I felt as though the world had slowed. I tugged instinctively on the reins, bracing my weight, and the team turned in a smooth arc. My heart pounded in my chest, light and free. I pulled a bit harder, and the horses responded, moving in a steady circle. The grin that split my face was not a conscious choice.

I snapped the reins and the chariot leapt forward, but I kept my balance. I was one with the wheels, the horses, the world. We danced our way across the field, until at last, the surge of power buoying me began to fade and I remembered my audience.

I climbed down from the chariot, trying to force my cheeks into a more reserved expression. Yudhajit's face was stony, his shoulders hunched in palpable frustration, and I felt a slight churn of guilt. "You were a good teacher," I said.

"No, I wasn't," he said, and seemed to shake himself. "But you—you were excellent, Kaikeyi!"

I had truly not been expecting such praise "Really?" I asked.

"You're a natural." He closed his eyes and took a deep breath, then gave me a small smile. "Maybe in this, you can teach me."

So Yudhajit passed on the words of his instructors and memories of how maneuvers were supposed to look while I figured out how to get the horses to actually respond, and in the end, we taught each other together.

We practiced through the harvest and the cooler season, bundling ourselves in coarse woolen cloaks to stay warm. It was cold enough to see our breath, but we knew that in a few months our chariot practice would have to halt for some time. As the air warmed, it came with a warning that rains would not be far behind. The ground would turn to mud, and while horse riding was still permissible, charioteering was not. The mud could break in one moment what craftsmen had labored over for months.

One evening, storm clouds loomed on the horizon and the air was almost damp with moisture. We rode out in silent agreement that this would be our last practice, but when we arrived at our usual place, I saw there was a second chariot already there, with horses.

I looked around, worried we had been found out by some disapproving advisor.

"Stop looking so serious," Yudhajit said with a laugh. "I brought it out here just before, then rode back to get you."

"But how?" I asked. "Wouldn't it be strange if—"

"Nobody asks such questions." Yudhajit hopped down, face bright with excitement at his own ingenuity, and I bit my tongue. I was questioned all the time by advisors, by the nobility—where was I going? What was I doing? Why was I not elsewhere? This was perhaps the most useful application of the Binding Plane—it was slowly becoming instinct to redirect any unwanted inquiries. I would grasp a bond with my mind, pulling ever so slightly on the rope between us while suggesting, *You have important business elsewhere,* or *Kaikeyi is very responsible and you need not worry.* "I thought we could practice against each other."

I eyed him, skeptical. "There's no point in two charioteers practicing against each other unless they are carrying warriors."

I could tell from the way he blinked up at me that he had not thought this fully through. His expression fell slightly, and I immediately felt sorry. He had gone to a lot of effort to surprise me with this. "You know what," I said. "Maybe we can make it a contest through the forest paths. There's plenty of obstacles. That would be wonderful practice."

Yudhajit smiled so widely I could have counted his teeth. "Shall we race to the river?" he asked, excited. There was a small river running several hundred paces away from where we stood at the edge between the forest and the hills. Soon it would be swollen and dangerous, but that was many hours away. I gave him a nod, and he clambered into his chariot, steering the team into place next to mine.

"Ready?" he called.

"Three, two..." I counted, drawing it out and tensing my body.

"One!" Yudhajit shouted, growing impatient. He took off.

I snapped the reins and sent the horses running to catch him. We jostled for room on the path, and he used his narrow lead to block me time and time again. I snarled in frustration, scanning the quickly passing surroundings for an opening.

Yudhajit let out a whoop as I slowed my horses slightly, then turned his head, confused, as I swung my team to the side. The chariot bumped uncomfortably over the uneven trail, giving a groan, but I gripped the reins and spurred the horses onward. They were racing now, the chariot lifting slightly into the air. When we burst back onto the main path, we nearly collided with Yudhajit. My heart leapt into my mouth, but I made myself hold firm, and he, in an equal moment of panic, slowed his team, allowing me to take the lead. He cursed behind me, and I felt his horses nudging my chariot. With a flick of my wrists, I sent the horses weaving along the path so that he could gain no advantage.

The river was in sight. With a whoop of my own, I spurred the horses, slowing only as we reached the edge, their hooves splashing into the shallow water, droplets cooling my flushed skin.

I leapt from my chariot, all decorum forgotten. I threw my arms up and cheered and spun around to find my brother.

Yudhajit climbed down from his chariot and stalked toward me, lips pressed into a line. I held up a conciliatory hand, but before I could ask if he was all right, he tackled me into the river. I shouted, indignant, as the cold water hit my back, the shock setting my teeth chattering. I wondered if this had been a bad idea. I should have let Yudhajit win. But he rolled away, laughing so hard he was nearly crying, and as I caught my breath lying in the shallows, I quickly entered the

Binding Plane. Our bright blue bond was calm, undisturbed, and so I turned to look at him. He was on his knees, preparing to stand, and was looking at me with open admiration. "You were incredible!" He offered me a hand up.

"Then why did you throw me into the water?" I asked, shivering slightly.

"You're too serious all the time," he said, putting his arm around me. Yudhajit radiated heat. "I wanted to set you off-balance. The look on your face when I threw you in?" He grinned. "Remember, Kaikeyi, never take your eyes off your enemy." He put on a serious face, but I snickered at his pronouncement, and soon we were both choking with laughter.

"You're not my enemy," I told him, elbowing him in the rib cage. "Just my competitor. But we should get back and change before we take ill." He gave a good-natured groan but willingly followed me home.

"Manthara, I need to practice my swordplay," I said one evening. The monsoons were well and truly here, and watching the ground become a lake of mud outside the palace was boring me to tears. I itched to *move*. "Can you help me?"

She laughed slightly. "I know nothing about swordplay."

"All you need to do is stand and hold a shield," I said. I could tell she was resistant to the idea, and so I sent a plea in the Binding Plane, *Kaikeyi most fervently desires this. It would make her happy.* I had learned that such entreaties worked best with Manthara. I worried sometimes that she only humored me because she had to, but then Manthara would, when she thought I was asleep, whisper in my ear how much she loved me, and I would put the thought from my mind.

She hummed, considering. "Stand and hold a shield?" she asked. "I don't have to use a sword?"

"No," I said, already turning to find the shield in anticipation of victory.

"All right." I picked up the wooden circle and turned back to her when she added, "Then you must do something for me."

"What do you want?" I asked cautiously. If Manthara needed something from me, would she not have already asked for it?

"I suppose really it will be helping you," she said. "For every blow you deal me, you must correctly answer a question about the court."

I groaned. "That's so boring. I know everything I need to."

"Do you?" Manthara took the shield from me and slotted her arm into place. "You attend all the functions, that is true, and you are well-liked among the staff. But I think you could be doing more. Though if, as you say, you know everything already, then this should be very easy."

I slipped into the Binding Plane, more than ready to convince her that I did not need such childish lessons. I touched our bond with my mind, and then actually listened to her words. She was right. This would be easy. And if I manipulated away her condition now, it would only come back in some other form later. Instead, I could prove to her that I already knew everything I needed.

I picked up my wooden sword and did a basic approach, rapping the shield with my blade to finish. It was a far cry from the double-edged khanda the best warriors fought with, but even so I struggled to maneuver with it. "Very nice," Manthara said, although I could tell she didn't really care. "Your father is inviting a guest this evening. What is his name?"

That was easy. "Tarush." I tried a more complicated maneuver, hitting the shield from the side. "Arya Tarush," I repeated, adding a title of respect.

"Why has he been invited here?"

I knew that too. "Father just took over his land." Kekaya's borders had remained stable for some time now. The kingdom of Kosala, which lay to the southeast, its territory beginning

59

just across the Sarasvati River, had recently conquered a cluster of smaller villages that had been causing us trouble. With our southern border secured, my father had taken this as an opportunity to wage war on some northern tribes that were posing a nuisance before they had the chance to become stronger.

Manthara lowered the shield and gave me a level stare. "You think your father invites all those whose land he has conquered to his home as an honored guest?"

I frowned at her. "He wants to make sure Arya Tarush won't try to fight this?"

"That's better." She lifted up her shield again. I took several spinning steps, tripped, and missed Manthara by several paces. She laughed, but there was no ridicule in it. I laughed as well, shaking my arm out before trying again, concentrating on my footwork. This time, I managed a weak hit against the shield.

"What should the palace do to ensure that your father's plan succeeds?"

I truly paused at that, the sword dropping to my side. "What do you mean? There's a feast for his arrival."

"You believe that's all it takes?" she asked.

"It's a great honor," I insisted.

"Would you be honored to sit in the hall of your enemy after you were defeated by their hands?"

I bit my lip. "I suppose not." It sounded rather humiliating.

I searched my mind for what else might be required. "He should be seated close to my father. And...perhaps the kitchens could prepare foods from the north? His people are almost from the mountains. We can serve mutton as a show of respect."

Manthara nodded. "That is one way." She lifted the shield once more, but now I was curious.

"What other ways are there?"

She raised an eyebrow at me. "I thought you knew everything." At my frustrated glare, she smiled slightly and continued, "We should ensure his chamber is comfortable and laid out in the fashion he is used to. Uncomfortable beds make for uncomfortable men. He should be served immediately after the king, before all others. He should be well attended, with a servant within shouting range at all times. And he has a friend in the court—do you know who that might be?" I shook my head. "Devi Tara is his sister, although she left his lands when she married Arya Karthik many years ago. We should make sure that she is seated near to him and treated as an important figure, so he knows his family is taken care of and respected."

"How do you know all this?" I asked, swordplay entirely forgotten.

"Because I listen. You should know all this too. Raise your weapon, Kaikeyi. We will practice until you are ready."

CHAPTER SIX

AS MANTHARA HAD INTENDED all along, my practice sessions with her changed me. Once I learned how to use information gathered around the palace, I wished to do it.

Over the years, trips to the kitchen to steal a snack became hours-long visits. I would mention to the head cook, "I believe my father intends to host a wedding at the palace next month."

"We have not been told yet," he said. He was a tall, willowy man who was unfailingly kind to everyone working below him. I wondered how he managed to still run such a competent kitchen.

"I know, I just heard it from Devi Megha." Despite my long-ago evasion of her sewing lessons, my old tutor had warmed to me over time. "I wanted to tell you first, to be sure you had enough notice."

"Whose wedding?" he asked.

"The chief of Singapura's son is to marry Devi Megha's niece." The marriage had been arranged over ten years ago when the son was still quite young, but the chief had recently begun making noise that he was unhappy with his grant of land and wanted more. My father had offered him a great celebration in the capital to avoid conflict breaking out. The kingdom was constantly engaged in a balancing act, keeping the men who governed its towns and villages happy without allowing them to come into dispute with one another. Of course, I did not say any of this to the cook. "I do not know how many people will be in attendance, but I believe it will be an outdoor celebration, monsoons willing."

I came back the next week, bearing information from Megha. "Her niece prefers milk sweets," I said. "And the chief has a sensitive stomach."

The cook frowned. "I can prepare a separate dish for him."

The point of this wedding was to soothe the chief's ambitions. It seemed to me that singling him out would make him feel weak, embarrassed. "Perhaps it might be easiest to prepare all the dishes with milder spices instead?"

He clucked his tongue. "A bland dinner will be savored by no one."

I found the grass-green bond between us, gave it a soothing touch. *You can do this*, I encouraged him. Out loud I said, "It will be a challenge, but you have never failed to impress before."

His expression became thoughtful. "I suppose I could. Do you know if he is simply sensitive to chili heat, or other foods as well? What about oil?"

"I will find out for you," I said, giving him a sunny smile, and watched our bond grow stronger before my eyes.

Over those same several weeks, I began readying the guest wing of the palace for heavy use. I took a survey of the rooms with Manthara and another servant, Shilpa.

The palace's dark stone structure, with its high windows and narrow corridors, did not seem restrictive to me. But I had heard that to some, the rooms felt chilly and unfriendly, and so with my father's complete ignorance of my activities at my disposal, I set about righting it. Despite their occasional usage, some of the furniture and linens had not been changed in years, and so I spoke to the head tailor, requesting brighter, lighter materials to soften the stone rooms and make them just slightly more hospitable.

I also met with our most skilled weaver, commissioning a fine tapestry for the wall, bearing out my prediction to Megha that I would not need such sewing skills myself. It arrived the night before the chief, and I supervised its hanging myself.

The next morning, I made sure to be present at the chief's arrival, meeting him and accompanying him to his rooms. Manthara had advised me to ask about his journey on the freshly maintained roads connecting Singapura to Kekaya, and the chief was more than happy to oblige, extolling the quality of the work. When we stopped outside his door, he paused to admire the tapestry. "The work is lovely. I believe I have seen this spiral pattern work on the temple of Brahma in the forest near Singapura."

"Thank you," I said, ducking my head so as to appear modest. "The weavers of this city are known for this particular pattern."

"You are a very poised young woman," he said when I took my leave. "Your father must be very proud."

That little shard of praise wrapped itself around my heart, but not as much as what happened at dinner the next evening.

I had just carefully sopped up some curry with a small piece of roti. It was mild, as the cook had promised, but nutty and fragrant with cardamom, the mutton melting like butter on my tongue. Next to me, Yudhajit made a happy noise. "The cook has done so well," he said. "It's not very spicy is it? But you hardly notice."

I said nothing, my gaze flicking up to the high table where my father sat next to the chief. The chief was gesturing to his plate, and my father's eyes connected with mine. He gave me a small smile—so small, I would have thought it was an accident, except he followed it with a brief nod.

My stomach fluttered with happiness, and I looked down at my plate. I knew, logically, that he would go back to ignoring me soon enough, that there would be no words of praise for my machinations. But I could not help my happiness.

After a week of wedding ceremonies and celebrations, the palace went back to normal. I had missed my usual weekly lesson with Yudhajit, but that was a more common occurrence than I would have liked. It had been almost three years since we started training together, and in those years we had acquired real responsibilities. I even found I had less and less time to take short trips to the cellars, though I had still managed to work my way through every scroll I could hunt down involving magic and meditation.

I slipped down there every so often and wound my way through the shelves, wondering what to read now that I had exhausted all the magic scrolls. I found myself drawn to the shelf that housed recent stories and histories, and my eyes instantly alighted on one scroll at the top of the pile, with a distinctive border of red vines on the outside. I remembered my mother's slender fingers unrolling it, for she had read it many times.

I opened the scroll, eager for this small scrap of connection, and found at the very top a short note. My breath caught.

My dear Kaikeyi,

I do not have much time to write this. I hope that when you find it, you will also find it in your heart to forgive me. I do not wish to leave any of you, but especially not you, for being a yuvradnyi is no easy task. But I know you are strong, Kaikeyi. Be careful. Remember the lessons of these scrolls. I know you will thrive.

There was no signature, but I did not need one to recognize my mother's elegant hand.

I dashed a hand across my eyes so my tears would not fall on the scroll. For years now, I thought she had left without saying goodbye. But she had thought of me. Believed in me. Told me things she had never said aloud.

After a few moments, I turned my attention to the rest of the scroll, to the story that had so captivated my mother that she had thought to leave a message buried within it. It was the tale of a sage from the southernmost end of Bharat named Gautama who had been blessed by the gods with centuries of longevity, and who had amassed several powerful boons with his piety besides. He had also won from the gods a prize: the beautiful bride Ahalya.

Brahma had fashioned Ahalya out of water to temper the pride of the apsaras, the dancers in Indra's heavenly court. All the gods wished to have Ahalya, and so Brahma declared that the first god to complete a race around all the worlds would win her hand in marriage. Indra, with his immense power, leapt into his golden chariot. His winged horses pulled him with ease around the heavens, the earth, and the home of the asuras. But when he returned, he found that Gautama was already married to Ahalya. He had walked in prayer around a cow giving birth to a calf, and this was equivalent to all the worlds.

Despite losing, Indra still coveted Ahalya for himself, so he bided his time, until one day Gautama left their home on some errand. Indra took Gautama's form and came to Ahalya, and they lay together. But as the day wore on, Ahalya realized she had been tricked. She begged Indra to leave, for she knew her husband's considerable wrath. It was too late, however, for as the god departed, he ran straight into Gautama.

Gautama recognized immediately what had happened, as he had long known Indra lusted after his wife. He cursed

Indra to wear his shame on his skin, covering his visage in lewd markings. When Indra returned to the heavens, Brahma took pity on him and turned those marks into eyes.

But Gautama saved his true wrath for his wife, for he believed she should have known the man at the door was Indra and resisted his advances. With another of his terrible boons, he turned Ahalya to stone and left her alone in their forest home.

The scroll ended there, and I knew there was no redemption for Ahalya—the gods would help Indra but never a woman who had slept with another man. It ate at me, for how was Ahalya to have known? The fault was Indra's from start to finish. Gautama could have chosen to understand and forgive her. But neither gods nor men had such mercy.

I understood too why my mother, living in a cold and forbidding court and exiled by her own husband, would write her missive to me on this particular story. It was a warning.

I took the scroll with me to my room and hid it among my things. I could not stop thinking about Ahalya, doomed to remain a stone statue in a forest, slowly eroding while her husband continued to wander the world. If a woman crafted by the gods themselves could be consigned to this fate, what hope was there for a woman born of a woman? Was that not what my mother had wished for me to know?

I read the scroll enough times to commit it to memory, absorbed in thoughts as overcast as the weather.

Eventually, the season passed and so did my mood. Yudhajit and I took advantage of the firmer ground by fighting particularly hard, beginning with spears and sparring until both our arms burned from effort, our breaths coming short and painful. "Father frets about the harvest from Sakala this year," Yudhajit said as we slumped against the cool ground, exhausted.

"Why? We have had ample rain." I plucked a stalk of long grass from the ground and shredded it as I spoke.

"I could not make much sense of it. He talked of blood and of the gods, but what would that have to do with the harvest?"

I closed my eyes and envisioned a map of Kekaya. Sakala was a small farming village on the southwestern border of the kingdom, near the Chandrabhaga River, which was sacred to Vishnu. Something about this pricked the back of my mind. During the rainy seasons, we had received a rare visit from some rich merchants from a town upriver of Sakala. Had I learned something then?

Of course—Manthara. She had told me of a strange event reported by the merchants' servants as we practiced—the river had split after a torrential downpour, adding a new bend. I hadn't thought much of it at the time, more focused on striking her shield with my sword. But now I said, "Oh!"

"Oh?" Yudhajit asked lazily, rolling to lie in a patch of sunlight.

"The outlying villages all perform animal sacrifice, including Sakala," I explained. "It's one of the few customs that Father has allowed them to keep, even after the sages declared the practice to be barbaric and contrary to the wishes of the gods. The village must not have realized that the new split of the Chandrabagha River runs right to them. Perhaps when they sacrificed their animals, some of the blood ran into the flooded river, offending Vishnu, as the sages had warned."

The color drained from Yudhajit's face. I understood his fear. Vishnu was among the most powerful gods. In his immortal form, he could turn fields to ash with only a thought. Just as the gods regularly answered the prayers of the pious, so too did they often visit destruction on those who they deemed immoral.

"What is Father to do about it, then?" Yudhajit had only recently been allowed into the Mantri Parishad. He often told me of their discussions, and we tried to find ways for him to prove himself to the others.

"Pray to Vishnu?" I phrased my words as a question, for I did not actually know the answer. "Perhaps if the people of Sakala make an elaborate offering, or—they could hold a Yagna! It would likely bankrupt the village, but that would surely appease Vishnu."

Yudhajit hummed thoughtfully, then threw a loose fistful of dirt at me. I supposed that meant *thank you*.

The thick, royal blue rope between us was so full and solid it seemed nearly made of metal. I could sense my brother plain as sunlight. It was difficult for Yudhajit to admit that I had a talent for matters of governance. To him, the throne was merely another tiresome responsibility. He knew well how to navigate the court and create spectacles but hated the intricacies that kept the kingdom running, the ones that I navigated as easily as I did the Binding Plane. Yudhajit liked to make fun of me for it, teasing me for how enthusiastically I threw myself into studies of history and administration.

"Ashvin is falling behind, have you noticed?" Yudhajit interrupted my daydreaming.

I pushed myself up onto my elbows. He had spoken quite casually, but this was not a casual matter. "Falling behind? In what?"

"Mostly his physical studies. He used to be a decent archer, but now he's merely passable, and he's not progressing at all in swordplay or riding."

"I hadn't noticed," I said, dismayed. I was rarely allowed out onto the practice field where my brothers trained. And Ashvin was the quietest of my brothers and least likely to complain.

"You don't have to notice everything on your own."

Yudhajit sat upright so he could face me. "That's why you have me. Should I talk to him?"

Ashvin had come down with a fever two moons ago and complained of pain so great that two servants carried him down to the deepest cellar and submerged him in the coolest bath they could draw. He had seemed to recover—but perhaps he hadn't, not fully. "I think it might be better if I speak to him," I said.

"If you insist." Yudhajit glanced up at the sky, noting the position of the sun. "Kaikeyi! We should go."

I collected and wrapped the spears and secured them to Yudhajit's horse. Despite my protests and attempts to kick him, he lifted me up onto mine, then mounted his in an easy motion.

"Race you back?" he asked.

"That's not fair, I have to let you win. Nobody can catch me riding at such an unladylike speed."

"I'll race you to the top of the first hill then," he said, smiling at me. I knew that smile worked wonders on all the court ladies, but I merely rolled my eyes.

"What will you give me if I win?" I asked.

"My undying love and affection?"

I snorted and spurred my horse. "I already have that!" I shouted over my shoulder as Yudhajit cursed at me.

My brothers adored me. But, now that Yudhajit had mentioned it, it occurred to me that Ashvin had not chosen to spend much time with me since his illness. I lingered by the stables, thinking I might speak to him after his riding practice, but was told he had missed it entirely. So I went instead to his rooms, and found him reclined on his cot, reading.

"What?" he asked sullenly when I entered the room. Out of all my brothers besides Yudhajit, Ashvin usually looked the most like me. But his small nose and tapered chin had become sunken over the past few months, giving him a sickly appearance that his shoulder-length curtain of black hair could not hide. Ashvin acted nothing like how I would have behaved had I had the privilege of being a boy, but then again, most boys knew nothing of their incredible luck. Instead of immersing himself in his weapons training or speaking his mind when invited to by my father, he always tried to shrink into the shadows and avoided the outdoors and the training fields whenever he could.

"How are your riding lessons going?" I kept my voice deliberately light and didn't look at him, instead moving to the paper window. He would wilt under too much attention.

"Fine."

"And your swordplay? How is it progressing?" I pressed.

"Fine."

"That's not what I've heard," I said gently, lowering myself to the edge of his bed.

He shrunk away from me ever so slightly.

"I think I will be dismissing your instructor. Clearly he is not doing a good job."

"No!" Ashvin protested, showing more emotion than he had for our whole conversation.

I hid a smile. "No? We cannot have you falling behind."

"It's not his fault," Ashvin whispered, almost to himself. I stayed silent, waiting and—

"I can't do it."

"Do what?" I asked.

He hung his head, and I clenched my fingers to stop myself from stroking his hair. It would only embarrass him. Instead, I found our bond, a strong white sinew, and sent him the lightest of suggestions. *Tell me.*

Ashvin sighed. "Ride. Or hold a sword properly. My elbows and my knees—" He stopped.

"Take your time," I said.

Ashvin shifted slightly. "They hurt. Ever since I got sick, they hurt all the time and even more when I'm in the practice yard."

"I see." At last I turned toward Ashvin. "Why didn't you tell me?"

"I thought it would get better," he said. The admission clearly bothered him. "What's wrong with me?"

"I don't know." To Ashvin, false vows were worse than worrisome truths. He hated the usual childhood promise that *everything will be fine.* "But I will speak to the healers. This is a side effect of some of the worst fevers; you are not alone. I think they have herbs and exercises that have helped others. They can help you."

"No," he said instantly.

"No?" I asked. "They can ease your pain."

"I don't want anyone else to know. Besides, I hate training. I hate warfare and anything to do with it. Please, didi, don't tell them," he begged. *Didi* simply meant elder sister. But even though he had used it as a term of endearment, to manipulate me, the word still filled me with warmth. The white cord between us thrummed.

"Have you always hated it?" I asked. "Or is this only because of the pain?"

"Don't act like I'm stupid," he said, turning away from me.

"Okay," I relented. "You really hate it. You can't abandon it altogether, but perhaps we can tell people you have taken an interest in healing and wish to pursue that. It's an important profession, and as the fourth-born, you would be allowed that path."

Ashvin's eyes widened. "I never thought of that."

"You're eleven. I'm sixteen," I reminded him, and finally gave in to the urge to ruffle his hair. He squirmed away from me, but I did not care, pleased with myself and my solution. "Besides, that's why I'm here."

* * *

When I received the summons to my father's private rooms, I assumed it was to discuss Ashvin's new placement. I silently rehearsed my reasons for the decision as I navigated the halls, and mentally prepared myself to try to use the thin, slippery string between us to bring him around.

But when I pushed open the door, ready for battle, I stopped short in surprise. My father and Yudhajit were seated together at a small table, papers fanned out before them. The high window and the squat flickering lamps placed in the wall niches did nothing to ease the coldness emanating from the room.

"Kaikeyi," Yudhajit said, smiling at me. It did not reach his eyes.

Dread pooled in my belly. The blue cord that connected Yudhajit and me in the Binding Plane vibrated a warning, and I imagined I could feel the thrum extend into my heart, sending a jolt through my limbs.

"Ah, Kaikeyi, thank you for joining us." My father did not sound grateful at all and did not lift his gaze from the letters in front of him. "Have a seat."

I obeyed, perching on a low wooden stool. My father's spare style did not even extend to his own comfort, although he did use a small footrest. When it became apparent he would not immediately speak, I drew a letter toward me. It was a flowery missive, extolling the virtues of some chieftain's son. My stomach flipped in awful anticipation as I read about the young man's skills in hunting and his fairness when adjudicating disputes among the clan. And there it was, right at the end: *the honor of your daughter's hand.*

Panic shot through me. I shoved the missive away from me. Only Yudhajit's quick reflexes stopped it from flying off the table.

Stay calm, he mouthed. I took a deep breath to keep myself from leaning across the table and shaking him. Calm? Father had summoned me here to discuss marriage.

Although I knew in a removed way that I would one day be wed, I could not believe it was happening now. Was I supposed to be eager for this? I felt no desire to take a man as a husband, to share a bed or a life with him. I had always assumed that I had more time to prepare myself—that it would come later, when I was older.

As if reading my thoughts, my father said, "You are already sixteen, and it is time to speak of your marriage, Kaikeyi." He finally lifted his head to look at me. "I should have arranged it years ago, but I thought your brothers needed you here, in your mother's place."

"They still need me," I protested. My voice sounded high, girlish. "I just helped Ashvin with—"

"But now I've realized your influence is making them soft," he interrupted coldly. "And we cannot postpone the matter of your marriage any longer. Our kingdom needs to make new alliances."

"Please," I began, but Yudhajit jerked his head at me and I swallowed my words. Instead, I plucked at the fragile thread between me and my father. I did not apply too much pressure, for fear it would break, even though a large part of me wanted to cut our bond straight in two.

"You bear the name of our kingdom," my father said. He seemed to soften as the thread between us quivered under my influence. "You are the first of your name and it is your duty to represent Kekaya. We are struggling. We need alliances. And you cannot stay here forever."

I bowed my head. I knew what small scraps he gave me were poor attempts at manipulation. He did not even care enough to put real effort into it. These pretty words about firsts and duty were only there to make me compliant.

When I stayed silent, he sighed. "These are the proposals we have received so far. Once we make it publicly known that you are ready, more will arrive—"

"I want a swayamvara," I said immediately, then clapped a

hand over my mouth. I had interrupted my father. For all my newfound sense of self-worth, I was still his daughter. I had broken every rule of decorum and protocol.

Anger clouded my father's features. "Don't you—"

"It's a good idea," Yudhajit said hastily. Gratitude flooded through me. I could rely on him blindly, without even going to the Binding Plane. "A swayamvara will bring attention to Kekaya. Such a contest for a woman's hand is only hosted by great kingdoms, and it can secure our place among them. And Kaikeyi will be able to pick a match among the best contestants, so she will not have to marry a man she has never met. Everyone will be happy."

I prayed for the possibility, however remote, that our father's love for Yudhajit might distract him from his anger, convince him of this plan. Yudhajit's hands were clasped, knuckles turning white. I realized he was praying too. The gods never listened to me, but perhaps they would bend for my brother. My father stared at Yudhajit for a long minute, and I held myself as still as possible, hoping to escape attention.

Finally, Raja Ashwapati nodded. "You make intelligent points, Yudhajit. You have a fine head on your shoulders."

"Thank you, Father," Yudhajit said. My father flapped a hand toward me, and I rose, thus dismissed from the preparations for my own engagement.

Yudhajit said little, leading us out past the hilly fields and into the cool forest. Unlike the densely wooded land south of Kekaya, the growth here was sparse and the brush presented little obstacle. There was no large game to be found among the trees, so hardly anyone ventured out here, giving us near total privacy. The only sounds were the thin cries of birds. For the first time, I wondered what it was they were saying.

I went to remove the weapons from his saddlebag, but he shook his head.

"Come sit," he said. I sat beside him on the slightly damp earth, leaning against rough bark and drawing my knees close to my chest. I took several slow breaths, enjoying the sharper scent of the air here. Yudhajit was silent, which was unusual. Just when I entered the Plane intending to suggest that he *speak*, he gave a small sigh.

"It will be a contest of strength," Yudhajit told me, turning so that his shoulder was against the trunk and he was facing me.

I groaned at his admission, but in truth I had not expected any less. Cleverness or charity were not much prized in a kingdom such as ours. Besides, while a swayamvara supposedly allowed a bride to pick among her suitors after they showed their skills in competition, in reality the bride's father always made clear which options were truly suitable.

But it was still better than having no choice at all. "How long do I have?"

"One year."

"Don't jest," I said. "How bad is it, really? A moon? A fortnight? Be honest."

"I am being honest. I convinced him that one year was the best option, that it would give us time to arrange a truly spectacular contest and ensure that the most powerful princes accepted our invitation. The young prince of Gandhara will certainly come—they have been seeking an alliance with us for some time. The Kambojas should send a delegation. Even Kosala might come."

Yudhajit took my hand, traced the lines of my palm with a finger. As young children, we had pretended to be soothsayers, reading each other's palms and mapping ludicrous futures. In hindsight, the stories he created for me were nowhere near absurd enough to describe the catastrophe of my life, but I had no way of knowing it then.

"A year," I breathed, nearly unable to comprehend the words. The litany of kingdoms, all powerful and important potential allies, did not excite me nearly as much as the gift that was time.

"And a choice—or at least more than you would have had," Yudhajit said. My heart surged and I tackled him into the dirt, embracing him.

"Thank you! Thank you, *thank you*, you are my favorite brother."

"Obviously," Yudhajit scoffed. "Who else would it be? Shantanu?"

"Ashvin," I said, rolling off to lie next to him in the dirt. "Ashvin is next."

"Of course. Our strangest brother."

"And who is your favorite brother?" I guessed, "Mohan?"

"You're my favorite," he said, sitting up and brushing himself off.

I remained on the ground, content. "I'm not your brother."

"You wrestle in the dirt, you like weapons and fast horses, you're smart," Yudhajit listed off. "I'd say you're more man than woman."

I rolled my eyes. "That's idiotic. Women can be all of those things. Intelligence doesn't make me less of a woman, and I would think that you knew that." The contentment faded. His words hurt, more than I could tell him.

"Don't take offense," Yudhajit said. "It's a compliment. Who wants to be a woman?"

The words were callous, careless, a joke. He was my brother, my twin, and I thought at the very least he believed me his equal. I had fooled myself into thinking I could be an exception, an intelligent woman in control of her own destiny. That he saw me that way too.

But now I was to be married off, and he would be a king.

For now, though, I was still his twin. I took his hand when he offered it, let him haul me up from the dirt, and walked with him shoulder to shoulder to our horses.

CHAPTER SEVEN

I RETURNED MANY TIMES to my mother's note, to Ahalya's story, and dreamed of finding a man who might allow me
some measure of power. Of possessing more control than my
mother had been granted. This hope made the idea of marriage seem easier to tolerate, and I made my peace with it. Perhaps I would only understand its pleasures once I was married.
And a swayamvara—some measure of choice—was something
to be savored.

Manthara was the only person I told of my impending marriage, well before my father announced the plan to the greater
court.

"I don't mind the thought of a husband, but I wish to be a
person my husband will *listen* to. How do I accomplish that?"

She cocked her head at me. "What do you want him to listen to you about?"

It was a hard question, for my future plans were so half-
formed I could not articulate them. "I want to live my life
freely," I said at last, and that much was true. "I do not want
the life my mother had."

"That is more a matter of choosing the right husband."

There may have been a time when Manthara watched her words around me, but it was long gone.

"Still," I said. "You have been preparing me for years. Certainly, you know what I must do."

"You're already doing it," she said. "Learn to run a palace and a household. And be irreplaceable."

I took her words to heart. And I returned fully to the Binding Plane.

I did not need to force anyone to do things against their will and put myself, or them, at risk. My relationship with Neeti had never recovered. She turned away from me in the halls, glared at me when nobody else was looking. Instead, I used my connections to solicit information. Rather than aiming to accomplish particular small goals, I used my connections now at random. I would often enter the Binding Plane without even realizing it, grasping my bond with a servant or minor noble and tugging to ask, *Do you have something to tell the princess?* One of the servants would tell me, "I think Arya Karan is ill." The next time Karan's cousin approached me at court, I would inquire about Arya Karan's health. My bonds within the palace increased in number and strength. This was armor of a different kind.

I sat with Manthara in the evenings, trying to work out how to manage it all. "I want to oversee Rahul's training tomorrow, as he was complaining about his instructor at dinner. And some of the ladies have invited me to a gathering, but I wonder whether it will be completely frivolous. Might I offend them if I do not go? Because there is to be an offering to the gods in the main square of the city at the end of the week, and I want to talk to some of the servants to make sure the preparations are moving smoothly."

"You do not need to attend the gathering," Manthara told me. "They want to discuss suitable matches for some of the younger nobles—you were invited as a courtesy."

"I can go to Rahul's lessons directly after my tutoring, then, and speak to the servants in the evening."

"Are you even learning anything in your lessons anymore?" Manthara asked. "Surely you can read and write better than your tutors."

My tutors did not even glance at my work. But I liked having the time to sit and read old texts and scrolls and write my thoughts, to learn new stories and histories and to think without interruption.

Similarly, my lessons with Yudhajit were no longer about new skills, but to hone my abilities. This had another purpose too. Through him, I could absorb as much information about the council and the men's work as possible.

But one evening, Yudhajit came to find me outside of our scheduled lessons, a nervous expression on his face. Before he even opened his mouth, I could tell he was about to shatter my fragile acceptance of my fate.

"Father's doing *what*?" I shoved Yudhajit into my room, slamming the door behind me.

Yudhajit raised his hands in surrender. "I'm sorry, I only just learned. I thought you would want to know right away."

"Did you say anything to him? Did you tell him it was a stupid idea?" I kicked my bed, hard, biting down a yelp of pain as my foot began to throb.

Yudhajit winced and backed away. "No."

I pushed air through my lungs, in, out, in, out, until my fists stopped trembling. I could not—should not—punch my brother, heir to Kekaya.

"So, you have some sort of plan, then?" Rage made the Binding Plane hard to summon, so in my mind I returned to the old meditation guide, reciting the mantra to find it. When the blue bond between us finally appeared, it throbbed with wild energy, resembling a skipping rope turned by two uncoordinated and excitable children. I let it slip away at once, conscious of my roiling emotions.

Yudhajit turned away and pressed his forehead against the door. He mumbled something that I couldn't make out.

"What was that?"

"I said, I don't think it's a stupid idea." He looked over his shoulder at me, but whatever expression I made must have frightened him, because he quickly dropped his head back against the door.

"I think I misheard you," I said after a moment, grinding the words out through my bared teeth. "Unless you meant to say that it is worse than stupid?"

Yudhajit shook his head. "I know you were promised a swayamvara. And I meant to see it through. But things are changing quickly. The harvests were terrible this year. We can barely find the coin for a swayamvara, let alone the full spectacle other kingdoms will expect of us. And the dowry would have to be immense. It can't happen the way you wanted, Kaikeyi. You need to get married soon," he said. "The bride price that they have asked is manageable, and Kosala is so prosperous that this alliance should improve Kekaya's situation. Raja Dasharath himself is respectable and—"

"*You're* not married," I countered.

"I'm not a woman," Yudhajit snapped, turning around. "You have a responsibility to your family."

"I have fulfilled the duties of the woman of the household," I all but shouted at him. "I raised our brothers. I have helped make our court one that is widely known, admired even, in our region. Please, tell me how I have not yet fulfilled my responsibility to my family."

"You—"

"No," I cut him off. In that moment, I hated him. "I will not be lectured on my responsibility by you. What have *you* done for this kingdom?"

"One day, I will be the raja," he said, as if that in and of itself was an achievement rather than a birthright. "This is a good match for you, Kaikeyi. You will be a radnyi."

"What a burden to be raja," I spat out. A deep, visceral anger had taken over my being. I could not believe he had the gall to act as though he knew best for me. "If I marry him, I will be his third radnyi, and the youngest. He has asked for me because he remains childless." I shook my head, unable to meet my brother's eyes. There were some things I could not share even with him, and my tangled knot of feelings about motherhood was one of them. "Everyone knows he wants a son. What does he believe? That Mother was fertile, so I must be too?"

"Is that so bad?"

"How can you be fine with consigning me to life as nothing but a brood mare? You're my brother, Yudhajit! You're my brother." I blinked back hot tears.

"It won't be like that. You will be radnyi of a great kingdom," Yudhajit said. He took a step toward me. "It is a great honor. Even when planning the swayamvara, we did not believe Dasharath would seek your hand. Kosala is a greater kingdom than ours, perhaps the greatest Bharat knows. It has the most fertile land, the most powerful army. Just think. One day your son could have that."

I knew rationally that Dasharath was an honorable match for me and, more importantly, my family. And yet—

"I wanted to have a choice," I said softly. "My swayamvara is only two months away. Surely, we can wait. I will at least be able to meet the men, pick among those who complete the task, have some control over my future."

Yudhajit snorted. "Did you really believe that at the swayamvara Father would let you have any choice among your suitors? None of us have a real choice. My first marriage has been arranged since I was seven years old. As a third wife, you may not have power, but you will have freedom."

I shook my head. What a fool he was, believing that some small portion of freedom was a better prize than power. "You don't understand. You're not a woman."

"Perhaps not," Yudhajit said. "But I understand you, Kaikeyi. This is best."

"I know what's best for me, not you, not Father, not anybody," I snapped. "Do not force me to go through with this!"

"I'm not forcing you to do anything. Father has made this choice. I am simply trying to counsel you in this matter."

"I don't need your counsel." I met his gaze squarely. "In fact, I don't need you at all."

Yudhajit reared back as if I had slapped him. Bitter satisfaction flowed through my veins as the cord connecting us, once full and vibrant—the strongest bond I had in the Binding Plane—began to wither like a dying flower. "You've always needed me. But the truth is I've only ever had myself." It wasn't true, not exactly, but I knew how to hurt him and so I did.

Yudhajit just stared at me, eyes wide.

"Get out of my room."

He blinked. I saw a tear upon his eyelashes. Another blink, it rolled down his face. He scrubbed at his eyes with the heels of his hands and looked back up at me, pleadingly. Our bond, now a delicate thing, quivered.

"I said, get out."

He went.

The next morning, several attendants were sent to my room to prepare me for court. I felt numb as I watched them unfold my sari, a bejeweled length of shining red silk adorned with delicate blossoms of gold. They wrapped it around me, the material surprisingly soft, although the regimented fan of knife-like pleats restricted my movements far more than I would have liked.

They pulled my dark hair back, coiling and pinning and

coiling and pinning until it sat in a heavy bun against my nape, then covered it with one end of the sari cloth, leaving only a few strands free to frame my face.

They laid an ornate ruby necklace around my throat in an attempt to draw attention away from my too-wide shoulders. Its gold links were studded intermittently with small red stones, and the large gem in the center gleamed like a drop of blood against my collarbone. I was grateful for the years of training that allowed me to stand tall beneath its weight. A delicate gold pendant hung down onto my forehead, all of Kekaya's supposed riches now on display for this mighty raja.

They applied rose water to my wrists and dark kohl to my eyes and painted my lips in a sticky red dye. I had to remind myself every few seconds not to rub the heaviness from my face.

When I looked in the mirror, I was surprised that I could still recognize myself. But all of my features were slightly altered, my eyes larger, my mouth more...noticeable. The drape of the sari pallu brought out my curves. For previous appearances at feasts and important occasions, I had been dressed well, but as one would dress a child, with little face paint and simple jewelry. But now—I looked like the other noblewomen of the court. And, with a jolt, I realized I looked a bit like my mother. She had been considered very beautiful, and I could see that maybe, accentuated by all this finery, I could be too.

I would not want to look like this every day. But it was nice, if strange, to see this other version of me.

I walked to the court accompanied by two guards, my chin lifted in a passable imitation of a radnyi. The finery gave me confidence to face whatever came next, like a thin layer of armor between me and the world.

A herald announced my entrance to the throne room, and I swept in with all the grace I could muster, avoiding the urge to look to the various nobles who lined the walls to gauge their reaction to my new appearance.

My father stood upon my arrival, as did the stranger next to him. I checked the cord connecting Yudhajit and me and found it recovered from yesterday. But it had undoubtedly diminished. I forced myself to look away from my twin and instead turned to the foreign man.

The first thing I noticed was that he was much younger than my father, and I might have sagged in relief. My lips quirked upward before I could stop my reaction, and his own mouth twitched in response. He was watching me intently, spine straight as a spear. I saw something in his expression, a ferocity, that I recognized as kin. But with a belated start, I realized everyone was waiting for me as I studied this man. I pressed my hands together and bowed to my father, and then to Raja Dasharath, my husband-to-be.

My father extolled the accomplishments of the fair-haired king, speaking not to me but to the assembled court. I barely paid attention to his words.

My conversation with Yudhajit had made clear one thing. If I wanted power, I would have to take it. And after spending half the night tossing sleeplessly, I thought I knew how.

Raja Dasharath was childless, and he needed me to give him a child.

"And, if you are amenable," my father concluded, "I will provide my blessing for the marriage and you will be wed in a fortnight."

If you are amenable. I knew the words he expected me to say, the expressions of gratitude and the praises of Dasharath, the acceptance of the marriage.

All I had to do now was make one simple request. One simple, improper request.

I turned to the man in question and asked, "You would have me as your third wife?"

If he was surprised at my forthrightness, it did not show on his face. But in the Binding Plane, a golden bond spun into existence between us.

"Yes, my lady." His reaction gave me the confidence to continue.

"And you are thus far without child?" I asked.

He leaned forward, resting his elbows on his knees, but his calm expression gave nothing away. "Yes, my lady."

"I would accept your proposal of marriage, but on one condition." I kept my gaze on his, my shoulders back, my chin high. I could not take back the words now.

"I will consider it," he said. Was that a smile playing on his lips?

I took a deep, steadying breath. "If I should bear you a son, he will be named your heir, regardless of any other sons you may have in the future. I may be your third wife, but my child will be first." As I spoke, I fed the idea into our golden connection as well.

My eyes stayed fixed on Dasharath, for I was too afraid to look at my father and see his rage and disappointment. There was every chance that Dasharath would refuse, and that I had made a fool of our entire kingdom. I could not even fathom what would become of me then.

My clasped hands grew damp with sweat and I clutched them tightly together so they would not shake. Each beat of my heart sounded in my ears. As the seconds went by, I regretted my decision.

"Done, my lady," Raja Dasharath said suddenly, rising and descending the steps.

I gave a small gasp, and then, as elation swept through me, I smiled. It was wide—too wide for court—but I could not hide my relief, my happiness. He smiled in return, the corners of his eyes crinkling. In that moment, he looked exceedingly kind.

"Then I am yours."

* * *

Whatever my father had initially thought of my foolhardy scheme, he had only words of praise once the decision was made.

"Our bloodlines will rule and unite two great kingdoms," he told Ashvin. "She has done well," he told Shantanu. It was the most genuine praise I had ever received from my father, albeit indirectly, and it was some consolation to know that I would be thought well of in Kekaya after my departure.

Manthara too seemed inordinately pleased at my maneuverings and gave me a crushing hug when she heard the story of my engagement. I knew that Manthara would always act in my best interests. She was the only person in my life I could truly rely on. And so, as the wedding preparations began and I readied myself to leave for the palace in Ayodhya, the capital city of Kosala, I insisted upon bringing her with me. Dasharath easily agreed. He must have been quite desperate for a son.

The only obstacle to my happiness, then, was Yudhajit. We studiously avoided each other, except regarding preparations for the various ceremonies. As the eldest of my brothers, he had duties to perform at the wedding. I did not want to bring dishonor upon the court by requesting that Shantanu act in his stead. Sometimes, in these moments, I thought I saw Yudhajit staring at me out of the corner of my eye, but when I turned toward him, he was never looking my way.

This time passed in a haze. I selected my wedding sari, a dark yellow silk creation with crimson embroidery and precious stones winking in swirls along the blouse. I conspired with the head cook over the menu, the two of us ensuring there were as many desserts as courses. I said my goodbyes to the palace staff and spent precious moments with my brothers.

On the day before my wedding, I walked through the halls, committing them to memory. And then, I made a special, final pilgrimage to the library cellar.

The scant light and strange stone shadows had made the room seem immense to me as a child, but now I could cross the room in twenty paces. I spent a full hour wandering there, running my hands down the rows of scrolls, trying to embed the most important place in the palace into my mind. I closed my eyes and tried to remember the feel of sitting next to my mother in the quiet corner. Her message to me, Ahalya's story, remained safely tucked among the few possessions I would bring to Ayodhya.

I emerged into the waning day.

Alone, I took one last ride on my favorite horse, a powerful gray mare who would not be making the journey southeast with me. When I reached the hilltop where Yudhajit and I had raced so many times, I watched the sun sink slowly away. From this height, I could just barely make out the stables. And if I closed my eyes, my heart remembered the feel of running through the grounds with my brothers, of sparring with Yudhajit and lying in the grasses talking for hours. I wished I could capture the feeling somehow, etch it into my bones so I would have it always.

That night, I lay in my near-empty room and stared up at the ceiling.

It occurred to me, as it often did while I waited for sleep to take me, that maybe the gods had marked me for my mother's sins. Sons could not be held responsible for maternal sins, but daughters? My mother had told me to remember Ahalya's lesson. Nothing protected me.

I was surprised to feel hot tears pricking my eyes. I blinked them away, helplessly infuriated. My mother should have been here. I needed her comfort and guidance. Manthara had helped me through my first moon cycle, and more recently had explained the mechanics of the acts Dasharath would expect from me, but she had never actually been married. If Manthara had done such things herself, she could never say, and so

I could not ask her my real questions. But perhaps I could have asked my mother: Did you feel the same disinterest contemplating such matters as I did?

For when I thought about the acts Manthara described, or when I studied the illustrations in some of the more well-hidden recesses of the library, I felt only indifference. I had heard serving girls talk in whispers and giggles about men they found charming, or how it felt to steal a covert kiss with their betrothed. I thought of Dasharath and searched for the same desire within myself, but nothing ever emerged.

The faintest of knocks sounded against my door, disturbing me from my thoughts. I held my breath, wondering if perhaps I had imagined it. But the knock came again. I slid out of bed, padded to the door, raised my hand, and then hesitated.

In all likelihood, Yudhajit stood on the other side. We had a secret signal. I would tap it out—four beats, a pause, four beats, then he would tap out a pattern of three beats with an emphasis on the last. But I did not know if I wanted to face Yudhajit right now.

Maybe he had come to apologize. Maybe I still had a chance to leave him on good terms. I rapped out the pattern, and he immediately knocked his reply. I opened the door a crack. He stepped inside and closed the door behind him.

I crossed my arms, trying my best to keep my face impassive. "Why are you here?"

"It's the night before your wedding!"

"It's the night before a wedding you pushed me into," I reminded him coldly. "This night is your fault."

"Kaikeyi, you can't hold this against *me*."

"I can and I will. It may not have been by your hand, but your silent agreement is just as bad. Had you stood with me as you promised, the both of us might have changed Father's mind."

Yudhajit frowned. "I thought perhaps the past few weeks

would have cleared your head. I prayed to the goddesses that you might realize your folly. But no. Do you really think either of us, or even both of us together, could have changed his mind? I was being reasonable. As you should've been."

Taking two steps back, moving as far away from Yudhajit as possible, I slipped into the Binding Plane. Once again, our diminished bond vibrated with angry energy, but today I was beyond caring. He had not come to apologize. He had not even bothered to see it through my eyes. "You think he is more reasonable than I am?"

"No! I mean, yes. But, Kaikeyi, *think*. You're leaving. Whether now or later, you were always going to go away, to leave me. I have to live with Father, stay in his graces. You can't understand. When he asked me if I thought Dasharath was a good match, I encouraged it. For *you*. He is a good man. He will take care of you."

"You encouraged it?" There was a familiar coldness in my voice, a tone that belonged not to me but to my father.

"I thought it was your best choice," he said quietly.

"*But I didn't choose.* You chose! That's not a choice."

"You're not the only person in this palace."

I groaned in disgust. "You sold me for what? A few peaceful months with Father?"

"This is all going wrong," he said. He sighed and moved to sit on my bed, but I stood in his way. He hung his head. "I came here to make things right. Before you left."

"Congratulations on another job well done." I pushed as much venom into my voice as I could. Yudhajit flinched. *Good.* "What you did is unforgivable. You will perform the rites at my wedding tomorrow and then we need never see each other again."

"Please, Kaikeyi, I didn't mean—" The thread between us shook with such emotion it was almost a blur. I tried to catch it with my mind, to still it somehow and force Yudhajit to see reason, but it slipped through my uncoordinated grasps.

"Leave, Yudhajit. This time, I mean it. I cannot wait until the moment we never have to see each other again."

"I did what I thought was best." He reached for my hand, squeezing it. I yanked it away.

"Go, now. I'll be someone else's problem soon enough."

"I do love you," he said sadly. "You'll always be my sister."

As though from far away, I heard myself say those poisoned words: "You are no brother of mine." Without my conscious thought, the idea passed through our dark blue connection, a black disease speeding its way toward my brother's chest with the force of a piercing arrow.

My aim struck true. The bond between us shattered, falling in a rain of blue pieces only I could see as Yudhajit fled my room.

PART TWO

CHAPTER EIGHT

THERE ARE THOSE WHO would blame Manthara for what I did, claim that she forced me to take her to Ayodhya and manipulated me from there. But my choices were my own, and to pull Manthara's name down with mine would be quite simply cruel. Because without Manthara's continued presence by my side, I would never have ridden off to battle or saved the king, and Kosala would have fallen, heirless, into the depths of time.

My first impression of Ayodhya was one of beauty. The sight of the palace and the grounds completely arrested me. A lush expanse of greenery sprawled to the edges of the walls, dotted with gracefully curving paths, framed by a rich profusion of flowers. Their fragrance perfumed the air, rose and jasmine mingling into a gentle and welcoming scent. It was a marked change from the tall grasses and simple, unadorned lawns of Kekaya. Before me, the palace rose upward, constructed out of light gray stone that glinted here and there in the light as though infused with gems. It was crowned by a curved dome that pointed toward the sky, proclaiming Ayodhya's power for all to see.

And the size—the grounds stretched outward, extending like an unfurled flower. A series of delicate open arches surrounded the interior of the palace, lending the structure depth. I took a few steps closer and was able to make out intricate carvings above the arches, patterns of intertwined stars and moons. Above the arches, I could see large windows covered in paper that must have let in much light during the day. Now I could understand why others had found my old home, with its dull stone and stark decoration, dark and foreboding. Just the sight of this place lightened my spirits.

"Do you like it?" Dasharath asked, smiling at me.

I nodded eagerly. "It's incredible."

I followed behind him in a daze, reveling in the tapestry-covered halls. In Kekaya, the fashion had been black figures patterned against a single color, when tapestries were hung at all. But here, it was all I could do not to stop and stare at each of the colorful scenes laid out in the weavings before me.

One was done in such vibrant hues of blue and green that I had to pause to look more closely. It was an image of a great fish pulling a boat, and I recognized the story of Matsya and Manu. Manu was a young man, a chief of a tribe, when he discovered a small fish in his drinking water—Matsya. Manu was a kind man, and when Matsya spoke of his fear of being eaten by bigger fish, Manu offered his protection. When the fish grew large enough to be safe, Manu released Matsya into a river. Before he left, Matsya instructed Manu to build a boat and board it on an appointed day. No sooner had Manu finished the boat and ushered his family onto it than a great flood swept through the land, destroying all in its path. But Matsya returned to Manu, carrying him to the safety of the Indra Mountains until the waters had receded. There, Matsya revealed his true form—for he was no ordinary fish, but an avatar of Lord Vishnu come to earth, and he was rewarding Manu for his kindness. It was fitting to see this tapestry here, for legend tells that when Manu descended from the mountains, he founded the first city of men—Ayodhya.

"It's one of my favorite stories," Dasharath said, coming to stand beside me. "The story of our city."

"I used to love it as a child." I suddenly wished to tell him about the library cellar, about sitting in the flickering light with my mother and reading through scrolls, but I found myself unable to share this piece of me. Still, our golden bond seemed to sparkle a bit more brightly.

"Are there other stories you enjoyed? We could have a tapestry made for you," he offered. I shook my head, for I was far too overwhelmed to think up other tales I might want to see. But it was a kind offer, and I was glad for his kindness.

Dasharath walked slowly after that, letting me take in the sights, until we arrived at the left wing of the palace. Fresh garlands of small white mogra hung from the walls, enveloping the whole corridor in sweetness. I wondered if this was how the halls were adorned every day, or if they had made special preparations for my arrival.

My husband threw open the doors of a vast chamber with a great papered window on the opposite wall that let light into all corners. It was a strange living space, though, for I could see no bed. As I hesitated, fumbling for what to say, Dasharath said, "Do you not wish to see the rest?"

"The rest?" I echoed, and he beckoned me inward. I realized only then, stupidly perhaps, that there were carved doors set in the walls on either side of us. The one on the left opened onto another spacious chamber, dominated by a great bed that four people easily could have slept on. A covering of dark red wool warmed the floor, and an exquisite wooden cabinet inlaid with intricate swirls of mother-of-pearl stood against the wall. I touched the decoration with my fingertips, tracing the carved vines and flowers.

"Do you like it?" he asked.

"It is beautiful," I said, unable to wrench my gaze away.

"Not unlike you, then." His voice was filled with a quality entirely foreign to me. I turned to look at him, but he was already striding past me, through the main room and onto the other side. There he revealed a small chamber mostly taken up by a table and cushioned seating.

"If there is anything you need, you can ask any of our servants." He sounded—nervous? Or perhaps impatient.

"Thank you, my lord," I said with a bow. "You honor me. I am sure you have more important matters to attend to."

"The happiness of my wife is one of the most important matters I can think of." He gave me a small smile. "I will leave you now, but not for long."

Manthara was waiting outside of the door, only entering when Dasharath had departed. I went back into the bed chamber, marveling at the space, while she examined every nook and sill. "He has done well," she said at last. "Now I must find some maidservants to help you prepare. Of course, you will have to choose your own staff eventually…"

Manthara bustled about, talking of preparations, as I sat and pondered what this new life might have to offer.

The next morning, Manthara and I set ourselves to the task of turning my quarters into a living space. My belongings had been moved into the room, and as Manthara unpacked, I cast a critical eye over each item I had brought, having taken in the opulence of Dasharath's court. All my best outfits appeared frumpy in comparison to the elegant eastern fashions. I tried to recapture my confidence from the day I had been adorned to meet Dasharath—the glimpse of my mother, the assurance to hold my head high—but I could not. I might have been worthy to be a radnyi in Kekaya, but here…

I lifted one blouse, which extended past my waistline. "Not one woman wore a blouse this long," I said.

"You can get it hemmed," Manthara answered without looking up from her work. "Or have new ones ordered."

I picked up one of my favorite saris, a lovely sky blue thing that I secretly had always believed suited me well. "This color is so dull."

"You have never cared much about such matters before," Manthara said. "Where is this concern coming from?"

"I never had to worry about whether what I wore was in fashion before," I replied. "I want the court to like me, not see me as backward."

"They will like you," Manthara said as a knock sounded on the door. I liked the sound of it, the solidity of the wood of the door and the slight echo that spoke to the size of my room. Manthara went to receive the caller while I stood by my bed, still considering what I could wear in the evening's court assembly.

"I apologize, but the radnyi is busy," I heard Manthara say.

"I won't be but a moment." The woman's voice sounded familiar, and I gave up on making a decision, dropping the fabric in a bundle and entering the main room in a plain cream dress, only to find Radnyi Kaushalya.

I panicked and bowed to her, before realizing I did not need to do any such thing, and straightened so abruptly that I stumbled forward a step. My face flushed with heat and Kaushalya's lips twisted into a barely concealed smirk. "Are you all right?" she asked.

"Yes," I whispered, embarrassment making me curt. She lifted a single eyebrow, and I added, "You honor me with your presence. Won't you come inside?"

She stepped into the main room, the scent of sandalwood sweeping in with her, and glanced around.

Kaushalya was Dasharath's first radnyi. She stood a head above me, but her graceful neck and perfect posture made her seem even taller. The drape of her rich orange sari suggested soft, womanly curves, at odds with her sharp bun and cutting cheekbones. Garnets glinted at her throat, setting off her luminous skin. The effect was so lovely that I wished to hide myself behind a curtain to avoid any attempt at comparison between us.

"It's quite bare," she said.

"No different than my rooms back home," I said immediately. Before I could give offense, I hastily added, "But these are much bigger."

Kaushalya turned to look at me, brow furrowed. Somehow even that was elegant. "This is your home now." She sounded kind, but I sensed an undercurrent of disapproval. I bit my tongue, annoyed that somehow every word I had said so far had come out completely wrong. "Do you need assistance?"

Perhaps her offer was genuine, but in that moment, it seemed like a challenge. She believed me a simpleton, a bumbling fool. "No, I am perfectly fine on my own." I straightened my shoulders and met her eyes.

"I see," she said. She glanced me up and down, then gave a little half shrug, casting me back into my girlhood and all of my early interactions with the Kekayan court. My cheeks burned. "I suppose you have no need of me, then." She turned neatly on her heel and departed, leaving me bewildered at the exchange. I entered the Binding Plane and found only a slim wisp of black between us. I grasped it, hoping to leave her with the impression that this conversation had not been a complete disaster, but even the slight brush of my mind against the cord caused it to tremble, and so I withdrew.

I had never been in this position before, where my bonds were so tremulous that I could not even attempt my usual methods of influencing people. I felt small, useless, as though I was twelve years old and without my mother for the first time, unable to comprehend the palace without her.

I soon discovered the same was true for Radnyi Sumitra,

who invited me to take my afternoon refreshment in her rooms. I assumed this would be much the same as the gatherings I had attended in Kekaya, with several noblewomen and much gossip. Instead, it was just Sumitra and I perched on delicate chairs, her watching me as I tried not to marvel at her rooms. They were laid out in a similar fashion to mine, but bursting with colorful ornaments, beautifully painted clay lamps, and divans adorned with emerald-colored cushions, all giving the place a full and joyful feeling.

"How have you been settling in?" she asked me. Unlike Kaushalya, Sumitra smelled of rosewater, and her clothing was always in light, pastel shades—today she wore blush. She was a much less intimidating figure, but her easy cheer still set me off-balance.

I gave her a small smile. "Well, and you?"

"I am glad to have you here," she said. She was only a few years older than I was but seemed to know so much more. "Do you need anything? I know all of this can be overwhelming at first. Especially for one as young as you."

I had been with her for all of three minutes and already it felt like she was poking fun at me. Had Kaushalya told her about our first meeting? Did she too think I was some naive yuvradnyi? "I assure you, I am fine."

"I am happy to introduce you to people, if you would like," she pressed on.

It would have been so nice to have someone guide me, to tell me who and what I needed to know. And yet, would she not think me weak for admitting so? "Perhaps," I said, hoping not to seem too eager. I was desperate for her to think of me as independent.

But instead, Sumitra's brow furrowed briefly before her expression smoothed over. "At your convenience, then." Her voice had taken on a distance. In the Binding Plane, our silver bond was as wispy as cotton.

It was no better with the other courtiers. I wondered if Kaushalya had spread rumors about me, or if the same things that had made me so off-putting to her were apparent to the rest of the court. I could barely touch any of my new Ayodhyan connections with my mind for fear of accidentally snapping them—they could not be of any real use to me. After a few awkward failed attempts at conversation with even lower nobility, I resigned myself to loneliness. Everyone remained polite, of course, greeting me at court or if they passed me in the corridors, but they did not seek me out or try to gain my favor. Word spread, I am sure, of the strangeness of Dasharath's new radnyi.

When I was able, I wandered the palace halls, learning my new home as best as I could on my own. I occasionally attended Dasharath's open courts in the main hall, seated in a balcony with the other women, or skirted the training fields when the men were too engrossed in practice to notice me. I made appearances at celebrations and rituals, observing all of the rites of the gods, knowing full well it would not help me even in this new land. I attended evening dance performances in the elegant main courtyard, a practice that had been confined to temples in Kekaya, and admired the talent of these men, who floated despite the weight of bells at their ankles, arms extending toward the sky, spinning and leaping as they told wordless stories that made my heart ache. I even tried to search out the library, but the cellars were hard to find in Ayodhya. I discovered one, near the kitchens, but it was filled with food, not scrolls. A servant happened upon me and hovered at my elbow, clearly wishing for me to leave. Fearful I would gain a reputation for being a glutton or a nuisance, I stopped searching.

Dasharath was the only person in Ayodhya I regularly spoke with, other than Manthara, for he summoned me to his rooms at least once a week, save when I was bleeding.

The first time he kissed me, on our wedding night, I had flinched away, and he laughed, presumably finding my strange virgin behavior endearing and amusing. The next time he kissed me, on my third night in Ayodhya, my body bucked involuntarily, and in desperation I had tried to use our cord to stop him. He did not find it endearing the second time. "Surely you cannot be surprised now," he had said, his voice gentle but firm. "You are the one who wanted a son." The look on his face worried me, for I needed him at least to like me, and so I held myself stiff but did not move away.

After several weeks in Ayodhya, I had become accustomed enough to his attentions that I had learned to mime the correct response, even though I did not understand why it was necessary. Our bond was not yet strong enough for me to influence or redirect his desires—perhaps it would never be. So I would bear his kissing for a few minutes, and then he would lead me by the hand toward his bed. He would set to my clothes with a brisk efficiency, the pleats of my sari unraveling under his hands as I stood still as a statue. He thought me submissive and meek in the bedroom, but that was better than him sensing my disinterest in the acts he wished to perform.

"It does not matter what you feel for him," Manthara had told me, one week before my wedding. "All that matters is what he thinks you feel for him. And perhaps, in time, you will grow to like it."

"I will never like it," I had said then.

Manthara had only chuckled. "That matters very little when you are a radnyi."

And she was right. For although I had no appetite for such things, I pretended to, and he pretended to care about what I felt, using his body and, on a few occasions, his tongue. In a way, I was thankful that I had a kind husband, one who at least wished for my pleasure as well as his. I knew I could have done far worse than this.

And yet, sometimes I found myself wishing that I did care for him in this way, that I could give myself to at least this duty of a radnyi. Men were allowed to be more open with their desires, but I had of course heard women speak of the wanting that accompanied marriage. They had all made such desire seem like one of the most important parts of becoming husband and wife. But I lacked it. What did that make my marriage?

Once, I came to Dasharath earlier than he had expected, and when he did not open the door, I let myself in. It was an old habit, formed by years of entering my brother's rooms without warning.

I found him poring over a cloth laid out on a large table. I approached it, curious, and saw a very detailed map of Kosala, beautifully and precisely inked, depicting the settlements within the kingdom.

I took a step closer, and at my movement, Dasharath glanced up.

"Kaikeyi, I did not expect you so soon!"

"I apologize for disturbing you, Raja," I said immediately. "I can leave if you are occupied."

He shook his head, smoothing out the map with one hand. "I was merely thinking."

I stared at the map for several moments more, taking it all in. I had seen versions of such maps of Kekaya in the library cellar but had never had the opportunity to study a map of Kosala. My eyes were immediately drawn to where the kingdom's borders began just east of the Sarasvati River, although to look at this map, that area was no longer well populated.

Despite my brother telling me about the might of Kosala, and my own distant awareness of it as our southeastern neighbor, I had not had a true awareness of how vast my husband's kingdom truly was. The Indra Mountains ran diagonally across the top of Bharat, forming the northernmost borders of

Kekaya and Kosala, which divided at the source of the Sarasvati River, high up in the mountain peaks. But in addition to
the section of the Indra Mountains within Kosala's control, its
borders encompassed an entire mountain range to the south,
as well as several cities beyond even that. I swept my eyes over
the map again, a bit awed.

A cluster of red markings just to the north of Kosala's borders caught my attention. I peered closer, to find dashed arrows
from villages at the foothills of the Indra Mountains running
in and out of Kosala's borders—raids, it seemed.

"Who are they?" I asked, brushing my fingertips against
the shading. I worried perhaps I was being too forward, but I
didn't wish to stop. I had not had any real conversation with
my husband since our unexpected moment in the throne room
so long ago.

He raised an eyebrow. "You read that quite fast."

"Thank you?" I said, uncertain.

Dasharath's eyes flicked up to my face before looking down
at the map with a sigh. "It is a newer kingdom, or at least, they
proclaim themselves to be a kingdom. In reality they are just a
collection of villages united by the warlord Sambarasura, who
has promised them a share of Kosala's riches if they only arm
themselves."

"They've been targeting trade routes," I observed.

"Yes, but you see there?" He pointed to a cluster of villages next to the River Ganga, and when I looked closer, I saw
annotations—*burned, thirty dead, harvest ruined.* "They have
made several forays into our farming towns and are growing
more violent. Stealing is one thing, but this—" He shook his
head.

This time, Dasharath actually studied my face, and I could
see him losing interest in the conversation as he remembered
why I was there. "You do not need to worry," he said, coming
around the table to take my hand. "It will be taken care of."

"All right," I told him. "Kosala is my home now too." I wanted to add, *If there is anything I can do*—but no, it was not worth going down that path. After all, what could he possibly need from me?

Without Manthara, I might never have survived those first months. In the privacy of my rooms, free from the restrictive dress and the formal speech of court, I was often too dispirited to do anything but spend hours lying in bed. Manthara would sit patiently beside me, embroidering and teaching me the names and roles of nobility I was certain I would never meet. Once she even offered to practice swordplay with me, as we used to do. I could tell from a glance at the Binding Plane she did not really want to, and it made me realize just how worried she was about me, so I rose from bed to stretch and pace, and then lift objects and review the footwork Yudhajit had once taught me.

But when Manthara was not around, I would lie back in bed and enter the Binding Plane and stare at the strings, despairing at how I had so quickly become useless. If there was other magic out there, something that might help me become a part of this foreign place, it was within the purview of the gods. I was alone.

On one such day, she returned early from whatever other work she did in the palace and found me lying in bed once again. Where before she often viewed me with sympathy, instead she clucked her tongue at me. "Get up," she ordered. I was so surprised to hear this tone in her voice, one that had been missing for so long, that I obeyed instantly. "Wear your pale blue sari, the one from Kekaya."

"The court will laugh," I muttered.

"We're not going to court." Her voice brooked no argument and so I dressed myself, intrigued despite the fog that still surrounded me. I followed her down the hallway to a small door, presumably the entrance to a servants' passage, designed to help them move more easily through the palace. After descending a rickety stair and navigating a short maze of walkways, Manthara pushed open a second door, giving a quick nod to the guard stationed there. He just yawned, barely glancing in our direction.

We had emerged onto a small side alley, on the other side of the palace wall.

"What—" I began, turning around. But Manthara gripped my arm and pulled me out of the alley and into a bustling road.

This was nothing like Kekaya, where the quarters nearest the palace were sparsely populated. Here, just beyond the palace, merchants sold their wares to the streams of city dwellers passing by on their business. Manthara's arm snaked around my shoulders, and she pulled the pallu of my sari up so the cloth covered my head.

"I have been asked to buy some things by the ladies of the palace. I do not work for them, of course, but it is good to do them favors from time to time. I thought you might want to accompany me. Stay close."

We set off, and I felt almost giddy to be swept up in the bustle. The thoroughfare next to the palace let out quickly into a large open square. Manthara approached one man who had laid out a gorgeous array of glass bangles in a rainbow of hues. I watched as Manthara haggled for a few minutes before sweeping up a collection, deep crimson and cobalt and saffron all glinting in the sunlight.

"What need have noblewomen of those?" I asked. The bangles were lovely, but not the type of thing the fine women of court arrayed themselves in.

"Trinkets for their children or grandchildren," Manthara said. "They do not have the money to let small fingers break their precious objects, wealthy though they may be."

At another stall, Manthara stopped to buy a bundle of

fragrant dried herbs. She carded through the selection with deft fingers before alighting on one that looked to me the same as the others. "Can these be mixed with milk?" she asked.

"Of course," the man said briskly.

"Are you sure?" Manthara pressed. "I have heard complaints of stomach pain after doing so, and I do not want to displease my mistress."

"Yes," he insisted, just as another voice said, "No."

A woman who had been crouched next to the stall and tending to a brazier that let off a smoky aroma rose to her feet. "Those should not be taken with milk. You are correct that it can sometimes cause digestive upset, and in that case won't take effect."

The man's hand darted out quick as a cobra, landing a slap on the back of the woman's head. "Did I ask you?" he hissed. Flinching, she shook her head and silently squatted back down to her work. To Manthara the man said, "Forgive her, she does not know her place. As I was saying, the herbs can be taken with or without milk. But if your mistress has difficulties with milk, there is no harm in trying without."

Manthara's mouth was pursed in a thin line of displeasure, and she haggled with the man for far longer than she had at the previous stall before exchanging the herbs for a scant few coins and moving on. As we pressed farther into the square, I turned back to look at the woman. I thought perhaps I would find her crying. But she was staring down at her brazier, turning the drying stems of her plants carefully, as if nothing had happened.

I had never been taken to a marketplace in Kekaya, but I was grateful to have the chance to witness such a thing in Ayodhya. The market seemed full of chaos, and possibility. People shouted and bartered, their anger at a bad bargain or pleasure at good craftsmanship flowing freely. There was something alive about this place. And yet as I swept my gaze over the stalls, I saw not a single woman standing alone behind one. There were women to be sure, folding fabric, rearranging their goods in preparation for customers. But all were accompanied by men, and none seemed in control.

"Kaikeyi?" Manthara said softly in my ear. "Are you ready to go?"

"Is it always like this?" I asked.

"Today is the busiest day of the week," she said, misunderstanding my question. "But that means the best wares are on offer."

There was nothing amiss to Manthara, I realized. Why would there be? Even in palaces, women were rarely heard. The gods did not wish for women and men to mingle overly much, and even in Kekaya the sages had created rules to keep such order in place.

I could not expect any different outside the palace walls, and yet I found myself hoping that the market, this place so full of life, might be better. In that moment, I felt like the old Kaikeyi, who had convinced her brother to teach her to fight and had negotiated the terms of her marriage. I could see myself again, just within reach.

CHAPTER NINE

THE TRIP TO THE marketplace woke me from the depressed fog I had been living in. I began asking questions of Manthara. *Can we go back? Can I go as myself? Are there other markets? Could I arrange a formal visit?* I knew I could not navigate the chaos alone, but Manthara promised me that we would work out a plan together. But before we could, she came back to me with a different sort of news.

Dasharath had decided to challenge the warlord in the north.

Radnyi Kaushalya, first among the wives, hated the war camps and had refused the raja's invitation to accompany him. Sumitra never even entertained the idea of going. But a war camp sounded exhilarating to me.

So, when Dasharath requested my presence in his chambers at the end of the week, I was prepared. Manthara chose a forest-green sari for me, one that lay soft and pliant against my body, and an attendant younger even than I wrapped my body in the gauzy fabric, lined my eyes with kohl, and decorated me with strands of delicate golden jewelry that I knew to be lovely, but to me just felt tiresome.

Dasharath did not so much as look at me when I entered the room, but thankfully years living in the same palace as my father had inured me to such treatment. I simply stood quietly, contemplating the golden cord that stretched between us in the Binding Plane.

"Ah, Kaikeyi," he said at last, as if only just noticing me there. "I wished to speak to you."

"Yes, Raja," I replied, keeping my head bowed. I grasped our cord firmly in my mind. It was the same thickness as my smallest finger.

"I am headed off to battle in a few days. The warlord Sambarasura has become too greedy, too arrogant. It is time for me to put him in his place."

"That is all," he added, when I did not respond. "Have you nothing to say to me?"

I met his eyes, opened my mouth, and discovered that words would not come out. Despite Manthara's information, I found myself tongue-tied.

Dasharath's face fell. He turned away from me. "You may go, then," he said, and the rudeness of the dismissal shook me from my stupor.

"Take me with you!" I blurted inelegantly.

Dasharath turned back around in shock.

"My king," I added, sending waves of deference and longing through our golden connection. "Please. It would be an honor to accompany you."

He squinted at me, then reached out and grasped my chin, tilting my head side to side as if searching for something. "You wish to come to the camps?"

"Yes," I said softly.

"They are filled with men. Soldiers. Far cruder and baser than you are used to."

I held my tongue, for now was not the time to remind him that I had been raised with seven brothers and had heard many crude and base things. "I can bear it, for the honor of staying by your side."

Pretty words, flattery. Such things may have been the art of women, but they were the weakness of powerful men. A well-placed strum of the cord between us with my mind certainly did not hurt my case.

"Very well," he said slowly. "I will consider your request."

He kissed me then and led me to his bed.

When he was spent, and we were lying beside each other, Dasharath raised himself on an elbow to look at me. "You may come with me to the battle," he said gruffly. "And you may spend the night here if you wish."

I wanted nothing more than to leave, to race barefoot to the women's quarters and climb into my own bed, alone. But I mustered a small smile. "You honor me, Raja. I will gladly stay by your side."

Soon Dasharath's breath turned soft and even, and I turned away, my back to him. I willed myself someplace else, in a vast field in Kekaya, astride my fastest horse, and as the imaginary wind whipped through my hair, I found brief haven in sleep's dominion.

I awoke the next day before Dasharath and slipped away. He did not like company in the morning, and I did not want to risk his good favor. I found my way back to my chambers without incident and sat on the edge of my bed, stroking the cool silk cover beneath my hands.

"Ah, there you are." Manthara's voice came from the next room. I jumped, despite myself.

"Manthara?" I called out.

"Who else would it be?" she replied, walking into my bedroom. "When you did not return last night, I assumed you would be accompanying Raja Dasharath today. I took the liberty of packing your garments and ensuring that a palanquin would be prepared."

"Why—I mean, of course," I said.

There was no point in protesting to Manthara, who did not have the power to change this arrangement. In Kekaya, palanquins were used only for the elderly and the sick, and it would have brought my father great shame to see me riding in one. But here, a radnyi would never be allowed to ride off on a horse. With a sudden pang, I thought of Yudhajit, imagined how he would have laughed at my predicament.

I banished that thought from my mind and rose. "Do you know when we depart? He told me nothing."

"Because you need to know nothing." Manthara put her hands on my shoulders. "You are a radnyi now. Do not worry yourself with details. You managed the hardest part. You persuaded the raja to take you with him. All the rest leave to me. You will depart in a few hours."

"And what am I to do once I get there? Dasharath will be fighting. Am I to manage his camp?"

Manthara shook her head. "His soldiers will handle that. You are simply there to provide your husband some comfort." That sounded—incredibly boring. Perhaps Manthara sensed my hesitation, because she added, "Was there something else you wanted to do?"

Now that she asked me, I felt foolish. "I...I want to fight alongside him. I know how, I am not some wilting flower."

Rather than laughing at me, Manthara only looked thoughtful. "I've heard that Raja Dasharath has recently grown dissatisfied with his charioteer. He feels that the man is more interested in proving himself with extraordinary maneuvers than listening to commands."

Manthara had deftly created her own circle of servants from which she gathered information for me, and for this I was grateful. "You believe the raja will allow me to be his charioteer?"

"I believe that you could convince him."

I closed my eyes and allowed myself for a moment to imagine it. Standing at the front of a war chariot, steering Dasharath out of danger, creating opportunities for him to destroy his enemies. I was an excellent charioteer. Even Yudhajit had said so, and he did not give out praise lightly. We had honed my gift with years of practice. I could feel the slap of the reins in my hands, hear the rhythm of the wheels against the ground...

A soft bump against the door startled me out of my reverie. Manthara had vanished to secure something or the other from my bedroom, so I opened it myself.

Radnyi Sumitra. I forced myself to smile and gesture her in.

"How are you?" she asked. She had not come to see me in months, but unlike Kaushalya, she at least gave me a kind smile or word in court.

"I'm well, and you?" I resisted the urge to fidget with my dress.

"I just came by to wish you a safe and blessed trip," she said, staring at my feet. I squinted at her, surprised she already knew. She looked up at me and gave me a small smile. "It wasn't hard to guess. You seem suited for it."

"Suited for it?" I echoed blankly.

Her face fell slightly. "Well, I suppose I have never been north, but from what I've heard—" She took a deep breath to stop the torrent of words and then started again. "I wanted to wish you well. For your trip. It is very kind of you to accompany Dasharath."

"I—thank you?" I stuttered.

"I've never gone myself," she continued with a shudder. "It is too much for me. Kaushalya used to go, but she felt it was..." Sumitra trailed off, but I could guess at what she meant to say. *Beneath her. Not ladylike. Unrefined.*

My cheeks grew hot. I considered shoving her, as I used to do to my brothers, or making a snide remark. But instead, I remembered my evenings practicing with Manthara for welcoming guests in Kekaya. Sumitra could give me veiled insults, and I would prove to her that I could receive them with a smile. "I am glad to be of help," I said instead. "Thank you for the kind wishes."

We reached the fields of battle within a week. The Indra Mountains loomed over us, rising up beyond the vast plains of rippling yellow grass, stark and foreboding against the pale skies. Sambarasura and Dasharath had agreed to fight here, in the flatlands, one army against the other for supremacy. I did not see much value in communicating intentions so clearly, but my people were considered half-barbaric in the western kingdoms for our war methods, so I did not voice such apprehensions to anybody.

The only company I had on the long trip was a young handmaiden named Asha. She had a round, cheerful face and wore her hair in two thick, oiled braids down her back. Ordinarily, Asha was in the service of Radnyi Kaushalya, but the raja had requested her presence for me.

I worried Asha might hate me, as Kaushalya obviously did, but to my surprise she did not seem to. Each night, she arranged my hair and dabbed at my face, and although I hated it, she made me look more lovely than I ever had, her clever fingers coaxing my hair to fall just so. And each day the leaf-green braid between us thickened with a new strand.

Before my nights with Dasharath, I had evenings, when the soldiers set up camp and Dasharath busied himself with his advisors, discussing strategy. Recalling my rides with Yudhajit, I used this time to slip away in the twilight gloom and visit the Master of Horses.

Ashwasen was a grizzled man who had once been the charioteer to Dasharath's father. His long brown hair was streaked through with gray and though he walked with stiffness and spoke with a certain gruffness, Dasharath still found him indispensable.

The first night, I told him I simply wished to spend time with the horses. "They remind me of home," I said, and as I did, I took a brush from one of the servants and began tending to a large brown stallion.

He observed me for a moment, arms crossed. "It's dirty work," he said at last.

"I don't mind," I murmured, and truly I didn't. Standing here, one hand rubbing the horse's warm flank as the other gently worked, was the most like myself I had felt in some time.

"Hmm."

"You have done a fine job caring for them," I said. "My father's own would not be treated better."

At this, his face softened slightly. He walked away, but as he did a friendly brown thread materialized between us in the Binding Plane. The next day, he offered me a ride on one of the smaller horses, a dappled gray mare, and I accepted eagerly. Our bond thickened without my even noticing it, so that when I checked it on the third evening, it had developed into a supple wood-like bow. One of my first true connections in Ayodhya.

That evening, I asked to see the king's chariot, fully prepared to use the Binding Plane if needed. But magic proved unnecessary—Ashwasen led me to it willingly. We discussed the chariot's properties at length, and he appeared suitably impressed by my knowledge.

On the fourth night, I asked him if I might drive the chariot, just for a few moments to ensure everything was in order. He was reluctant at first, but I told him how Yudhajit's chariot had once lost a wheel, during one of his first skirmishes—and added a gentle push in the Binding Plane. He gave in, harnessing the team and cautioning me to drive no farther than a short stretch of dirt road.

The chariot was magnificent, with massive wooden wheels and a beautifully curved partition between charioteer and warrior. I stood in the front, knees bent slightly for balance as I wielded the reins. I pretended that a warrior stood behind me, loosing a volley of arrows, each hitting their mark guided by the smooth motion of the wheels, and life surged through me. Something of my old spirit came back to me with every second I drove those horses.

I longed to race off farther down the path, to race away into the distance, to some unknown future. Instead, I obeyed Ashwasen's parameters, finishing a loop in barely a minute.

"The left back wheel is indeed loose," I said as I carefully hopped down.

Kaikeyi is an excellent charioteer, I told him in our connection, watching as the thought raced along the relaxed curve of the bond like a reflection on polished wood.

The fifth evening, the Master of Horses sought me out by asking Asha to relay a message to me. I met him barely an hour later, buoyant and eager, and he handed me the reins of the chariot, already prepared for riding.

"Try a few maneuvers," he said. "I wish to watch."

He had attached two powerful Madhuvan bays to the chariot in a field at the edge of camp. I set them into motion with just a flick of my wrist, then pulled them to a quick stop. A fierce grin spread across my face at their responsiveness. I could not erase it as I imagined a battlefield before me. Instincts from the obstacle courses Yudhajit and I once raced through came rushing back, and I urged them forward, riding down soldiers separated from the pack. Then I brought the horses to a sudden halt so the raja could launch a spear. The moment he let it fly, I brought the horses into a tight circle, fleeing from an enemy chariot bearing down upon us. I slowed our pace while they were in pursuit, so they passed us, turning from hunters into hunted. Then, with a cry, I urged the horses to charge down the gap. I imagined Dasharath leaning out of the chariot and carving through enemies with his khanda.

I lost myself in the feeling of movement, of power, until a familiar voice pierced through my happiness. "Kaikeyi?"

Dasharath.

I pulled the horses to a halt. In the Binding Plane, our golden thread vibrated dangerously. I dismounted, windswept and sweating, nearly stumbling in my haste, and dipped into a shaky bow.

"Raja."

The bond between us jittered. I focused on sending waves of calming energy across our link, though I was hardly calm myself.

In that moment, it occurred to me that perhaps I had been misusing the Plane in Ayodhya. In Kekaya, where all my bonds had once been solid and sure, it was easy to send suggestions and accomplish my goals—so that was all I did. But I did not have that luxury here. So perhaps I could instead try to strengthen the bond ever so slightly rather than use it to influence. It would not help me immediately, but over time...

My mind rushed with adrenaline, crystallizing the idea. And as the bond between me and Dasharath began to quiet, I suddenly noticed a third thread, fully unconnected to me.

I blinked, and it disappeared. I blinked again, and it reappeared, more solid than before.

A thick maroon cable connected Dasharath and the Master of Horses. As I focused my attention upon it, Dasharath turned to Ashwasen, who was smiling smugly.

"What is the meaning of this?" he demanded. His face was thunderous.

"Your radnyi comes from a kingdom renowned for their riders and their war horses. I sought to consult her on such matters, to ensure everything was in order for you," he lied. Their bond was the width of a forearm and rippled with vitality. Clearly, they held each other in high esteem.

Could I manipulate that cord? I wondered. *Even though it is not connected to me?*

"And why is the radnyi driving a chariot?" Dasharath demanded. I tried to grasp their cord with my mind, but it slipped away from me, disappearing for good.

"She has a talent for it. You watched her just as I did. Do you not agree, my raja?" He was far more brazen than I could ever be. I hid my amusement as Dasharath opened and closed his mouth, unable to find a response.

Finally, he turned to me. "Where did you learn to drive like that?" he asked.

"My brother Yudhajit," I said, averting my eyes in a poor facsimile of humility. Our golden cord had fully calmed, so I knew there was little danger of it breaking. "When I was a child, he included me in his games and lessons. I apologize if I have caused you any offense."

"Offense?" Dasharath closed his eyes. "You drive better than my own charioteer."

"Thank you," I said demurely, hoping my triumphant pleasure was not evident in my face.

"You were looking to replace him," said the Master of Horses. "I think you have found your match." He walked out toward the chariot and began unhooking the team, as if the discussion had already ended.

"My match," Dasharath repeated, as if pondering the words. And then, "I do not wish to ask you to risk your life for me." I met his eyes, and there was no anger there. "The heat of battle is no place for a woman. You would not be wielding a weapon—the gods forbid that, and we would not disobey them—but it is still dangerous. But Ashwasen is right. You are excellent. Would you be my charioteer?"

"I accept." I had to force myself to modulate my voice. I did not think my husband would appreciate my shouting with excitement. "Yes. I will gladly stay by your side." As I said the words, the thread between us thickened into a chain of metal, and the smile that crept onto my face was entirely genuine.

The following evenings, Ashwasen had me put through my paces, conscripting other soldiers on horseback so I might practice formations. The men all respected Dasharath so deeply that if they were surprised at their raja's decision, they did not show it or question it. They approached the task with discipline and rigidity.

Despite the rigors of the tiring practice, on the appointed day of battle I woke before Dasharath—before even Asha lifted the flap of my tent. She had somehow managed to procure a set of men's breeches and armor, and we had spent the past two days furiously fitting them to my body.

I slipped them on and beamed. I could finally move comfortably.

When I had made the request, I worried that my bond with her would fray from my unladylike conduct. Instead, it had grown stronger.

"You look excellent, my lady," she said now. "It suits you."

"It suits me?" I repeated. Sumitra had said something quite similar just a week ago. Was Asha mocking me as well? Had I judged her too highly? But when I checked the Binding Plane, I found no evidence of the cloudiness of deceit that I had come to recognize on some cords.

"I only meant you wear it well. Not that you are suited to men's clothing. My apologies. You look excellent in anything." Her voice and face painted a picture of perfect sincerity.

"You have done a masterful job on this in such a short time," I said by way of apology. "Perhaps when we return to Ayodhya you might create a similar suit for me, in a more feminine material? They can be my riding clothes."

"You would wear breeches in the city?" Asha looked me up and down, and I tried not to show any traces of self-consciousness.

"I would wear breeches that look to others like normal women's clothing. If you are up to such a task."

Asha was missing a front tooth and unafraid to show it in her smile. "Very well, my lady. Survive the battle and I will make you breeches."

"Sambarasura is a minor warlord," I scoffed. "I am not afraid of him."

In truth, he was more than that. He had carved a small kingdom for himself, which took willpower and steel at the very least. But there was no room for me to let fear in here.

She shook her head. "Do not underestimate him, my lady. I have heard he is a formidable warrior." She bent her head. "Lord Vishnu, please protect Radnyi Kaikeyi and Raja Dasharath and the armies of Kosala. Allow the righteous to prevail."

I gazed at her bent head. Would prayers made for me fall into the same empty void as prayers made by me? Only Manthara had ever mentioned praying for me, so I had no way of knowing. But I appreciated Asha's sentiment all the same.

I had heard that the gods of war had long favored Kosala, allowing them to emerge victorious in battle after battle, ensuring the kingdom was the largest in the land. My presence could not change that. I hoped.

The sun had not yet risen, but by now the men were stirring in the camp. I made my way to where the Master of Horses waited for me. I spoke to each of the animals in turn, stroking their manes. Being with them, working with my hands and doing something useful, calmed my fraying nerves.

I harnessed Dasharath's team myself, inspected every turn of the chariot.

Then I watched the bloody sunrise as I waited for the battle to begin.

CHAPTER TEN

THE BATTLEFIELD OVERWHELMED ME.

The horses had been trained for war, but I was unprepared. The moment the archers began shooting, any semblance of my control slipped away. The neat lines of men broke into chaos, assaulting my senses. The screams of men dying, the scent of blood—it churned my stomach and slackened my grip dangerously. I forgot my lessons with Yudhajit and my drills with Ashwasen. I breathed through my mouth, trying to get calming air into my lungs, but my body had seized with panic. The horses slowed, making us a target. I watched a few men turn to us, readying their spears. It was this fear that finally penetrated through the haze, somewhat clearing my head.

I spurred the chariot onward, my shaking hands pulling the horses into an arc. Dasharath leaned out of the bay, the powerful strokes of his khanda cutting through three of Sambarasura's men.

"Excellent, Kaikeyi!" he shouted out to me. I would have responded, but the battlefield was rapidly devolving into a tangle I could not parse. As the long yellow grass was trampled into a mess of matted red, as bodies fell and the rising dust coated the men on foot in a haze of gray, it became impossible to discern our formations—let alone who held the upper hand.

The glint of a spear cut toward me. I jerked the reins in a panic, and Dasharath gave a shout of surprise behind me. Icy fear coursed through my veins and shook my hands, and the noise of the battle and sounds of death became too much to bear. I turned this way and that, desperate for a reprieve, and nearly drove our chariot over a group of our own men. An arrow flew past the horses, and although they were well-trained beasts of war, the front horse reared up. I pulled them all in, bringing us to a near standstill, when another arrow came whistling through the air, shearing through my sleeve. I barely felt the sting of it, for I was driving the team forward again, trying to keep my head.

Dasharath, for his part, did not shout angered instructions, but I could feel his frustration radiating from behind me. He threw another spear, but I twisted the chariot at the last moment and we both watched as it went wide.

"I'm sorry!" I shouted, knowing it was absolutely inadequate. Words were meaningless right now; he needed action. I scanned the battlefield, trying to pick out places where our men were struggling or locate Sambarasura's own chariot, but I was so disoriented that my vision blurred. Tears pricked at my eyes, and I dashed them away with my hand, ignoring the sharp pain in my arm at the motion.

Yet another spear came toward us, and Dasharath dove to one side of the chariot to avoid it for I was too slow. We tilted precariously as I fought for control, both of the team and of myself. An arrow embedded itself in the chariot's rail next to me. Inches higher, and it would have pierced my husband.

My heart beat so hard I thought I felt faint from the force of it. My failures were putting my husband, my raja, and maybe even my friend in danger. Right now, I was responsible for his life, and I was getting nowhere in this panicked, frenzied state.

So, I stopped.

For just a brief moment, I brought our chariot to a standstill, closed my eyes, and filled my lungs with air. As my heart calmed, I opened my eyes and entered the Binding Plane, muttering the mantra to myself for the first time in years. As I gazed across the battlefield, I saw the faint, gossamer threads that connected me to Dasharath's men. And I saw the places where there were no threads at all.

I heard Dasharath inhale sharply behind me, but before he could speak, I set us back in motion. This time, I was grounded. Focused. While I could not tell the soldiers apart visually, I used the Binding Plane to steer us to a group of men who lacked any connection to me at all. As we approached, I was able to differentiate their mismatched armor from that of our own soldiers and I let out a bark of triumphant laughter.

Dasharath expertly launched a spear at the man in front, then drew his khanda, slashing with speed and precision. He gave a whoop as his blade connected, and then I pivoted the chariot so that it collided with another two soldiers. Something crunched and I flinched. But Dasharath shouted "Well spotted!" and urged us on.

There was no time to think, let alone to question the way I had just crushed the life out of a man. I blocked out everything but the Plane, seeking out new gaps to pursue. We took down knot after knot of enemy, and I grew more confident, bringing us to the edges of clashes to the aid of our men. My blood sang with the cruel work, and Dasharath's weapons brutalized Sambarasura's army.

A spear rammed hard into the side of the chariot.

Dasharath stumbled, and this time it took him several moments to regain his balance. As I twisted around to check on him, I realized—I was wasting time. I was helping our men, yes. But the battle would only end when Sambarasura was defeated.

I kept the chariot moving at a steady pace, searching for only one man who mattered. Fallen standards kept catching my eye, but none of them were Sambarasura's. Of course he had not fallen—we would not be so lucky, nor his men still fighting were that the case. Some banners still whipped in the wind, but most were our own, the brilliant gold stark against the pale sky.

Dasharath's men were gaining the upper hand, and the field was scattered with broken chariots. For several moments, my focus was fully directed to navigating around the dead and the dying. It was almost frightening how quickly I had acclimated to the suffering. I lifted my gaze once more, sweeping across the battlefield, and something caught my eye. I flicked the reins, pushing the horses to move more quickly, and a standard came fully into view. It was the enemy's: embroidered with the snarling face of a tiger but dyed in a deep green that made it stand apart. Sambarasura.

We raced toward him, and I knew that Dasharath immediately understood my plan. He loosed an arrow at Sambarasura that barely missed when the enemy's charioteer swerved at exactly the right moment. We careened toward each other, and just as I put Dasharath within spear range of Sambarasura, our opponent hurled his own with a triumphant cry.

The spear glanced off one of our wheels with a crack, and the horses reared in fear as the chariot came to a bone-halt. I do not think it would be arrogant to say that with my driving, Dasharath's chariot itself had become a brutal weapon. Sambarasura had not been trying to kill us, not yet. He had been trying to stop us.

"Get down!" I cried, all decorum lost in the face of danger. I crouched low as the horses' hooves churned the ground.

"I'm not a coward," he called back. He drew his khanda with a rasp of steel.

"Get down!" I repeated, but he was a raja under no obligation to listen to his charioteer—or his wife. Sambarasura's chariot raced toward us. The warlord hefted another spear in his hand and, with a great cry, sent it soaring through the air.

Time seemed to slow, then came rushing back far too quickly as the weapon pierced Dasharath's chest.

Never take your eyes off your enemy, Yudhajit's voice cried in my ears. So I did not turn to help him.

Instead, as Sambarasura drew closer, preparing to finish us, I pulled off my helmet for a better view of the whole field. I could see his eyes now and watched with a grim sense of satisfaction as they widened in surprise. A woman charioteer was not a common sight.

And then he made his last mistake. He hesitated.

Take the opening, Yudhajit said, but I did not need his advice.

Holding the reins of the horses firmly in my left hand, I reached behind me and grabbed the smooth wooden shaft of one of Dasharath's mighty spears. Relying on instinct, on the muscle memory of years of old lessons, I adjusted my grasp on the haft, finding the center of gravity. I threw, my breath rushing out of me in a shout.

By the time obsidian-tipped death found Sambarasura, piercing his neck and shoulder in a deadly blow, I had jumped down from my injured husband's chariot to examine the damage, conscious it was our only form of escape.

My hands shook as I examined the smashed wheel, two spokes broken, the whole thing fallen off its axis. Steel clanged behind me, the shouts of fighters mixing with the cries of dying men. My magic could not help me now.

"Indra, please," I whispered, desperate.

Indra was the god of charioteers and had long been considered a protector of Kosala. Perhaps he would help me to save a favored raja. "Guide my hand."

No inspiration struck me. Maybe the gods were punishing me for joining the fight after all. And Dasharath…He might already be dead.

I grabbed the bottom of the wheel and tugged with all my strength, trying to push it back into place. My shoulder blade pressed back into the splintered spoke. I strained with the effort, eyes clenched shut, until a battle cry sounded too near for comfort.

Never take your eyes off your enemy!

I opened my eyes as the wheel popped back into place. A soldier lunged toward me, sword ready.

I rolled out of the way and he buried his blade into the earth as I swung myself back into the charioteer's seat. If only Yudhajit could see me now—he would laugh and call me as agile as a monkey for clambering back up so quickly. I spared a moment of gratitude for my brother's words, for they had kept me alive. Then I snapped the horses into motion, barely hearing the soldier scream beneath the wheels as I carved a path away from the battlefield, my mind fixed firmly on my husband.

Dasharath's troops parted for me like ghee on a warm summer day. An observant rider outstripped me, racing back to camp to prepare them for our arrival. In the broken chariot, it took us several precious minutes in which I felt as though with every breath I was the one bleeding and not my husband. If he died in a chariot I drove into battle, they might as well put me on the pyre with him.

I pulled up into the middle of camp, and healers swarmed us before I'd completely stopped.

"Is he alive?" I asked, leaping onto the dirt, uncaring of who might witness my unwomanly behavior. Not that it mattered, because nobody so much as looked at me. Their chattering overlapped into an undecipherable din.

I slipped into the Binding Plane and studied the fragile ties binding me to the men around me. The threads were thin, brittle, and dull besides, as though I was trapped in an aged wheel. Magic would not work.

"Is. My. Husband. Alive?" I made each word ring like metal blades.

The raja's retinue all turned to me with varying expressions of confusion, contempt, and horror. A small man next to Dasharath's prone form nodded. "Yes, Radnyi. He still draws breath."

The work resumed, but now the advisors encircled me.

"What happened?" one demanded.

"Sambarasura cracked one of the chariot's wheels, and in the ensuing confusion, his spear struck true." Skepticism radiated through each on the Binding Plane.

"And where is Sambarasura now?" This voice I knew. Virendra, the Minister of War. He was Dasharath's favorite advisor. He shouldered his way into the circle. The string between us was orange, made thicker than the rest through familiarity, although I knew that did not mean much.

"Dead," I said, turning to face him. "The raja slew him before succumbing to his wounds."

The lie was easy. It felt as though I prepared my whole life to tell it.

Their discussion subsided as they stared.

"How did you escape?" another asked.

"I jumped down from the chariot and pushed the wheel back into place," I said. "And then I brought him here immediately."

In the corner of my eye, I saw the healers lift the raja onto a hammock and carry him off to another tent. I thought his arm moved, but perhaps that was simply the jostling motion.

"You?" the advisor said, pulling my attention back. He looked me up and down, just as Asha had that morning. But whereas I had felt at ease under Asha's gaze, under his I felt disgusting. His mouth pulled into a slight grimace. "How could *you* fix the wheel of a war chariot?"

"I prayed to Indra, and he guided my hand." Another lie. The only one that would quiet them, for of course the gods would assist in saving their beloved raja.

Accepting that as truth, they turned away from me and followed Dasharath into the tent.

CHAPTER ELEVEN

DASHARATH'S DEATH WAS, IN some ways, my fault. In the end he was a casualty of a much greater war, his undoing meant as a punishment for me. Let it be known that I did not wish it so; on the contrary, even when I stopped all other prayer, I always prayed for my husband's long life.

Perhaps that was his doom.

For two days and two nights, Dasharath lay pale and still in the healing tent. The camp physicians assured me that they had diagnosed and treated him according to the most comprehensive Ayurvedic texts, but still the outcome was uncertain.

I sat by his bedside, leaving only to eat and bathe. I constantly slipped into the Binding Plane to look at our golden cable, just to ensure Dasharath still lived. *Live*, I instructed him. *Wake up*. But he did not respond. I slept on a straw mat next to his bedside for the first night, and on the second, Asha managed to construct a more comfortable makeshift bedroll.

On the third day, Dasharath woke every few hours, disoriented and confused. Each time, I patiently explained what happened. Each time, he subsided back into sleep upon learning that he had dealt the decisive blow, and our men had routed Sambarasura's remaining forces.

The next day, Dasharath woke at dawn in full possession of his faculties. He managed to sit up, drink water, and consume a light broth. I wished for him to stay secluded and rest, but soon his advisors crowded around him. I was relegated to the corner of the tent until one of them noticed my presence and tartly informed me that this was no place for a woman. Somehow my daring rescue had not endeared me to them.

Feeling low, I went to visit the horses. Dasharath's team had escaped unscathed, and the brown stallion I had first met greeted me eagerly, pressing his soft nose into my hand. I stretched out to rub his neck and heard someone clear their throat behind me.

"You did well," said Ashwasen.

I did not turn around to meet his eyes. "The raja almost died."

"But he did not. And the battle was won." I said nothing, and after a moment he continued, "I have seen many charioteers in my time. You are not the most skilled I have ever seen, but you are certainly the most determined. I doubt any other would have brought him back alive."

At this I did spin around. The Master of Horses was smiling at me, and I felt hot tears rush into my eyes. I blinked rapidly before they could spill. "Thank you," I whispered.

"Take as long as you need," he said. "I find they are quite calming."

But I did not feel calm. As I pet the horses, tears began falling down my cheeks, until I pressed my face into the side of the chestnut horse and wept. I cried not just for Dasharath, but for the men I had killed, and for the horror I had seen. Battle was nothing like the glorious martial exercise I had thought it would be. My hands shook as I stroked the horse's mane, whispering praise to it just to calm myself.

Once the adrenaline of battle had faded, I had been left with only despair. I had been wrong, I saw now, to think war glorious. Nothing could be further from glory, from righteousness. I knew that I would never go back to battle, never seek out war.

Eventually, the storm passed. I felt spent, and I suddenly craved company. I returned to my tent, where Asha sat waiting for me.

"How are you, Radnyi?" she asked, setting aside her needlework. If she noticed my swollen eyes, she made no comment.

"Fine," I said. "I just wish to sit with you for a time."

At this she gave me a smile. "You are very kind. And not at all what I expected. The radnyis, sometimes they—" She stopped talking and stared down at her needle and thread.

"Sometimes they what?" I asked.

"Well, they are very close. Radnyi Kaushalya and Radnyi Sumitra. And they wonder why you don't seek them out." Asha did not meet my eyes.

"Why would I seek them out?" This conversation, however awkward, was so much better than being alone with my thoughts. "I am an intruder in their home."

"The raja has the right to take as many wives as he pleases," Asha said, looking up with surprise. "They do not begrudge him this."

"Then why have they never sought *me* out?" I added a gentle push for information along the emerald strand of our bond.

Asha furrowed her brow but gave in as my magic bumped lightly against her sternum. "They have sent you several invitations to join them, for private meals, walks in the gardens. You have ignored them all."

"I have done no such thing," I insisted. But as she spoke, I remembered Manthara telling me that she had received several missives. In my fog of unhappiness, I had ignored her, unwilling to read their words after I had humiliated myself before them. "Oh."

"Oh?" Asha repeated.

"I suppose I may not have properly...opened them."

Asha snickered, then covered her mouth in horror. "I did not mean any offense, my lady."

"None taken. I suppose it is somewhat amusing that a radnyi could be so incompetent," I said wryly.

Asha looked at me with appraising eyes. "And here everyone has been wondering whether you are shy or superior."

"Instead, I am simply a fool," I said with a small smile.

Asha giggled, and soon we were both laughing with abandon.

Of course, that was the moment Virendra arrived at the tent. The Minister of War pushed open the flap and ducked inside, looking strange and out of place. I sat up straight. Asha became quiet, suddenly busy with her needle, but by his expression, he had witnessed our moment of levity and disapproved.

"Raja Dasharath has requested your presence, Radnyi," he intoned after a few uncomfortable seconds.

I rose immediately and strode from the tent, keeping my back straight, wanting to mask my apprehension from Virendra, who stayed a disconcerting two paces behind me. After all, I had no reason to be nervous. Dasharath, unconscious as he had been, would have no reason to question my story.

But perhaps he would be angry, or embarrassed that I had been the one to save him.

"Go on," Virendra said when we arrived. "He's waiting for you."

"Why does he want to speak with me?" I asked, spinning around to face him in an attempt to stall for time. I carefully plucked the small string between us.

Virendra pressed his lips together. "I imagine he simply wants to be with his wife. He is in pain and has dealt with important affairs of the state all day." It did not feel like a lie.

"Oh." I turned to face the entrance again. Would Dasharath want to bed me? It normally took considerable exertion on his part, and he was sorely wounded. No. He probably wanted companionship, someone to talk to.

I took another breath, released my hold on the Plane, and entered the tent.

Dasharath lay in his bed, propped up against several pillows. Strips of cloth covered his torso, and he had dark smudges under his bright hazel eyes. But he smiled up at me when I entered, showing all his teeth, and gestured to the place next to him with a careful motion of his arm. "Please, sit."

I perched on the edge of the cot, sandals sliding for purchase in the dirt floor. "How are you feeling?"

"Like I was grievously wounded in battle," he said in a teasing tone. He had never used such with me before. "But better injured than dead. I was informed that I have you to thank for that."

I gave him my best impression of a demure smile. "I only drove the chariot to safety. You did all the work."

"Did I?" Dasharath asked, and my heart sank. "You see, my sweet wife, I do not remember throwing any spear. In fact, when Sambarasura broke the chariot wheel, I recall drawing my khanda."

He had trapped me. I could not contradict my husband. Neither could I agree with his remembrances. My head throbbed, whirling in panicked circles, and in my panic, I could not focus enough to find the Binding Plane. I was reduced to averting my eyes.

"Have you nothing to say?" he asked.

"No, Raja."

"Then you agree that I could not have slain him. And yet we have his body. How can this be?"

"Perhaps a spear from another one of our soldiers?" I offered. My whole body tensed, and I fought the urge to spring up from the bed and flee. *If you cannot fight, run,* Yudhajit used to say, but this was not combat. Dasharath could banish me for lying, for unwomanly conduct. For defying the will of the gods by raising a weapon. Would my father take me back? I doubted it.

"Perhaps. Though my advisors tell me that when they received the body, it was my spear that was embedded within it."

I forced myself to look at Dasharath and accept his judgment. But his face was blank. Somehow this neutrality calmed my heart just enough for me to slip into the webs of magic around us. Our armored thread had somehow thickened into a rope the breadth of a strong arm. Only Manthara and I had a stronger connection.

"That is strange, my husband," I said at last.

"Do you find it so?" he asked. "Because I do not. My wife grew up among the ferocious Kekaya people. She has seven brothers. She can drive a chariot better than most men I've seen. That she can also throw a spear is not strange."

I stood up from the bed and knelt, knees in the dirt. "I am sorry. Please, I beg for your forgiveness."

Dasharath struggled for a moment, then managed to lever himself off his pillows, and swing his feet off the edge of the bed. "Kaikeyi, there is nothing to forgive."

His words stunned me. "There isn't?"

"You slew my enemy and saved my life," he said simply, laying a hand on my shoulder. "Why would I be angry?" Before I could answer, he continued, "I understand why you lied to my advisors, although I would be remiss if I did not request that you refrain from doing so in the future. But between you and me there should be no secrets."

"Yes, Raja." My voice shook. To my shame, tears welled in my eyes. Through my blurry vision I watched our connection grow ever stronger, a shining beacon of gold.

Dasharath cleared his throat. "For your valor on the field of battle, I grant you one boon. For your efforts in saving my life, I grant you a second boon. I place no restrictions on these. You may ask anything of me, anytime you wish, and I will do everything in my power to fulfill your request. This I swear by the River Ganga, by the Indra Mountains, and by the gods themselves."

I rocked back onto my heels in shock.

"Two boons?" I asked, just to be sure I had heard correctly.

Dasharath kept his face stern, but his eyes were soft. "Yes, Kaikeyi. Now please, help me lie down again."

I scrambled up, helping guide his body back against the pillows. "Will you tell your advisors the truth?"

"Do you want me to?" he asked. In the six months we had been married, he had never once asked what I wanted.

I considered carefully. I had risen in Dasharath's esteem after he learned the truth, and after my conversation with Asha, I thought it possible that I had misjudged the Ayodhyan court as a whole. Perhaps his advisors would like me better if they knew what I had done. But I also knew how fragile my connections with all of them were, and experience had taught me that lying was considered more unbecoming on a woman than on a man. "No, Raja. That is not necessary."

"Would you have told me? Had I not surmised the truth?"

"I don't know," I said. But of course, I would not have.

Dasharath made a small humming noise. "Are you afraid of me? Is that why you lied?"

I studied him, injured on the bed. Was I afraid of him? I was certainly afraid of the power he held over me, and perhaps before today I had feared him. But just now, when he gave me two unrestricted boons, he had made himself vulnerable. I might order him to make me his chief radnyi or to abdicate the throne, and he would be forced to obey. Those were the laws of the gods, and while they may not have ever governed me, they certainly still governed Dasharath. I thought, improbably, of Ahalya. Had she possessed a boon from her husband, she would not have been turned to stone. I had power too now.

"That's not why I lied," I said at last.

Dasharath laughed and his body folded over in pain. "You're witty," he said when he had recovered. "I had never noticed that about you before. But you did not fully answer my question."

You're smart. I had never noticed that about you before, I wanted to say, but I held my tongue. "Perhaps I once was afraid. When you came to Kekaya and sought my hand, I was certainly afraid of you then. Not anymore."

His fingers found my own in an oddly comforting gesture. "I was the supplicant then. You had no reason to fear me."

"I had no choice in the matter. You and my father and my brother made all the decisions. I had no part in it. No part in determining my own future. Of course, I feared that. I did not know what kind of man you were, did not know what kind of husband you would be."

"And what sort of husband have I proven myself?" he asked.

"A fair one," I said without hesitation. "And kind."

"I could do worse." His thumb stroked my hand.

"You could," I agreed.

"But is that what you wanted?" he asked after a moment. "A fair and kind husband?"

"Isn't that what every woman wants?"

"I asked what *you* wanted," Dasharath said with a grin. "I hope you learn to answer my questions directly one day."

"Very well," I conceded. Manthara had instructed me to trust my instincts, and my instincts had led me true so far. Given the strength of the cord between Dasharath and myself, I thought I could risk this. "I did want a kind and fair man. And I wanted more than that. I wanted to be able to speak my mind and make decisions for myself. To be trusted by my husband, to have responsibility beyond child-rearing."

Dasharath's expression grew serious. "And what responsibility do you desire?"

"A seat on your council," I said, before I could convince myself not to say it.

He gave a slight laugh at that. But our golden bond shimmered as though lit with sunlight, and I realized his amusement did not come at my expense. "Might I ask why a radnyi would need to sit on the Mantri Parishad?"

"I—" My truthful answer—that I mistrusted men and wanted my own independence—would likely offend him, but neither did I want to start such a momentous step with a lie.

My hesitation was obvious to him. "What is it? I promise I will not make light, whatever your reasons."

As I searched for what to say, I thought of the marketplace I had seen with Manthara. The women there were capable, some perhaps more so than the men who ran the stalls. "I want to help others," I answered at last.

"Do you feel my council does not already do that?" His tone was curious, not defensive.

"You help some of the kingdom," I conceded. "But there are others who might benefit if they had someone to champion their interests."

To his credit, he understood immediately. "Other women, you mean to say."

"Yes." I met his gaze and found no judgment. "I would help them however I might."

"Why?" he asked.

"Excuse me?" I asked, too quickly. "I'm sorry. I don't understand your question."

"You are free to do what you please from now on, and your situation is far removed from your serving girl's."

He had a good point, and my thoughts on the matter were as of yet half-formed. But the more I thought about what I had seen, the less sense it made. "It is possible to want something for others too. Is that not my responsibility as radnyi? They are also your subjects, and they are capable."

Dasharath was silent, and I hesitated to look at our connection. But when at last I did, I found it swaying only slightly, as though in a contented breeze. "And to that end, you want a seat on the council."

"I would not ask you to change things on a whim or without consideration, for I know that you will undertake to do so only when you are satisfied it is truly best for the kingdom. But on your council, I might be able to prove to you that change could benefit us all. So yes." I kept hold of his gaze.

"Would you ask that of me? As one of your boons?"

"No," I said at once. I would not use up so precious a gift mere moments after receiving it, and I did not have to. "Now that you know this is my dear wish, I would ask it of you as your wife. If you feel I have proven myself, then it would be in your own interests to trust me, to consult me as an equal, would it not?"

He looked at me, and for once I let him see the true Kaikeyi. No averted, soft eyes, but as much fierce flint as I could muster.

An eternity passed in nervous silence, and then Dasharath closed his eyes. His lips tugged upward into a smile. "Six months we have been married. Six months. And you reside in your rooms, only attend court when summoned, seem a shy recluse. And here you are, a warrior, a woman who wishes to be made an advisor."

My cheeks burned hot. I did not think he intended to shame me. And yet, like Yudhajit's accidental barbs that had marked my childhood, his words stung. "I am sorry. I meant no offense."

"No, I am sorry. I have done little to ease your transition to Ayodhya, preoccupied as I was with Sambarasura and other matters. I will grant your wish, allow you access to my Mantri Parishad. But in return, you must promise me something."

I took a deep breath before I spoke. It helped, giving me time to bury the urge to agree immediately no matter the terms. "What would you ask of me?"

"That you actually talk to Kaushalya and Sumitra, and that you properly fulfill your duties as my wife. I am granting you an unconventional request, but you must obey convention too."

The request was reasonable and, perhaps, a way to finally end my seclusion. A seat on the council would be worthless if I remained in hiding the rest of the time. "Yes, Raja. We have an agreement."

He took my hand in his again even as he closed his eyes, and his thumb moved in slow circles. I covered his hand with my own, stopping the movement so that he knew he could rest. He did not pull away, and neither did I, content to sit in the comfortable silence until his breaths deepened and he slipped into a healing sleep.

CHAPTER TWELVE

WE RETURNED TO THE palace one week later, when Dasharath was well enough to travel. There was a huge feast in honor of the victory, and I sat at Dasharath's right hand. It was a joy to have a palace cooked meal, and even more of a joy to lie on my bed. I slept for half a day and woke feeling ready to start the work Dasharath had set for me.

I approached Radnyi Sumitra first. I still had the memory of her well-wishes fresh in my mind, and she appeared less intimidating, with her pleasantly rounded cheeks and ever-present smile.

Sumitra responded with enthusiasm when invited to my chambers for an afternoon repast. As we ate the colorful milk-sweets, Sumitra gossiped about a servant who had allegedly been asked to leave Kaushalya's service. I nodded along, but my attention was in the Binding Plane, trying out the idea that had struck me the evening Dasharath made me his charioteer. I shaped our bond, doing my best to augment it, and I watched as the thin filament thickened into a robust embroidery thread. But by that point, the string was shaking side to side quite dangerously, so I let go of the Plane entirely.

Sumitra was talking about some sewing project she was working on, and so I decided to take a risk. In a drastic maneuver, I dug out my own haphazard work I had occupied myself with in the carriage to the battlegrounds. Sumitra laughed so hard that she cried, and our bond strengthened tenfold to a firm cable that looked like thick wool, more than I could have done with my magic.

Toward the end of our time, the topic turned to a ceremony that was being planned in a few moons' time. I listened with half an ear, for a radnyi's job at such events was to observe and look beautiful, until Sumitra said, "Of course, because it is for the goddess, we will take part in the ritual."

"What?" I asked, bemused. That had certainly not been the custom in Kekaya. The sages performed all rites, with the occasional assistance of the men.

"It will not be much work, don't worry." Sumitra patted my hand, as though my concern was with the difficulty of the task. "We will wash the statue and make the offerings. Lakshmi has blessed this kingdom with prosperity."

I had not given much thought to the rules of public rituals, for I cared little about trying to please the gods. But now Sumitra's words struck me differently. Here was yet another place where women were largely pushed aside—even the most devout.

I barely heard the rest of what Sumitra said as we bade each other farewell, wrapped up in my own thoughts.

The next day, I attended the Mantri Parishad for the first time.

None seemed surprised to see me—Dasharath must have warned them—but I caught several men glaring at me when they thought I was not looking. In the Binding Plane, my connections to most were nonexistent wisps. But despite his severity, Virendra seemed to respect me, as did the Minister of Finance. These two men, along with the religious advisor,

Manav—an elderly man with whom I shared no bond at all—
formed Dasharath's inner council. I focused on strengthening
the few cords I had ever so slightly, but even by the end I had
not yet built adequate rapport to contribute to the council's
deliberations. Even many of the men seemed bored, for the
meeting was primarily occupied by a few ministers seeking
custodianship of Sambarasura's old territories. I doubted I
would ever build the necessary connections to shout *You are
idiots* at the arguing men without severe consequences.

When the meeting was over, I returned directly to my
chambers, wanting to remove my heavy jewelry. Only after
stripping off my necklace and one jhumka did I realize I had
company.

Kaushalya stood at the other end of my room, half-hidden
in the shadows near the window.

I dropped into an instinctual bow and then committed to it
rather than repeat my first error. "Radnyi, I did not notice you
there." If she had wanted a better reception, she should not
have entered my chambers and gone into my bedroom without
permission.

"That much is apparent." Kaushalya walked slowly toward
me. She looked lovely as always, dark kohl framing her eyes
and delicate gold gracing her long neck. "I came here to talk
to you after court, but it has been some time since the public
audiences adjourned."

"I was listening to the meeting of the Mantri Parishad," I
said, gesturing behind me in a useless motion. Kaushalya knew
where the court was located.

If Kaushalya was surprised, she hid it well. "A council meeting. That is no place for a young woman."

I wanted to protest that I was not a young woman, but pet-
ulance would hardly sway her. Besides, to all others the council
was no place for any woman at all.

"I am sorry you feel that way," I said at last, blinking into the Binding Plane and finding the black bond between us. It flickered in and out of my vision, which was concerning, to say the least. I had long ago trained myself to only look at my magic from the corner of my eye, but part of me wanted to stare at Kaushalya's chest and watch the bond. I could hardly do that though.

"You have been here half a year," Kaushalya said, arriving in front of me. "In that time, you have barely attended court, never spoken to me or Sumitra without prompting, and shown little interest in the affairs of the king. Now you accompany him to battle, invite Sumitra to your rooms, attend council meetings, and steal my best servant."

"I've done *what*?" I squeaked. Most women considered poaching help to be one of the most despicable sins.

"Asha. All she has done for the past several days is speak about you."

I remembered with a start that Sumitra had talked about Kaushalya dismissing a servant just the day before. "Oh—oh, please, do not dismiss her. She was forced to attend me during the battle, and perhaps something about that frightening experience stuck in her mind."

"Dismiss her?" Kaushalya asked, her lips disappearing entirely into a thin line. "Why on earth would I do that? No, I simply assigned her to the kitchens for a week as punishment. It was annoying, hearing her tell stories of the camp and your deeds for the fifth time. Then who should visit me yesterday but Sumitra, also talking about the great Kaikeyi. It seems I cannot escape you." Her manner conveyed the utmost annoyance, but at the end of her tirade the bond between us had flared into firm existence.

I ducked my head to hide my grin and examined the bond. It was delicate and gleaming, like molten obsidian, and I imagined that it would feel exquisitely polished to the touch. "I am sorry, Radnyi."

"You do not sound sorry," Kaushalya said. "And you do not need to call me Radnyi. We are equals."

"You will always be the first among us," I said.

Kaushalya's nostrils flared as she inhaled and exhaled dramatically, and still her high cheekbones and large eyes kept her face the picture of beauty. "What do you want?" That was now twice in the span of a moon someone had asked me that, when I had gone most of my life never hearing it.

As I had with Dasharath, I decided to answer her honestly. "I would like to rest. It is a hot day, and I have been wrapped in these stifling layers of silk for hours. You are the one who came to my room. I think the question is: What is it that you want?"

Kaushalya smirked. "I wanted to speak to you. I wish to know your plans, to know why you have suddenly decided to act the part of a radnyi. And I want to know what you hope to gain from Sumitra. She is a sweet woman, kind, unassuming. I won't have you using her for your own ends."

"You—" I spluttered. "You—you should speak to your husband."

"What does our raja have to do with this?" Kaushalya asked.

"He requested I take up my duties with the court. No— as a matter of fact, he ordered me to take up my duties with the court." The words poured out of me in indignation. "He brought it to my attention that I am a radnyi and should act like one. You are correct, I have neglected my responsibilities for months. I have been remiss, uncertain in this new environment. And yet you too have neglected your duties. I did not ask for this marriage. Whatever resentment you have because of it should not fall on my shoulders. I am eighteen years old; you are nine and twenty. You are Dasharath's first wife. You should have helped me."

By the end of this speech, I was breathing heavily and had

advanced several steps, forcing Kaushalya back. But improbably, in the face of this onslaught, Kaushalya laughed.

"Why are you laughing?" I demanded, unsure whether to be mortified or livid.

"Of course this was Dasharath's idea," Kaushalya gasped out. Her lovely features had transformed with the laughter, smoothing her furrowed brow and opening up her expression so that it appeared nearly inviting. "I should not be surprised. And you are quite young. It did not occur to me. I married Dasharath at your age, but he was younger then, still yuvraja. And I had no other wives to contend with."

I could tell this was the closest I would get to an apology. "Sumitra and I walk in the gardens almost every morning," Kaushalya continued. "From now on, you may join us. But do not be late." And she swept past me and out of the room, leaving me gaping.

My tirade had pushed me out of the Plane, and I forced myself back into it. Our bond had thickened in a matter of minutes, vibrant and polished as the jet-black rocks on the banks of the Sarasvati River. Had my anger somehow endeared me to her? I prodded it with my mind, and it rippled lightly, cool water flowing over a stone.

I thought over the conversation, hardly able to understand what had happened. Why had Kaushalya's suspicions been so easily allayed? Had her defense of Sumitra been genuine?

I removed my other earring and my silk shawl and lay on top of my covers, the questions circling about in my mind.

A knock on the door startled me awake. Drowsily, I wondered if Kaushalya had come back to further interrogate me. But when I opened the door, I found Asha, fidgeting in the hallway.

"Radnyi!" Asha said, brightening. "Radnyi Kaushalya sent me to you. She thought you might appreciate having another lady-in-waiting."

My mind immediately provided every possible negative interpretation. Asha might be a spy, beholden to report back to Kaushalya. Or Kaushalya might have used this as an opportunity to be rid of Asha for some imagined fault.

As if sensing my hesitance, Asha added, "She wanted me to tell you this is a gift, and that if you do not want my service, she would gladly have me back. She said that everything is shared between sisters."

Between sisters. I could not push aside the warmth that radiated through me at her words. "She said that?" I asked, unable to believe it.

"Yes, my lady."

I smiled even as my body sagged in relief. My prospects in Ayodhya were rapidly brightening. "Please, come inside."

The next morning, I stood at the entrance to the gardens at sunrise. I filled my lungs with the crisp morning air, delighting in the slight chill that reminded me of home.

When would Sumitra and Kaushalya come down? I had not asked what time they usually met.

As the minutes went by, I began to wonder again whether this had been a ruse on Kaushalya's part to humiliate me, to prove my powerlessness. The confidence I'd felt upon finding Asha at my door yesterday quickly dissipated.

I checked the Binding Plane several times as I waited, for once glad that I had so few true bonds with people here. It made my search for Kaushalya's easy. Our thread remained the same, black and shining. I picked out my bonds with Dasharath, with Manthara and Asha, grounding me in Ayodhya from all directions. I did not often go into the Binding Plane without a particular person nearby to focus on, so I spent some time making a game of determining who the thinner tangle of threads might represent.

After what felt like an hour of standing at the entrance, I

gave up. Slowly, I turned toward my rooms. Absorbed in my shame, I rounded the corner—and ran right into the women I had been waiting for.

"Where are you going?" Kaushalya asked from behind Sumitra as I scrambled to maintain my balance.

"I thought I had missed you," I hedged, hoping that would be an adequate answer.

Both women were wearing light, plain kurtas and simple sandals. I felt mortifyingly overdressed in comparison. Manthara had suggested something less formal, but I had insisted I knew better, donning the elaborate skirt of a mint green ghagra. The stiff silk was heavy against my legs as I walked, and the embroidered hem dragged against the ground if I was not careful.

Kaushalya walked past me toward the garden's entrance and gestured toward the sundial in the center of the courtyard.

"If you arrive by the time the dial is here, you will not be late," she said, indicating a time only a few minutes earlier.

Sumitra offered me a smile as she walked toward the gardens. "I'm so pleased you could join us today."

We wandered the looping paths, me on the left, Sumitra in the middle, Kaushalya on the right. I had come out here only once or twice, months ago when I first arrived. At that time, many of the flowers had not yet bloomed, and the walls of identical greenery seemed an unsolvable maze that had deterred future visits.

Now, walking among silky blossoms of blue and purple and red, I could almost enjoy the surroundings and the company. Jasmine scented the air with a light sweetness, and the hum of insects provided a pleasant accompaniment to the conversation. I had noticed very few birds in Ayodhya's palace garden. But then, birds always made me think of my father and my banished mother, so perhaps it was a blessing in disguise.

"Kaikeyi was there when it happened," Kaushalya said suddenly, pulling me from my reverie. "She not only accompanied Dasharath to the camps but drove his chariot into battle."

"What?" Sumitra stopped walking and grasped my wrist. I made a half-hearted attempt to tug it away before realizing that would be rude. After all, I had spoken quite noncommittally about my time away at battle in hopes of avoiding any mention of such unwomanly conduct. "Is this true?"

"Yes," I said, deeply uncomfortable with the attention. *Don't blush*, I instructed myself, as if that might help. I could feel the heat staining my cheeks.

"Dasharath himself told me," Kaushalya added. "He said you were the bravest person on the battlefield that day. That you saved his life."

I flushed further at the praise, hating my face for giving me away so easily. Dasharath had stayed true to his word. He had kept the truth hidden from the outside world—but had given me my due all the same.

"After he was wounded, I drove him to safety. That is all."

"That is all?" Sumitra repeated. "That is a great feat. Why did you not tell us?"

"Anybody would have done the same."

Kaushalya snorted. "Neither of us could drive a chariot down a wide road, let alone through a battlefield."

"The gods guided me," I lied.

"All the same. The gods do not assist the unworthy. They cannot make talent where there is none." Sumitra reached out and embraced me.

I stiffened for a moment, not expecting such a thing—but then I forced myself to relax and return the embrace. It was sincere. "Thank you," I said with a smile.

We resumed our stroll. I was trying to think what new subject I could introduce when Kaushalya spoke again.

"Perhaps that is why you are so ill at ease among women,

talking about women's work," she said. "You were raised by men to perform the tasks of men."

I considered correcting her, telling her that the men I had been raised with had never thought of me as one of them, but thought better of it. "Perhaps," I agreed. "Perhaps."

We had completed a circle of the garden. As we reached the sundial, Sumitra begged leave to go back to her chambers and prepare for the day. I wanted to do the same—but Kaushalya's friendship would dramatically improve my life in Ayodhya. By the same token, her enmity could make it intolerable.

So I lingered, quiet, as she crossed her arms and stared at the muddied hem of my skirts for what seemed like an eternity. I wondered if I would ever feel put together in her presence.

"We meet outside my chambers," she said at last, the hint of a smile playing on her lips. "In the mornings, when we take our walk, that's where we meet. When we want to present a unified front to the court—typically in the wake of scandals or threats—we also meet there." Kaushalya lifted her gaze to my face as she spoke.

I was unsure of how she wanted me to respond. Anger had worked well for me before, in my chambers, but it no longer seemed appropriate.

"And we will all go to court together today. There is to be a performance by dancers who have traveled all the way from Videha. They are renowned for their Shiva Tandava." Kaushalya started walking away from me, then turned back around. "You will want to change out of that dress. And in the future, you need not dress so formally."

I smiled ruefully. "I hope the mud will come out."

"If not," Kaushalya said, her voice dropping to a dramatic whisper, "just have a new one made. You are a radnyi."

CHAPTER
THIRTEEN

AFTER THAT, I SETTLED into the pattern of court life. On a typical day, I would wake and stretch, until I was warm and loose-limbed enough to practice fighting forms. I had no wish to go back to the horrors of the battlefield, but I still enjoyed pushing my body, feeling the rhythm of the movement. I borrowed a wooden sword from the training grounds and would occasionally practice with it in the main room for variety. But still it held less wonder than it once had, for I could remember how these objects had been used to steal life before my eyes.

After this, on most days I would join Sumitra and Kaushalya in the gardens for a walk, learning about the workings of the palace. Some of these mornings, Dasharath would hold open court as well, and men from across the kingdom would come to plead their cases and causes before the raja, asking him to settle their land disputes, requesting he revise taxation agreements, and so on. I would infrequently observe from the balcony, but there was little part for me to play, and I preferred the company of my fellow wives.

After that, if there was no council meeting, I would

study, determined to understand the workings of Kosala's administration.

The evenings were devoted to court pastimes, far more varied than the austere Kekayan palaces. There were feasts, of course, but also dance and musical performances, and traveling troupes of storytellers. These last groups were my favorite, for they gave voice to the stories I had long loved—the men dressed in fantastical costumes and unearthed different voices for each character, setting the scenes with lyrical ease. The esteemed artists of the city were sometimes in attendance to paint portraits or views of the palace, and it was a pleasure to observe their work. Often we would sit and enjoy the entertainments of court until the torches burned low.

But by far, what I enjoyed most were my infrequent trips into the world beyond the palace, whenever Manthara was able to slip me away. For even as I grew to know my fellow queens, I realized I had so much to learn about the lives of other women. I had long cared only for my own independence, but there were so many who were far less free. Knowing this bothered me for reasons I could not quite understand.

On one such occasion, Manthara brought me to a small mud home where a friend of hers resided, farther from the market than I had previously ventured. When I complained— for I had been hoping to once again drink in the sights and bustle of the stalls and vendors—she shook her head. "Not today. There is only so much you can do watching. Here is a chance for you to listen."

I was about to ask what I was meant to learn, when a woman my own age opened the door and ushered us inside. "Manthara-ji, it is so good to see you! And I see you brought—" Her eyes widened, and she brought her hands together and bent deeply into a formal bow.

"Please, there is no need for that," I said, stepping inside. A small etching of Lord Ganesha hung above her door.

"Radnyi Kaikeyi, you honor me with your presence," she said, her voice several pitches higher. "If I had realized you were coming, I would have prepared." She turned from us and walked quickly across the packed dirt floor toward the stove. Her entire home appeared no bigger than my room in Kekaya. From here I could see the low cot she slept on and a small shrine filled with statues of the gods.

I slipped off my sandals as Manthara did the same. "Truly, there is no need for that," I said. "What is your name?"

"Riddhi," she said, ducking her head. It meant wealth and prosperity—a kind, hopeful name for a commoner.

"Riddhi is an excellent cook, employed in the palace kitchens," Manthara said. "But recently there has been some trouble."

"What sort of trouble?" I asked her.

She shook her head. "It is no matter," she whispered, looking down and playing with her fingers. "I am used to it."

She was obviously lying. "Perhaps if you tell me—"

"It is no matter, Radnyi Kaikeyi," she said, speaking more firmly now. Clearly, something was upsetting her, enough so that she risked interrupting me. "Nothing to bother yourself with."

"I would like to help, for you are a friend of Manthara's," I said, trying to imbue my voice with kindness.

Manthara had been quietly observing, but now she said, "You can trust the radnyi. I am sure she will be able to assist."

The furrow in Riddhi's forehead deepened. "Nobody can help, unless the gods decide to change the circumstances of my birth." She sighed. "If you must know, I am...illegitimate. And there are some who dislike that my father found me a position in the palace—the only thing he ever did for me."

"Your father is a noble?" I asked.

She nodded. "Yes. But it is not his fault. After all, he did not decree that illegitimate daughters were unmarriageable."

She was right, of course. It was the sages who had made it so, for an illegitimate daughter was deeply inauspicious and impure—unmarriageable, a terrible curse for a woman. But of course the gods and sages had nothing to say about illegitimate sons, who were still able to quietly inherit both money and power. Suddenly her name took on a much crueler cast.

"That is no matter. It does not mean you should be mistreated," I said at last.

"I am not being mistreated," she protested. "But there have been...remarks made to the head cook, and when it comes to me, my father can only do so much. If the head cook decides to throw me out—well, I doubt there will be another chance for me."

"Who is making these remarks?" I asked. "Perhaps I can talk to them."

Riddhi shrugged. "I cannot tell you. My father has many rivals in court, and I am sure that is all this is. This is my burden to carry."

"But—"

"How are your neighbors?" Manthara asked, cutting me off. She shook her head slightly at me. I wanted to ask many more questions, but instead I sat back, half listening as they chatted, my mind spinning. Riddhi was being punished for something entirely beyond her control, but I did not see how I could help her. I had no power to oppose the words of the sages or to change the laws themselves.

I had long thought of Ahalya as the foremost example of how a man might devastate a woman, but as I saw more of the world, I was realizing there were many ways to ruin a person's life. Most women were not cursed by their husbands, but they suffered all the same. Manthara was right—I had learned something.

And yet, Riddhi did not have to suffer or carry her burden

alone. She worked in the palace where I was a radnyi. What good was learning if I did not take action?

That afternoon, I made my way down to the kitchens.

The space was cramped, far more than I would have expected and a strange contrast to Kekaya given that the rest of the palace in Ayodhya felt so much grander. The room was dim with smoke and bustling with movement, the scent of garlic, ginger, and cumin mingling in the air.

"Radnyi Kaikeyi, can I help you?" A stout older woman stood before me, head bent in deference.

She spoke with a slight air of authority. This must be the head cook. "I was hoping to speak to you about Riddhi," I said, making sure there was no trace of uncertainty in my voice.

"What is it now?" the woman asked with a sigh.

"No complaints," I said quickly. "I wanted to tell you that if you receive any further complaints about her, you may direct them to me. Unless you believe their grievances are legitimate, of course."

The head cook squinted at me through the smoke, as if trying to determine whether I was serious. I held still, waiting, until she relaxed and gave me a small smile. "That is a most generous offer, Radnyi, although I doubt when they hear you have favored her, there will be any further complaints. The girl is smart and skilled. I would not have wanted her to leave."

I had not meant to go so far as to favor her, but by protecting her I supposed I had indeed done just that. Instead, I gave the woman a nod.

"Riddhi!" she called.

Riddhi emerged from the back, bearing a plate of saffron-hued sweets arranged in a many-petaled flower. "It is ready, I am sorry for the delay—oh, Radnyi Kaikeyi." She bowed, balancing the plate aloft to preserve the design.

"I do not wish to disturb you," I said. "Only to tell you that you need not worry any longer."

Her face flitted through emotions quickly—confusion, shock, then happiness. "Truly?" I nodded. After a moment, she smiled broadly, bouncing slightly on her toes as if unable to contain herself. "Thank you, Radnyi."

"It was my pleasure," I said.

"I don't know how I can ever repay you—" She looked around frantically, then said, "Wait one moment. Please." She walked quickly to one of the storerooms.

"You have not shown interest in the kitchens before," the head cook said to me. "Although we appreciate your attentions."

I knew that she was really asking *why*. "She did not deserve to suffer."

The head cook studied me, hands on her hips, a twinkle in her eye. In the Binding Plane, a rose-hued thread unspooled between us. I knew from my time in Kekaya how useful it was to have the goodwill of the kitchen staff, and now with one act of kindness I seemed to have accomplished that here.

In helping another woman, I had in fact helped myself. The head cook's favor would increase my own power in court.

At that moment, Riddhi emerged again with a smaller dish of the same saffron-hued sweets and offered the plate to me. "I think you will like these," she said.

As I lifted one, I caught the faint scent of mango. I took a bite, and a delicious burst of flavor danced across my tongue, the rich sweetness of sugar, the tart vibrance of mango, and the creamy undertones of milk. I had eaten such boiled sweets before and enjoyed them, but here there was an extra hint of nuttiness that made them divine. With a noise of pleasure, I put the whole thing in my mouth.

"That was extraordinary, Riddhi, thank you."

The young woman grinned again, and I quickly took two more before departing, delighted with my success.

*　　*　　*

I entirely forgot the festival of the full moon, until Asha approached me to show me what she had chosen for me to wear that evening.

The sari was a diaphanous white, for the full moon, heavily embroidered with exquisite silver branches that danced like shadows on water when I moved. The necklace she had laid out held three obsidian stones nestled among intricately woven webs of gold. Her taste was excellent—the delicate necklace and embroidery would suit me well.

Because all other happenings had been canceled for the day, I decided to take a stroll in the gardens and enjoy a moment of solitude. There would be a great feast tonight, to celebrate the end of the fasting period for the sages, all of whom would be in attendance. Their day would be occupied in ceremonies for Shiva, but women were not permitted to attend those, for fear it may anger him and lead to a poor monsoon season. It seemed absurd to me that such a great god would care about such a small thing. Still, we had all heard of Videha, the kingdom to our west, where an entire harvest had been lost when they failed to properly observe the same rites. They were much closer to the mountains, and catastrophic mudslides from the slopes had killed many. It was not worth the risk.

But for the moment, I was content to wander in the breeze and enjoy the beauty of my surroundings. Lost in thought, I rounded the corner of a hedge and promptly collided with what felt like a stone pillar and fell with a thump. *Have they added a new statue?* I blinked up at the object. After a moment, I realize that it was in fact a very tall man who was staring down at me in concern.

"I am so sorry, Devi. May I assist you?" I took the proffered hand, strangely delicate compared to his size, and he hoisted me to my feet.

"Thank you. I apologize for my clumsiness. I thought

myself alone here." I did not recognize him, but he was finely dressed. Most likely he was a noble visiting for the feast.

"There is no need for an apology—I thought the same. I don't believe we've been introduced, Arya. I'm Kaikeyi." I deliberately omitted my title. Knocking over royalty could be a criminal offense, and I did not want to scare him—though on second glance, he did not look like an easily intimidated man.

In fact...he looked like he might not be fully a man at all.

His deep brown skin seemed to have the faintest glow—or was that the light of the waning sun? His hair was curled so tightly it may have had muscles of its own, styled in a manner unfamiliar to me. And his eyes shone like gemstones, a brilliant deep orange flecked with red. Inhuman eyes. I had seen those eyes once before, deep in a forest near the banks of the Sarasvati River. My heart beat quicker, and I took a small step back without thinking.

But the recognition that flared in his expression was quite human, halting my panicked response. "Radnyi Kaikeyi!" he exclaimed. "It's a pleasure to meet you. I am Ravana, of Lanka."

This surprised me. I had known Ravana would be our guest for the evening, but I had not expected to find him wandering the gardens. Immediately, I swept into a bow. "Raja. A pleasure to meet you."

Ravana's territory existed on an island at the very southern tip of the known world. His kingdom had long been plagued by the disapproval and punishments of the gods, and he was making pilgrimage to the high mountains in order to seek Lord Shiva's grace. It was a long, fraught journey, and everyone knew he hoped it would bring his people better fortune.

When Dasharath had told me of his coming, I had wondered why such a seemingly devout leader would have the need for such a pilgrimage. But looking at him now, I knew. He had rakshasa blood in his veins.

"I am not sure how pleasant being knocked over was for you," he said, and I found myself laughing. The disconcerting color of his eyes was softened by the kindness held within them.

I shook my head. "It was my fault. As I said, I should have paid more attention to where I was going."

"I understand. Sometimes I find myself lost in thought for hours on end." He sat down on a nearby bench, and drawn in by his easy manner, I sat down next to him.

"Lost in thought about what?" I asked.

He raised his eyebrows as though surprised to be asked. "Flight, for one thing," he said.

"Flight? Like birds?" I was intrigued.

"Yes. I am trying to find a way to make it possible for us intelligent creatures to take to the sky," he explained, his eyes taking on a distant look. "If birds, with no language or tools, can fly, then why shouldn't we?"

"Birds can speak," I said immediately. "You and I cannot understand them, but that does not mean they don't communicate."

He looked at me as if seeing me for the first time. "And how would you know such a thing?"

My cheeks reddened. "I have read of it," I mumbled. I would not reveal my father's boon, especially not to a stranger.

"That does not sound like information one would find in a scroll," Ravana pressed. "But I am fascinated by this. If I were to wear a pair of wings and flap as hard as I could, I would still not take flight. Something else must buoy birds. If I could only speak to them, I might be able to divine what allows them to fly."

I laughed at the thought of little sparrows or finches relating the secrets of their wings to this man. I wondered if this was one of the many things my father knew and could never share. "They are far more trouble than they are worth."

Ravana turned to face me fully. "Now, Radnyi Kaikeyi, you really must tell me. How have you come by such knowledge?"

I had talked myself into a predicament. I needed to distract him, and for want of a better option, I entered the Binding Plane. Happily, we had already formed a bond, a cord the color of the cloudless sky. I could work with that. I sent him a gentle suggestion: *Drop the matter.*

His brow furrowed, and he shook his head as if to clear a fly away.

To my shock, I felt the suggestion recoil from him, the same way I had bounced off him on the garden path. Such a thing had never happened before. I frowned, concentrating this time, and sent the message again, more firmly.

Ravana sprang to his feet. "What are you doing?"

"Nothing!" I insisted, too quickly.

"Are you a witch?" he demanded, taking a step away from me. His features twisted, eyebrows knitted together and lips pulling back into a scowl. For a moment, he looked like a creature from the tales, from my nightmare in the forest. And yet, however frightening he looked, his actions betrayed his own, mortal fear.

"No, of course not!"

"I received a suggestion in my mind," he said. "Some sort of magic is afoot."

"That's absurd." I rose to my feet, pretending insult. "I will not be maligned in such a way."

But he stepped in front of me, blocking my path. "Why such an extreme reaction?" he asked. "I am sorry. I was rude just now, but please do not leave."

"What do you want?" I asked, eyes darting to the path behind him.

"Only to talk," he said. "I mean no insult, but you have magic. I know it; I felt it. Look, here. I will swear that I mean no harm. Would that put your mind at ease?"

Cautiously, I nodded. He would be honor bound to such an oath.

"I swear to the great Lord Shiva that I will not tell another soul anything you share with me about this matter of magic, and furthermore, that I mean you no ill will on its account."

I repeated his words back to myself, searching for any gap in his statement, but found none.

"What would you like to know?" I finally said.

"Everything," Ravana replied. "Shall we walk back to my rooms? There is something I wish to show you, which I think will be of great interest to you."

And so, for the first time in my life, I revealed my secret. I told someone about the text I had discovered in the library cellar of Kekaya's palace. I told of the Binding Plane and my ability to influence others. I had always feared that my story would sound like madness—or worse, like heresy—for the gods were the origins of all magic, and my power came from no god. I could not tell anyone—not even Manthara—for fear they would never trust me again. But Ravana could not be so easily influenced. I felt protected by his vow, and flattered by his interest, and the words spilled out of me.

When we reached his rooms, Ravana checked to make sure no servants were present, then unlocked one of his trunks and rummaged inside. After a moment, he pulled out four scrolls, each made of fine leather.

"These are my texts on magic," he said to me. "I thought I would bring them to the mountain of Lord Shiva, in the hope that perhaps in that sacred place I would be able to use them. I thought they might help me with my investigations into flight. But I have never wielded magic myself. And now I see that these were never meant for me. They were meant for you."

This was a precious gift indeed to give to anyone, let alone a near stranger. I shook my head. "That is too much."

"Read them," he insisted. "You have time. If they make

sense to you, then you should keep them. Knowledge is meant to be shared."

I knew that politeness dictated I protest more vigorously, but in truth I ached to read the scrolls. I had never succeeded in discovering more of my own in Kekaya's library and had been too fearful to even look in Ayodhya. So, I gave in to the desire, carrying them to the fine teakwood desk in the corner.

The first was a treatise with faded illustrations of the five elements sketched in feathery ink and painted: orange and red fire, dark blue water, pale gray wind, green and brown earth, and yellow lightning. Below each element was listed a mantra. Ostensibly to create it?

I mouthed each mantra in turn, concentrating as I did when I entered the Binding Plane. When I recited the final one, my fingers brushed against the page and I felt a light tingling sensation. Excitement jolted through me—but I could not seem to replicate the sensation.

The next text was nearly impossible to decipher. I managed to discern that whatever power it contained had been discovered by devotees of Lord Brahma, but that was all.

Most magic in this world belonged to the gods, this I knew. But it was still discouraging to see it laid out this way. I opened the third, expecting the same, but—

The third dealt with the Binding Plane. I recognized the language immediately.

I read it quickly, my vision nearly blurring in my haste. And then, puzzled, slowly read it again.

It had nothing to do with personal connections. It took me several moments to understand that it was referring to other people's bindings. The scroll contained a different mantra to the one that was now as familiar to me as breathing. This mantra supposedly allowed me to access a new aspect of the Plane. Beneath it was an explanation of concentration techniques to strengthen or weaken these connections as one pleased.

My heart thrummed in my chest as I recalled that day on the field, when Dasharath had seen me maneuvering the chariot and confronted the Master of Horses. I had seen such a connection then. At the time, the bond between them had been slippery, unwilling to come into my grasp. But if I had known this mantra, perhaps I might have touched it.

I could feel anticipation pooling in my stomach at the idea of sitting at the council table and changing not just my own relationships but the alliances and rivalries themselves. Incredible potential unspooled before me, and I fought to keep my excitement in check.

I glanced around and realized Ravana had retired to the other room, offering me privacy to read the scrolls.

"Raja?" I called. Ravana returned immediately. "May I try something on you?"

"Of course." His face lit up, his excitement mirroring my own. "What should I do?"

"Just stand there," I said. I focused my eyes on his solar plexus and repeated the mantra to myself. I sensed the faintest glimmer of something but lost it. No matter.

I tried again, emptying my mind of all else and repeating the words with more force. The world *shifted*, as though the mat beneath me had been lightly jerked.

A strange veil fell over my surroundings, shrouding them in gray. And at the center of this faded world was Ravana, and the web of bonds that radiated from him in a tapestry of light.

"Incredible," I breathed, walking toward him. I resisted the urge to duck, knowing that the threads of the Binding Plane were not real; I had never seen threads that did not move with me. It felt as though I could get tangled and trapped in them, as though I could reach out and touch one. Underneath my feet, the world was solid, even though it had dulled to a distant gray. But I could tell that I was not quite fully in my reality

163

anymore. I lifted my hand and lightly touched a bond—but my fingers passed right through. It was only magic, after all.

"What is it?" Ravana asked.

"You could sense earlier when I tried to use my ability on you, yes?" I asked. He nodded. "Tell me what you feel right now." I found the brightest, strongest bond and sent an aimless thrum of energy at it, not changing or suggesting anything, but trying to merely sound it out.

"My wife," he said instantly. "Mandodari. Whatever you did, I am now thinking quite strongly about her. You would like her. She's brilliant and beautiful and a great asset to our kingdom. I love her so—" He frowned. "I think that is your influence, pulling this out of me."

"Amazing," I said, hardly able to believe it. "If you would permit me, I would like to try something regarding someone you do not care for very much."

"Not my wife, then," he said immediately.

"No, no." My eyes fell upon a very fine green floss. "Who is this?" I plucked it just barely.

"I am picturing a stranger I met on my travels a few years ago. We both camped in the same cave for a night, when it rained."

"He is of no matter to you?" I asked.

"None. I had not thought of him since that night."

"Lovely," I said, and focused on the bond, feeding it with energy. Before my eyes, it swelled to twice, then thrice its size.

"I liked him," Ravana told me thoughtfully. The bond quavered, and I could not calm it. My mind's grasp slid from it again and again. "I liked him immensely. Should I have offered him a position in Lanka?"

I sent one final push, but it was too much. The bond frayed and snapped even as I tried to prevent it, the two ends crumbling like ash just as had happened to my bond with Neeti so many years ago.

"No. I hate him." Ravana sounded bemused. "I have no idea why, but I do. Did you change something? Is this usual for your workings?"

I blinked, and my shoulders sagged with exhaustion. I let the Binding Plane drop away, and the gray veil lifted. Color snapped back in the world, and a wave of dizziness washed over me.

What was the strange, colorless place I had just been? I looked around, disoriented for a few moments, before the realization hit me. That world *was* the Binding Plane—truly another world, a half step from our own. In the past, I had glimpsed only a small part of it, seeing only my own connections. But this was the true Plane, foreign and wondrous. Already I could not fathom that I had been so ignorant.

But using it was *difficult*. When I had been a girl and had first discovered the threads, using them would leave me feeling like I had sprinted the length of the palace thrice over. I had grown comfortable, complacent with time. And now I could hardly stand.

I would have to strengthen myself all over again for this new world.

I looked up at Ravana and realized he was waiting for an answer. "Not usual. I have never done such a thing before. And it is you who are most unusual. You are the first to have been able to discern any of my workings. I had never thought that possible until meeting you. Thank you for allowing me to experiment in such a way. This scroll is very valuable." I held it to my chest, a sense of wonderment energizing me.

"I am half-rakshasa," Ravana admitted. "That is how I can feel your magic. And why I have some immunity to it. Radnyi Kaikeyi, you should keep the scroll. Keep all of them. You have a talent."

"You hardly know me," I protested. "Why would you give me such a gift?"

He said simply, "I think it incredible that anybody in our world can harness magic. I am happy to do my part in helping yours." Through our bond, I could feel he told the truth.

"A raja cannot be so altruistic," I warned him, because I liked him and did not wish to take advantage of his kindness.

"Perhaps. You have shared your secret with me, so I will do the same. What if I were to tell you that I wish for magic in the world, because I hope it can move us out from under the thumb of those with more power?"

"You mean the gods?" I whispered, as though they were not capable of hearing every conversation among mortals.

"Their rules hold us back, do they not?" Ravana shrugged, as though he was not speaking complete blasphemy. But my stomach clenched, for if we were overheard—or if the gods took notice—we would suffer greatly, royalty or not. "My kingdom is constantly punished for every improvement we make, every step we take toward healing and science. I am going to Lord Shiva to beg him to spare us, to let us go forward and bring others into enlightenment as we see fit."

"What are you talking about?" I hissed. "The gods—" I wanted to say *always have our best interests at heart*, but my mouth said, "protect us."

He stepped toward me. "Are you sure about that? Then why should they punish me for progress? Or you, or anyone else for that matter?"

I moved toward the door, studiously ignoring his question, for I did not want to admit what it stirred inside me. Some part of me heard Ravana's words and recognized truth.

But it was all too much. A whole world had just opened up to me, and with it, opportunities I did not yet fully understand.

Maybe Ravana had a grander vision for the future. But he was a man, and could dream like that. This new Binding Plane, the potential of the present—that was enough for me.

"I am still not sure I can take the scrolls from you," I said. "It does not seem fair."

He sighed. "All right. Let us simply say that in exchange for the scrolls you owe me a favor, should it be in your power to give it, and leave it there."

The symbolism of the gesture felt right.

"Thank you, Raja Ravana. I truly hope one day I can repay you." I clutched the scrolls to my heart and left his rooms, wondering what favor I could possibly ever grant him. But I quickly put it out of my mind: I doubted our paths would ever cross again, and I had other things to concern myself with.

CHAPTER FOURTEEN

THANKS TO RAVANA'S INCREDIBLE gift, the whole world opened up to me in a burst of color. I learned how to view all of the Binding Plane at once and lost myself for hours in the brilliant webs. Thin skeins of orange and red created tracks of fire around the palace, while threads of blues and greens sent beautiful rivers through every part of the court. Against the faded gray hues my surroundings took on when I entered the Binding Plane, the bonds and connections stood out ever more brightly. The Plane had its own landscape, and I came to feel like its god.

But one problem remained that couldn't be solved with the Binding Plane. As the weeks went by and I went again and again to my husband's bed, my moon cycle did not change. Every moon I bled, and every moon I failed to produce an heir.

In the privacy of my own room, I worried over the many possibilities for my childlessness. My occasional evening horseback rides. My work in the Binding Plane.

My divine abandonment.

Hardest to bear was the disappointment of Kaushalya and Sumitra. Kaushalya especially had given up on the idea that she would ever bear the raja a child, and I had come to consider her a true friend. Letting her down filled me with shame, and sadness at causing her such pain. Despite all my maneuverings in becoming Dasharath's bride, I was now a worthless third queen.

When Dasharath summoned me to his chambers nearly fifteen moons after my move to Ayodhya, I delayed as long as possible. Just the idea of trying again twisted up my insides. Manthara forced me out the door, reminding me that no matter how I felt about it, Dasharath was my raja and I had to obey.

My treacherous feet bore me forward even as my mind protested. I stood outside his rooms, considering for a fleeting moment using my influence over Dasharath to make him forget his desires. Finally, I lifted my hand to knock. The door swung open before I even touched it, and Sumitra's cheerful face peered out at me.

I blinked. Did Dasharath now want two of us at a time?

"Here she is! No need to send a servant out to find her," Sumitra said, beckoning me inside. I followed her through the chambers.

"Good." Dasharath sat on the edge of his bed, and Kaushalya sat on the floor by his feet. Sumitra knelt beside her, and I forced myself to assume the same submissive posture. At least it seemed that I would not be expected to perform any conjugal acts tonight.

"I believe there is a reason why all of your wombs have failed to bear a child," Dasharath said. He spoke quickly, as though he did not like the words. "That reason is me."

I nearly toppled into Sumitra, trying to hide my surprise. Men never took responsibility for infertility—that was a woman's curse.

"I have not performed the proper rituals for the gods. I have been too preoccupied with expanding our territories and administering to the needs of the kingdom, and so neglected my spiritual role. This kingdom has not had a Yagna in a generation. The gods are punishing me by withholding an heir."

Ah. That made more sense.

"How will we rectify this, Raja?" Kaushalya murmured.

"I have arranged to perform a great Yagna in a fortnight. We will sacrifice our best animals, offer our best foods, and pray that one of you will bear a child."

Sumitra clapped her hands together, but I had her measure well enough by then to know without checking that she only feigned enthusiasm. She believed herself fully barren, despite evidence it might be Dasharath's fault.

"What should we do to prepare?" she asked.

"I have consulted the city's sages. They tell me there are purification rituals you must undertake. Our court sage will instruct you. And you must fast for the next fortnight."

Despite knowing such rituals were unlikely to work for me, I was willing to try, not only for myself and my kingdom, but for the promise Dasharath had made me in my father's throne room.

And so, I forced myself to observe every preparation for the Yagna. I fasted for two weeks, subsisting on water and the occasional fruit, hiding my irritation that Dasharath, as a man, was allowed to eat freely. It was another inequality that I had been ignorant of. How many poor women had undergone similar rituals, forced to go about their days with only a few sips of water? How many were forced to fast during their cycle? It was a small indignity, not as bad as the laws that prohibited women from speaking in public or forced illegitimate daughters into a life of poverty, but it rankled me.

By the day of the Yagna, none of us could contain our irritation. Dasharath had promised us an enormous feast afterward, but that seemed so far away when servants woke us before dawn to bathe.

"Sage Rishyasringa better move quickly," Sumitra griped as we began dressing. Her usually sunny disposition had fully faded in the face of the court sage's potential long-windedness.

"I might eat whatever animals they sacrifice," Kaushalya added, pulling on her shift with more force than strictly necessary.

I groaned. "I might eat Sage Rishyasringa himself."

They both stared at me, and I thought I had gone too far—but then the room echoed with their peals of laughter.

"Not nearly meaty enough," Sumitra joked.

"Well, he has those horns and a little tail. Perhaps he would taste like goat meat," Kaushalya said, her voice remarkably even for someone speaking so ludicrously. It was common knowledge among the court that Rishyasringa's mother had been an apsara, a dancing spirit in the court of the gods, who had been cursed to live in the form of a deer. The gods liked to remind apsaras of their place, lest they get too arrogant in their beauty—Brahma had fashioned Ahalya to humble the apsaras too.

Born of a human father and a divine deer, Rishyasringa was a renowned sage, even if he took after his mother in some respects.

"Just a few more hours. When the sun sets, we can eat." My stomach rumbled agreement.

"You know what I want?" Sumitra asked. "Kheer. I want kheer."

I made a fake gagging sound. "I hate kheer. I don't think even now I'm hungry enough to eat it. It's so...grainy."

Kaushalya flicked my shoulder. "If you can eat Sage Rishyasringa, you can eat kheer."

"I wouldn't be so sure," I said. "But there will be many other desserts at the feast. Gulab jamun—I could eat one hundred of those." The delicious fried dough soaked in rose-flavored sugar syrup had been my favorite dessert for as long as I could remember.

"Only if there's a hundred for me too," Kaushalya said. "Otherwise, I will fight you for them."

I laughed. "You would lose."

"Would I?" Kaushalya asked, voice cool, and I worried again that hunger had loosened my tongue overmuch. Then Kaushalya dissolved into a fit of giggles. The hunger had turned us all hysterical. We struggled to dress ourselves. When our handmaidens entered the preparation rooms, the sun had barely risen over the horizon. Their deft fingers undid and redid our clothes, fastened jewelry.

Asha snuck each of us a small peach, and despite the fact that we were not supposed to eat until the feast, we devoured them as if they were the choicest dish in the entire kingdom.

"That just made me hungrier," I groaned. When no one was looking, I quickly licked a drop of juice from my finger.

Asha only grinned at me. "You're welcome." She acted far more familiar toward me than a servant normally would. She had become a friend, and the thick braid of green between us proved that.

A sudden pang of sorrow shot through me, for the way she treated me made me think of Yudhajit. I missed him dearly. He had been wrong to send me away, even if he had been right about my life in Ayodhya. I might have swallowed my pride and apologized for the chance to get my brother back. But the door was closed, and the bond broken.

I walked to the Yagna, shivering in the cool morning air. We had all been dressed in plain yellow cotton saris that did little to warm our bodies. Sage Rishyasringa lit the sacred fire, and despite the smoke, I was grateful for the beacon of warmth before me.

Much of the ceremony passed in a fog of sadness and hunger and exhaustion. The sage would intone prayers and instruct Dasharath to repeat holy words after him. Every so often, we would be instructed to sprinkle water into the fire and speak a mantra or make offerings of flowers or fruits to the flames. The sage scraped ashes from the fire and used his thumb to apply them to our foreheads, marking us as Dasharath's wives. At his command, we rose to our feet and completed three pradakshina, circling the statues of the gods and the flames while we repented any sinful acts of our past. I thought of Neeti, how I had so foolishly lost her friendship. I thought of Yudhajit, how even though he had been at fault, my cruelty had sealed our fate. And even though I had not forced her away, my mother's face flashed before me. I had lost so many people.

I walked around the flame in a daze, not looking up from my own feet. My mind felt hazy, half-removed from the world. Perhaps that is why I did not notice anything amiss until Sumitra shrieked my name, her hand pulling me back. I stumbled, not quite reaching her, and felt at my back an all-consuming heat.

Never take your eyes off—

I spun back toward the sacred fire. But it was gone, replaced by a column of pure flame towering above me. Before I could move away from the radius of destruction, a male form coalesced out of the blaze. He stepped forward, eyes falling immediately on me. Despite the heat, a shiver ran down my spine. I recognized him.

Agni, god of fire.

His hair and eyes were molten gold, his skin a searing red. Bright light fell off him as though he was the sun. He towered over me, taller even than the half-rakshasa Ravana had been.

"Why do you not bow before me?" he asked, voice crackling. Out of the corner of my eye I saw that all the others, even Dasharath, had dropped to their knees.

"I do not know," I answered. My lips were incapable of forming a lie. Raw power came from him in waves.

"Kaikeyi," he intoned, each syllable like the strike of a gong in my head. He approached me and placed a single finger under my chin. Instant pain rose where he touched me. He tilted my face up toward his, and I fought down a scream at the unbearable heat.

Instead, I made myself look into his burning golden eyes. I would not show the gods weakness, no matter how they hurt me.

His lips quirked upward into a smirk. "Radnyi Kaikeyi. We have expected you."

I blinked at that. "Expected me?" I echoed, jerking my chin from his grasp. Cool relief.

"You think we ignore you for our amusement?" he asked, voice a whisper. "There is a reason."

"Why?" I demanded. "What have I done?" I hated that I needed so badly to know.

"It's not what you have done," he said. All mirth had left him. "It is what you will do."

"What will I do?" I asked. "Tell me and let me be done with it." Behind me I could sense the quiet murmurs of the watching crowd. Half of Ayodhya had turned out to witness the spectacle of the Yagna. And now they watched as Agni singled out the third wife of the raja. How would I explain this to Dasharath, to the others?

"I cannot tell you that," he said. "But the gods-touched are immune to the charms of the gods. Forsaken. You are forsaken." He brushed past me then and strode purposefully toward Dasharath.

"Gods-touched?" I called after him. "What does that mean?"

But he had already forgotten me, turning instead to the raja. In the god's hands appeared a small silver pot, and Dasharath was nodding, smiling, prostrating himself to touch Agni's feet.

I managed to gain enough control over myself to find the Binding Plane. I did not know why, but my instinct in this frightening situation was to flee there, to a place where I had power. Gray overlaid the world and I searched for Agni, hoping to demand answers.

He was not there.

In the Binding Plane, even his shadow had disappeared. The space in front of me stood empty, and I reached out a hand, hoping to touch the blank spot where I knew a god should stand. But there was nothing.

"Feed this kheer to your three wives," Agni rumbled, and I jerked my hand back, exiting the Plane to see Agni still standing by Dasharath. I blinked the magical threads back into existence, and once again, the god disappeared.

"Once they have consumed it," Agni continued, "they will bear you strong sons." His voice had amplified so the whole crowd could hear him. Perhaps the whole city.

"Thank you, my lord," Dasharath said. "We are unworthy of your blessing."

Agni stepped back and back into the fountain of fire and the flames rose up around him, consuming him until he was indistinguishable from the towering blaze. In the blink of an eye, the fire died down to its normal, mortal size.

I raised my hand to my chin, expecting to feel a blistering burn, but my fingers met only smooth skin.

"What did he say to you?" Sumitra whispered, coming to stand beside me. Kaushalya stood on Sumitra's other side.

"He wanted to know why I had dared not to bow," I whispered back. "I apologized. I explained that the hunger had made me faint and I was not in my right mind."

"What did you shout after him?"

"I was begging forgiveness," I said. My explanation was flimsy, so I gave our connection a quick strum.

"If you begged for forgiveness, he granted it. Put that out of your mind. The gods are not cruel." Sumitra straightened as Dasharath approached Kaushalya with the kheer. I reached for her hand and squeezed it, trying to thank her. She squeezed back.

Kaushalya lifted the kheer to her lips and drank long and deep. As Kaushalya's throat bobbed, my stomach roiled. I really did despise kheer. It tasted sickly sweet, like fruit that was several days overripe. It was the only sweet I could not stomach. Even in this, the gods mocked me.

Kaushalya finished drinking and passed the vessel to Sumitra. Sumitra took several swallows, then handed the vessel to me. I looked into the silver pot, and the sight of the creamy rice pudding made my empty stomach turn. I lifted it to my lips, held my breath, and took two fast swallows. When I paused to breathe, the thick coating on my tongue choked me. I could not make myself drink again.

I passed the vessel back to Sumitra. "I don't wish to take more than my due," I gasped out. Perhaps the others would view it as generosity and humility, rather than simply a deep hatred of kheer. I watched Sumitra struggle and could tell the moment that hunger and a desire to be out of the intense scrutiny of the public won out. She gulped down all that remained.

Dasharath raised the empty pot up to show the crowd. "It is done!"

The kheer churned in my belly. I focused on breathing in, out, in, out. Soon we would be in the palace, soon we would be at the feast, soon, soon, soon.

CHAPTER FIFTEEN

"WHAT DID AGNI SAY to you?" Manthara asked the instant I entered my rooms.

I knew I could not lie to her. "He said they have expected me."

"They?"

"I assume he meant the gods," I said, sinking down onto my bed. I turned my face to the side slightly so that Manthara could hear my next words. I did not want to repeat the ugly truth. "He admitted that the gods have forsaken me."

Manthara was silent. "I am sorry," she finally said.

I glanced up at her, shocked by the gravity of her voice. The dupatta she often wore over her hair had ridden forward, casting shadows over her face. Her dark eyes were black, sorrowful.

"All this time I insisted that you must be mistaken, when you said the gods didn't hear you. I treated you like a foolish child." Her words warmed me. She believed me.

"I *am* foolish," I admitted after a moment. "Sometimes. But I knew this to be true."

"Did he tell you why they did such a thing to you? You have not committed any great sins."

"He said—" I stopped myself, considering what Agni had told me, and despair coursed through my veins. Agni was a powerful god who acted as a conduit to bring mortal offerings to the heavens. But this time he had brought something from the gods to us—and he had brought me a message besides. Such a reversal could mean nothing good for me. "He said I was gods-touched. That the power of the gods could not work on people such as me."

"Gods-touched," Manthara echoed, placing a cool hand on my head. I told myself I was imagining the reverent wonder in her voice. I knew in my heart Agni's words were a curse, not a blessing. "I always knew you were destined for something great, but this..."

"I am not destined for something *great*, Manthara. I am destined for something terrible. He said I was forsaken because of what I will do." I buried my face back in my bed to mask the tears that slipped down my cheeks. I could not fathom what I might do. But to have incurred such divine wrath from birth—

Is this how Ahalya felt, knowing Indra's eye was always upon her? Or when her husband returned and she stood in that moment between innocence and condemnation, knowing what was to happen and yet powerless to stop it?

I had wished merely for a measure of freedom for myself, and perhaps now for others. There was nothing evil in that. Was there?

"The gods would smite you down if they thought you would be the source of terrible deeds." Manthara ran her fingers through my hair, and I relaxed despite myself. "You are meant to help the world."

"He didn't look at me like I would help the world," I told her. But she couldn't possibly understand. She loved me. "He looked at me like I was wicked."

"I've known you your whole life," Manthara said to me. "You don't have a wicked bone in your body."

"Then maybe I am to become wicked," I said. My voice trembled, but Manthara had seen worse weakness from me. I needed her reassurance right now.

She did not disappoint. "That is entirely within your power. Now, if you are done with this foolishness, you should rest. Your body has work to do." She sat on a chair next to my bedside. "Shall I tell you a story?"

I was not a child anymore, and it had been many years since Manthara had spun me a tale. But I nodded anyway, lying back and letting her voice wash over me as she spoke of Savitri and Satyavana. I had heard this story before, of how brave Savitri bargained with Yama, the god of death himself, for the life of her husband, Satyavana. Yama offered her any wish, except for the life of Satyavana, and so she wished she would have one hundred children with her husband. Impressed, Yama brought Satyavana back to life.

I had found it a boring story as a child, for there was no fighting or danger, no wondrous gifts or thrilling escapes—just a woman and a god, speaking. But now I heard it anew. A woman, speaking to a god as her equal. A woman, saving her husband. A woman, outsmarting death. It soothed me, for a few minutes, to imagine myself as Savitri, even if I knew deep in my heart that hers was not my path.

After the story was done, I felt calmer, more peaceful. And when I briefly opened my eyes, before I slipped at last into sleep, Manthara was still there.

I might have been immune to the magic of the gods, but Dasharath was not. The kheer we all consumed allowed his seed to stick inside us, and soon we all swelled with child.

I knew that if I bore a son, Dasharath's vow would make me the most important woman in the kingdom. I also firmly believed that, although they had promised Dasharath strong sons, the gods would give me a daughter just to laugh at me.

I did not wish to bring a daughter into this world of men, into a world that would silence her thoughts before she could even speak them. I wondered how many women had felt this same fear, deep in their bones. If my mother had. It turned my stomach, kept me awake at night, thinking of all that might go wrong.

I had to change it.

I had to build a world where my daughter would not be exiled by her husband on a whim, where her opinion could be valued without first having to save her husband's life in battle. The thought of my daughter marching to war was like an ache I could not shed. I lay awake night after night unable to breathe for fear of it. I would not always be there to protect her myself. Confined to only the least strenuous of activities, I had far too much time to think of these remote possibilities, for myself and my daughter, until I felt my chest would break with the fear, my ribs crackling like brittle wood under the weight of it.

But in time, the fear also brought clarity. I was a radnyi and had a seat on the council—if anyone could change this, it was me. I had to try.

The sages had made the wishes of the gods clear, putting rules in place to keep women separate and protected. But in truth, it was little protection. If the gods had already ordained my evil deeds, then I had nothing to lose by defying them now. So, I would defy them.

I could not change the minds of the gods, but I could change the minds of men. Ravana had given me a monumental gift, and I began to wonder what I might be able to accomplish with it. How I might make this kingdom a better home for my daughter than Kekaya had been for me, or my mother. Opening the court to women. Permitting women to learn in the open market schools. Allowing women to maintain their own stalls in the market—and perhaps even hold property. Being unmarriageable would no longer be a life sentence then.

I spun out the possibilities like strings in the Binding Plane, identifying the difficulties. The more traditional men, I knew, would be unhappy—Dasharath's religious advisor still barely tolerated my presence in the room, although he held his tongue around my husband. But perhaps I could weaken their ties with Dasharath and his closest advisors and bind the others to me instead.

It would take slow and careful work, work that I could not begin until after my pregnancy—the court healers had told me in no uncertain terms I could not tax my mind or body—but I began to believe in myself again.

After my second missed cycle, I wrote to my father, explaining briefly about the Yagna, the kheer of the gods, and the simultaneous pregnancies of all of Dasharath's wives. I reminded him of Dasharath's promise not so long ago and asked for his prayers that I bear a son, playing the part of a dutiful daughter. I imagined that he would be pleased when he read it, and it warmed me to think that he might be proud—though I still believed I would bear a daughter.

And even though we had not spoken in well over a year, I tried to write to Yudhajit as well. My first attempt—a meandering and apologetic ramble—I tossed into the fire. Perhaps I had something to apologize for, but the fault was not mine alone. My pride, lessened though it was, still would not allow me to be the first to bend.

In the end, I essentially copied my letter to my father and made no mention of my emotions at all. That way, I told myself, his eventual failure to respond would not hurt me.

Manthara handed me a thick package from Kekaya nearly a moon later. I ignored it for a few days, assuming that my other brothers and various courtiers had likely been conscripted into sending bland well-wishes.

This assumption was right, and I wanted to scream as I

contemplated the thin strips of reed paper and realized how many I would be obligated to return. I almost ignored the final letter in the package. But as I idly turned it over, I recognized—

Yudhajit's handwriting. Just the sight of it transported me to our childhood, practicing our letters in that cold stone room and racing each other to finish. I was filled with a homesick longing for my brother. *He had written to me.*

My eyes blurred for a moment. I blinked furiously, desperate to read.

Dear Kaikeyi,

I am heartened to hear of your pregnancy and have nothing but the best of wishes for you as you carry this child. I hope you are taking care of yourself in Ayodhya. Father tells me that you have taken to court well, and that he hears nothing but praise of you. I would expect no less.

I miss you desperately, and I apologize for not writing you sooner. I confess I was quite angry at what you said, but I am sure you now regret it—as I regret my role in your departure. My previously arranged marriage has fallen apart, and Father has set a new match with the princess of a mountain clan that will soon be joined with Kekaya. I think I understand a bit, now, of what you must have felt when I told you of your imminent wedding, and I do not even have to leave my home. For that, I am as sorry as I am glad that things have worked out for the best.

I know you and your propensity to assume the worst in all situations, so you must be well convinced by now that you are carrying a daughter. But I am confident that you will bear Dasharath a son.

Love always,
Yudhajit

Heart pounding in my chest, I reached for the Binding Plane, welcoming the familiar tug as the world shifted slightly underneath me. I rose from my chair and spun in a slow circle, finding and discarding in turn each bond that lay shimmering against the drab curtain covering the world.

There. It was smaller than before, which is perhaps how I had missed it in the time it took the letter to reach me, but the deep, rich blue was unmistakable. It extended out through the west-facing wall of my window, and I imagined it crossing the plains and fording the rivers, navigating the city and entering the vast stone palace of Kekaya, until it arrived at the heart of my beloved twin.

CHAPTER
SIXTEEN

YUDHAJIT WAS RIGHT. FOR all my plans in bearing a daughter—all I had begun to do to prepare to raise a girl in this world—I bore a son.

At first, when the midwife proclaimed my child was a boy, I did not understand her meaning. Then I shook with the force of my shock and relief, for I had truly never believed I might bear a child who could live an unconstrained life. Remembering that my father had named me for his kingdom, I named my son Bharata, after our entire continent.

Kaushalya's son was Rama, born the day before my Bharata. Sumitra followed us one week later with sweet-natured twins, Lakshmana and Shatrugna.

In the span of a fortnight, childless Dasharath became the father of four heirs. The sages proclaimed his sons to be evidence that the gods smiled upon Dasharath, and they recognized him as a great and pious ruler.

In the moments after I gave birth to Bharata, as I lay foolish and sweaty, I looked into his beautiful face and believed with all my being that one day he would rule.

The relief I felt at having a son was indescribable, so bright and hot that I nearly fainted from it. Instead, I cradled him, his soft skin filling me with a joy so deep it dwarfed the relief. I looked into his eyes, and I made him two promises: I would never leave him, not the way my mother had left my brothers and me. And I would never use the Binding Plane on him, never risk that destruction.

I had wondered, in the weeks leading up to the birth, whether I would be a good mother. What if I was too strange, too war-like and rebellious for it? But I need not have worried. I took to child-rearing quickly. After all, I had years of experience help-ing to raise my brothers, and I had far more help in prosperous Kosala than had been provided in Kekaya.

At first, Kaushalya and Sumitra and I tended separately to our children, our camaraderie ignored as we jealously guarded every precious moment we could spend with our sons. But one evening, several moons after their birth, Kaushalya arrived in Bharata's nursery, bouncing a sobbing Rama.

"He won't stop crying," she explained, the dark shadows under her unadorned eyes telling all. "He is perfectly fine, but...I heard from someone that you always know how to soothe Bharata, and I thought..." The long gaps in her speech, as though she could barely cling to thought, cut through my own tired reluctance.

"Give him here," I said, glancing at Bharata, who lay coo-ing on his mat, waving his small fists in the air at the arrival of his brother. I held Rama close and gently bounced him, stroking the down of his hair and pressing kisses on his soft cheeks. He continued to cry, but his wails softened, and with-out thinking I began to sing to him, a nonsense song I had sung to my littlest brother, Rahul, when he was upset. A song I hazily remembered my mother singing to me and Yudhajit long, long ago.

Rama quieted, looking up at me with wide eyes and trying to grab at my lips, and I felt my heart melt for him. I bounced and swayed, still singing, as Kaushalya leaned against the wall and slowly sank to the floor. "How did you do that?" she whispered.

Rama's eyes were closing now, and I hugged him close to my chest, lowering my voice to a soothing hum. In a few more minutes he was fast asleep, and Bharata had also drifted off. I did not want to let him go, but exhaustion clung to me too. I lay Rama down by his brother, smiling as they unconsciously turned toward each other, and then went to sit by Kaushalya. "Practice," I said.

"Even I want to sleep now." Kaushalya leaned against my shoulder, the weight of her head inexplicably comforting. It was the closest we had ever been.

We both awoke some time later to the sounds of Rama and Bharata babbling to each other.

From then on, we spent much of our time together. I quickly found myself thinking of Rama and Lakshmana and Shatrugna as my own, and I believe Kaushalya and Sumitra thought of Bharata as theirs. And in my heart I vowed that I would raise all of them to be good men—men like their father, not like mine.

In the exhausted fog of those first few moons and the bittersweet relief of bearing a son, I had little time to think about the daughters of my kingdom. But it remained in the back of my mind, a seed of understanding that even if Bharata and his brothers were not going to suffer, someone else's child would. And as I began to get my bearings once again, I realized Bharata's birth brought me a gift: He solidified my position in the eyes of the court.

The first time it happened, I nearly fell out of my chair. "Radnyi Kaikeyi, do you think the harvest will be sufficient to increase the tribute?" Arya Suresh asked. I had learned through my acquaintanceship with Riddhi that he was her father. My bond with Suresh had grown since I helped her, so I imagined that he knew what I had done.

Still, I was so shocked at hearing my name that I barely heard the rest of the question, and I felt heat rise in my cheeks. I took a deep breath, collecting my thoughts about the tax the rest of the men had been discussing. "Perhaps it would be best to keep the tribute the same?" I said, then chastised myself for answering a question with a question. "The rains have been sufficient, it is true, but the gods must also bless our fields. The contributions were set based on last year's harvest, which was abundant, so keeping it the same would not hurt us. If the harvest is worse than expected, the people will be glad there was no increase, and if the harvest is better, they will remember our generosity."

I glanced toward my husband as I finished. Dasharath was practically beaming at me.

I had the power to change my kingdom.

Bharata was all of six moons old when I finally decided to raise the subject of the marketplace.

My suggestion was to modify the law to allow women to sell at the stalls twice a week. As I spoke, I kept an eye on the Binding Plane. A few of my bonds trembled, but my golden connection to Dasharath was like sunlight on a cloudless day.

Virendra, the Minister of War, cleared his throat when I had finished. I still did not know him well, although our relationship was respectful. I had always gotten the impression that he found me too strange after the whole affair with Sambarasura, as though he suspected I had not told him everything.

My heart sank. This subject had little to do with him. If he was speaking now, it was surely to rebuff the proposal.

"That is a fine idea," he said. I gaped at him. His eyebrow went up slightly, and I snapped my mouth shut. "Our merchants may be more willing to part with their sons if they know their daughters may help them. We are always in need of more soldiers."

I had truly not even thought of that benefit, although it now seemed an obvious way to appeal to a Minister of War who cared about recruiting soldiers, if not aiding women. I saw a few men nodding along. But on a Mantri Parishad with fifteen members, I would need more than a few.

Another man cleared his throat, and this time I knew it would not be in my favor. Manav rarely spoke, but as religious advisor he was quite devout and traditional. "That is blasphemy. The sages have been clear on this point—allowing women to sell in the market would certainly offend the gods." He spoke as if it were the last word on the matter.

But I had prepared for this objection. "The sages would defer to our king, if he thought it in the best interests of the kingdom. After all, they want Ayodhya to prosper, as do the gods who have blessed us with their favor. If this new rule improved our city, I do not think the sages would have objections."

At this, Suresh joined in, "Allowing women to sell might encourage trade too, for merchants could make more trips and leave their wives to tend their stalls."

One after the other, most of the advisors spoke up briefly. I counted nine who agreed with my proposal. Ultimately, though, the decision lay with Dasharath.

I looked up at him, giving him a small smile, and entered the Binding Plane. My husband seemed in agreement, but I was gripped with a sudden worry that my first proposal would fail. I hesitated for a moment, then found the strong cord between us and gave it a featherlight touch. *It is a good idea. Most of your council supports it.* The idea traveled down our bond, and when it reached Dasharath he gave a small nod. "I am convinced," he said. "This seems a wise decision."

I could not hold back my beaming grin.

As the men filed out, I sought to catch and thank Virendra. But before I could, Manav loomed before me, blocking my path to the door. "I wish you would reconsider, Radnyi Kaikeyi," he said softly. His voice held a disquieting energy. I did not step back, but I entered the Binding Plane as a precaution. The thin bond between us jumped this way and that.

"I am sorry we disagree," I said politely. "But why not give this idea a chance? There is wisdom in it, and benefit to our people."

"Perhaps. But you cast aside the words of the gods so easily," he said. "This will anger many."

I did not respond, for I could tell he would not listen. But neither did I pay him any heed.

On quiet evenings, when there was to be no dancing or music in court and the children were soundly sleeping, Sumitra, Kaushalya, and I would gather with our favorite ladies and servants and talk. We would pretend to busy ourselves in embroidery or the like, but mostly we would sit on the soft cushions in our rooms, lamps lit like so many tiny stars flickering around us, and tell stories about what we had heard around the palace.

One such night, we sat in my quarters sampling delicate sweets made of crushed pistachio and spun sugar—Riddhi's magical creation—giggling at Sumitra's story of happening upon a newlywed noble couple acting amorously in the corridor outside the main hall. Kaushalya gave a quite undignified snort, and the shock of that sound coming from the most elegant of us sent us into another round of laughter. It was at this moment that a knock sounded on the door.

This quieted us, for it was unusual for anyone to call at such an hour—everyone who might have done so was already here.

We straightened, trying to recapture a sense of decorum, and Asha answered, opening the door only a crack. I heard the voices of two other women speaking in hushed tones. My lady-in-waiting turned to us. "It is two serving girls from the kitchens," she explained. "They seek an audience."

It was strange to hear such a formal request, but seeing that my fellow radnyis had regained their composure, I waved the girls in and asked Manthara to serve them tea. Only once they were settled and drinking did I ask, "How can we help you?"

One of the girls, the younger of the two, straightened her spine and stared right at me. I immediately liked her. She looked to be fourteen or fifteen, with large brown eyes that held a barely contained spark.

"My name is Saralaa, Radnyi. Hers is Mugdha. We are from Chedi."

I knew of Chedi—it was a small village in the farthest southwest reaches of Kosala. They bred fine sheep and were known for their lovely textile weaving—I had a quilt from Chedi that was as light as a simple sheet and yet as warm as a summer day. But of course, that fact was no use now.

"We have heard a rumor, my lady, that Kosala intends to make war against the southern villages. I was hoping you could tell us...Should our family flee?" She spoke haltingly, tripping over her words so I could barely make out her meaning. I glanced at Manthara, who came to stand beside me. Perhaps an elder servant's presence would calm the girl.

"Let me make sure I understand." I took a sip of tea, forcing myself to go slowly. "You and your friend are from Chedi." A nod from Saralaa. "You heard a rumor that Kosala wants to declare war on Chedi." Nod. "And your family plans to leave?"

The girl shook her head. "No, my lady. My brother has just arrived, to take up a position in the stables. He's the one who said that the village elders in Chedi are preparing for a war with Kosala. I just want to make sure my family is safe."

We had in fact discussed Chedi at last week's council meeting. Their village council had refused to pay its tax this year, so one of the Minister of Finance's men would accompany a small group of soldiers there to collect payment.

But to a village like Chedi, on the outskirts of Kosala, that might seem like a declaration of war, a possibility we had not considered.

"King Dasharath does not plan to wage war on Chedi," I said at last. "He is simply sending a delegation."

"A what?" Mugdha asked softly. She seemed a few years older than her friend and spoke to her hands instead of to me.

"A...small group of people," I explained. "Some soldiers, some officials. They have matters to discuss with your elders. I would not worry. I would, however, tell your brother to stop spreading such rumors." As I spoke, I found the threads of trust between us and added some firmness to my words.

Saralaa grabbed my hand between both of hers and bowed over it. "Oh, thank you, Radnyi! We were so worried." Her friend elbowed her, and she dropped my hand, a look of horror drawing over her face. "I'm so sorry, Radnyi."

I reached out and squeezed her fingers. She had spirit, and I did not want her to fear me. "Thank you for trusting me with this matter."

After they left, I looked at Asha. She seemed a bit too pleased by the exchange. "How strange, that they should come to my door so late," I said mildly.

"They call us the Women's Circle," Asha said, not looking up from the small tunic she was hemming for Bharata.

"Who calls us that?"

"Almost the entire palace," Sumitra chimed in. She too had picked up her sewing. Sumitra embroidered beautifully and was currently sewing tiny jewels onto small dhotis for each of the boys.

"What does it mean?" I pressed, and wondered, *How did I not hear about this?*

Perhaps I relied too heavily on the Binding Plane for

information. It could never help me answer questions I did not know to ask.

"People know that we gather in the evenings in this manner. Not all of them use the term in a kind way, but I think the women in the palace do." Asha put aside her work to look at me, leaning forward onto her elbows. "They wish for invitations. Some of the servants ask me for them."

Like lightning, a revelation coursed through me.

This social gathering had become something more without my even trying. People wanted to come and speak to me, to us, because we had power. Here was my chance to do what I had always wanted, handed to me on a silver platter.

"If you trust them, bring them here," I said. "It's our responsibility."

A few days later, Kaushalya and I sat suffering together through a particularly boring kavita performance. Sumitra had begged off as too tired, and I silently envied her brilliant thinking.

The man was telling the history of a tribe of monkey people to the far south of Bharat. Although they appeared fully like monkeys, they had built a great city among the trees. They were ruled by kings and waged wars just like us, and so it should have been a fascinating recitation. But as the man plucked at his veena and droned on in a nasal tone, all I could think was that this was an insult to that monkey tribe.

After some time, Kaushalya leaned in toward me, pulling her pallu forward to mask her whisper. "What do you think of the Women's Circle business?" she asked.

I chanced a glance at Dasharath, who sat several feet away and looked half-asleep. "I'm glad of it," I said. "Why do you ask?" I did not think Kaushalya would harbor reservations about it, at least not in secret.

She shuffled the cushion on which she was seated closer to

me, in a movement that should have been ungainly but looked completely graceful on her. "It seems a silly name, does it not?" she whispered. In the Binding Plane, our ebony bond was solid and still, and I chanced a glance at Kaushalya. She was giving me a mischievous smile, her golden jhumkas winking in the torchlight as if they too knew her joke. "Your advice the other day stopped a panic that might have spread dangerously. It's the sort of work the Mantri Parishad could do, if they bothered with the problems of serving girls."

I smothered a laugh, for I did not want to attract too much attention. "Agreed. But you do not like us being called the Women's Circle?"

"I would not say I have a particularly strong feeling about it," Kaushalya said. "Just that it sounds frivolous."

"We could make it less frivolous in other ways," I offered, the idea coming to me as I spoke. "Asha spoke of invitations. But instead, we could hold an open audience, the way Dasharath does. The radnyis of Kosala attending to the people's problems. It is certainly more imposing an image than the idea of a...matron's sewing circle."

"The people?" Kaushalya raised an eyebrow at me, astute as always. "Beyond the servants, you mean?"

The music quieted for a moment, and we both split away, sitting up straight for several moments as the man hummed. I saw Dasharath open his eyes hopefully and only barely school his disappointed expression into feigned interest as the man launched into the next verse. Next to me, Kaushalya shook her head, an affectionate smile on her face.

When it was safe to continue the conversation, I whispered, "We could use the public gardens, near the main marketplace. It's like you said. The men do not—" I narrowly stopped myself from saying *care* and glanced around to make sure I had not been overheard. "They do not have time to listen to such small matters. But we do. We already are."

I could sense Kaushalya was skeptical, and so I plucked at our bond, holding in my head the image of us, providing counsel to women, giving aid and comfort as we stood among our people. I could see it now, women young and old gathered before us, all of us filled with hope at what futures we might build together.

"Perhaps," she said, considering. "But who would come to such a thing? Only the most desperate, surely."

"Is that not who we should seek to aid?" I asked. "We are radnyis, are we not?"

At that moment, the man finally finished with a flourish. There was an awkward silence for a moment, before Dasharath began giving lukewarm applause. Kaushalya and I joined in, politely tapping fingers against our palms until the moment was over and we could rise to our feet. "There are those who would be offended," Kaushalya said. "First the new rules about the marketplace—no, don't say anything, I know that was your proposal—and now this? Surely if it pleased the gods, this type of council would have been established long ago."

"Those rules were written long ago," I argued. "But these are different times."

"Different times indeed," she murmured thoughtfully. "I have an idea, then. Let us simply call it the Women's Council."

And so, once a week, in the evening, Sumitra and Kaushalya and I went to the public gardens in the heart of Ayodhya with several of our staff and held audiences. It came together in fits and starts, such that it was hard to say the first time we truly became a council. The first meeting, a few palace servants who we had turned away throughout the week sought our audience, and it was as if we were simply back in our rooms. The next time, it was much the same, small and unassuming. I struggled to ignore the gaping of passersby, the imagined titters.

But slowly, week by week, the number grew. The gaping stopped. It began to feel like something more. Like a Women's Council.

I was the unspoken leader of the group, and both Sumitra and Kaushalya deferred to me when it came to major disputes. And yet without them, the Women's Council could never have been. For they spread the word among the noblewomen, the elite social web that I still remained on the outskirts of, despite the fact that I now dressed fashionably and moved confidently about the palace. I supposed that I had made more efforts to strengthen my relationships with the noblemen of the palace than the women—but now, with this council, that was slowly changing.

After the first moon, people stopped watching to see if the gods would punish us for so flagrantly disregarding their edicts. Instead, members of the city trickled in to seek audiences: the poor who could not make trips to the palace for open court, those with problems they did not wish to bring to male advisors, and those whose pleas for help had been turned away everywhere else.

Was Dasharath proud, I wondered, that we were saving women from husbands who spoke only with their fists? That Kaushalya and I had modified grain storage quotas to distribute food to children on the streets, that Sumitra had employed homeless women in the palace kitchens? That we were conceiving of projects at the Women's Council that I would then bring to the Mantri Parishad to complete?

The last was not our only work, of course, but it was what I loved the most. I think Kaushalya enjoyed resolving disputes, and Sumitra loved best matters of the heart. On occasion we would get young couples, who professed their love for each other despite their families' disapproval, hoping for the Women's Council's blessing. Sumitra loved to hear their stories and bless the matches. Even Kaushalya occasionally became interested and joined in. They thought me shy when it came to such matters, for I would sit back quietly, but in fact I had nothing to add. No such feelings for Dasharath, or any person, had ever surfaced in me. I was comfortable with my husband, loved him as a dear friend, but the pull of romance meant nothing to me. I could be happy for those in love, but I could not understand.

Fortunately, most of the Women's Council's business concerned matters at which I was more skilled.

This particular day was quite cool, clouds covering the sun and a brisk breeze stirring through the gardens. "Step up," I called to the next person in line, and shifted my shawl over my arms as an older woman approached. Her sari pallu obscured part of her face. "What is your name?"

"Dhanteri, your majesty," the woman said.

It was like someone had plucked me from my seat and dropped me back into that chilly stone corridor in my father's palace, standing by a door next to Yudhajit, both of us longing for our mother.

I could not forget that voice. Instantly I began to sweat, despite the cool air. I tried to recall the face of the woman who always stood behind my mother, but it kept slipping away.

I checked the Binding Plane almost instinctively and quickly recognized it: one of the first threads I had ever followed. It was merely a wisp now, and perhaps I would have once struggled to locate it. But in the washed-out world of the true Binding Plane, even the smallest bonds stood out in stark relief.

"Dhanteri," I said, grateful that my voice remained steady. "Former lady-in-waiting to my mother, Kekaya."

"Yes. I am so glad to see you again, Radnyi Kaikeyi. You have grown so much."

An inane comment, considering I had been barely out of girlhood when she had departed. Of course I had grown. And

Dhanteri did not sound glad to see me in the slightest. She had lowered her pallu but still held herself rigid, like a single hard line connected her creased forehead and her clenched legs. The stiff pleats of her light blue sari and the severe bun sitting high atop her head did little to soften her image.

"It is good to see you too," I said, but I leaned back in my chair. "How can I help you?"

"The last time I saw you, you were only twelve? Thirteen? To see you now, a radnyi of the Kosala kingdom, brings me great joy."

"Indeed, I was thirteen." I kept my tone neutral. Dhanteri's face fell an infinitesimal amount. Had she really expected such mundane flattery to work? At our last meeting, she had threatened Manthara.

I crossed my ankles and waited.

Dhanteri approached me, and the palace guard that typically accompanied us stepped forward to intercept her. It must have galled her, to be treated like a commoner. I lifted my hand in a purposefully lazy motion and the guard fell back.

"There are others who seek an audience," I said. "What is it you want?"

"I have news," Dhanteri said. "About your mother."

And there it was.

She must be after money, or a job in the palace, and she planned to blackmail me with my mother's shame. It would not work. "What sort of news?"

"Perhaps it would be best to speak of it in private," Dhanteri suggested.

"You came to the Women's Council to seek an audience with me," I said. "And now you have it. Please tell me what you wish to say."

"Your mother did not leave the court of her own choosing." Dhanteri lowered her voice as if to keep her words between us, but I knew she intended others to hear.

"I am aware. My father banished her, did he not?" She thought to blindside me with something I had learned long ago. I smirked at her shock. "Do you have anything else you wish to tell me?"

"She lives now in Janasthana."

This I had not known, but I did not want to admit it. Still, traitorous interest built under my skin.

Interest, and anger, for clearly she had a permanent enough residence that Dhanteri might know about it. And yet she had not written to me in the decade since she left, not even to provide well wishes for my wedding or the birth of my son. Dasharath's Yagna, from the appearance of a god himself to the birth of four sons, was the kind of story that had been proclaimed across the kingdoms.

Someone with a shred more self-respect would not care about this news. But it turned out that beneath all my confidence, I was still a child.

"Janasthana," I repeated. "That must be...nice...for her." I tried to put the mildest hint of distaste in my words. Janasthana meant little to me. It was a faraway city, two moons' journey at least, beyond Chedi. One had to cross mountains and jungles to get there, and for what? A few exotic goods. And apparently my mother.

Dhanteri's disappointment was obvious. "That was all I wished to tell you. Thank you for speaking with me." She turned to leave, her movements slow as molasses.

I sighed. "Wait." A woman like Dhanteri would not resort to such desperate measures lightly, and no matter my dislike for her, I had sworn to myself to help all women who came before me.

"Yes, Radnyi?"

"What do you do now?"

"I recently came to Ayodhya. I am still seeking work. Nobody wants to hire an old lady like me."

I leaned over to Kaushalya, who I knew had been listening to the exchange with great interest, although her expression was serene. "I owe you for Asha," I said quietly. "This one is caustic, but also a hard worker and an excellent servant." I could sense my sister queen's skepticism, and I hoped she could in turn sense my need.

Kaushalya nodded. "You may join my staff, if you wish," she said to Dhanteri, with the perfect cool composure I could never mimic, even though I occasionally practiced.

Dhanteri's face lit up—she had come to try to weasel into a position on the third radnyi's service and gotten one on the first radnyi's instead.

I spent the rest of the council session on edge, worried Kaushalya might press me on the matter or judge me poorly for my family's secrets once we were in private. But when we arrived at the palace, she simply squeezed my arm and whispered, "We are lucky to be in Ayodhya, are we not?" And that was the end of the matter.

"I ran into an interesting person on my way to your chambers," Manthara said, and I startled. I hadn't even noticed her entrance. Her arms were crossed and her mouth pressed thin, the lines around her eyes more pronounced, as though I was an unruly child skipping my classes once again. I remembered the enmity that had always existed between her and Dhanteri, and I bit back a groan.

"She came to speak with me at the Women's Council. She wanted a position and I pitied her. But she will work under Kaushalya, not under me."

Manthara's eyed me. "That is all?"

Somehow, after all these years, I was still foolish enough to try to hide things from Manthara. "No. She told me that my mother lives in Janasthana." Now as I said the words aloud, they filled me with some unidentifiable emotion, loosening my tongue. "Why would she go there? I always assumed that... that she had died, and that was why she never contacted us. But to know this? That she simply did not care enough? That makes me—" The torrent of words stopped as I realized I had no idea how I felt.

A small child standing in her father's throne room. Alone.

Manthara, however, made no move to comfort me. "And here I thought you were intelligent, child."

"Excuse me?"

"What, you thought that your father would let her send you letters or visit you on important occasions? You think that she could show her face even in Kosala after being banished by her husband? Kekaya had no choice. If she is still alive, I am sure that it eats at her every day. She was not heartless. A woman wishes to see her children. To meet her grandson."

I sank abruptly to the floor. Manthara's words made sense, and yet they sounded like an excuse. In my heart, I still felt there was no justification good enough for my mother to leave me and my brothers.

Manthara must have sensed my skepticism. "Come, Kaikeyi. You have seen this happen enough times to others. You know this is the truth."

And she was right. How many women had come before me in this exact situation? I did not blame them for leaving their husbands and children. But this felt different, because it had happened to me. I was being unfair, but I felt twelve and alone again, and that had been unfair too. I wasn't yet who I wanted to be, unquestioningly just. I had so much work left to do. So much to learn.

Watching the realizations play out across my face, Manthara sighed. "You carry on as bold as a man, and as clever too. It has served you well so far, but you cannot assume it will always be so. Or that others will do the same. You are unusual."

"I do not carry on like a man," I protested, sprawling on the floor dramatically.

Manthara knelt down next to me and rubbed my head. "Only you see it that way, Kaikeyi."

I closed my eyes and accepted the comfort of Manthara's touch.

CHAPTER
SEVENTEEN

THE WOMEN'S COUNCIL AND Mantri Parishad took up most of my time, and I thrived on the work. I loved stepping into the world of the Binding Plane, that gray world that was fully my own, and walking through it as its mistress. And I enjoyed the careful shaping and altering of bonds, and the sweet thrill of victory that came with success. Here I could solve the kingdom's problems with the strength of my own power, strategizing and pushing and arranging the council to best serve the people. Perhaps the only thing more satisfying was watching my sons grow older.

It was my blood son, Bharata, and Sumitra's Shatrugna who got into the most trouble. As twins, I had expected Shatrugna and Lakshmana to be inseparable, as Yudhajit and I had been. But I suppose that all the boys were born so near to one another that the idea of twins did not take hold with them. Shatrugna and Bharata frequently ran from their nurses and tutors and would be found hours later hiding in various corners of the palace. They would feign injury and cause everyone to panic, only to spring up, laughing. They played pranks on their brothers and, on one memorable occasion, evaded various palace guards to burst into the throne room in the middle of a diplomatic meeting.

All children must learn right from wrong, and princes more than most. Sumitra and Kaushalya hated disciplining the children, could not bring themselves to cause the princes to cry or feel ashamed. And so, it often fell to me.

With Shatrugna and Bharata, punishment was simple: I separated them until they learned their lesson. I had vowed at Bharata's birth that I would never manipulate him with my magic, and I quickly extended this promise to the other children. The heart-wrenching pain of what had happened when Yudhajit's bond had snapped would never be fully gone from my mind, even if, all these years later, we had spun it back into existence with our steady correspondence. With my sons I could not risk it. I never even allowed myself to enter the Plane around them.

Lakshmana acted like Brahma incarnate, although between his light hair and hazel eyes he appeared to all the world as Dasharath made small. He never misbehaved, unless one of his brothers talked him into it, and even then, he would only serve as a lookout—or earnestly take the fall for his brothers. I never truly disciplined him for that, for it was adorable to watch him attempt to explain how the fault was his. And looking out for one's family was a virtue.

Rama was the most difficult to manage. As a young boy, he barely cried. I remembered only one true tantrum from him from his early years. At maybe two or three years of age, he had begun sobbing one evening about not being able to play with his friend. When asked what friend he missed, Rama replied, "The moon." Kaushalya's attempts to explain the moon was far away and could not play with Rama only made matters worse, and at last she sent for me, unable to bear his tears. When I arrived, Rama was sitting in the corner hiccuping, fat droplets rolling down his flushed cheeks. He held his chubby arms out to me, and I scooped him up.

"Ma, I want to play with the moon!" he cried, burying his face in my shoulder.

"I know, I know," I said, bouncing him up and down while I tried to think of some way to calm him.

Finally, my eyes landed on a small hand mirror propped on top of a chest. Still holding Rama with one arm, I snatched up the mirror and carried him out onto the veranda, where the vast expanse of the night sky arched above us. The sight of the full silver moon hanging there only made him wail more loudly. I deposited him on the ground and turned him away from the moon.

"I'm going to give you a magic toy," I said. "And it will bring the moon into your hands."

He quieted and stretched his hands toward me. I gave him the mirror and maneuvered it until the moon shone brightly in its reflection. Rama gasped in delight, then looked up at me. The brilliant smile on his face sent a pang straight through my heart. I ruffled his short black hair and sat next to him. Kaushalya brought me his plate of food, and I fed Rama as he happily babbled at the moon.

When they were a bit older, seven or eight, I taught the boys games from my childhood. Kaushalya and Sumitra hadn't wrestled their siblings in the dirt, it turned out, and the boys' tutors were only interested in formal instruction. The boys all ran about the palace halls in a pack, and while they did not mean to cause disruptions, they generally created chaos. So one evening I brought them outside to a grassy courtyard behind the palace.

"What is this, Ma?" Rama asked, his small hands on his hips, looking at the empty space in confusion.

"We're going to play a game," I said. "I used to play it with my brothers. One person closes their eyes and counts to twenty. Everyone else hides. When you find someone, you have to catch them. The first person to get caught becomes the next finder, and the last person to be caught wins the round."

The boys all nodded to me, faces serious. "It's a game," I repeated. "It is meant to be fun. It is not a test. I will count first." I covered my eyes and began counting slowly and loudly. Behind me, the boys whispered, arguing among themselves. I wondered if I would have to count for longer, but eventually the argument stopped and I could hear them running off.

I opened my eyes, squinting across the courtyard. There was a bench some distance away that was slightly askew, and at the farthest corner of the grounds, I could see someone crouching behind a large urn. I decided to make my way toward it, creeping forward until I could make out Bharata's form, kneeling and trying not to laugh.

"Go, run," I whispered to Bharata. "You're supposed to start running."

He got to his feet slowly and I waved him along until he took a few hesitant steps. As I started to chase him he picked up his pace, but I kept jogging slowly so he would feel like he had a chance. As he ran toward the bench where I knew another son was hidden, I spotted Rama, who had peeked his head out from behind a pillar to watch the scene. Without warning, I turned to catch him instead. His eyes widened in surprise, and then he sprinted away in the opposite direction of Bharata, his laughter ringing out. I loved the sound of that laughter so much, I almost stopped to listen to it.

Bharata, meanwhile, dashed for the corner of a shed, where he must have found Shatrugna, because each of them tried to push the other until they both tumbled out, laughing so hard they could barely move. I remembered the feeling, lying in the tall grass of Kekaya with my brothers, and wished I could somehow preserve this moment so they would always have it.

They picked themselves up, and I changed directions to run after them, adding speed to reach Shatrugna and tap him on the shoulder. His face fell, until I said to him, "Chase your brothers with me." It was not part of the game, but he immediately whooped and ran after Bharata while I spun back to Rama.

In the end, both were caught before we found Lakshmana, who had rolled himself up and squeezed himself into an empty water barrel. He tried to stand when Rama finally found him, but he was stuck. His face turned red with effort as he wriggled about. We had to pull on him, me and the other three boys tugging at his arms, until he burst free with a *pop* and we all fell in an undignified heap.

"You're really fast, Ma," Bharata said. I laughed at his tone of wonderment, because of course even my jog would seem fast to a seven-year-old boy.

"You all should play again," I said. "Shatrugna will be counting this time. I'll watch."

I stayed in the courtyard, the sun warming my shoulders, watching them hide and chase and wrestle one another.

And yet, as I watched Rama take a turn finding his brothers, his soft face set in determination, a strange wave of foreboding came over me. We had played this game the day my mother was exiled. The day that everything had changed. I couldn't preserve this moment. This precious happiness could not last.

These are different children, I reminded myself. *And you are their mother, not Kekaya.*

I took a deep breath and turned to go inside. But even in the warm summer air, the chill remained.

I was not my mother, but just as importantly, Dasharath was nothing like my father.

A few days after I taught the boys this game, I happened upon Dasharath tiptoeing through the children's wing of the palace. When he saw me, he shook his head with a slight smile and put a finger over his lips. I covered my mouth to stop my laughter, for I knew instantly he had been pulled into one of the boys' games. Dasharath carefully opened Bharata's bed-room door and disappeared inside for a few moments.

"I have checked every room," he grumbled when he emerged empty-handed. "They told me they would be hiding somewhere in this corridor."

"And are you sure you have searched thoroughly?" I teased.

Dasharath drew himself up, feigning indignance. "I am the raja of Ayodhya. I think I am capable of finding some chil-dren." His eyes belied his tone, pinching at the corners as he tried not to smile.

"It appears your children have outsmarted you, raja or not," I said, not bothering to hide the laughter in my voice now.

"Oh, and I am sure you know where they are," he said, voice light. He took a step toward me, boxing me in toward the wall.

"I have my suspicions." I leaned back carefully against a tapestry, crossing my arms.

"As your raja, I command you to tell me."

"Alas, Raja, my loyalty belongs to my sons," I said as seriously as I could.

He kissed me very quickly, for we were in a hallway. "What if I command you as your husband?"

I pretended to consider. "I still feel bound to keep their secret. Who can they trust, if not their mother?" I said inno-cently, and he groaned.

"Ah, but you are one of my wisest advisors," he tried again. "Please advise me."

I gave a put-upon sigh. "Very well, if I must." I paused, and Dasharath gestured at me to go on. "They are not here. They let you count and ran off outside. You have been duped, oh great Raja." I had seen them play such tricks on their caretak-ers before, and I knew they would leap at the chance to do it to their father too.

He threw his hands up. "I have spent half of an hour

searching their rooms and they left?" Dasharath took off down the corridor, toward the training grounds, and I followed. We emerged blinking into the sunlight, to find Bharata, Shatrugna, Lakshmana, and Rama holding wooden swords, seeming for all the world like they were studiously practicing their sparring. But Bharata's shoulders were shaking slightly, and Lakshmana kept glancing toward the entrance.

"You thought it would be funny to trick your poor father," Dasharath called out, and they all whirled around. "But I have found you, and you cannot outrun me!"

He began chasing after them, and the boys shrieked and scattered. I thought of what my father would have done had my brothers tried anything similar. He would have been furious, I was sure.

But this was a different time, of different kings. My father did not even sit on the throne of Kekaya anymore—he had abdicated in favor of Yudhajit so that he could receive treatment for an old war injury.

Dasharath caught Lakshmana first, gently tackling him into the dirt. "I have captured your brother," he shouted to the rest. "Are you going to defend him?"

He picked up one of the wooden swords that had been discarded in the dirt and gestured for Rama, Bharata, and Shatrugna to take up the rest. Bharata charged first, shouting out, but Dasharath easily batted his sword away. I watched as he expertly fended off all three at once, a grin of delight on his face. Behind Dasharath, Lakshmana got to his feet, and I silently cheered him on, watching as he quietly approached his father and then jumped on his back. Dasharath fell to his knees dramatically and the rest of the boys swarmed onto him. He gave a great cry as he tussled with them on the ground.

"Radnyi Kaikeyi, help me!"

I stepped forward, and the boys turned to look at me. "What do you think?" I asked them. "Should I help him?"

"No, Ma—" "Stay there—" Their shouts overlapped.

I looked to Dasharath, lying on the ground. "I am sorry, my raja. It seems there is nothing I can do."

"I have been betrayed," he moaned.

I could no longer contain my laughter. It spilled out of me, echoing around the grounds, and soon the rest of my family was laughing too.

I felt peaceful, light in a way I hadn't been in years. I had a place here, with four perfect, beautiful sons, who could be happy in a way I had never been as a child. I had a family, and they loved me.

CHAPTER
EIGHTEEN

LONG AFTER I RIPPED apart the entire kingdom, old servants claimed that they saw me behave cruelly toward Rama when he was a child. They said it was proof that I disliked him from the beginning. They had always seen me as neglectful, and indeed I was busy, for by the time my children were ten years old and I had acquired twenty-nine years, the idea of a Women's Council had spread beyond Ayodhya, brought there by the wives of nobility and diplomats who had witnessed our success and wished to find their own. I wondered how they would fare, for they did not see, of course, the continued— if ineffective—opposition of the more traditional men, like Manav. They were not privy to Dasharath's occasional meetings pacifying our sages, who performed their public duties to bless the kingdom and praise its ruler but privately warned that the Women's Council was a step too far. They certainly did not see the retaliation some of the poorer women who came before us faced, including one who was banished from her husband's home and her father's after telling us of the beatings she was forced to endure.

But these women who aspired to start their own councils

were right about one thing—there was a power in listening, in trust between women.

By the age of ten, all of the boys were polite and well-spoken, but Rama especially so, and so I did not notice at first when things began to go wrong. In fact, Asha was the first one to realize it. She had volunteered to watch the boys one afternoon, and when I returned to my rooms, she was waiting for me.

"Have you noticed anything odd about Rama recently?" she asked me.

I shook my head, alarmed. "Is he ill?"

"No! No, nothing like that, but..."

I breathed a sigh of relief. "I have some work I need to do for tomorrow's council meeting—perhaps we could discuss this later?"

"He is physically well, but this is urgent nonetheless, Radnyi."

Asha almost never addressed me so formally when we were alone. I finally took a good look at her. She was biting her lip and twisting her hands. Incredibly nervous, by Asha's standards.

"What is it?" I asked.

"Rama and I were talking. He asked where everyone else had gone, so I explained. I think the nurses and tutors don't speak frankly with the boys, because he had never heard of the Women's Council."

"That's hardly a sin," I told her. "He's young. I'm sure you provided him with a good explanation."

Asha's face fell. "I thought I did. He stayed silent for a few minutes and I went to check on Bharata and Shatrugna. I hadn't heard anything from them for some time, and that got me worried. But they were just painting with intense concentration." She smiled slightly.

"That's lovely," I said. "But what does this have to do with Rama?"

"When I came back, he told me that he had been thinking carefully about what I said. And that he believed we should stop." She looked at me, uncertainty in her eyes. I nodded encouragement. "He said that women shouldn't hold a council because it was immodest. That it defies the laws of the sages, and thus of the gods."

My stomach tightened. My son, accusing me of behaving immodestly. He was only ten years of age.

"Why?" I exclaimed. "Do you have any idea what led him to say such a thing?" Could it be one of his tutors, filling his head with such ideas? It wasn't impossible. Though their tutors were considered the brightest scholars Kosala had to offer, we hardly interrogated them about their views on reform when appointing them.

Miserable, Asha shook her head. "I asked him who told him such things and he said nobody did. He informed me that it was a fact of life and everybody should know it. And then he told me not question him, and he tried to send me away."

"Send you away?" I echoed weakly. It *must* have been his tutors. He would not have learned such behavior from Dasharath, who allowed us to create the Women's Council and continue it without complaint. His tutors must have taught him this, or perhaps other men and boys he interacted with at court. I had not considered the possibility that my sons might learn such old-fashioned attitudes from others.

Asha stepped forward, her warm hand reaching out to gently rub my arm. I realized I was hugging myself around the middle. "I told him I answered to you, not him."

A wet laugh bubbled out of me. I could imagine Asha, arms crossed, telling the prince of Ayodhya she wasn't going anywhere. "I'm sure he didn't like that."

"Oh no. His sweet little face turned so red. I thought he would burst into tears, or maybe kick me. But he just yelled that I was lying and ran off."

I dashed away the tears pooling in my eyes with the heel of my hand. So Rama had, despite the best efforts of all of his mothers and even his father, adopted a poor attitude toward women. I could still fix this. I would speak to Lakshmana, who was Rama's confidante and the most observant of my four sons. I would try to determine if all the boys felt the same way, and then regardless I would dismiss all of their tutors. I had always taken an interest in the boys' learning, teaching Bharata his letters, observing Rama's physical training, telling Lakshmana and Shatrugna old stories about great heroes that I recalled from my childhood trips to the library cellar. But maybe I needed to do more. Perhaps I could even find a female scholar for one of their subjects, just to make sure the boys understood that women could be learned as well, and could hold many respected positions.

"I'm sorry, my lady," Asha said.

"Why are you apologizing? This is not your fault. It is mine. Rest assured I will impress upon Rama the rudeness of the way he spoke to you."

"There's no need. I am just a servant, and the princes can speak to us however they wish. I should apologize to him, for refusing his orders." Asha enjoyed walking the edge of impropriety with me, but she did her best to be perfectly courteous to all others.

"If you apologize, it will further reinforce for him that women should know their place and be submissive and modest and all of the rest. Please do not."

She bowed her head. "As you wish."

That evening, I hurried to the courtyard, intent on finding Rama and giving him a piece of my mind. Instead, I rounded the corner straight into a familiar stone.

"We must stop meeting this way," a booming voice said, chuckling as he helped me up.

I looked up and up, a smile splitting my face despite my worries. "Raja Ravana! It is so good to see you."

He chuckled. "It is wonderful to see you, Radnyi. How long has it been?"

"Ten years," I said. "How times change."

"I think about you often," he said. While the years had given me the first glints of silver in my hair, and deepened the lines around my mouth, Ravana appeared completely unchanged, his glowing skin still perfectly smooth and his black curls gleaming in the evening light. He lowered his voice. "How goes the magic?"

"Very well," I told him. "Does your vow still hold?"

"Of course." He placed a hand on his heart. "Whatever you tell me will stay between us alone."

"Ayodhya has a Women's Council now, and it is thanks to you and your scrolls."

"I have heard all about that—indeed, we have one of our own in Lanka," he said. "But having met you, I think all credit is due to you, and not any paltry scroll. I believe you could have accomplished the same without magic."

I blushed at his praise, warmed by the thought that even faraway Lanka had embraced what I had begun. "How have you been? How is your flying machine?"

"Almost ready." A hint of bitterness colored his tone. "I can now get it to go up, but not come back down without utter destruction."

"That is a difficulty. But I have no doubt you will figure it out eventually."

"Mm. I hope so." He looked down at me. "Are you not going to ask me why I am here? Have you become all-knowing since last we met?"

"No, no, that is still reserved for the gods." His lips quirked and I returned his smile. "Would you tell me why you are here?"

"I am going back to Lord Shiva," Ravana told me. "After I completed the necessary penance, he granted my request to spare Lanka for a time. But in the past few years, some villages at the southern tip of the continent requested Lanka's protection, and they brought with them new troubles."

"What troubles?" I asked.

"A wave of illness. Sudden and ferocious lightning storms. Destruction that is obviously divine in nature. Have you not experienced such things when your kingdom expanded its territory?"

I shook my head, thinking of the vast expanse of Kosala. "No. Dasharath accepts new tribes often, and without unhappy incident."

Ravana's mouth twisted, and he looked forlorn. "Well, I always knew the gods disliked me particularly."

"They have no fondness for me either," I told him, placing my hand on his. "I am sure Lord Shiva will see your piety and grant you reprieve."

"My piety is in short supply these days. But thank you." We both stood in silence for a moment. "Where were you rushing off to, if I may ask?"

"A matter regarding one of my sons. I must have a difficult conversation with him."

"A very important matter, then," he said seriously.

"Do you have children of your own?" I said with a smile. He spoke as if he did.

The sadness in his face deepened. "No. Mandodari gave birth to a daughter, but…she is no longer with us."

I could see from his expression that I had stumbled into his greatest pain. "I am so sorry. That is a terrible loss to bear."

"She would have been almost your son's age," he said. "Nine."

"Perhaps you and your wife will have another child, if that is what you wish."

Ravana gave me a small, sad smile. "I hope so. But none will ever replace her. I do not think Mandodari will ever be the same, and neither will I." He shook his head, as if throwing off his sorrow. "What an unseemly topic of conversation. I apologize, Radnyi. Will I see you at the feast tonight?"

"Yes, of course, Raja."

How strange, I thought as we parted ways, that I had run into this faraway king twice in my life. Then I put him out of mind. If only I had paid more attention to his troubles, recognized them as warning, perhaps things would have ended differently. But I remained blissfully unaware of the gods' disapproval.

Later, I would sit next to Ravana at the feast, laughing and swapping stories of Mandodari and Dasharath, of battles and victories, of Kekaya and Lanka. I wonder if anyone else remembers the feast, remembers how friendly we were. Maybe they recalled it years later, after the start of the great war, and believed I had been a traitor all along.

But before the feast, there remained the problem of Rama. By the time I made it to the courtyard, the boys' studies had ended for the day. I found Rama playing a complicated game that involved the throwing of various stones with his brothers.

"Rama?" I called out to him. "Come here."

He dropped his stones immediately and ran over.

"Hi, Ma," he said, giving me a hug without prompting. I buried my face in his mess of hair, then pulled away to study his face. His large, light eyes stared up at me, bright and loving, fringed with thick, long lashes. Seeing all my sons arrayed before me, I could feel in my chest a love so bright it nearly hurt. Hope tingled inside me. Asha might have been mistaken—or maybe Rama had merely been joking, in a silly ten-year-old way.

"How was your day?" I asked, taking his hand and leading him a few steps away, out of earshot of his brothers.

"Good."

Experience with my brothers had taught me that directness would get me nowhere. I idly wished that the men in my life could be as straightforward as the women, but I had to pick my battles.

"Did you do anything fun?"

"No." As he shook his head, one perfect curl fell over his forehead. He was the most handsome of his brothers, and I knew that in a few years he would be invited to every swayamvara in Bharat.

"I did something fun today," I told him, lowering my voice to get him interested.

"What did you do?" It worked. I had his attention.

"I went out to the public gardens and held a Council. Just like your father does sometimes. Your other mothers came with me."

Rama wrinkled his nose. "You shouldn't have."

"Why not?" I asked.

"You shouldn't leave the palace. What if men come and see you when you're out?"

I put my hand on his shoulder and smiled at him. "Plenty of men come to us with their problems, and we help them. We always have guards with us. It's quite safe."

Rama's eyes narrowed, as if I had only confirmed his suspicions.

"What is the matter?" I asked.

"Women are meant for the eyes of their husbands only," Rama said, as though in recitation. "Aren't women who invite the attention of other men whores?"

I slapped him.

I had always sworn I would never raise a hand to my children, and I have been ashamed of my actions ever since. Rama cried out and all the servants in the yard turned to look at us. Lakshmana and Shatrugna and Bharata stared with wide, horrified eyes.

Rama drew himself up. For a moment he appeared far larger than ten, far larger than even an adult man.

"How dare you raise your hand to me?" he cried, and it was as though a hundred resounding voices spoke with his tongue. I stumbled back.

His eyes flashed a clear, unnatural blue, and he seemed to loom over me. The air sparked as it would before a storm.

The day of the Yagna flashed in my mind. His presence felt as Agni's had. Like a god.

But that was impossible. I had been there when he was born, had held Kaushalya's hand. It was impossible.

Rama collapsed back into himself, a normal child once more. He began crying, his cheeks turning red. I moved immediately to comfort him.

"I'm sorry, I should not have done that," I said in his ear, holding him tight.

"I'm sorry, Ma, I'm sorry, I don't know why I said that, please don't be angry, I'm sorry, I didn't mean it," he babbled, small body racked with sobs. Sympathy made my own eyes water. He was only ten; of course he did not mean it.

"Shh, shh, don't cry." I kissed the top of his head and rocked back and forth to soothe him. "You should not call any woman such a word," I told him.

"I'm sorry, Ma," he said. "I won't do it again, I promise."

When he was calm again, I surveyed the courtyard. Everyone had studiously averted their gaze, but I was certain that others had seen. But I doubted from their reaction that they had seen Rama's form as I had.

"Where did you learn to say such things about women?" I asked gently.

"I am sorry," he whispered again, his fingers clutching at my dress. "I heard some soldiers talking on the field. Our soldiers are good men, are they not? I just said what they said."

"Our soldiers are very brave," I agreed softly. "But many

of them hold beliefs from a different time. Our kingdom has changed, and as a prince of this city, you should be glad of that. You must not take every word you hear from others as the truth. You must learn to listen and decide for yourself."

"But I asked my tutor, Sage Vamadeva," Rama protested. "He told me—he told me women who behave too freely are bad, and that I should not associate myself with them."

"Did he tell you that your own mothers were such women?" I asked, making a mental note of the name. Dasharath had spoken to me about the man before—he had been excited that the sage had agreed to tutor the boys in their religious studies, for he was renowned for his piety.

Rama shook his head against me. "Then you do not have to worry about us, all right?" I rubbed his back a few more times before releasing him. "I'm so sorry I raised my hand to you."

Rama shrugged, eyes downcast.

"No matter how badly you behave, I should be better than that." I said it half to him, half to myself, as a reminder. "I will never do it again, I promise. Now, go play with your brothers?"

He hugged me briefly. Then he ran off, and I stood, a wave of exhaustion sweeping through me. What had come over me? What had come over Rama?

Maybe I had imagined that flash of godliness, my mind try-ing to teach me a lesson after my body had done something so horrifying.

Maybe there had been something more in the kheer than just rice.

No. We would already know. Wouldn't we? I distrusted the gods, but I had been with Rama his whole life. No. Rama was just a normal ten-year-old boy. That was all.

Sumitra and Kaushalya were not angry with me for slapping Rama.

"I am surprised you have not raised your hand to any of them yet," Sumitra said, offering me some tea.

"Did your mother hit you?" I asked, curious. Manthara had been the closest thing I had to a mother, and aside from yanking my hair once or twice while combing it, she had never physically punished me.

"All the time," Kaushalya said wryly. "It helped me to remember to stand straight, and lower my eyes, and memorize my recitations. Rama said such a foul thing—he deserved it. Nobody will think any less of you. It's a mother's prerogative, after all."

I hummed an acknowledgment, considering the possibility that perhaps Manthara had never hit me because she couldn't. The fact that she was a servant did not stop her sharp words, but it might have stayed her hand. My mother had never raised a hand to me, but she had been distant through my childhood. I thought of her, suddenly, in faraway Janasthana, living an entirely new life. What might she think of what I had done?

Kaushalya continued on, oblivious to my musings, "With Rama especially, it is important to train this out of him. Imagine otherwise how he might treat his subjects."

This shook me from my reverie. I stared at her, utterly bewildered. On instinct, I entered the Binding Plane—but our bond lay calm and assured.

Kaushalya believed Rama would be raja.

Had Dasharath never told them? I racked my brain, trying to think if he and I had ever discussed his promise to me in the years since the boys had been born.

We had not.

I excused myself, sending a quick thought through the Binding Plane, *She's still upset about what happened, give her time.* But as I walked toward my own rooms, my thoughts were consumed by Dasharath's promise.

*　　*　　*

That evening, I went to Dasharath's bedchambers unannounced after checking that neither Kaushalya nor Sumitra had been summoned. He smiled widely when he saw me, embracing me. For all I did not care for acts in his bed, I had developed a taste for his hugs. It was soothing to be held in his firm arms, to feel the heat of his body warming me.

"It is good to see you," he said. "I was just reading the most recent report from the governor of Sripura. That is Kaushalya's birthplace, and I am sure she would be pleased to hear that they are prospering. And for you, it even mentions that he has appointed a woman to oversee their grain reserves."

I smiled at this, for he knew me so well and shared such tidings because they would bring me joy. "That is indeed good to hear," I said to him as he set the papers aside. "But I have something else to tell you." I worried, as I told him what had happened with Rama, that he might grow angry, but he seemed just quietly contemplative.

"Boys need a firm hand, and you are the strictest of my radnyis." He unclasped my ornate necklace as he spoke.

"He implied we were whores. That's why I slapped him."

At this, my husband spun me around to face him. "He really said such a thing?" I nodded. "Why did he believe that?"

"Because we go out in public and hold the Women's Council."

Dasharath's brow furrowed. "Your reaction was warranted. I will need to speak with the children." It warmed me, that he trusted me enough that he would not even consider my actions to be anything but necessary.

"No, no. He is just a boy. He apologized profusely. Leave him be. Although…he did mention that Sage Vamadeva helped plant the ideas in his head."

"How so?" Dasharath looked even more concerned at this. "He is a very holy man. He has held the gods' favor for years.

At one point he was able to divert the course of an entire river to prevent a flood—I could think of no better tutor for them in religious morals."

"Rama asked him about what he overheard the soldiers saying, and Vamadeva warned him of the dangers of impropriety in a woman."

At this Dasharath's expression relaxed. "Well, that is of course his job, to explain such values. Even you agree that impropriety is a danger. So long as he did not insult you."

I tried again, sending the smallest of nudges in the Binding Plane. "I am sure there is another who can teach Rama and the others just as well."

Dasharath gave a small laugh. "Kaikeyi, we cannot dismiss a venerable man for such a small matter."

There was only warmth in Dasharath's voice and so I forced myself to accept his rebuke. After all, I too was imperfect—I still could not quite forgive myself for slapping Rama, no matter what everyone else thought.

Besides, I had other matters to discuss with Dasharath. "I was talking with Kaushalya afterward, and she mentioned something about Rama taking the throne. She seemed to believe that he would be your heir."

"Did she?" Dasharath had busied himself with unwinding my elaborate bun as I spoke, and I could tell that he was not really paying attention to my words.

I twisted slightly to face him. "I thought, perhaps, you might have told them about our arrangement already. The promise you made to me and to my father before we were wed."

Understanding dawned on his face. "No, no I have not. But rest assured, Kaikeyi, our promise still stands. Bharata is yuvraja of Kosala." Tension bled from my shoulders as he called Bharata the crown prince, and I fully relaxed against him. He brushed some hair from my face. "Would you like for me to tell them now? I did not wish to make things strange between all of you."

I thought about how much I valued their friendship, Kaushalya's steadiness and Sumitra's optimism. I did not believe this revelation would damage our relationship, but I could not take the risk. If they liked me less, or even began to dislike me... They were the sisters I hadn't realized I needed—my family. I could not lose them.

"It is all right," I murmured. "I would not want to cause them any pain. When they are older, and Bharata can prove himself..."

Dasharath smiled and embraced me again. "You may be the strictest of my radnyis, but you are still too kind," he murmured. "The way you hold your court, always speaking for the lowest of our citizens, and even now thinking of Kaushalya's and Sumitra's happiness. You have a bleeding heart."

"Do you mind it?" I asked him, genuinely curious.

"No." He lifted me onto his bed. "It's an attractive quality, in a woman."

"And in a man," I said.

"I should hope so," he replied. "Or else there is really no point in how much of my treasury I've set aside for my radnyis' projects, is there?"

I laughed at that, then quieted as he began removing my blouse. "It helps your people, that should be reason enough. Not seduction."

"Yes, yes," he grumbled, and when I looked to the Plane for sincerity, our thick, gold-plated bond stayed still and clear.

CHAPTER NINETEEN

ON A SEEMINGLY RANDOM session of the Women's Council, just after midday break as the sun began its slow descent, Sumitra leaned in and whispered to me, "Is that the royal procession?"

Sure enough, over the amassed crowd, I spied several guards on horseback, and then the top of the royal palanquin only used when Dasharath wished to make an entrance.

"It is. But why is he here?" I whispered back.

"If anyone knows, it would be you," Sumitra said, no trace of malice in her voice.

I gave my head a small shake and tried to pay attention to the woman speaking to Kaushalya while keeping one eye on my husband as he drew closer. Kaushalya's patient questioning uncovered that the young mother was a widow with a mind for sums, and so we provided her a reference for the treasury. After several tearful expressions of gratitude, the woman turned around to leave, then froze, nearly stumbling on the edge of the steps.

The rest of the crowd followed her gaze. Like tall grasses under a strong wind, they all sank into low bows.

"So much for subtlety," I muttered. Sumitra laughed, but Kaushalya did not say anything at all.

"Did he tell you about this?" I asked her. "You seem unsurprised."

Kaushalya only smiled enigmatically. "It will all be clear in a moment." I found the cord between us but decided at the last minute not to use it. She would have cautioned me if I needed more preparation.

Dasharath dismounted and came toward us. He was dressed in an ornate kurta with glinting gold embroidery, and his ceremonial khanda was strapped to his waist. He reached the steps to the dais where we sat, then ascended to stand in the place of our usual petitioners. "I have a matter for the Women's Council," he declared, his voice echoing over the hush.

Sumitra and I blinked in bewilderment. It was Kaushalya who spoke. "State your case, Raja."

"I come seeking advice."

"Tell us of the matter, and perhaps we may be able to help you."

Dasharath knelt, one knee on the ground, and looked up at us. "I am searching for a way to reward a member of my Mantri Parishad."

"What have they done to earn such a reward?" Kaushalya asked immediately, and I realized: They had rehearsed this little performance. But why?

"This person has made themselves an asset to the kingdom of Kosala. I trust their advice above that of almost anybody else. They are kind, hardworking, and beloved by all of Ayodhya."

"And you need help in determining a reward?" Kaushalya asked. "Land and jewels, perhaps."

Dasharath shook his head. "They have no need of that."

"Fine clothes or servants?" Kaushalya suggested.

"They have no need of that."

Kaushalya smiled. "Are they your most trusted minister?"

"They are not a minister." A minister was the highest position one could obtain—either a member of Dasharath's inner council or a governor of a piece of Dasharath's vast territory. They had the ears of the raja, their counsel trusted above all. It was certainly strange for Dasharath to so revere someone who did not already hold such a title.

"Then make them a minister," Kaushalya said simply. "That is an excellent reward."

Dasharath smiled at me again. "I would have to create a new position for them."

"I see." Kaushalya paused, seeming to ponder for a moment. "If they are your most trusted councillor, then make them saciva." Saciva was an old title, out of use in most kingdoms. It referred to a king's chief advisor. They used to be members of every raja's inner council, perhaps the most powerful member, but over the years too many of them had attempted coups or other forms of dissent, and so the position had fallen out of favor.

"You have excellent judgment, Radnyi," Dasharath said, bowing his head and rising to his feet. He turned to face the crowd, now grown several times larger as word had spread of the king's arrival. "Today I create a new minister for my council—Saciva Kaikeyi!"

It was lucky that I was seated, for even as it was, I almost fell over. Lucky too that he stood between me and the citizens of Ayodhya, so most could not see the dumb expression on my face. He spoke words I knew, and yet their meaning was incomprehensible.

"Get up," Kaushalya hissed at me. "Go stand beside him."

"What?" I asked stupidly.

"Kaikeyi, he's naming you saciva!" she said. "Get up!"

"But...I'm a woman," I said.

Kaushalya rose from her chair, took my hand, and pulled

me to my feet. "And you are always the one claiming that women can provide value to their kingdoms beyond bearing children, are you not?" She smiled, nudging me, and I stumbled forward a few steps to stand by Dasharath. The crowd cheered as Dasharath presented me to them.

"Congratulations, my saciva." His voice was too soft for anyone else to hear.

"I don't understand," I said, equally softly.

He raised my hand and pressed a kiss to it. "You have already been my saciva for a long time. And after what you told me about the boys, I had to make sure they understood that their mother—all of their mothers—are strong and valuable women."

They held a feast in my honor that evening, a joy-filled occasion where Sumitra, Kaushalya, and I finished an entire carafe of sweet wine, and I drank enough to shed a few tears when Kaushalya presented me with a stunning necklace of emeralds set in gold and arranged like the petals of a flower. For nearly a full day, I believed that Dasharath had created this spectacle solely out of his love for me. But when the next meeting of the Mantri Parishad adjourned, he asked me to stay behind.

"I need to send an emissary to Kekaya," he said, once we were alone.

I understood immediately. He wanted to send me, former yuvradnyi of the kingdom, to negotiate some favorable conditions on his behalf, and so he had made a public declaration of my virtues in order to bolster my position. All of this... spectacle...was merely a way to convince Kekaya that sending a woman rather than another minister—or attending himself—was not a snub.

"Stop that," Dasharath ordered.

"What?"

"You think I named you saciva solely so I could send you off to Kekaya."

It was irritating how well he could read my thoughts. "Did you not?" I retorted.

"Of course not, Kaikeyi. I have been planning this for a long time. I have counted you an advisor for nearly ten years. You have proven yourself to this kingdom and to me many times over. But the incident with Rama and the need for an ambassador forced me to move more quickly. Otherwise, I wanted to throw a parade in your honor."

I laughed despite myself. What he said made sense. Was this not what I had always wished for? I had wanted Dasharath to value me, to treat me as equal to his male ministers. He already did. And wanting his motives to be pure was ridiculous—a king with pure motives was at best inept and at worst injurious.

"Really, you must believe me. I am your raja." His tone only made me laugh harder, and his stern glare dissolved into mirth. As it faded away, we both stood there in the comfortable silence.

"Kekaya," he said at last.

"Yes. Kekaya. Why do you need to send an emissary? Has something happened?"

Dasharath sighed. "Since your brother took the throne two years ago, our traders have reported that Kekaya is providing highly unreasonable terms. Our merchants are returning with only half of what they expect. One trading season I would think it a random chance, but two we must respond to."

That sounded like Yudhajit. He had always claimed that other kingdoms took advantage of Kekaya, and that when he was raja, he would make them respect his value. I assumed that when the time came, his temper would have calmed, but apparently this had not come to pass.

"I can reason with Yudhajit. I'm sure I can make him understand that this stance will only hurt Kekaya."

"Thank you," Dasharath said. "I will, of course, provide you with a carriage and gifts for the court."

I imagined Yudhajit's face if I arrived in a carriage. "No, that will not work."

"Why not?" he asked, but he did not sound angry. He had become accustomed to my mulishness.

"In Kekaya, only those who cannot ride on horseback ride in carriages. To arrive in that way would signal weakness."

Dasharath raised an eyebrow at me. "I arrived in a carriage when I came to seek your hand."

"And my father and brother probably interpreted that as eastern foolishness. But I was a yuvradnyi of Kekaya once, and I know better. If I want to show them that I still have their interests at heart, that I might have gone east but my blood is still of the west, then I must arrive on horseback."

"Very well. What would I do without you, my radnyi?" he asked, drawing me close.

"You would do just fine." He kissed me, and after a moment I drew away. "May I take Bharata with me? He should see the court of his forefathers."

"Yes, of course. But he will need company, on the road. Take Rama as well. He should see more of the world."

"Why not all the boys?" I asked, because I knew Bharata would want Shatrugna to come along, and Rama would miss Lakshmana's company. "They can ride in a carriage, of course, and I'll take a few more servants to accompany them. And when we get there, I am sure my brother will treat them as his own children."

"I do not want all four of them to leave at once," Dasharath said. "What if something were to happen during the journey?"

He had a point. "Very well. I will take Bharata and Rama with me. When should we leave?"

"In the morning, if you can be ready."

The first day of our journey, I had the boys ride. I reveled in the feeling of being on horseback again, at the breeze in my hair and the easy rhythm of the horse beneath me. Until the sun reached its peak, the boys did too, enjoying this glimpse at the settlements west of the city. It was refreshing to see a place so uncrowded and unhurried, the yellow straw roofs an exciting novelty for the boys who would never see such a fire risk in the city itself. But as Surya began his lazy arc down the horizon, and the villages surrounding Ayodhya faded into the distance, the complaints began. We were riding through flat plains, a sea of yellow before us and behind us—and I could sense not only boredom but weariness. I did not countenance any of it to their faces, but told Asha to ensure they could have a warm soak that evening.

The next day, I asked if they wanted to move to the carriage. Bharata agreed immediately, but Rama insisted he would continue on horseback. Once he heard this, Bharata quickly changed his mind, eager to be with his brother.

By midday I knew they must be desperately sore—even I was feeling the pain of the ride, despite our relaxed pace—but they bore it bravely.

That evening Bharata limped into my tent and flopped onto my bedroll. He would soon be too old to show such easy affection, and I felt a pang of loss at the idea.

"How did you do it?" he asked.

"Do what?" I gave him a hint of a smile to let him know I was teasing him. "You should be more specific."

He groaned. "Horseback riding. My legs hurt."

I knew he must be in quite a bit of pain to admit it so freely. I rubbed his legs, and he gave a deep sigh of contentment. "Practice," I said. "Where I grew up, I rode almost every day, and I still do it when I can."

"And we are going to the kingdom you grew up in?"

"Yes. I'm sure my brother would love to give you a riding lesson."

At this, Bharata sat up. "The raja?" he asked. "Won't he be busy?"

"For you he would make time," I said, remembering the escapades of my youth. I wondered if Yudhajit had become more serious since then, if out from the thumb of our father he had come into his own.

Given his recent actions, I doubted it.

"What was it like?" Bharata lay back down, then added very quickly before I could chide him for being too vague, "Kekaya, what was it like?"

"I grew up in a palace, as you and your brothers do," I said. None of my children had ever asked me this question before, and I found myself at a loss. I certainly could not tell them of my mother and father, absent in different ways. "It is colder there than in Ayodhya, and there were fewer people around. We had many magnificent horses, and the palace was surrounded by huge open fields—perfect for riding. It was good that we had so much space, because I had seven brothers."

I wondered what would they look like now, as adults. It had been so long since I saw them.

"I wish I had seven brothers," Bharata said wistfully. "A younger brother would be nice."

I stroked his hair. "Why do you want a younger brother?"

Bharata blushed and turned his head away from me. I stayed silent, knowing that he would tell me eventually. Finally, he said, in a small voice, "So I can be first at something."

I put a hand on his cheek and turned his head back toward me, looking into his troubled eyes. "What do you mean? You are first at many things. I know you are excellent at sums, and your tutors tell me that you are one of the fastest readers they have ever seen." I remembered these things vividly, because while I loved all my sons, I took the most pride in Bharata. I was happy when any of the boys succeeded, but Bharata's triumphs made me want to smile all day. It helped that he was a very bright young man when he decided to sit with his tutors instead of causing mischief.

He shook his head slightly, adjusting his legs and then wincing. "Those things don't matter. Rama says a raja must be a warrior first. I want to be a good one. A *great* one. So I must become a better warrior."

"Your father is a raja, is he not?" I leaned forward and started massaging his legs again, wondering if it was Rama's insistence on toughness that had caused the boys to ride all day without asking for the carriage.

"Yes?" Bharata squinted up at me, clearly sensing a trick but unable to figure out exactly what it was.

"And how many wars have you seen him fight?"

Bharata looked up at the canvas ceiling for several moments trying to recall. "I can't remember any."

"That's because since you and your brothers were born, he hasn't fought any. He has ridden with his soldiers a few times on patrols, and of course there are small skirmishes at our borders every so often. But the last major battle he fought was before you were born. Almost twelve years ago."

I did not think about it often, but sometimes in my dreams I would revisit that bloody battlefield and wake up in a cold fear that Dasharath was dead, that I had failed. I did not want my children to ever have such dreams.

"I didn't know that." He turned toward me, resting his head in my lap.

"Your father is a great raja—the greatest in Bharat—and he spends most of his days looking at numbers and reading reports so he can make the best decisions for the kingdom. That is the work of a raja, and you excel at it. Being a warrior is worthy. But war is not something to wish for. It destroys people, destroys kingdoms. A raja should not wish for it. There is far more to being a ruler than that."

I couldn't see Bharata's face, but when he said, "Thanks, Ma," I could sense the happiness in his tone. He fell asleep in my lap, and I let him stay all night in my tent, treasuring each moment before he would grow too old to want this proximity anymore. And when he staggered to his feet the next morning, legs shaking, I ordered both boys to the carriage with no room for argument. Rulers had to be wise as well as strong.

One week into the trip, the boys reached the edge of the world they knew. They had never been farther than this while hunting, and they did not want to stay trapped inside the carriage any longer. They rode beside me for as much of the day as they could manage, commenting with wonder on everything they saw: the cone-like trees bristling with slender needles, the vast rolling hills, the roaming herds of shaggy goats and horned sheep.

Their enthusiasm gave me fresh eyes, and I viewed it all with pleasure. I remembered all too well feeling trapped inside the carriage on my bridal journey from Kekaya to Ayodhya.

At the end of the second week, we reached the bridge that spanned the Sarasvati River. I remembered my adventure with Yudhajit near its banks long ago, that surreal glimpse of the rakshasa in the hush of the forest, and apprehension rippled through me.

As we had written back and forth over the last eleven years, our blue bond had grown. But it did not even approach its former strength. The love and tranquility of his letters, filled primarily with news of our respective courts and memories of childhood, might not translate when he set his eyes upon me.

Even though I could gain no real assistance from the goddess, when I saw the river, I longed for the calming ritual familiarity of taking its blessings.

I stopped our party on the banks and instructed everyone to bathe their faces in the water. Manthara waded in several steps, an expression of true contentment on her features. She had insisted on accompanying me, for she was getting older and might not be able to make the long journey back to her homeland again.

"Why is Manthara so cheerful?" Rama asked me. Excitement shone in his features, boyish enthusiasm propelling him onto his toes.

"The Sarasvati River is sacred to us," I answered. "We say that it is the pathway to heaven and the stars. The goddess protects our rivers and waters and expands the minds of men."

Rama shook his head. "Lord Vishnu is the protector, not Sri Sarasvati," he argued.

I turned to look at him. "Rama, you cannot say such a thing in the presence of this holy river. Apologize at once."

"Why? What can she do to me?"

Irritation flashed through me at his dismissal of the goddess, followed closely by fear. If Sarasvati heard such blasphemous words, she might rise up to strike my son.

I positioned my body between Rama and the river. "Sarasvati is a goddess, and worthy of your respect."

"I respect her. Of course I do," Rama said quickly. "But I do not—"

A scream came from behind me, and I spun around, pushing Rama farther back. The steady waters of the river had become a churning menace, creeping up the banks toward us. The servants were scrambling backward and away. With the cloudless, sunny sky above us, there could be no question what was causing this.

"Move," I told Rama. "You need to run."

"I am not afraid. I will not flee."

"Go!" I begged him. "Rama, please!"

"No," he said calmly. "But if you are so afraid, you may leave."

I could not abandon my child. The waves surged higher, white and frothing like a great beast, defying all laws of nature. I stood over Rama and braced myself, determined to protect him at all costs.

The water crashed over us in a shock of icy cold that

drenched my body and numbed my mind. Still, I held Rama tightly in my arms and prayed, knowing full well it would have no effect. I could feel the utter powerlessness of our position. But no matter what happened, I would not lose my son.

The waves beat at us again, pulling us forward. I slipped and caught myself, digging my heels as deep as I could into the muddy bank.

"I'm sorry," I whispered. "He is sorry. Please, he is only a child. Please, please."

I clung to Rama, bracing for another wave—but none came.

I twisted around to watch the last of the torrent subside and the water slide back into its place. In a moment, it was serene, the very picture of stillness. A sob caught in my throat. Had the goddess heard me?

"I told you I was not afraid," said Rama, and I turned to look at him. I was soaked to the skin, water and clothes plastered against me, but Rama was—

Rama was completely dry. In fact, he was glowing. A halo of white light circled his head, and he shone from within as though he had the sun itself under his skin.

A cry came from the hill where the rest of the party had fled.

"My lord!" someone shouted.

"My lord!" another cried.

They knelt in awe, bowing to Rama. He raised his hand toward them in the universal sign of divine benediction.

Fear made bile rise in my throat. I stumbled back a step, and I could see it more clearly, the aura that surrounded him.

"He is gods-touched!" someone proclaimed, and the rest took up the chant.

To them, it must have looked like the river had crowned Rama, had put on that performance just to show his holiness, but I knew better. My son had angered Sarasvati. Perhaps my love for Rama had saved me, or perhaps the fact that I was gods-touched had prevented me from feeling the worst of her wrath. But Rama was *not* gods-touched. The fools on the hill did not know what that meant.

Heart pounding, I broke my own sacred rule, that which I had sworn never to do around my sons. I entered the Binding Plane.

I briefly leaned into the feeling of control as the world shifted and grayed until only the bonds were colored, and then looked up to find—nothing.

Rama was not there. I let the threads around me disappear, and Rama's glowing form came into view.

Only then did I know it for sure.

My son was a god.

CHAPTER
TWENTY

"HOW DID IT FEEL?" Bharata kept asking Rama during the final week of our journey. "When the river blessed you?"

Terrifying, I wanted to say. *I thought I would lose my son.* But he had not asked me. And Rama only laughed.

I wondered if he knew he was a god, or if his immortal memory had somehow been suppressed when born here on earth.

Over the remainder of our journey, I became convinced that Agni himself had been reincarnated. After all, Agni had provided the kheer at the Yagna, and it would follow that Agni could repel an attack from a river.

But *why*? Why would Agni have come down to the earth? In the stories, the gods only took human form in times of great strife. Bharat was mostly at peace. Rama had some higher purpose here, that much I knew. But I could not figure out what.

It was a relief to arrive in Kekaya, its narrow streets like an embrace. The city had changed only slightly, just enough that I knew time had passed. The wood and brick homes were dark, darker than the sandstone buildings of Ayodhya, but they welcomed me home. A familiar warmth blossomed in my chest.

I had missed this place, perhaps more desperately than I had ever realized given the stinging in my eyes.

I spied a figure standing at the gates of the palace. Yudhajit. I spurred my horse forward, and the moment I saw the smile on my twin's face, all apprehension melted away. My horse outstripped the guards in front of me and as soon as we halted, I threw myself off the steed and into his waiting arms.

"Kaikeyi," he said into my hair. "Kaikeyi, I have missed you so much."

I buried my face in his shoulder to hide my tears, but I could hear his breath hitch as well. "I missed you. I am so sorry, Yudhajit."

"Don't you dare ask me to forgive you. I was in the wrong too. We were young, and stupid. There is no need to apologize. I love you."

I pulled away to take a long look at him as he scrubbed a hand over his eyes. "When did you get so wise?" A few strands of gray streaked his hair, a mirror image of mine. The beginnings of lines had formed in his features. I had left him at seventeen and returned at twenty-nine. Of course he had aged.

"When did you become saciva?" he countered. Pride shone on his face. "There will be a celebration in your honor tonight."

I grinned at him. "In my honor only? What about your nephews?"

He turned toward them as if only just remembering I had come with a retinue and my sons. "Yes, of course."

"Bharata, Rama!" I called out. My sons dismounted eagerly and came to stand beside me. "Brother, this is Prince Bharata, and this is Prince Rama."

Bharata stepped forward and bent to touch Yudhajit's feet, but Yudhajit caught him around the middle and embraced him instead. He did the same to Rama.

"Welcome to Kekaya, my nephews."

My grin split my wind-chapped lips, but I did not care.

Our whole party streamed inside. The servants took our belongings while Yudhajit gave the boys a tour of the palace, rambling on as he led us from one room to the next, clearly trying to impress his nephews. When his enthusiasm became embarrassing, I sent him a slight suggestion of calm through the Binding Plane, and the torrent of his words slowed.

Still, I had to admit, Yudhajit's staff had done an excellent job—every room hinted at more wealth around the edges, moving away from the forbidding austerity of my father's time. The harsh stone chambers of my childhood had a softer cast, maybe because of the patterned tapestries in the hallways and the soft fabrics on the floors and furniture. While such decorations were commonplace in Ayodhya, I never recalled seeing them in Kekaya. Or perhaps the years had cast my childhood in the strange light of hindsight.

I lingered in the familiar maze of corridors. Did the palace feel smaller because I had grown accustomed to larger or because I myself had grown?

As I stood there, several paces behind the rest of the group, strong arms wrapped around me and lifted me up into the air.

I screamed, kicking at my attacker as my guards spun around, drawing their swords. Yudhajit ran toward me.

My attacker dropped me with a strangled yelp as my elbow landed in his belly. Yudhajit stopped and...doubled over in laughter?

I turned, holding up a hand to stop my guards.

"Missed me?" my attacker asked, his mouth twisting up in a familiar smile.

"*Ashvin,*" I said, gaping up at him. Then, "Do that again and I will ensure you cannot have children."

Ashvin shrugged, lifting one enormous shoulder. "Good thing I have plenty of brothers to carry on the family line."

We embraced, my arms barely wrapping around him. The slight, sickly boy who had taken up with the healers had grown into a giant.

"It is good to see you again, didi."

"Didi?" Bharata echoed, eyes widening at the sight of Ashvin's bulk.

"It means 'older sister,' " explained Yudhajit. "It's common only to the western dialects."

"An honorific," Rama said, confident even though he had never heard the word before.

"Yes." Ashvin smiled down at me. He wore a crisp white dhoti and a deep-orange cloth wrapped around his torso—the raiment of a healer or a sage. "And Kaikeyi is most deserving."

"Ashvin is Court Healer," Yudhajit informed me. "He has you to thank for that, *didi*."

"I had very little to do with it," I said, hiding my pride. "And by the way, I am your didi too, so you should not be so mocking."

"That does not count," Yudhajit countered immediately. It was the oldest argument between us.

"Were you the firstborn?" Bharata asked, eyes wide.

Yudhajit put an arm around me, and I pretended to shrug it off. "Kaikeyi is supposedly firstborn."

"Supposedly?" I repeated. "What does that mean? I was born several minutes before you."

"Oh, you're twins," Bharata observed, surprised. "Like Shatrugna and Lakshmana. Why did you never tell us?"

"Does it matter?" I asked. "It would be very boring for you to know every detail of my life."

"Boring? No, annoying," Ashvin said, his voice a deep rumble.

"Annoying? I see. And did you find it annoying when we worked together to get you apprenticed to the healers?" Within these walls, everything transformed, and we were children again, bickering back and forth.

"No, I found it annoying when my two siblings would run off into the hills every evening and leave us behind."

"You *knew*?"

"They figured it out," Yudhajit said. "We were not as stealthy as we hoped."

"Also, we were insufferable, and we followed you more than once."

"That I believe," I said with a grin. "I'm just ashamed we did not notice you."

"You were rather preoccupied," came another voice. My brother Mohan stood in the doorway at the opposite end of the room, easily identifiable by the scar on his cheek. He had once convinced Shantanu to shoot an arrow at a mango balanced on his head, in the manner of the heroes of myth. Shantanu had missed and cut Mohan's cheek open instead. Yudhajit and I had yelled ourselves hoarse after that particular incident.

I beckoned him forward and he too lifted me off the ground in an embrace. "I can't imagine what you mean," I said.

Mohan said, "None of us were surprised when just a few moons after you left, we heard wild tales of you on the battlefield. Driving chariots, shooting arrows. A true warrior queen." There was an undercurrent of pride in his teasing.

"You are trained in archery?" Rama asked, eyes lighting up, and I remembered that the boys were watching this entire conversation.

"Yudhajit taught me a few things. That is all."

"More than a few things. And she's excellent," Yudhajit said, ruining my attempt at deflection. "But far better at spear-throwing."

"Come show us!" Rama begged. "Can you? Please?" He

seemed so like an eleven-year-old boy that it was nearly impossible to think of what he had become at the banks of the river. I studied his excited face, trying to reconcile the heart-stopping fear with the love that filled me at his enthusiasm. I wrapped an arm around him in a quick hug, feeling a sense of relief.

"Well, Kaikeyi?" Yudhajit asked. "Have you kept up with it?"

I had, though with decreasing frequency over the last few years.

"Are you not raja?" I teased. "Have you nowhere more important to be?"

"Nothing more important than diplomacy on behalf of the kingdom," Yudhajit answered, winking at me.

We all followed Yudhajit down to the training yard. It was strange to walk there without any questioning looks—and stranger still to have Yudhajit freely accompanying me. I had spent many hours staring longingly down at my brothers from an upstairs window.

In my mind, the training fields of Kekaya had always been a large, shadowy place, but now in the open I realized they were smaller than the grounds in Ayodhya's palace, although they were far better equipped. Kosala, with its strangely polite rules about war, liked to limit its weaponry to swords and spears and arrows.

"Well, what do you think?" Yudhajit asked.

Rama and Bharata looked around in delight, gravitating immediately to the stands of heavy iron clubs. Bharata reached to take a flail off the rack and nearly dropped it on his foot.

"Careful!" I called out, walking briskly toward them. As I approached, Rama picked the flail up, moved a few paces from Bharata, and gave it a measured, perfect swing with an ease uncommon even in a fully grown man.

"Strong boy," Yudhajit said, catching up with me.

"Yes, he is," I said softly.

Yudhajit looked down at me, sensing my distress, so I forced a smile onto my face and tried to dispel his concerns with a tug in the Binding Plane. The radiant blue cable shifted slightly, and his attention glanced off my discomfort. By then, such little manipulations came as naturally to me as breathing. It would have taken more effort *not* to use my magic. "We are very proud. He will be a great warrior."

Yudhajit studied me for another moment, then turned toward Bharata and Rama. "Boys, have you ever seen your mother throw a spear? She is absolutely deadly."

Bharata ran up to me and threw his arms around me in a rare display of affection. "Could you, Ma?" His manipulation was so obvious, and yet I could not resist. I nodded to my brother, and he waved a hand at an attendant at the other end of the yard.

A straw target was set two hundred paces away. It was far, but within distance for me, even with my skills rusty from lack of use.

Yudhajit pointed me toward the array of spears. "Practice or—" He broke off as I reached for one that called out to me, long and slim with a wickedly sharp point. I weighed it carefully, my palms recognizing the feel of the polished shaft like an old friend.

"This is the one."

As I reacquainted myself with the spear, I noted more and more people stopping at the edge of the field. There appeared to be servants and courtiers alike gathering.

"I think news has spread," Yudhajit murmured. "We have an audience."

"Why?"

"The story of the warrior princess of Kekaya has inspired people here. We even have a few noble daughters who train now. They do not fight in battle, but they can defend themselves. Several are excellent at driving chariots."

Change. Even here, despite the censure of the gods, things were changing. To my mortification, tears welled in my eyes.

"Are you crying, Kaikeyi? Some warrior radnyi you are," Yudhajit teased, but he rubbed the tears from my face with his thumb.

"I'm going to hit the target," I said, then strode past him.

In the short walk to the mark, my hands turned clammy. I took a deep breath but could not shake the intense awareness of the crowd behind me, watching. If I missed, would they remove the young girls from their lessons? Would years of progress be erased? Would news of my failure reach Dasharath? Despite all the accomplishments I had accrued over these many years, my old insecurities rushed in to greet me here on the grounds of my childhood home.

I closed my eyes and let the whispers of the noblemen turn into the cries of the battlefield.

Never take your eyes off the enemy, Yudhajit liked to say, but right now, the people watching me were not the enemy. The target was my enemy.

I leaned the spear against my body and wiped my hands against my traveling breeches, designed by Asha. They were an iteration of the warrior garb she had cobbled together in an encampment over a decade ago, and that memory gave me adrenaline now. The target was my enemy. My nerves stilled. My muscles tensed. I hauled the spear into position. There was a taut silence, broken only by my grunt as I released the spear with a mighty heave.

The spear ripped through the center of the target. I stayed motionless for a moment, legs spread, one arm forward, basking in the sheer joy of it.

Cheers rang out behind me. Rama and Bharata rushed forward, jumping up and down with glee. "That was incredible, Ma!" Bharata called.

My eyes sought Yudhajit, my lips automatically responding

to his ridiculous grin. He ran toward me, lifting me up in the air and spinning me. "Put me down!" I scolded him, acutely aware of the number of eyes on us. "I am the ambassador from Kosala! You cannot treat me this way in public."

He laughed and set me down, not looking at all contrite. "I am so happy to have you back," he said.

"I thought Father had returned to the palace," I said to Yudhajit when we convened in his council room after the feast. I had met Yudhajit's wife, Mohan's wife, and Rahul's wife, which still amazed me. Rahul had been only eight when I left. Now he was twenty, married, and considered the most brilliant warrior Kekaya had produced in decades.

While the rest of the palace had changed, in the council room my father's presence hung heavy all around. As a child I had never been allowed in here, relying on Yudhajit to report its happenings to me. But looking at it now, I could see Yudhajit's descriptions had been quite faithful: a bare stone room, a window covered in stretched animal-hide, a large circular table. Yudhajit had clearly not made any alterations, and the severity of it brought memories of my father flooding back.

"He went back north to the mountains, to take in the air."

"The moment he found out I was coming, I presume."

Yudhajit tipped his chair back. "He left a week before we even found out. He does not hate you, you know."

"I doubt that."

"He did not know what to do with you. He wanted sons, and he got them, and he didn't know how to speak to a daughter, so he didn't. But he never hated you."

I shook my head, but something compelled me to enter the Binding Plane. Our bond lay quiet, the truth of Yudhajit's belief evident. For a moment, I considered telling him what I had learned from Dhanteri about our mother. But I thought better of it. I did not know what her life there might be like, or what would be accomplished by spreading the pain of the knowledge that she lived just beyond our reach.

"Kaikeyi, Father has grown ill, more gravely than I even let on in my letters." Yudhajit had apparently taken my conflicted silence as leave to keep talking. "Resigning the kingship has not eased his sickness. Ashvin thought his only chance of seeing out the year was going north and consulting with some of the sages who reside there."

I looked at him in shock, then looked away, both ashamed of my stubbornness and unwilling to concede. "In that case, we should talk about why I'm here," I said at last, changing the subject. "We need to discuss our kingdoms' trade relations."

Yudhajit rubbed the back of his neck, looking sheepish. "Would it be terrible if I told you that I only did it to get you to come here?"

"I'm sorry, you...What did you just say?" I blinked, certain I must have misheard.

"I know it was foolish policy. But I couldn't swallow my pride enough to beg you to come, and I did not think you would come of your own accord after everything that happened between us. I had heard about your Women's Council and Dasharath's deep trust of you and knew that he would send you to negotiate in the event of poor relations with Kekaya. My advisors were appalled, of course. It will probably take me a year to undo the damage I've done. But I wanted you to come."

I stood up, knocking my chair back. "Yudhajit! I cannot believe you! You jeopardized trade relations, ruined people's livelihoods—"

"The kingdom of Kekaya has compensated our traders for its losses, and we will send you home with enough gifted gold to cover whatever deficits you may have experienced."

I covered my face with my hand. "Would it really have been *that* difficult to ask?"

Yudhajit shrugged.

"You can't just do things like this!" I could not believe he had been so careless. "Next time, behave like an adult." I poured the suggestion into our bond as well, making it as near to a command as I could.

"Next time, I will." The corners of his mouth turned down. "But I can do whatever I like, Kaikeyi. I am raja, after all."

I turned away from him and set my chair to rights. He was correct. As raja, he could make whatever decisions he wished, however stupid. *Would Dasharath ever behave so foolishly?* I wondered. No. I knew he would not.

But it had all worked out in the end, had it not? It was the same luck I had often resented Yudhajit for when we were children. And now Yudhajit would stop his ridiculous charade. Relations between our kingdoms would be fine, with no effort required on my part. I was in Kekaya, sitting beside my brother who loved me. There were worse things in the world. I sighed and shook my head even as I smiled at him. "It was an idiotic decision, Raja Yudhajit," I said at last. "But I am here now."

We stayed almost two full moons in Kekaya. Yudhajit and I waited a week before dispatching an emissary to Dasharath, spelling out the new trade terms we had agreed upon, and I sent Dasharath a letter that heavily implied how hard I had pushed for Kosala's interest. There was no harm in using this to increase my stature, after all.

I also sat with Yudhajit's Mantri Parishad to help rehabilitate him in the eyes of his advisors. I strengthened the weakest threads among them until I could leave confident in the knowledge that Yudhajit had not lost anything on my account.

Just once, I snuck out of my rooms at night and made my way to the library cellar. It was as I remembered it—as though time had not touched this room.

I breathed in the scent of paper and dust. It was like stepping into a memory, as though if I rounded the corner I would find myself squatting next to my mother, squinting to make out the geography of Kekaya on a faded scroll. Would she be proud of what I had done? I touched the shelf where I had found her note to me, scrawled on the story of Ahalya. I still had it, hidden in a chest in my rooms in Ayodhya. She had been right—I had proven myself strong, capable.

I stayed in the room for a long time. But in the end, I took nothing, shutting the teak door firmly and leaving the cellar to guard its secrets.

I spent the rest of the trip showing the children around Kekaya, riding with them across the hills, and traveling to meet the rest of my brothers.

After the first moon, Rama seemed to have little interest in repeating treks we had already made, instead preferring to train with Kekaya's warriors. He was quite skilled, and he would find no such instruction for Kekayan weapons in Ayodhya, so I allowed him to continue what clearly brought him joy. But Yudhajit and Bharata and I would ride out for short picnics in the cool forest where I had spent many youthful evenings. Yudhajit would set up a target and teach Bharata how to shoot two or three arrows at once, a trick that delighted my son to no end. Other times they would wrestle in the dirt and proudly present themselves to me covered head to toe in mud, both so similar in their delight that I could only laugh.

The afternoon before our going-away feast, Yudhajit and Bharata took one final ride together, returning after an hour with red eyes. I would not use the Plane on Bharata, but I did not need to—their love and affection were clear, and I knew our departure would be difficult for them both.

So it was that by the time we left, hearts and bellies full, I had almost forgotten what had happened on our journey here.

But as we approached the Sarasvati River, I could think of

nothing else. It was evident by the murmurs around me that nobody else in our party could either.

I called for us to make camp early that evening, not wanting to cross the river in the dark, and lay down in my bedroll without eating. I stared up at the canvas of the tent, a single candle casting eerie shadows around me, and came to a conclusion. There was only one thing I could do to protect my son. And so, even though I was unaccustomed to it, I clasped my hands upon my chest and tried to pray to Sarasvati. *I am sorry for my son. Please let us pass safely.* I repeated it over and over again, my eyelids falling shut, and then—

I was standing on the banks of the river. Mist rose from the waters. How did I get here? I turned to look behind me, but there were no footprints in the damp earth. "What—" I began to ask, but a gust of wind whipped through the clearing, carrying the rest of my words away. The river surged up until it was almost to my knees. I tried to take a step backward, to flee to safer ground, but my feet had sunk into the earth. I was rooted fast.

"Sri Sarasvati," I whispered. Ice ran through my veins. Was this real?

The water rippled, and I felt her presence all around me, my shoulders bowing with the weight.

"Please," I called out. "Spare my son. I am begging you."

He is in no danger. She spoke with a thousand voices, both in my head and from outside, as though I was pressed between two great forces. My teeth rung with the force of it. *He needed to be reminded.*

"Reminded of what?" I asked.

The mortal world corrupts, but he will be stronger than you. He was sent to this world for a reason.

As the echo of her words faded, I turned them over in my head. "He...he is a god?" There was only silence, as if to reproach my asking a question I already knew the answer to. "Why was Rama sent here?" I asked instead.

To cleanse your world of injustice.

A singularly unhelpful answer. I opened my mouth to ask another question, but the river before me was dissolving into shining blue wisps of mist. *Cross without fear.* The voice was still in my head and yet sounded distant, as if she was speaking from the heavens. The water receded and I felt myself falling back and back—

I startled awake in my bedroll, breathing hard in the darkness. The candle had been extinguished.

I blinked, heart pounding wildly. Had that truly been Sri Sarasvati, speaking to me in a dream? Or had I been so preoccupied with my fears about Rama and the river that I had imagined it?

No. Something about it had felt divine, her presence unknowable. I could not have invented that myself.

He will be stronger than you, she had said.

She likely had meant mortals generally. She probably meant to cast aspersions on human vice.

But... she was a goddess. And not just any goddess, but the goddess of scholars, of the wise, of intelligence and knowledge.

And she had chosen to say *you*.

CHAPTER TWENTY-ONE

"WHAT IS THIS I heard about Rama controlling a river?"
Dasharath asked. I lay in his bed, studying the pattern of light
on the ceiling. We had returned to Ayodhya a few days prior.

"He did not control a river. We were crossing the Sarasvati,
and I stopped to pay my respects. Rama wanted to know why
we were asking the river for its blessing." A revised version of
events, to be sure, but Sarasvati's words were still fresh in my
mind. "His question must have provoked the goddess, because
the river became very angry and advanced toward where
Rama and I stood."

"Why did you not take Rama and flee?" Dasharath asked,
turning onto his side to face me.

"I begged him to flee, but he insisted on standing his
ground. I had no time to pull him away against his will, so I
stood over him and tried to bear the brunt of it."

Dasharath sat up, an expression of horror on his face. "You
did what?"

"What would you have done?" I countered. "Would you
rather I have run away and left Rama to face the wrath of a
goddess?"

He huffed but did not respond to that.

"The waves beat against us, and then after some time they retreated. I was unharmed but completely drenched. Rama was dry. He seemed to shine with light—or perhaps that was just the sun. I do not know."

"Gods-touched," Dasharath breathed, sinking back down. "He was able to protect himself from the river."

I shook my head. "I do not know if he is gods-touched, or something else."

Dasharath stretched out his large hand to trace patterns on my stomach. "Something else?"

"I think . . ." I bit my lip. "I think he might have some piece of a god inside him."

Surprise made him laugh. "What?"

"Maybe, when Agni came to us . . ." I hesitated, worried the suggestion might give offense.

"You think some part of him has incarnated within Rama?"

"I do not know. But there is something within him. I can sense it."

His warm palm settled on my belly. The heat felt good, even if I was indifferent to desire. "How do you know so much about all this?"

"I liked to read stories about the gods, when I was young." It was not quite a lie.

Dasharath wrinkled his brow. "Does it matter what Rama is? Gods-touched or part-god?"

Yes, I wanted to say. *Yes, being gods-touched is a curse.*

Except . . . it was not. I had made a blessed life for myself, even without the approval of the gods. I had learned a power of my own and used it.

Yes, I wanted to say. *Yes, being a god is a blessing.*

Except . . . it was not. My flesh-and-blood son, Bharata, the son of a woman abandoned by the gods, would still rule Kosala.

"No," I said. "It does not matter."

"You are worrying too much about a gift," Dasharath said. "If you would like something to worry about, there are plenty of reports waiting for you."

That surprised a laugh out of me. At this encouragement he added, "I am sure the palace staff have been missing your visits. And of course, the horses in the stables, how they have suffered without you. In fact, why are you still here? You should be working through the night."

His arm kept me in place, happy and secure, and I did not even pretend to carry out his order. Instead, we lay there, content. I am sure I was still smiling when I drifted off.

A few weeks after our return, I went to see my sons before their morning lessons and was nearly knocked over by the four of them rushing down the corridor. "Slow down!" I called. "Why are you in such a hurry?"

Rama turned. "We don't want to be late! Sage Vamadeva said we had a special lesson today."

"A special lesson?" I echoed. "I have never seen you boys so excited for that."

"It's a surprise," Shatrugna said. "But Rama said it's going to be amazing."

It made a bit more sense now—Rama's excitement looked to be contagious. "Perhaps I should come see this incredible lesson for myself," I said, half-teasing. I had a meeting of the Mantri Parishad soon.

But Rama's face brightened, and he reached out to take my hand. "Yes! Ma, you have to come!" I found myself tugged along with them, unable to stop myself from smiling as we made our way to one of their lesson rooms. I supposed I could stay for a few minutes.

The boys calmed themselves before entering, filing through the door and bowing their heads to an elderly man dressed in crisp ascetic robes—Sage Vamadeva. I dipped my chin to him as well. "My son invited me," I said by way of explanation.

Sage Vamadeva gave me a curt nod but did not acknowledge my presence further. The boys arranged themselves on the floor next to four low desks, and I leaned against the wall in the back of the room. After a moment, Sage Vamadeva said, "As you boys know, today's lesson will be different. I have invited some of the eminent men of our city to come speak to you and offer their thoughts on the matters we have been studying. Why is this important?"

Rama's hand shot up. "Because a good leader must listen to others."

Sage Vamadeva's stony expression softened ever so slightly. "Very good. Lakshmana, please summarize what we studied in our last class."

"We studied the responsibilities and duties within family relationships," Lakshmana said. "The role of the husband and the wife, of the parents and children."

Although the answer was apparently right, Sage Vamadeva did not praise Lakshmana. Instead, he opened the far door of the chamber and gestured three men inside.

One was dressed similarly to Sage Vamadeva—another sage, then. The second man was clad in a richly dyed crimson tunic, but I did not recognize him, so he was likely a wealthy merchant rather than a noble. The final man was a commoner, judging from his cleanly pressed, worn-looking cotton dhoti. He could have been anyone plucked from the stalls of Ayodhya's main market.

"It is important we listen to all men, regardless of stature," Sage Vamadeva said, a sentiment I could heartily agree with. "Vikram will speak first. You are a father and a husband, yes?"

"Yes," the man in the dhoti—Vikram—said. He sounded nervous, his eyes flicking around the room but never alighting on any face.

"And how do you carry out your duties to your family?" Sage Vamadeva asked.

At this, Vikram stood a bit taller. "I am a builder. I work hard every day to ensure my family has enough to eat and a good home to live in."

I could not imagine that this was the exciting lesson the boys had been hoping for, but I was glad they were hearing about lives so different from their own. Sage Vamadeva gave Vikram an approving nod. "And what about their duties to you? To each other?"

"When we build, we enter into an agreement that we will be paid in exchange for our work," Vikram said. "A family also has such agreements with one another. I support my family in every way, and so they obey me and attend to my needs. And my wife has a duty to our children to raise them and care for them, and my children in turn have a duty to obey my wife until they are grown."

Nothing he said was incorrect, I supposed—but I was less enthused with every word he spoke.

"Now, these boys will one day rule Kosala," Sage Vamadeva said. "Is there anything important they should know about families like yours?"

For the first time, Vikram's eyes met mine. He swallowed. "Nobody will be angry for anything you say here," Sage Vamadeva added.

"Some of my wife's friends have started to go out and work themselves," Vikram said, fixing his eyes back on my sons. "They bring their children along or leave them to be watched by older children. Some have been left in the roadside schools for many hours. This is not how children should be raised. I can provide enough for my family. There is no need for my wife to work as well."

As Vikram spoke, Sage Vamadeva glanced at me. Was that a small smile on his lips? I did not believe this laborer was speaking from any place of ill will, but regardless, his words were entirely inappropriate as teaching material for the princes of Kosala. The future could not be taught by the past.

"Thank you, Vikram," Sage Vamadeva said. "That was quite enlightening. Do the princes have any questions?"

Rama's hand flew up once again, but I did not stay to hear his question. I had learned enough.

After the meeting of the Mantri Parishad, I returned to the lesson chamber, hoping to catch Sage Vamadeva before he departed. In a moment of luck, he was gathering his books, his eyes firmly on his work as I approached him. When the silence became too awkward to bear, I coughed, put on a small, polite smile and asked, "How did the remainder of the lesson go?"

Still he did not look up from his work. "It went well, although I know you did not come here to talk to me about that."

I tilted my head, keeping my gaze upon him. "Then tell me why you think I'm here."

Vamadeva braced his hands on the table and slowly lifted his head to look at me. His eyes were light, gray like mist against the dark brown of his skin. Absentmindedly, I wondered whether one of his parents had been from the south, for he did not look fully like a man from Videha, the northern kingdom he hailed from. "You were unhappy with what you heard."

He had addressed me twice now but had yet to use my title. I pushed past the disrespect. "Do you truly think that was a worthy use of their lesson?"

His stare was cold, and I remembered that despite his age this man had the blessings of many gods and had performed miraculous works on their behalf. There was a reason Dasharath had sought him out. "It is important for them to hear other perspectives. No one person can know everything—not even you."

So I had not misinterpreted the disrespect.

"I never claimed to know everything," I said evenly. "But you are instructing them in religion and morals. Hearing about how one man prefers his wife and children to live is not instructive."

"I am their teacher, and I find it instructive." He looked back down at his books. "Your sons do not seem to mind."

"My sons are children," I said. "It is your duty to guide them. Surely you would not take them to the irreputable parts of the city, though one might argue that certain knowledge resides there."

"Of course *I* would not do such a thing," he said, shaking his head slowly, his white hair catching the waning sun from the window and throwing flashes of light as though he was anointed. "But I will not argue with you about this. The will of the gods is immutable. They must learn these truths somewhere."

My temper was fraying quickly. I slipped instinctively into the Binding Plane, but there was nothing between us. I needed to goad him into saying something he would regret, something I could use to get him dismissed and end this foolishness. "And they will not learn it from me? Is that what you're implying?"

Vamadeva quirked his lips as though I had said something funny. "I have no problem with you. But this world is awash with immorality, and I do not see you stepping up to stop it."

I was appalled that this loathsome man had been teaching my sons for so long, that I had not sought to speak to him before. But this was enough. I could tell Dasharath, quite truthfully, that he had disrespected me. "I see. Well, thank you for speaking with me," I said.

I did not wait to hear his response, but swept from the room without a backward glance.

* * *

As I had thought, Dasharath proved easy enough to convince. I had first come to him with implications that I had heard secondhand from Rama, but now—

"And he did not even call you radnyi?" he confirmed.

"Why would he do that, when he plainly thought me immoral?" I said. And although I rarely did so anymore, I found the golden bond between us and tugged on it for good measure.

Dasharath sighed. "He may be a pious man, but plainly he can no longer serve as a tutor. I will have him dismissed in the morning."

It was far harder to explain things to Rama. "Sage Vamadeva has left," he cried.

"I am sorry," I said, reaching out my hand to him. "I had to send him away."

Rama did not take my hand, and instead looked at me with suspicion. "*You* sent him away?"

"Yes. His teachings are not fit for princes of Kosala."

"But I liked him," Rama said. "He was an excellent teacher."

"You have many fine teachers," I told him. "There was nothing special about this one, I assure you."

"But he knew," Rama protested. "He knew I was a god, and he wanted to help me."

He said it simply, but those words caused my heart to catch in my throat. Rama knew what he was. Rama knew of his godhood and had spoken about it with this sage rather than his own family. "I did not realize you knew who you were," I said, my voice sounding strangely raspy.

"I have always known something was special about me, that something else is inside of me." Rama spoke so matter-of-factly, I hardly knew what to say. "Sage Vamadeva taught us that gods come to Bharat to rid it of evil. He was going to prepare me."

"You don't need him." I said the words too quickly, and I hoped he could not sense my jealousy toward a man whom we would never see again. "You will have other teachers. And I am always here to help you."

Rama did not care for my platitudes. "But I wanted *him* to help me." His lower lip trembled. "I don't understand why you have to do this!" A few fat tears slipped down his cheeks, and he stomped his foot in frustration. Despite my anger at Sage Vamadeva for commanding such a place of prominence in Rama's life so quickly, I felt bad for my son, who was blameless.

"What he was teaching you was wrong," I said. "You don't want to take guidance from someone who does not even understand how the kingdom should work, do you?"

"What did he say that was wrong?"

I considered how best to explain this to Rama. "Kosala is changing. Women like me and your other mothers are doing important work. Some people don't like that, and he is one of them. You need a more modern tutor."

"I don't want someone else," Rama said softly, and I could tell no explanation would be satisfying to him.

"Oh, Rama," I said. "Come here." This time he took my hand and I held him close. I understood in many ways how he was feeling, although I had not realized he was so attached to Sage Vamadeva. I thought briefly of my mother. "Sometimes people we want to stay with us cannot. I am sorry to have done that to you."

And I was sorry to have caused him pain, even if I knew it was for the best. I had to do what was right for Rama, even if it went against his wishes. But this pain would pass, and I could ease it along. "How about we go to the kitchens, hmm? I am sure we could sneak some sweets before lunch."

Rama nodded enthusiastically, extricating himself from me. The hurt was already forgotten. He was a god, but he was also just a boy, and I was determined to let him stay one.

PART THREE

CHAPTER
TWENTY-TWO

JEALOUS WHORE. THE GREEN-EYED radnyi. I have heard every name people have called me behind my back. Some claim I sent Rama into the forest because I could not bear for Kaushalya to become Queen Mother, because I could not bear for a son I had not carried in my womb to take the throne.

If only it were that simple.

For five perfect years, I suspected nothing at all. Not of Rama, nor of discontent in our kingdom, nor that any plan of mine could go awry. Time carried me along its current, ignorant and happy.

In being named saciva, I had achieved all the freedom I could hope to. But I found myself continuing to work, for if it was in my power to assist other women, I felt I had to. And there were still plenty of women who needed help, for attitudes changed slowly. Even outside of the Women's Council, people brought their problems to me, and I did my best to help.

One evening, after I returned from a meeting of the Women's Council, Rama came to me. "Do you have a moment?" he asked.

"Of course." We spoke often, but today he looked unusually pensive. "What is it?"

"Have you spoken recently to the sages of the city temple?"

Whatever I had expected, it was not this. In truth, I avoided the sages as much as I could, both because of my discomfort with worshipping the gods and because I knew they disliked me. "I have not. Have you?"

Rama nodded. "Please do not be angry."

"Why would I be angry?" I asked, still confused. "You can tell me anything."

"I have been seeing the sages, to further my religious studies. Our tutor on the subject—well, he is not perfect." I could hear, running below Rama's words, some hint of years-old annoyance that Sage Vamadeva had been dismissed. The prince's new tutor was not a sage, but rather a low-ranking noble who was very studied in the religious texts.

But I could not fault Rama for wishing to learn more about this—about who he was. "Of course I would not be angry. It is admirable to seek out more knowledge, so long as you form your own opinions."

Rama's posture loosened slightly in relief. "I have been speaking to them, and I think they are unhappy, and I thought—you help everyone. You could help them. They do not wish to be a burden to the palace, for they are separated from our affairs, but they have told me some of what they fear, and I would like to help them if I can."

"Why have they come to you? You know they can go to your father if they need assistance," I reminded him, uneasy at the idea that these men would put responsibility on the shoulders of such a young man.

"I suppose they feel a special connection to me," Rama said. "Perhaps because they believe me gods-touched, although I am not. They care so much for the gods and their will—for me, although they do not know it—that I wish to repay them. But I have found it to be a difficult problem."

"I do not understand," I said. "Are the temples struggling for donations?"

He shook his head. "It is difficult to explain. Perhaps I could show you, though? I would value your thoughts."

"Of course," I said. I did not particularly want to visit the temples or talk to the sages. But I cared about one god, my son standing before me, who had come to me for help. If it would ease his mind then I could swallow my discomfort for a few hours.

We agreed to go the next morning, just after sunrise when the sages would have completed their morning rituals but before the city's inhabitants would arrive for their daily prayers. The palace had its own temple, with an impressive marble floor that was always cool underfoot. In the center of the room stood impassive murtis, gracefully carved from granite, and the air was fragrant with cinnamon and sage incense. Many members of the palace went here to pray and complete pradakshina around the unseeing stone. But while I attended public rituals and observances as a radnyi must, I had only ever been to this more private place a handful of times, and had never exchanged more than a few words with the sages who attended it.

I had never been to the city's main temple, though I had seen it in passing before, a building of smooth red stone laid so precisely it was impossible to see where one stone met the next. The main chamber stood open and exposed to the elements on three sides, and the roads leading up to the temple were lined with trees. The roof was held up by pillars of the same red stone, carved with depictions of the gods' triumphs in battle. It was Sumitra who had once told me that a different artisan had decorated each pillar, so that the temple had the craftsmanship of Ayodhya itself imbued within it.

Rama and I took a palanquin there, upon his insistence, and he offered me his arm as we made our way up the temple steps. It was a beautiful, cool morning, the sky streaked with pink and gold, and I shivered slightly when I slipped off my sandals at the entryway. The foliage muffled the sounds of the city, giving the temple an air of calm, although I felt anything but.

"We should pray first," Rama whispered, approaching the statue of Shiva on the farthest right and kneeling. I made to follow him, but he twisted around and inclined his head toward my left. "Women pray on that side." I looked down at the floor and saw a faint white chalk line dividing the room in half.

The temple was nearly deserted, with only a few attendants sweeping or making other preparations for the day, replacing the old flowers with crimson and amber blooms and filling the small brass lamps with golden oil. Slowly, I moved to the other side of the line, faced the statues of the gods that lined the back wall, and bowed my head.

After some time, I heard Rama's soft footfalls approaching and rose to my feet. "They have their private chamber, where we can talk to them," he said, gesturing toward the back wall.

It was unnerving that he knew so much of this place. I had followed the boys' lessons less closely as they had grown older, once I had ascertained that none of their other tutors were of Sage Vamadeva's ilk. But surely someone should have told me if Rama was regularly leaving the palace to take lessons at the temple?

Together, we entered a large room with a curved dome ceiling. It reminded me of a smaller version of the palace. Great paper windows, as tall as a man, took up two walls, letting in streams of morning light. Still, the sages had lit several small lamps on the tables—perhaps so they could more easily read some of the texts that lined the other two walls of the place. Wooden shelves ran from floor to ceiling, filled to bursting with scrolls. Some part of me wanted to approach the nearest stack, dig through it, and lose myself in the knowledge held here. It was, in truth, a beautiful room, one designed for reading and learning. If only it wasn't set in a temple, for this place had been built for the gods.

The sages—evident by their saffron robes—grew silent upon our entrance. I pushed away the part of me that longed to know what they were saying, to participate myself. This was not the time and certainly not the place.

One sage stood, inclining his head to Rama. "Welcome, Yuvraja." Rama did not share my surprise at the title, inclining his head to the sage. But then again, he did not know that the title belonged to Bharata. For the first time, I wondered how Rama would feel when he learned of his father's vow. He clearly cared deeply about the people of the city and thought himself heir. Would it hurt him, to learn he would not be Kosala's raja? "I see you brought a guest today? Welcome, Radnyi Kaikeyi." The man's tone was distant rather than welcoming, but I ignored it. I knew nothing about him. Perhaps he was simply forbidding to all strangers.

I bowed my head, hands clasped together in greeting. "Thank you for allowing me to come here," I said.

"We did not allow anything," he replied. "Your son did not tell us he was bringing you. We do not permit women in this area of the temple, but for Yuvraja Rama I suppose an exception can be made."

Rama stepped forward. "You have my apologies. I did not realize that was the case. We can go—"

"No need," the man cut him off. "Today is not your lesson day. Can we assist you or the radnyi?"

"I was telling my mother of your concerns about the future of this temple, and she wished to speak to you herself, to see how she might assist."

A flicker of surprise rippled across the man's face before he schooled it back into sternness. "You wish to assist?" he asked me.

"Should I not?" I smiled, but his expression remained stony. "If it is in my power to aid any member of this kingdom, I would like to."

"You have told me of your concerns that people no longer respect the temples or worship the gods or respect their will as devoutly as they should. I am sure if my mother was to hear more, she would try to help," Rama said.

"There is not much more to say," the sage said slowly, as if he was trying to stall for time to decide how best to respond. I slipped into the Binding Plane, worried that he might attempt to spin some type of falsehood. Unlike Rama, the sage was present in the gray world, but there was not even a wisp of connection between us. "It is simply that many in the city no longer hold the temples in as high a regard."

"Has attendance fallen?" I asked, wondering how he was measuring regard.

"I suppose," he said. "But we do not count day to day; such things are not our concern. We worry that even the people who attend are falling further from the teachings of the gods."

I chanced a glance at Rama, who was frowning in concern and nodding along. But I could not fathom what this man was talking about. "And what have they done to make you so worried?"

"All of us here have devoted our lives to ensuring our kingdom retains the blessings of divine favor, but people no longer come to us seeking guidance," he explained, growing more animated. "Our teachings are meant to ensure that people live good lives—pious lives—but now so many in the city think they know better. It is a dangerous path."

"What teachings would these be?" I asked, glancing at the walls of scrolls. For the first time, I considered that they might not be full of the kinds of knowledge Kekaya's cellar had held. Perhaps instead they held page after page about the rules of the gods, and their interpretations. Even though the room had brightened as the sun rose, it felt far less inviting now.

"I think you know," he said.

"I do not believe so," I replied coolly.

"Are you certain? You interfere with the natural order, the gods-given order. The women who come to your council are the same ones who step out of their homes, leaving their husbands and children to fill roles they should not have to."

I had not expected him to say such a thing directly to me. Sages were not obligated to show deference to their rulers; they did not fall under the purview of the traditional hierarchy. But blatant disrespect was another thing altogether—it had gotten Sage Vamadeva removed from the palace, as these men surely knew. "Who is to say that is the natural order?" I asked him. "The Women's Council has improved many people's lives. Including those of men and children."

"Perhaps it has improved their material station, but at the expense of spiritual poverty," he countered. "We are the keepers of the gods' wisdom, and it falls to us to interpret their desires. We study for years to do this. It is a sacred calling. And yet somehow you think you know better?"

I glanced at Rama. He had a hand on his chin, and his eyes were distant. "I do not understand. If your temple is still fully attended, receiving faithful worshippers and donations, how does it harm you if women in this city have some small say in their lives? I have seen no sign the gods themselves are displeased."

The man shook his head, nose crinkling in disgust, and turned to Rama. "Why would you bring her? She has shown herself uncaring of our plight. She is, in some ways, the cause of it."

"She only wishes to help," Rama said, and I felt a flash of warmth for my son. "She is wise and capable."

"You are always welcome, Yuvraja," said the man. "But I do not think she should be here any longer."

"How dare you?" I demanded. "I have done nothing but help the people of Ayodhya—"

"You may have your own ways at the palace, but we are not

269

beholden to you." The man took a step away from me, a clear dismissal. "You will keep your peace and leave."

"You cannot—"

"Ma, let us go," Rama murmured in my ear.

Part of me wished to stay, to argue with these pompous men who believed they knew better because they had surrounded themselves with scrolls and shut themselves off from progress. But I had fought these kinds of battles many times before, and I knew I could not shout them down, nor could I stoop to their level. Instead, I let my son guide me away, out through the now-bustling main chamber of the temple and into our waiting palanquin, and reassured myself that the fact that the sages had needed to ask for help proved that I had already won.

"Do you see?" I asked him, sinking against the cushion behind me. My face felt hot. "They are fine. They are merely unhappy at the thought of change, any change."

Rama's handsome face was clouded. "They treated you quite rudely, and I am displeased about it. But perhaps I should not have brought you into their space at all. That is my fault. I simply thought—we are meant to serve all members of this city, are we not?"

"We are," I replied. "But we do not have to agree with all of them."

He nodded. "I am sorry that went so poorly," he said. "I just wanted you to understand their view. I believed you could help."

"There was nothing to understand," I said. "The sages must learn to accept what they do not like, just as we all must."

Rama looked down at his hands, mouth twisting. "I want all people of this kingdom to be happy, for I am here to help them."

"Are not the women who wish for more members of this kingdom?" I asked him. "Their happiness matters equally. Why should the sages decide the course of their lives?"

"They have devoted their lives to worship, a noble pursuit," Rama said. "But you make a good point that I must also consider."

To me, that was tantamount to agreement. "He never told me his name," I said after a moment of silence, a peace offering.

"He really was unkind to you," he agreed, shaking his head in irritation.

We talked of other things the rest of the way home.

We did not speak of the visit to the temple again, for less than a week later, as I sat with Dasharath on our favorite divan in his rooms, sipping cardamom tea, he asked without warning, "Were any of your brothers sent away to train when you were children?"

I put down my cup to stare at him. "No, although Ashvin traveled to learn from healers in other cities after I left. What prompted this?"

"I am considering sending Rama, and perhaps one of his brothers, to an ashram, to continue his martial training. I wondered what you thought of the idea."

"We live in one of the largest, most celebrated cities that history has known. What could the boys learn in a secluded religious community that they could not learn here?" I countered. I was not necessarily opposed to it. But I also did not want to part with any of my sons.

"I was sent away for two years when I was their age, and it helped me to see the world more clearly, away from the immediacy of the city," Dasharath explained, taking my hand in his. "I have been assured that Sage Vishvamitra himself will be there to supervise their training."

Sage Vishvamitra was legendary. Before Dasharath was born, he had been a warlord and feared warrior in the eastern part of Kosala. He had coveted the prosperity of a nearby ashram and amassed several talented soldiers to storm the hermitage. But their weapons turned to dust in their hands. Upon seeing this, Vishvamitra renounced his rulership and turned to a life of penance and devotion to the gods. He had become one of the most powerful and pious men in the land, a wanderer and a scholar who rarely took pupils. Some of the greatest kings of Bharat had studied under him.

"Why Rama?" I asked, suddenly realizing how strange this arrangement was. "Shouldn't it be Bharata who goes, if any of them must?"

Dasharath lowered his eyes.

I stared at him, uncomprehending for a moment. Then the traitorous part of my mind asked, *How could Bharata compete with a god?*

Blood pounded in my ears as though my body was bracing for a fight. But there was no fight. "Why Rama?" I asked again, more quietly. I needed to hear him say it.

"Kaikeyi, I am sorry," Dasharath said.

"You made a promise." My voice was cold. For the first time in weeks, in moons, I entered the Binding Plane in the presence of my husband. The gold cord that connected Dasharath and me still had prominence, but to my eyes it looked slightly thinner, duller, where before it had seemed luminous. I went to touch the cord, then stopped. Dasharath had broken his wedding vow and betrayed my trust. Perhaps it was this broken promise that had thinned our bond. But he was raja. He had the power—the right—to name his own heir.

"Rama is the most gifted in his studies, the most dedicated," Dasharath said. "He is a superb warrior. He will make a fine ruler."

"I accepted your proposal only after you made your vow. This marriage is—" *built on a lie*, I wanted to say, but with difficulty I swallowed the phrase down.

Dasharath sighed. He reached out to touch me, then seemed

to think better of it. "And I am very sorry. But I do not think Bharata has any interest in ruling the kingdom. Kosala is vast. I will make certain Bharata governs one of our most important territories. He will be powerful, and a brilliant asset to Rama."

I opened my mouth, but no sound came out.

"You will always be the first of my radnyis, Kaikeyi. Kaushalya and Sumitra know it, and they love you more for it. When you asked me to vow that your son would be heir, you were about to be my third radnyi, and the youngest besides. You needed power, am I right?"

I nodded slowly.

"You don't need that anymore. And I must think of what's best for the future of Kosala. I love all my sons, but I also love my kingdom. I cannot deny that Rama is what is best for its future. And I think, in your heart, neither can you."

This felt like a betrayal. Dasharath had asked me about the ashram knowing I would realize that Rama was to become heir. He must have been thinking about this for some time and kept it from me. This deceit had diminished our bond, and it filled me with anger to think about it.

And yet—Dasharath believed in the truth of what he said, and upon evaluation, he had a strong argument. Rama's kingship would not hurt my position in court. Kaushalya might become Queen Mother, but I would still preside over the Women's Council. It was a part of the fabric of Kosala now, and no line of succession could take that away from me. I would still be saciva to Dasharath. I would have the loyalty of the palace staff, the loyalty of the women in the kingdom. I would still be loved in Kekaya. Kosala was my home now. I should want the best for it.

I forced myself to take several deep breaths, and with each moment, calm returned. It was true that Rama was preparing for the responsibility. The visit to the temple had made that clear. And I knew, deep in my heart, that Dasharath's decision would not hurt Bharata, who did not seem to share this same interest in the burden of rule.

"Very well," I said, despite my sorrow at the breaking of my husband's promise and the loss of a future I had long imagined. "I too want what's best for Kosala." I released my self-pity as best I could. "The opportunity to train with Sage Vishvamitra is one he must take. You ought to send Lakshmana with him. They are close companions."

Dasharath did reach for me now, stroking my hand with his thumb. "Thank you, Kaikeyi." His love for me was clear in his eyes, unchanged despite our bond.

CHAPTER
TWENTY-THREE

THE PALACE FELT EMPTIER without Rama and Lakshmana. For a time, even Bharata and Shatrugna seemed quieter,
as though they were lost without their constant companions.
But as with all things, we adjusted to their departure, for
despite their absence most things in Ayodhya remained much
the same.

And then, a year after they had left, rumors about Rama
began reaching the city, each more astonishing than the last.

We heard he had brought forth water from a well dried for
decades. We heard he had shot a meteor from the sky with a
simple wooden bow. And then we heard that Rama had single-
handedly slain a rakshasa threatening the ashram. The story
spread like wildfire in whispers throughout the palace, and I
heard rumors in snatches of conversation.

"The rakshasa was taller than two men, and still the yuvraja faced him—"

"I heard the yuvraja slew it in just one blow—"

"The gods have truly smiled—"

"Do you think it is true?" Dasharath asked me as I sat on
the edge of his bed watching him prepare for sleep.

I remembered watching Rama's presence grow, seeing his godhood within him. "Yes," I said. "I could believe it."

"He truly has a gift." Dasharath's expression was filled with wonder. "Just imagine what he will do as raja."

"I hope he will be more sedate by then," I said. "A king should not risk himself."

"Are you accusing me of being boring?"

"*I* did not use the word *boring*," I said archly, and he pretended to lunge toward me, even as he laughed.

Less than one moon later, news reached us that Rama and Lakshmana had embarked with Vishvamitra on a journey through several northern kingdoms. The official messenger provided us no other information, but throughout the palace it seemed everyone knew something about our sons.

"My sister lives on the border of Videha, and she said the princes passed through last week, hunting rakshasas," one serving girl whispered to another in the corridor outside my room. The door wasn't fully closed, and I stood on the other side of it, fear freezing me in place. "Some sort of beast has been slaughtering their cows, and when the yuvraja heard, he went toward the mountains in pursuit."

"He's so brave," the other girl said, a hushed awe tinging her voice. "We are fortunate indeed."

They moved down the hall and away from my perception. *They are just rumors*, I told myself. And I might have believed it, if the very next day Kaushalya hadn't told us her distant cousin sent her a missive repeating the same story.

"Why is he putting himself in such danger?" I asked, my heart in my throat. Our children were so far away, so far from our protection.

"He is gods-touched," Sumitra said, her voice bright. Confident. "And he is sharing his blessing."

I could hardly breathe, living with the fear day in and day out. Sometimes it would lie dormant, half-forgotten, but never for long, for the whole city was consumed with stories about Rama, each more far-fetched than the last. He had ridden on a white elephant. He had healed all the sick of a village. He had defeated a six-armed asura with one perfect shot to the heart.

Only when a messenger came to us directly from Rama and Lakshmana to tell us that they were safe did the knot in my chest loosen. They wrote that they had indeed tracked down and slain two rakshasas in combat, an incredible feat, and were now safe in a small city. I could scarcely comprehend how my two boys had done such a thing. I thought of them fighting their father with wooden swords, thinking only of fun and games. But they were grown now, and knowing they were safe was a gift.

The next day, Dasharath summoned us to his rooms.

"We have all heard of Rama's and Lakshmana's triumphs," he said proudly. "It has reminded me that the boys are almost seventeen, and well accomplished. It is time for them to marry."

The last time he had called all of us to his chambers, we'd sat on the ground by his feet as he bid us sacrifice our bodies to his quest for an heir. This time we sat on cushioned benches in Dasharath's study, meeting one another as equals.

The years had aged all of us, but Dasharath remained vital as ever, laboring each day to ensure the kingdom's prosperity. While he did not ride out to fight anymore, there was hardly any occasion for it—the villages and tribes to the north had been completely folded into our kingdom under Dasharath's reign, and the southwest of Kosala had become more settled and therefore less hospitable to bandit encampments.

Kaushalya had retained her serene elegance and biting wit and still masterfully followed all the inner workings of the court and palace. And Sumitra's constant cheerful wisdom was a balm, her laugh lines only accentuating her beauty.

I did not know what the others saw when they looked at me,

or what they thought my governing quality might be, but I knew that my hard edges and raw ambition had softened with time.

"Who did you have in mind?" Kaushalya asked, pulling me out of my musings.

"King Janaka of Videha is holding a swayamvara in his capital of Mithila for his daughter Sita. She is rumored to be a girl of great beauty and compassion. And Janaka and his brothers have other fine daughters besides. If Rama wins Sita's hand, there is no reason we cannot bind Kosala and Videha with several ties of marriage."

Videha. It was a powerful kingdom to our east and had long been our ally. Although smaller than Kosala in size, it was renowned for its cultivation of spices and therefore highly prosperous. This would indeed be a strong match.

"You should all prepare to travel within one moon," Dasharath said. "Rama and Lakshmana will meet us there, and I expect we will not leave until there has been a wedding."

Mithila, the capital of Videha, was located at the base of the mountains. Its deep swathes of forest and crisp, clean air sent a sharp pang of longing through me, for it resembled the landscape of my childhood. But unlike in Kekaya, the people of the Videhan court wore the same dress and practiced the same customs as those in Kosala.

We were among the first to arrive for the swayamvara. Raja Janaka had invited Dasharath to discuss matters of state beforehand. Whoever married Sita would likely take the throne of Videha, and Dasharath wanted to ensure that if it was not Rama, Kosala's alliance would still be secure.

Secretly, I had no doubt it would be my son. I had heard a rumor that Janaka had convinced Lord Shiva himself to provide his bow for the swayamvara. The suitor who could lift the Shiva Dhanush, string it, and shoot an arrow from it would win Sita's hand in marriage. It was the kind of challenge that would live on in stories and in song, outlasting any mortal heart. Rama had grown into a warrior capable of slaying rakshasas unaided, and he had his divinity besides. I did not know what man could match him.

The palace was busy with preparations for the swayamvara, so one afternoon, while Janaka and Dasharath held council and Kaushalya and Sumitra took rest in their rooms, I decided to walk down to the stables. Even if I could not ride here, I always enjoyed spending time with horses.

Along the way, I passed a girl dressed in the garb of a servant. She hurried past me up the path toward the castle, and I stopped to watch her go, for she carried herself quite gracefully. In fact, there was something familiar about her...

"Sita?" I called. She froze, and I knew I was right. "Yuvradnyi Sita. We met at the welcome feast."

Slowly she turned back around. "Radnyi Kaikeyi, how good to see you again. Please, pardon my rudeness."

I shook my head. "There's nothing to pardon. Were you visiting the stables?"

She bit her lip, but nodded. "I like to ride out in the mornings. When I can. To pray." Sita was quite pretty, with long black hair woven in a thick braid, shining black eyes, and a full mouth. But she had been given away by the stripe of luminous silver running through the front of her hair and the tiny flower-shaped birthmark at the corner of her right eye. Not a face one forgot easily.

"I see. Are you very devout?" I asked. "I've never heard of prayer on horseback."

She laughed, then covered her mouth as if horrified that the sound had slipped out. "I think I am. I pray every day, many times, to many gods."

I think I am, she had said. Someone who prayed many times a day to many gods was certainly devout, unless— "And do the gods listen?"

She took a step back from me. "What a strange thing to ask."

I blinked into the Binding Plane, but we had only a slip of silver string between us. That would not work. I smiled at her, a small smile of commiseration. "What you said reminded me of myself when I was your age." I paused, but something compelled me onward. "The gods have forsaken me as well," I said gently.

Sita looked around as if worried someone might be spying on us. She took several steps closer, then whispered, "Do you know of the circumstances of my birth?"

I shook my head, mystified.

"My father found me buried in the earth. He was plowing the land, praying for the famine that had befallen Videha to end, when his plow stuck fast. My father began to dig out the plow and found me enfolded beneath the dirt. He said to survive there, I must have been gods-touched. Except it can't be true. The gods never listen to me, and now I am to be married, and how can I be married if the gods are blind to my existence?" She burst into tears. "The gods must give their blessing to all marriages."

I stood for a moment, shocked into silence. *Buried in the earth?* Though I had heard of many improbable wonders, even I had never heard of a child surviving in the ground. But as she continued to cry, she looked so miserable, so lost, that my instincts took over. "Calm down. Breathe." She took a shallow, shaky breath. "Another. Another." Finally, she took a deep, even breath and nodded her head.

"I'm sorry. That was unseemly."

"Do not worry yourself. I understand," I told her, rubbing her back. "As I said, I felt the same way once."

"You were buried in the earth too?" she asked, and I pulled away in surprise. Then I noticed her shy smile and gave a small chuckle.

"When I was a girl, my brothers would pray for good aim and then hit a perfect bull's-eye. My father would pray for rains and they would come the next day. But it seemed that whenever I prayed for something, nearly the opposite would happen." The words inspired far less pain than I had expected. They were simply a fact now.

Her face crumpled, and I thought she might cry again. But when she said, "That's exactly what happens to me," her voice was remarkably steady.

"I have a marriage," I told her. "A marriage in which I am loved and trusted. Without the help of the gods." My disinterest in the marital bed and my lack of desire for Dasharath did not matter. I loved him like I would love a dear friend, and he had never caused me pain. For a woman, even in our new world, that was more than plenty.

"But how? If the gods have forsaken me, then how will my marriage be real?"

I sighed. Of all the things I had learned about Sita prior to our arrival, no one had mentioned the girl's apparently rigid piousness. "You said it is your father who claims you are gods-touched?"

"Yes."

"The truth about the gods-touched is that they cannot be influenced by the magic of the gods. Their power cannot sway us, for we have a higher purpose."

"What is my purpose?" Her eyes held a hunger, one I recognized.

"I cannot guess your purpose," I said. But I had very strong suspicions. If she was gods-touched, then she was probably intended to be Rama's bride and his queen and, in that way, would serve her purpose. It would be ideal for Rama to have a wife he could not instantly read, to have a wife he could not compel to obey.

"What is yours?" she asked. "Have you completed it yet?"

I shook my head. "That I also do not know."

Her face fell. "I see."

"But that does not mean you cannot make your own purpose," I said quickly, for as a child it would have been a blessing to hear from someone also forsaken by the gods that I could be more. Could aspire to greatness. "I am Raja Dasharath's saciva." This time, I smiled with all my teeth, sharp and predatory and not like a proper radnyi at all. She would need a fire in her belly too, if she wanted to thrive as Rama's wife.

To her credit, Sita met my smile with one of her own. "I have heard that. They say you even rode out into battle once, as the raja's charioteer."

"I did," I said. "Many years ago."

"My father was impressed by that story," she said. "When my sister and I were young, he allowed us to take lessons in archery and spear-throwing. He said that your skill had saved your husband's life."

I blinked at her, my heart unexpectedly full. "That is wonderful," I said.

"It was a pleasant break from sitting and reading," she said. "I do enjoy archery."

"Is that why the swayamvara contest will be archery?" I asked. It was no longer a secret, for Janaka had told us upon our arrival of his coup in being granted the Shiva Dhanush.

She shook her head. "I do not think they are related. My father simply wanted a task that only the most powerful of suitors could accomplish. The Shiva Dhanush was supposedly carried into the palace by four men. Although I think they must have exaggerated that."

"Oh? Why is that?"

"Well, I wished to see it for myself, so I slipped into the room where it is kept when everyone was sleeping. I thought perhaps it would be fun to see how heavy it was. But I lifted it with little difficulty—it is not much heavier than a normal bow." She said it without guile, her shrug dismissing the incident. But I bit on the inside of my cheek to keep from gaping at her.

Janaka would not have lied about the weight of the bow, nor its origins. It seemed much more likely that Sita had simply lifted a bow made for a god.

She was a worthy match for Rama indeed.

CHAPTER
TWENTY-FOUR

RAMA AND LAKSHMANA ARRIVED the day before the swayamvara.

We had not seen them in two years, and Bharata, Shatrugna, Kaushalya, Sumitra, and I waited in their empty chambers to greet them together on their arrival. We all began shouting when the door opened, but it revealed only Dasharath, who gave a sheepish grin and came to stand with us.

"You might look less disappointed to see me," he muttered, and I was about to tease him back when the door opened again, this time revealing my two sons.

I could not stop the tears that sprang to my eyes as we swarmed around them, embracing and laughing. They both were over a full head taller than when they had left, and all traces of childhood had vanished from their faces. Our boys were gone. They had become men. They had become warriors.

I was grateful to see that Kaushalya and Sumitra also had tears running down their faces at the sight of our sons, and even Dasharath dashed a hand across his eyes when he thought nobody was looking. I clutched Lakshmana close and then Rama, my heart overflowing.

But we had little time to ourselves, for they had to clean away the dust of their travels and prepare for the swayamvara itself.

When I saw the Shiva Dhanush the next morning, my heart sank. It was even larger than I had imagined, nearly the length of two men.

The wood was a rich, deep maroon, rare and precious indeed, and lustrous as though lit from within. Although there were no carvings, a spiraling ribbon of gold was inlaid in its surface, like a curl of fire. It lay, unstrung, in the middle of the training field, carried out by four strong men. The eyes of the suitors grew to comical proportions when they realized the magnitude of the task at hand. The idea that Sita might have lifted it seemed laughable and yet...

Lots were drawn for the order of the competition, and Rama's was drawn last.

Before him, among all the other suitors, only one man managed to even lift the bow: Ravana of Lanka.

News of the death of Ravana's beloved Mandodari had reached Ayodhya some two years past. Had Rama not been competing, Ravana would not have been the worst match for Sita. He was old enough to be her father, but I knew he would treat her kindly, for he had treated me with kindness even without cause to do so. Kindness was still not a custom for brides across the land.

Ravana was in the middle of stringing the bow, arms trembling with effort and sweat drenching his brow, when he glanced up at Sita, seated on a dais. Something about her—perhaps her beauty or perhaps some sense that warned him she was gods-touched—seemed to greatly move him, because the string slipped from his finger and he dropped the bow with a resounding boom that shook the very earth. In the silence that followed, Sita giggled, and the bell-like sound echoed around the field.

Ravana flushed a bright red and hurried off the field.

I felt sorry for him, but I could not follow my old friend now. So I put it from my mind as my son took the field.

There was a strange, almost palpable hush that fell over the watching crowd as Rama stepped up to the Shiva Dhanush and grasped it. He lifted it in one easy motion, and the silence broke with a collective intake of breath.

With his other hand, he slipped the bowstring into place and pulled upward. The bow bent like the neck of a swan, held steady by Rama's hand, and he finished stringing it with ease. He held the bow loosely at his side as he stepped up to the mark and inspected the arrows provided in the quiver.

I felt it then—that strange sense of foreboding that had passed through me so long ago, playing with my children. That I might stand on the jagged cliff face of loss. But the feeling passed quickly, washed away as Rama selected a golden arrow, then half turned to look at the spectators. He spotted Sumitra and Kaushalya and smiled slightly. Then he locked eyes with me and gave a single nod. I nodded back and tried to pretend I had not spied the halo around his head, tried to pretend his divinity was not throwing diamond sparks against his jet-black hair, tried to pretend that a young man of sixteen wasn't casting a shadow twenty feet long.

In a motion as fluid and beautiful as a dancer, Rama faced the target, nocked the arrow, and took aim.

The arrow ripped through the center of the target, and the splintering echoed in the absolute silence. Even I took a second to comprehend the sheer effortlessness of it. In the next moment, we were all on our feet cheering. Even the other suitors were shouting their approval of his feat.

I turned to look at Sita. She was gazing at Rama with a small smile on her face, and he was staring back at her. After a moment, she stood and climbed down from the dais, a white lotus garland in hand.

As she walked toward the center of the field, the celebrations quieted. There was no doubt in anyone's mind that Sita would take Rama as her husband. And yet we all knew we were witnessing something holy. Marriage was common, but the joining of two kingdoms—of a yuvradnyi born of the earth and a yuvraja who had performed an impossible feat—felt different.

As Sita approached, Rama walked toward her, smiling. He looked every bit a yuvraja, and every bit a god. He came to a stop before her and bowed his head, pressing his hands together. "Yuvradnyi," he said, voice ringing for all to hear. "I have completed the tasks you set for me. I have lifted the bow, and strung it, and hit the target besides. If I have performed to your satisfaction, I ask for the honor of your hand in marriage." He kept his eyes fixed on Sita as he spoke.

Sita met Rama's gaze, her hands steady around the flowers. She looped the garland around his neck, and her demure smile blossomed into a grin. "Yuvraja Rama, I choose you as my husband."

Kaushalya grabbed my elbow. "Our son, wed," she whispered in my ear. "Only yesterday he was born."

I leaned my head against her shoulder. "Congratulations, Queen Mother."

Afterward, I went to find Ravana, hoping a friendly face would help temper his humiliation. There was also the distinct possibility my presence would rub salt in the wound, but our bond looked strong and I decided to risk it.

"Hello?" I called into his chambers. The door had been left slightly open, but no servants appeared to be present.

From inside came a soft sound of movement. The hall was deserted, so I entered his rooms and closed the door behind me. "Ravana?" I called. "It's me, Kaikeyi."

I moved past the antechamber and found him leaning

against a casement in his bedroom, arms crossed. Tears glinted on his cheeks. He did not even look at me.

"Mandodari died," he said, startling me.

"I had heard. I am so sorry." I came to stand beside him.

"I waited years to find another bride, and now...this." Despite the tears, his voice was remarkably even. Emotionless.

I rested a hand lightly on his arm. "You were the only other who even managed to lift the bow. That is nothing to be ashamed of."

"I am not ashamed!" he bellowed. I jerked my hand away in alarm. "Did you hear her laugh?"

"She is young, naive—she meant no harm by it."

"It was the most beautiful sound. She sounded so like Mandodari." He heaved a great breath. One hand reached up to wipe the wetness from his face. "Your son Rama won the contest, I assume?"

"Yes."

"Is he a good boy? Will he treat her well?" So he was smitten with her. I had not expected this turn of events.

"He is the best of boys," I said. "Please, Ravana, do not despair. There will be other women, of course—"

"How dare you?" He snarled, rage transforming his features into ugliness. I stumbled back several steps. Ravana looked dangerous—demonic. "How dare you? Leave me!"

I ran from his quarters, only slowing when I reached my own chambers.

I did not see Ravana again and did not have the time to ponder his strange turn of behavior, for all the boys were wed on the trip. Bharata and Shatrugna were joined with Sita's cousins, Mandavi and Shrutakirti, both happy, vivacious girls who seemed well matched for the boys. Lakshmana married Sita's younger sister, Urmila, their quiet temperaments beautifully suited.

The joint wedding had all the usual pomp and ceremony

of such a momentous occasion. The yuvrajas and rajas of the other kingdoms largely stayed for the wedding. There were weeks of feasting in the great hall in Mithila, and for each of the seven days of ceremony, Janaka sacrificed several prize animals to the wedding fires.

Sita outshone all others in the wedding. Her neck and arms were heavy with pure gold, crafted into intricate loops and whorls so that it appeared to be embroidered onto her glowing brown skin. She wore a yellow sari in the custom of Videha, but it had been embroidered with tiny jewels that flickered and shifted constantly. As she took seven steps with Rama around the sacred flame to sanctify their marriage, it was as though she herself was made of flame.

My own wedding had been exhausting, but the wedding of my children was a time of joy. It was selfish, in a way, because men did not leave home after a marriage—so I was losing nothing. I could tell Janaka truly grieved to part with his daughters and his nieces all at once. I imagined the palace at Mithila would seem quiet, desolate without them, and I was sad for him.

But there was much to do, both in Videha and awaiting us in Kosala, and so at last we took our leave.

For all the pain it might have caused Janaka, it was a pleasure to have all our sons back, and their wives besides. And we needed some bright moments for it was harvest time, and the monsoons had not come with their usual strength. It was Kosala's second such year in a row, and there would not be enough grain to feed the entire kingdom. Our small stockpiles provided barely enough grain to last one bad harvest. Usually in such a situation, our traders in Southern Kosala, beyond the Riksha Mountains, could obtain supplies from the fertile southern kingdoms. The region surrounding the city of Janasthana was especially productive and traded away their surplus in exchange for cloth and tapestries and other beautiful wares.

But this year our caravans were returning empty-handed, with tales of hostile guards and forest fiends. I hardly had time to think on it, though, for the situation at home was dire.

One morning, a quiet knock startled me as I prepared for yet another meeting of the Mantri Parishad. Manthara went to answer it, then quickly reappeared.

"You should come."

I followed her to my antechamber, necklace still in hand, to find Sita sitting on a stool, her mouth downturned and trembling as though she might cry at any moment.

"Sita?" I asked, shocked to see her looking so distraught. "What is it?"

She lifted her head and I saw dark shadows under her eyes. Her hands shook as she brushed her hair from her face.

"What has happened?" I asked. "Are you ill?"

She shook her head, and her eyes darted to Manthara. Before I could even turn, Manthara made an excuse and quietly left the room. Of course, I would tell her everything that transpired later, but for now Sita's comfort was paramount.

"I think I am losing my mind," Sita whispered. "Or else I have been cursed. I did not know who else to turn to, but I remembered our conversation by the stables, and I thought—" She rose to her feet, and the stool fell with a clatter. "I am being stupid. This was a mistake."

"What is it?" I asked. I entered the Binding Plane and sent a suggestion of comfort through our silver bond. "You can tell me anything."

"When we spoke that day, you said that the gods never answered your prayers."

"That is true," I said. "Is there something you need? If the gods won't answer—"

"The gods are answering," Sita whispered. "Or I suppose, they are speaking to me, for I never asked a question for them to answer."

I had not expected this. "What...what do you mean?"

"A few days ago, Rama and I argued. It was small, really—he mentioned that he had seen a wife contradict her husband in public and he hoped I would never do so. I told him that I would not contradict him in public so long as he did not say anything that needed correcting. I was partially jesting." At this I gave a slight laugh, and the corners of her lips turned up in response. I could imagine myself saying something similar to Dasharath.

"That night, I dreamed of the goddess Lakshmi. She told me that my husband was destined for greatness and that my first job was to support him. She said it would bring me great prosperity. I thought it was just a dream, but at the end of it, she handed me a gold coin, and when I woke..." Sita reached into her blouse and handed me a golden disk. It was unlike any coin I had ever seen before, perfectly round and smooth, decorated with an eight-pointed star.

I swallowed, considering my response carefully before speaking. "That is very strange. But between you and me, the gods have talked to me before once or twice too." I pictured the blistering heat of Agni and my own dream of Sarasvati. But even that dream had not been like this, for she had not actually appeared to me nor given me any token. Still, I added, "I do not think it is cause to worry."

"It was not just her," Sita said. "Last night I dreamed again, this time of Parvati. She told me Rama would go nowhere without my assistance. In return, she said my heirs would rule the kingdom for generations. I woke up holding a lotus in perfect bloom. But I don't understand why they are coming to me and saying these things."

"Did you ask them?" I did not mean to seem rude, but I too was curious.

"Yes. I asked Parvati, and she said that the mortal world held many temptations. She said...she said that Rama was divine, and I needed to help him restore order to the world."

So now she knew. "And what did you make of that?" I asked quietly.

"Rama already told me himself, once. I didn't believe him then. I laughed at him, in fact. But now I…" She buried her face in her hands, clearly shaken.

I gently placed my hand on her shoulder. "Rama is a god, it is true. He was sent to this world to do something great."

"To restore order?" Sita interrupted looking up. "What does that mean?"

"I do not know," I said. "I do not think we are meant to know. But they have come to you so that you know the truth. So that you may help him on his journey."

"They never cared about me before." Sita sounded bitter, and I sympathized with her resentment. The gods spoke to us as it suited them. We were important enough to be part of their plans and yet completely abandoned otherwise.

"I know. And you do not have to listen to them now. You are gods-touched, remember? They cannot force you to do anything you do not wish to do."

At that, Sita's tired eyes filled with steel. "I am devoted to him, but I do not want to be subservient. And Rama might be more traditional, but he has not asked it of me either."

"Then I would put it from your mind," I said. "And get some rest."

But as she left, her chin set and step steady, I felt less certain. The goddesses had come to her for a reason—because they were trying to influence Rama's path. It seemed they were worried. And I wondered if that meant I should worry too.

The next evening, Dasharath and I looked over the map of Kosala as we discussed plans.

"The south, beyond the Riksha Mountains, had a good harvest," he said. "That is a relief."

"And the northern reaches, near the Indra Mountains, have

never used much grain in their diet. So they can do with a bit less."

Dasharath rested his chin on my shoulder. "Do you remember, when we were first married—that territory was not ours."

"Believe me, I could not forget," I said, and he laughed out loud.

"You have done a fine job with making arrangements for the rest of the kingdom. Even if we must pay a higher price to Videha, or Kekaya, this is what is best."

"Thank you," I said, feeling content, as I always did when we had executed an idea well. "The root of our troubles is not just poor weather. We have received less grain in trade than is usual."

"It is," he agreed. "I have been meaning to speak with you about this. I have heard concerning rumors from our traders who go past Southern Kosala to Janasthana. All of them returned empty-handed this year, despite fertile fields in that region. And there have been other happenings too. The raja of Janasthana recently died in a fire."

This struck me, for I had heard a strange tale from a female trader at a Council meeting. She spoke of a frightening presence emerging from the woods and threatening violence upon her for daring to venture far from home. It had been only one story, and I had thought it more likely a bad dream, for she had returned safe and whole. Now, though, with these other omens, I could see that perhaps I had missed a vital sign. "I have heard of a beast or presence in the forest that blocked the passage of some traders. But I have not heard about this fire. It is altogether very odd."

Dasharath's eyes widened. "One of my messengers claimed that a hostile force near Janasthana has plans to attack Ayodhya."

The idea was preposterous. In order to reach Ayodhya's gates, enemies from Janasthana would have to travel through a deep wilderness, and then the entire region of Southern Kosala. Such an enemy would have to have an army strong enough to sustain that grueling march and defeat Kosala's armies at the border before they could even *approach* Ayodhya.

"I assume they meant Kosala, for attempting to reach Ayodhya would be absurd," Dasharath continued, echoing my thoughts. "I have spoken to Virendra privately and made sure to allocate more soldiers to Sripura and Southern Kosala." The Minister of War was elderly but sharp as ever. "But now, saying it aloud—have we grown dull with age?" He chuckled, but there was no mirth in it. "This seems more dire than I believed, and all the while we sit here reading grain reports and lamenting that we did not have the foresight to build a new granary."

Whatever enemy this was, they had proven they did not need to march armies upon us. They could starve us instead. And that was indeed worth taking seriously. Still, we could not just ready our soldiers for battle based on suppositions. We might be reading shapes where there was only fog.

"You need to send someone to Janasthana itself," I said, thinking aloud. "Someone whose sole job is to understand the threat. Someone who cannot be bought." Now that I had spoken it, I was filled with the desire to go.

I had tried my best to put her from my mind, but in discussing Janasthana, I could not help but think that my mother might still be there. I had wondered for so long about who she might be now, what she might say to me. This was my opportunity to serve my kingdom and my own curiosity all at once.

"There is no one to send. Aside from you and myself, I trust only Virendra for such a task, and he is far too old to make the journey."

"I will go," I said.

Dasharath's brows rose in alarm. "You want to go to a city

supposedly overrun by some evil force. A city two moons'
journey south through treacherous forests."

"Yes." As I spoke, it made more and more sense. "I can
move quickly and I have the influence to negotiate on our
behalf. I am easily underestimated but can protect myself. If it
would put your mind at ease to send someone south, I can go."

"I cannot allow that," he said immediately. In the low light,
he looked exhausted. "You are my radnyi. My saciva. I would
not risk your safety."

"It is because I am your radnyi and saciva that I should go,"
I argued. "Who better to execute your will than me? But if you
think I need protection, Rama can accompany me." After all,
he had slayed a rakshasa and lifted the bow of a god—whatever
beast loomed in the forest would be child's play for him.

"Absolutely not," Dasharath said without even considering
my proposal. "I cannot send away the yuvraja of Kosala and
my saciva both."

"No harm will befall us," I insisted. "And besides, three of
your sons will remain here. Surely that is ample security for
the kingdom."

He did not seem moved, so I decided to send a suggestion
down our bond. It moved sluggishly and seemed to flash blue
as it dissipated at Dasharath's chest. I had never seen such a
thing happen before, and I worried that perhaps my disuse of
the Binding Plane had made my power there weaker. Still, it
seemed as though the idea had been absorbed. "Rama would
benefit from such a trip. You came to the throne in a time of
war, but he has no experience of such things."

Dasharath met my gaze, considering, and then his expression shuttered. "No. I cannot allow it. He only just returned,
and I need him here."

"But—"

"I said no, Kaikeyi!" he snapped, and I clamped my mouth
shut. In all of our years of marriage, Dasharath had never

spoken to me that way before. He must have seen my shock, for he added in a milder tone, "You will not take Rama, but it would certainly alleviate my worries if you had accompaniment. You should take Lakshmana."

"That is a fine suggestion," I said softly. I was hurt by his sudden anger but reminded myself he was under an enormous amount of stress. And Lakshmana was just as skilled as Rama. "We will leave in a week."

Dasharath closed his eyes. "You may go to Southern Kosala, but no farther. You should be able to learn more about matters from there. I will not have you going to Janasthana. If any of the rumored danger is real, it will be too great a risk."

My heart sank further. "I doubt I can fix the situation without visiting the seat of the problem," I argued.

"If you go all the way to Janasthana and anything befalls you, I will not know what has happened for near half a year." Acute worry pinched his features. I did not want to cause him any more concern.

"As you say," I told him. "Do not fear. All will be well."

CHAPTER TWENTY-FIVE

WE TOLD THE REST of the palace that we were going away on a ceremonial trip to replenish our offerings at a small shrine in the Riksha Mountains so as not to cause panic. Our real destination, Sripura, was a large town in Southern Kosala. Kaushalya hailed from there—she had been yuvradnyi of the region before her marriage with Dasharath. If we had disclosed our true purpose, news of our arrival might have preceded us. I could not even tell Manthara or Asha. Lakshmana remained ignorant too, out of fear he might reveal the truth to his brothers.

We snuck away the night before our announced departure so that we could take up our guise of mere travelers, and not until the following morning did Lakshmana ask me any questions.

"Where are we really going, Ma?" His voice was so quiet I almost thought I had imagined it.

"Sripura," I said.

He did not respond, so I turned to see his reaction. He was frowning as he mouthed the name to himself. "Your mother, Radnyi Kaushalya, is from there," I added.

"I know. It is just past the Riksha Mountains on the banks of the Mahanadi River."

I pulled up my horse in surprise, watching his back as he continued on for a few paces before also stopping. He twisted around. "Is something the matter?"

"How do you know that?" I demanded. "Did you hear about our true destination and study the maps before we left?"

Lakshmana narrowed his eyes. "No, of course not. Why would I ask where we're going otherwise? We were instructed in the geography of Bharat at the ashram."

I spurred my horse back into motion. "I did not mean to accuse you of lying, Lakshmana. You have my apology. It's just—your memory is quite impressive."

"Oh," he said, almost sadly.

"Is something the matter?"

"Do you really think it's impressive?" he asked.

I glanced at him out of the corner of my eye. He held himself rigid, gaze fixed straight ahead. "Very. I have met only one other person with such recall."

"I don't understand." He sounded lost, much younger than his years.

"Has nobody told you so before? Surely your tutors have had reason to observe your memory."

"No," he said simply. "I have always taken my lessons with Rama, and he is far smarter than I. At the ashram, Sage Vamadeva said that being second to a man such as Rama is nothing to be ashamed of."

I nearly toppled off my horse. "Did you say Sage Vamadeva?"

Lakshmana did not seem to pick up on my unease. "I did. He was our tutor for a year, long ago—you may not remember. He left to meditate at the ashram."

My head spun. Sage Vamadeva had spent two years with my children, with *Rama*, without my knowing. And on top of my old grievance with the man, I was filled with new ire at his words to Lakshmana. Calm, quiet, patient Lakshmana would never begrudge his brothers anything, this I knew. For while Rama was highly charismatic and gifted with weapons, he had been attending the Mantri Parishad meetings since his return, and I knew he had little head for sums or maps or city planning. But his godly presence spilled into every corner of every room he walked into, convincing all—almost all—that they witnessed greatness.

"Rama cannot do what you can do," I said after a moment, for I did not wish to get into the topic of Sage Vamadeva right away.

"Rama is brilliant," he said, an edge I had never heard before in his voice.

I stared at him, confused. Clearly something was happening under the surface to distress him. If we were to travel together, if I was to know him and help him recognize his value, perhaps I would have to break my own rules. With some reluctance, I entered the Binding Plane.

We had a dark yellow thread of acquaintanceship between us, attenuated—I assumed—by our years apart. Respectable, but not strong enough to provide the answers I wanted.

My eyes flicked up to Lakshmana's face, and that was when I saw it, extending from his neck—a blue cord, so bright it almost hurt to look at. I had never seen such a thing before, but...

It came to me in the next moment, what this must be: Rama. They had spent two years with only each other, and in that time Rama's godliness must have ensnared Lakshmana.

"Ma? Are you well?" Lakshmana's words brought me back into myself.

"Yes," I managed to say. "I am merely thinking."

"I am sorry for getting sharp with you," he said. "I don't know what came over me. Please do not be angry, Ma."

"Have I ever been angry with you?"

He shrugged, exaggerated enough for me to see. Even now he was considerate. "When I go along with Bharata's plans."

I laughed. "They're Bharata's plans?"

"You didn't know?" he asked, all anger seemingly forgotten. "Bharata comes up with the ideas, and he claims the riskiest parts for himself. Shatrugna does all the rest."

"Shatrugna does the smartest tasks," I corrected teasingly. "That's why I thought he came up with all their nonsense."

"We always thought you only pretended not to know. Because Bharata is your son." Once again, his voice was matter-of-fact.

"What?" I asked, shocked. "No. You are all my sons."

"You believe that?" When I met his gaze, his light eyes were dark with emotion. He looked so much like Dasharath had the first time I met him in my father's palace.

"*Yes*. Because it's true."

"I see," he said, and his voice trembled ever so slightly.

"I'm not angry with you, Lakshmana. I promise. I'm angry at myself for letting you think that."

"It's not that important," he said.

"I get to decide what I find important," I told him. "And I think that you are important, you and all your brothers equally."

He snorted, amused. "Rama is yuvraja. He is the most important. There's no need to hide that truth. We are happy for him."

It was a noble sentiment, if misguided, and I needed to respond with care. "My brother, your uncle Yudhajit, was the crown prince of Kekaya. I loved him and was happy for him. But that did not mean that I thought he was better than me at everything we tried, or that I deferred to him in every matter. And back then I was just a girl, considered a burden on my family."

Lakshmana sighed, loud enough that I could hear it over

the horses and the wind. "Rama is...something more than us. I cannot explain it, but I know it is my duty to support him, to follow him. I have no problem with this," he added hastily.

"Don't say such things about yourself," I insisted, knowing he would not heed my words.

It did not matter, though, for I had nearly half a year of time away from home to forge a stronger connection with my son and try to change his perspective.

"Why are we going to Sripura?" Lakshmana asked the next day. I enjoyed riding with him—he was quiet enough that I could concentrate on the feel of horseback, the rhythm that reminded me of my childhood, but willing to talk when the hours felt long and the scenery grew dull.

"I have heard rumors of new forces at work past the borders of Southern Kosala, whispers about some sort of beast interfering with our trade caravans. I volunteered to go alone, but your father thought it best I have protection. And I knew I could trust you." There was no need for him to know that I had first suggested Rama as a companion, and even less reason for him to know that his father and I thought these threats quite serious.

"Rama would have been the better choice. My skills with a bow and a sword are acceptable, but he would have protected you far better. I was there when he slew the rakshasas."

I wanted to reach out and shake him, jolt this inferiority out of his skull, for it sounded to my estimation that Lakshmana had done plenty. But horseback and propriety prevented me from doing so.

"I trust *you*. You will not give up our secrets for any reason, you will be reliable and loyal, and I have seen your work on the training field. You are more than capable of protecting yourself, and me should it come to that."

Lakshmana frowned. "This is a long journey. Rama might need me at home," he said.

"Really?" It was time to test their bond. I entered the Binding Plane. "If Rama is so capable, why would he not be able to do without you for the span of a few moons?"

The blue bond flared into existence immediately. "Why do you hate Rama?" Lakshmana asked coldly.

I focused my energy on the otherworldly chain. It fought back, and I surrendered control of movement to my horse and instincts so I could give this task my full attention. As I pressed, the bond shuddered, dimming an infinitesimal amount. I swayed, clutching at the reins and leaning forward to steady myself.

That small task had sapped all of my strength.

Lakshmana was staring at me, expression defiant, waiting for a response. "I do not hate Rama," I said, voice rasping as though I had not had water all day.

His expression changed, first to bewilderment and then to mortification. "I know you don't, Ma. I'm sorry."

"You do not have to apologize," I said as my energy slowly returned. "I am simply trying to point out inconsistencies in your logic—and no, I do not hate you either. Rama is fallible, as are you. He has your other brothers to help him should he need it. I know the two of you are used to being together without any family to rely upon, but Rama is back in Ayodhya. Why are you so worried?"

He turned away, his expression so sorrowful that I decided not to push any further. I kept glancing over at him, but he kept his eyes on the road ahead, his throat bobbing every few minutes as though he was working up the courage to say something. Watching him, I felt a streak of shame run through me. How had I never realized?

At last, when the sun was high in the sky, we stopped for a meal. I turned away from Lakshmana to remove some food from our packs. "I don't know," he said suddenly, and I whirled around. "I don't know." His face crumpled slightly, and I put my arms around him.

"Loyalty to your family is an excellent quality, and to be commended. But you can be someone beyond your loyalty—and you should be, because you have so much to offer."

"I feel so strange," he said. "I don't know what to do with myself." Each word took him several seconds to speak, as though he was swimming through sugar syrup. My mind flashed back, strangely enough, to Ashvin, and my long-ago attempts to help him.

"I am glad you are so close to your brother. When he is king, he will need advisors he can trust. You will make a wonderful advisor, with your memory and devotion. And if you want more, you should not be afraid to ask."

"I don't understand." He pulled away from me and scrubbed a hand across his eyes. "What do you mean?"

I had gone far enough for today. "We can talk about this later," I said. "For now, we should eat."

For the next several days, we conversed about lighter topics as we crossed into the scrublands. I figured out how to whittle away Rama's hold on him more gently, although every time I weakened their bond, the world spun around me and I often lost my grasp on the Plane. But in between those episodes, I learned that Lakshmana's great skill with visual memory extended to conversations—he could recall nearly everything he had ever heard. Had Dasharath known this, when he asked me to take Lakshmana along? I could not think of a better companion for such a lengthy mission.

Our path took us through the thorn forests, a place I had heard of only in scrolls. To my surprise, the short thorn trees were not all that spiky, or painful to touch, but rather dotted the landscape like large, twisted bushes. We saw herds of elephants roaming the grasses, snapping branches off the shrubs to eat. Lakshmana's sheer delight at the sight, his whoop of excitement every time he spotted another elephant, was almost contagious.

But as Lakshmana became more friendly, more open, my heart sank deeper into my stomach. I knew I wasn't alone in thinking of Lakshmana as shy and reserved, but clearly that was not quite the case. He was very much like Sumitra: kind, loyal, wise, free with love. And his deeply buried wit, his sense of humor, was all Dasharath. I wondered if even Shatrugna, his twin brother, had any idea of who Lakshmana was underneath his silence.

"Ma, I see you looking at me. I am not blind," he said to me one morning. We had made good time on our journey—we were out of the scrub and on the last stretch of the winding pass through the Riksha Mountains.

They were nothing like the snowy and forbidding peaks to the north of Kosala and Kekaya, which had always reminded me of jagged teeth reaching to devour the sky. The valleys we traveled through were filled with lush forests, alive with chittering monkeys and brightly feathered birds, and even the higher passages were sun dappled and warm. When I craned my neck to look at the peaks, I couldn't discern any snow on their crowns.

"I'm not looking at you," I said. It was true only because I hadn't snuck a glance at him in nearly an hour. But he was right—my eyes kept seeking him out, studying him, trying to make up for lost time by discovering what else I might have missed. Dasharath and I had estimated this journey would take nearly two moons, but we had anticipated much more difficulty in the passes than had been borne out. I had less time with Lakshmana than I thought—but the same responsibilities.

"Something is wrong with me, is it not?" he asked, sounding

dejected. "You can tell me what it is. I may not have presented the best face to you, but I'm strong enough. I am."

He said the words so earnestly that I wanted to reach out and ruffle his hair, try to cheer him up. Instead, I checked our bond, which was a shining construct of amber, strengthened over the weeks. But it held no answers.

"What do you mean?" I asked. "I don't think there's anything wrong with you. If this is about Rama again…" I trailed off as the blue rope flared into existence.

It was thin now, and I set my will to breaking it. This was a yoke, not a relationship. I examined it, readying myself to sever it once and for all, took a deep breath…and shouted in fright.

Our surroundings had disappeared.

Alarm coursed through me as I exited the Binding Plane. The thick forest blinked back into existence in such a way that I felt dizzy.

"Ma?" Lakshmana was beside me at once.

I held a hand to silence him. "One moment," I said in a low voice, dismounting.

I pressed my hand to the nearest tree. It felt real enough. The bark was rough against my palm, and I could smell the faint scent of sap and damp earth. But when I reentered the Binding Plane, my hand was touching nothing.

At the farthest point visible on the road, I could see trees and birds and plants all cast in the gray mist that defined the Binding Plane. But here there was no veil. Only blinding white.

Magic was at work. And nothing good came of things I could not see in the Binding Plane.

"Lakshmana, what do you know about this area?" I asked quietly.

I heard him dismount behind me. "It is not particularly remarkable, if I recall the maps correctly."

"Are there any holy sites or shrines nearby?" I asked,

slipping back into the real world. The longer we stood, the more I noticed the air had a chill to it that felt out of place.

"Not here." He stepped up next to me, squinting into the dense forest. "Why?"

I considered the odds that I would find an entire section of forest that seemed to be gods-made so close to Sripura—and to the border beyond which a great beast lay. It was nearly impossible.

"Stay here with the horses," I ordered. "If I have not come back by the time the sun is at its peak, ride fast to Sripura and bring a search party. We are no more than a half day's journey away, and you can make better time alone."

"I do not wish to leave you, Ma," he said at once. "What do you see in there?"

"Nothing," I said, and it was the truth. "I simply have a hunch that something important lies within."

"I'm coming with you. I know you are trying to protect me, but I am also here to protect you. If you leave me here, I will follow. So you might as well just bring me now."

I considered him. He stood tall, chest thrown back, and I saw Dasharath within him. "All right, then. Be ready with your sword."

He secured the horses while I examined the surroundings further, and then we pushed our way through a lighter area of the brush.

After about a hundred paces, we could no longer see the path. Next to me, Lakshmana shivered, and I realized gooseflesh was running up my arms. The forest was cold—unnaturally so—and far too quiet. There should have been small animals chattering, running up and down the trees, but they were nowhere to be found. There was no birdsong, no movement in the undergrowth. Without it, the forest seemed an eerie place.

I entered the Binding Plane, standing firm as the ground shifted slightly and cast Lakshmana in its colorless palette.

The forest was unmoving, and so the sudden crunch of Lakshmana's boot against the ground reverberated, and we both startled before looking down. Brittle leaves of brilliant red and saffron had drifted over the path. I glanced up to see that the trees above had turned color, a blaze of flame. We rarely saw such things in Kosala, but the forests of Kekaya had been like this…in the late autumn. Not in the middle of summer.

"How is this happening?" Lakshmana asked, reaching down to pick up a leaf.

"I don't know," I said. And truly, I did not know what sort of magic this was. We pressed on more quickly, the movement keeping us warm as our breath came in clouds of white. Each step felt more and more *wrong*…

A low whine sounded from ahead of us.

"Do you hear that?" I asked Lakshmana.

We stopped, and the sound came again.

An icy crust coated the plants now, a field of deadly, glimmering frost under a canopy so dense we could hardly see five paces ahead. I knew we must be close to whatever lived in the heart of this strange place.

I reached out to grasp a fallen branch and fumbled in my pouch for a flint. It took a few tries, my fingers clumsy with cold, but finally the end of the branch flared up. I used it to light a second branch, which I passed on to Lakshmana. In the flicker of firelight, the woods were otherworldly. I took every step as carefully as possible, trying not to make any noise.

A clearing appeared ahead of us.

"Come, child," came a whisper. Lakshmana whirled around, and I grabbed his shoulder to steady him. "Come forward," the voice said. "There is no need to be afraid."

I was, naturally, very afraid. But the god—for that is who it must have been, for who else could spin into being entire forests that did not exist in the Binding Plane?—already had the measure of us. So I lifted my chin and strode into the clearing.

A man stood before us, petting the head of a magnificent pure-white wolf. He stopped the motion, and the wolf gave another low whine. The man shook his head, and the wolf trotted away into the forest. I looked more closely at the man and realized he was hardly a man at all. What had looked at first like gray robes actually appeared to be his skin, pale and marbled. His dark hair looked more like pine needles the longer I stared. Something cool and wet stung my face, and I glanced up to see fat snowflakes drifting down toward the clearing.

I knew who this was.

"Very good." The god smiled, revealing wolfish teeth. "It is not often mortals can find me."

"Shishir," I said.

"*Lord* Shishir," he corrected, and I bit back on a triumphant smile. My childhood obsession with the gods was good for something after all. "God of the winter and the changing seasons," he continued, taking a few steps toward us.

Next to me, Lakshmana dropped to his knees, the sword falling from his fingers. "Get up," I hissed.

The god gave a laugh. "That is no way to treat a god, is it? Kneel, for you are a mortal woman."

I knew I should. But that feeling of wrongness remained thrumming through me. It kept me on my feet. "Why should I kneel?" I asked instead.

Lakshmana twisted to look at me, horror on his face.

Lord Shishir studied me. "I know who you are," he said after a moment. "Kaikeyi. You pervert the will of the gods at every turn. Your insubordination does not surprise me, but you must know there are consequences."

The snow fell more quickly now, and I clenched my jaw to stop my teeth from chattering. Somehow my branch was still lit, but I knew it could not last for long. "Why are you here?" I gritted out. "What is this place?"

He smiled again, that wolf's smile. "I was on my way to see you."

The ice that gripped my spine had nothing to do with the cold. "To see me?" I repeated.

"In Ayodhya."

"Ayodhya?" Lakshmana mumbled through blue lips. "Why are you going to Ayodhya?"

Lord Shishir strolled toward us, and I held out the lit branch in warning. He made a motion toward it, and a gust of wind rattled across the clearing, but the flame did not go out. "We have been summoned," he said. "For too long you have tried to bend nature. You cannot continue."

Then, in a motion too swift for me to meet, he leapt toward Lakshmana and pressed a hand to his forehead.

I lunged forward, driving the burning branch into the god. He fell back, just as Lakshmana rose and turned toward me.

"That's right, boy," Shishir said, and without warning Lakshmana shoved me hard. His eyes were an unnatural blue. I fell back, hands scraping against the frigid ground as my makeshift torch rolled away from me. Still the fire did not go out.

"End it," Shishir commanded.

Lakshmana hesitated for a moment, the blue of his eyes flickering. I stumbled to my feet, thanking my luck that he had dropped his sword earlier. It took me a moment to enter the Binding Plane, but then the dark clearing was replaced by stark blankness. Lakshmana lurched toward me, the thin blue cord that connected him to Rama—to divine power, I realized— pulling him forward.

I reached into the depths of my strength, of the power inside me I still did not fully understand, and envisioned breaking the bond.

Lakshmana staggered. With a cry, I shoved again, imagining not just a simple unraveling but total obliteration.

The bond shattered and Lakshmana fell. Sharp shards of sickly blue swirled in the cold air before dissipating like so much mist.

"No!" cried Shishir's voice, and I returned to the god's forest.

"Ma?" Lakshmana asked, his voice shaking. He tried to stand but could not rise.

"Stay back," I told him, and he obeyed, a measure of just how shaken he was. Shishir advanced toward me, and I scrambled to pick up my branch. The flame had burned through half of it, but it was all I had. "What do you want?" I snarled.

"It is not a matter of what I want," he told me, even as a shard of ice crystallized in his hand. "Even if you prevail against me, a reckoning will come for your precious city."

The shard flew toward me. I swung the branch, somehow managing to strike it with the flame, and it splintered and fell.

"Who comes to Ayodhya?" I demanded, backing away from him toward the trees at the edge of the clearing.

Shishir stalked forward, and the wind whipped snow in my eyes, ice stinging my skin. "You already know, or you would not be here."

I had no idea what he meant, but I had reached my destination. I pressed the flaming branch against the trunk of the nearest tree, and as it caught, Shishir howled. *How dare you? This is a sacred grove.*

"Why do you want to kill me?" I shouted. The trees were catching one by one, crackling and spitting as the flames spread unusually fast.

"Because you stand in our way," he growled, lunging again. I swung the branch to meet him, and he jumped back.

"Run, Lakshmana," I cried, reaching out for his hand. He took it, and we began to race, stumbling out of the clearing and back toward the road as the flames licked the trees behind us.

I heard Shishir scream, a sound of pure agony—or maybe it was simply the keening of the wind.

By the time we reached our horses, the air was once again warm, and our limbs were damp with sweat. We burst onto the road, panting, and held each other as we watched the fire consume the god's grove. The trees crumbled into ash, the flames dying as they reached the true forest farther down the path. After a few more moments, it was gone. Before us was a charred swathe of land.

You are forsaken, Agni had said. Today those words had been a blessing. The forest and the snow and the wind had been gods-made and so had been powerless to stop the flames lit by my hand.

Lakshmana squeezed my arm, and I turned to look at him. He had the same confused look as he had worn in the forest. "I—I don't..." He trailed off, before groaning in pain, a sound that rattled inside my core. I only just caught his head before it hit the ground.

CHAPTER TWENTY-SIX

I BROUGHT LAKSHMANA TO Sripura, half-crazed with worry, and found a healer.

All I could think about was that I had brought my son into the grove and shattered that bond without a thought for the effect it might have. He might never heal.

It was only after the healer assured me several times that Lakshmana was suffering from a simple fever common to these parts and would be fine with a few days of rest and medicine that I calmed. That I had broken Rama's bond moments before Lakshmana's collapse could not be a coincidence, but I had no better remedy.

As soon as the healer left, I asked the innkeeper to send a message to Dasharath's man, a trader by the name of Hirav, telling him that his cousin was visiting. The innkeeper brought Hirav to my room shortly after—and his grim expression only confirmed my worst fears.

"I have written many missives to Ayodhya," he said immediately. "But I am worried they have not arrived."

"Raja Dasharath received a letter. He sent soldiers. Did they not arrive?"

"No! Did you get my letter about the siege of Janasthana? I fear Sripura may be next."

"A *siege*?" I repeated.

Hirav shuddered. "Yes, my lady. It is a rakshasa and a menagerie of feral, slavering monsters. They have attacked many who dare risk the path to Janasthana. And when last I tried to go, I found my way blocked by a ring of fire, leaping toward the stars. I thought it better to return."

This was far worse than Dasharath and I had imagined. A *rakshasa*? "Why do you fear Sripura is next? Has the rakshasa come here?"

"Not yet. But nothing has arrived from Kosala. No letters, no soldiers, no supplies. It is only a matter of time."

I held my alarm in check, trying to make sense of the mystery before me. How could the rakshasa be on both sides of Sripura?

The realization came to me, absurd, impossible, and yet—it fit. For I had encountered someone on the other side of Sripura who may have barred the way.

But Shishir was a god. It couldn't be. For all my frustrations with the gods, I did not think them evil. The gods would not aid the rakshasas. Would they?

And yet, I already knew the answer. Dread seeped through my limbs as I recalled the story of the churning of the ocean, the one I had loved as a child. Had the gods not long ago joined forces with the asuras because they needed one another to succeed? Shishir had threatened a reckoning. But what had he planned, this god, that would have required the help of a rakshasa?

"I believe the road to Kosala is clear now. We could send a missive to Dasharath. But even if we send a messenger, it will be several moons before soldiers arrive."

Hirav swallowed, looking down at his hands. "It is hard to describe, Radnyi, but I do not think we have that much time.

The whole city is living in fear. And I don't think we can stop this rakshasa alone. If it wants to burn a path to Ayodhya—"

"What does Ayodhya have to do with this?" I asked sharply.

"The rakshasa speaks of conquering the city."

It was my worst fear come true. A common goal. We had laughed, Dasharath and I, at the idea that anyone might reach Ayodhya from here. But a powerful rakshasa with an army could wreak such destruction as to destroy entire kingdoms.

Though Dasharath had asked me not to go, I could not just abandon Janasthana to its fate.

I thanked Hirav for his time, then watched over Lakshmana as he slept fitfully. I tried to compose a letter for Dasharath that would not alarm him when he could do nothing, but would impress the seriousness of the situation. I could not bring myself to mention Lakshmana's illness.

Dasharath—matters in Sripura are worse than feared. I have reason to believe there is a threat to Ayodhya in the forests of Janasthana. Lakshmana and I will take all precautions in looking into the matter, and Hirav will be waiting in a nearby village for us. It would not go amiss to fortify the roads into Ayodhya.

It took three days for Lakshmana to wake, and when he did, he fell out of his bed. The crash startled me from a doze, and I reached for my sword before realizing what had happened.

"Lakshmana!" I moved quickly to his side. "How are you feeling?"

"Tired." Lakshmana pushed himself up onto his elbows. "Thirsty. Hungry."

"Good, good." I helped him back into his bed and then went to the sill to fetch him a cup of boiled water.

"What happened, Ma?" he asked. "I had the strangest dream, about the cold and then a fire."

"It's been a few days since you collapsed. And that wasn't a dream."

He fell back on his pillow. "I had a fever." It was not a question.

"Yes. You did." I brushed my hand against his forehead. It was blessedly cool. "It has broken now. But you need to regain your strength."

"Wait, did you say *days*?" Lakshmana surged forward, and I pushed him back down, until he was fully lying prone. "We need to keep moving. You heard what Lord Shishir said."

"How are you feeling?" I asked again, more firmly.

He closed his eyes. "It is gone now. The presence. The one that Lord Shishir used to control me. I think…I think it was there before we ever met him." Lakshmana hesitated. "Do you think Rama had anything to do with this?" I thought back to how Rama had unconsciously pushed toward my mind. Was it possible that the rest of Ayodhya had these bonds too? I knew for certain only that Sita and I were free from them. And now Lakshmana. But no—Rama would not do something like this.

"I think he loves you dearly, but that he does not know how to control his power or influence," I responded. If doubt lingered in my mind, if part of me was desperate to return to Ayodhya, now was not the time. There was a real threat before us.

"Ma." Lakshmana took a deep breath. "I love Rama. He is my closest brother. But I have held my tongue all my life in his presence because my tongue has been held for me, and until you pointed it out I did not even realize it. Even then my thoughts were all trapped in my head and I was stuck."

"Slowly, go slowly," I said. "Do you mean to tell me that Rama's influence has kept you quiet in his presence? Literally quiet?"

"Yes." He took another deep, shuddering breath. "I feel like a different person now. There is no other way to describe it."

"If you could have spoken freely in our first conversation,

what would you have said?" I asked, struggling still to understand this new truth.

"I know that I am more intelligent than Rama, although he is far more skilled in the war arts. And I know that Rama's influence is the only reason our tutors think he is perfect. He cares too much about what others will think of him, or what others are saying about him. I think that is why he argues sometimes with Sita. And it is why he holds you at a distance—because he knows you think him foolish for it."

I sat down on the edge of Lakshmana's bed. "He holds me at a distance?" I asked at last.

Lakshmana squinted at me. "I thought you knew."

"I don't understand. Why would he do that? How do you know this?" The desperation poured out of me without warning, and I had to stop myself from alarming Lakshmana further.

"See? Rama has even gotten to you." Lakshmana sat up again and placed a hand on my shoulder. "You are his mother and you have done a great deal for the kingdom. But at the ashram, he asked Sage Vamadeva many questions I hardly knew Rama had. The sage said he thinks it shameful for women to be out in the open, believes that women are weak and foolish and will ruin Kosala. And Rama cares very much about what Sage Vamadeva has to say, and the opinions of those the sage introduced to Rama while we were there. They do not like you, which leaves Rama most conflicted."

"When did you learn so much about this?" I whispered.

"Those two years we were on our own were illuminating. Rama has always been kind to me, and he is my brother. In some ways, he is very wise. I do not want you to think I hate him or find only fault with him. But even the people we love can be flawed, no?"

"Yes," I said, voice thick with unshed tears. Lakshmana lay back down and I took the opportunity to dash a hand across my eyes. I had missed everything important about my sons.

"He is not ready to be king," Lakshmana said. He paused to gauge my reaction, and I motioned for him to continue. "Not yet. He will be a great ruler only for some. He is good to me and Bharata and Shatrugna, and to even the lowest of manservants. He listens to their opinions, respects them, and he will do great things for the men of the kingdom. His rule will be excellent for many people."

"But not all of them," I finished. And then we both fell silent.

Of all the rumors I have heard about me, the ones involving Lakshmana are some of the most laughable. Many people seem to believe our journey together was the time when he recognized my wickedness and realized he needed to protect Rama from my evil. But it is perhaps the least true out of all the varied theories, because by the end of our trip, Lakshmana found me quite fragile and in need of protection.

By the following day, he had recovered much of his energy. I gave the letter I had written to Hirav, with instructions to send it as quickly as possible and then ride hard for Bhojakata, and then we departed.

Over the course of our journey, I came to one conclusion: Rama could not take the throne until he became more secure in his bearing, able to sort through the clamor around him. I worried in particular about the two years he had spent learning under Sage Vamadeva. How long would it take to undo? But that problem was not insurmountable. After all, Rama wanted to please those around him. There was nothing strange about that. Hadn't I wanted to do the same? I had grown out of it in time and realized I could not stand to allow others to suffer when it was in my power to help. Rama would see that too, and learn the difference between whims and needs.

The forests grew darker as we approached Janasthana, the sounds of birds more haunting than melodic, and the nights a little blacker, with fewer stars scattered across the skies.

After our adventure in Shishir's grove, we were far more careful. Our conversations grew quieter and less frequent as we contemplated our surroundings with a wary eye. We alternated sleeping, so that someone could always keep watch on the encroaching shadows.

On the final day of our journey, we were exhausted to our bones. When it was my turn to sleep, I passed into unconsciousness in a blink.

I awoke to a brightness behind my lids. For a moment, I thought it was simply daylight, and that I had woken naturally.

But as I opened my eyes, a bright flame burned itself into my vision. I pushed myself to my feet, blinking rapidly as the image before me clarified itself into a man holding a burning branch toward me, just as I had done to Shishir not so long ago.

No, not a man.

The lips of his bull head pulled back into a grotesque smile. "You do not look like a trader, woman."

"Who are you?" I demanded. Over his shoulder, I saw Lakshmana slumped against a rock, almost unnaturally still, chest moving in shallow motions. "Lakshmana!" I shouted, but he did not stir. "What have you done to my son?"

"You must be Radnyi Kaikeyi," he said, stepping closer. Behind me stretched the dark forest, no safer than what lay before me. I stood my ground.

"How do you know who I am?"

"I have been waiting for you."

A sharp prick of fear slipped down my spine. Shishir had been waiting for me too. "Who are you?"

He extended the burning branch, and I watched the flames lick up his hand but leave no mark. My blood ran cold. I had thought him a rakshasa, a fearsome monster indeed, but such powers seemed beyond a mere rakshasa's control. My mind rapidly sorted through all the information I had heard about the demonic presence that plagued Janasthana. He commanded an army. He commanded real magic.

This was no mere rakshasa—this was an asura. A being whose powers rivaled those of the gods, who fought the gods for control. I was about to die.

"Pity," said the asura, tilting his head and blinking slowly at me. "I thought you might know."

I stumbled back under the canopy of trees and he followed, letting his weapon drop casually to the ground. The brush lit up immediately, and the fire snaked its way toward me faster than I could move.

I glanced around for water, for damp earth, for anything to save me. The flames circled around me, and I coughed once, twice, struggling to stay on my feet. I was dimly aware of the hem of my dhoti catching, and I beat uselessly at it with my hands. Hysterical panic built up in my throat.

"Goodbye, Radnyi—"

His voice cut off with a gurgle. I looked up to find a sword protruding from the asura's chest.

"Ma!" Lakshmana shouted. A moment later, he came barreling through the circle of flames, a cloth wrapped around his mouth. He lifted me up and rushed back through, dropping me before falling to his knees. I rolled for a moment on the ground, trying to catch my breath as waves of agony suffused my burned skin.

After a moment, I managed to turn my head. The fire was dying down. Lakshmana was standing above a pool of orange blood. The body of the asura was gone.

"What happened?" he asked, coughing.

"I don't know," I gasped out. Lakshmana helped me to my feet, and I limped toward our camp at the edge of the road, now a hundred paces away. I did not remember traveling so far into the forest.

Lakshmana sat me down and brought me water, lifting it to my mouth as though I were a child.

"The—rakshasa, he woke me up." There was no point in scaring Lakshmana further with my guess as to its true nature. "He had put you to sleep, I think. He said he had been waiting for me."

Lakshmana understood remarkably quickly. "It was a trap?"

I nodded. "We must make haste for Janasthana."

"If it was a trap, does he not want us to go there? Should we not turn around?"

"I do not believe we could outrun him in the other direction." My throat hurt fiercely, each word the thorn of a rose.

"Can you ride?" Lakshmana was already saddling our horses.

"What other choice do I have?"

I slipped in and out of a haze of pain until we reached the city. The midday sun beat against my wounds with a throbbing ferocity. The gate was closed and barred, but at our cry, a guard immediately appeared.

"What is your business here?" he demanded.

Lakshmana looked at me. "I'm here to visit my mother," I said, my voice a raspy whisper. "This is my son, her grandson."

The sun was at the guard's back, so I could not tell what he was doing. After a moment, he disappeared. Another guard, or perhaps the same one, emerged from the bottom of the watchtower moments later.

"Who is your mother?"

"Kekaya," I answered. My mouth was painfully dry. I coughed and fumbled for my waterskin, lifting it to my lips with shaking hands.

The guard studied me while I drank. "You saw it, did you not?"

"Yes," I whispered.

"We cannot offer you protection. But you may enter for now," the guard said, gesturing us forward as the gate opened. "Devi Kekaya lives in the Noble Quarter, by the palace. Ask a guard to point out her dwelling."

He beckoned me close. "If you venture anywhere else in the city, we will know," he said, and then slapped the back of my horse, sending me jerking ahead.

"What was that?" Lakshmana demanded as soon as we were out of earshot. "Does your mother really live here?"

I gave a sharp nod, hoping to forestall further questioning.

The streets around us were swept clean. Low, squat mud-and-straw dwellings lined the roads, the structures reflecting away some of the southern heat. There were few people outside, and those who we saw seemed wary, hurrying about their business. As we got closer to the city center, the Noble Quarter came into view. The dwellings sprawled out, with graceful arches of stone and brick, small gardens, and groves of mango trees.

But I could not appreciate the sight, for every moment I remained on my horse felt interminable. When I dismounted, stiff as though I had been sitting for days, pain coursed through me. I stumbled. Lakshmana hurried to my side and held my elbow carefully as we walked toward the guard posted on the corner.

"I am looking for Kekaya," I whispered.

The guard pointed to one of the dwellings. "You can find her there."

Lakshmana and I walked slowly. With every step, my burns throbbed, and my head pounded.

"Ma?" Lakshmana asked. "Would you like me to carry you?" I shook my head, and he seemed to understand. "I am sure she will be happy to see you, after so long a time."

"Yes," I said, for I could not manage more words.

A man stepped forward from the gatehouse, dressed in a

stiffly pressed white tunic. My mother had done well for herself. "What is your business?"

"I am here to see Kekaya," I said, groping blindly for the mix of haughty and kind that usually served me so well. I failed utterly, my words slurring together as though I had imbibed too much wine.

"*Minister* Kekaya," he corrected, turning up his nose. "Many people come to see her. Her time is both precious and limited."

I snorted before I could stop myself. "Well, that's nothing new," I muttered under my breath.

"Excuse me?"

"I'm her daughter," I said, enunciating more clearly.

The man looked me up and down. "That you are not."

"Excuse me?"

"You are most certainly not Devi Meena." He looked past me. "Ah, Minister, my apologies."

I turned in a jerky movement. There before me was my mother.

It reminded me of entering the Binding Plane, a veil of age overlaying a face I recognized well. Her hair had grayed and thinned slightly, but her uplifted chin and steely eyes had not changed.

She was dressed ornately, in a style unfamiliar to me, with a robe of deep blue, richly embroidered with silver flowers, elegantly draped over her white and silver silk sari. I felt like a child again, scruffy, unimpressive, intimidated by her cool grace. I opened my mouth to say something, anything, and only a pitiful croak came out.

"This woman came here asking to see you, Minister. She claimed she was your daughter. I was about to send her away." My mother lifted a hand, a gesture so familiar to me that my throat ached. The man stopped talking at once.

"Kaikeyi?" she whispered. I pressed my lips together and managed a shaky bob of the head.

Her face crumpled, and in that moment, she was transformed from the mother I had known into the mother I had wished for. She looked confused, bereft, loving. I used to pray she would show any one of those emotions to me, and now I had all of them and I simply wanted to cry. She reached toward me with weathered hands and I flinched away. The world spun, arms caught me, and that was the last thing I knew.

CHAPTER TWENTY-SEVEN

MY BONES ACHED. I blinked against heavy eyelids to find an unfamiliar room. But my hands and throat felt pleasantly cool.

"Kaikeyi? Kaikeyi! You're awake." And there was my mother again, looking over me as I lay in bed. I had to choke back a wild laugh at this wonder.

"How long?" I asked instead. It no longer hurt to talk.

"A full day has passed."

"And you ... have been here?"

I watched my mother's face flit through several emotions as though she was picking a story, and I entered the Binding Plane. A slender chain of purple connected us. "I just sent your son away to bathe," she said truthfully. "A healer has attended to your burns, and they are much better already. Lakshmana explained how you came to have them. We have gotten very skilled at treating such injuries here."

I had so many questions. "How did you recognize me?"

My mother's eyebrows arched in surprise. "You are my daughter."

"You barely looked at me as a child. How can you recognize

me as an adult?" I asked. I hated that my voice sounded young, a petulant whine.

"I have seen a painting of you," she said, leaning forward to brush my hair from my face. "I know I was not a good mother to you and your brothers. I was unhappy at court, and you deserved better. But it broke my heart when I realized I would never see you again."

There was a lump in my throat, blocking my words. And anyway, what was there to say? She had done what she had done, and neither of us could go back.

Her expression fell slightly at my silence, but her fingers continued to card through my hair. "I am very happy to see you," she said. "But I know you did not simply come to visit. Would you like to tell me why you are here?"

The question was a relief, allowing me to push aside emotion in favor of business. "I am here to speak to the governor of Janasthana," I improvised. "Our traders have complained of various harassments, and we wished to come to an agreement about dealing with those threats. I volunteered."

"A party of two?" She pursed her lips.

"It is a long journey. I did not wish to take others from their homes unnecessarily. And I did not realize the severity of the problems when we left. Clearly."

She crossed her arms, radiating skepticism. "As you say. Well, it will be difficult for you to speak with the governor."

"Why is that?" I asked, pushing myself upright.

"He won't be arriving from Lanka for another week."

"Lanka?" I asked, completely bewildered. Surely she could not be referring to—

"Ravana is the governor of Janasthana," my mother said with a tight smile.

"When did he become governor?" This news had not reached Ayodhya.

"Not long ago. He was on his way here when he heard tell

of the evil lurking in our forest. Raja Danda and his son were killed in a fire shortly before his arrival, and we were trapped in the city, besieged by all manner of foul creatures. His soldiers helped drive them away and build a wall, and he decided to stay. To protect us."

The magnitude of our ignorance in Ayodhya astounded me. Shishir had truly duped us. But I still did not understand *why* the asura had tried to take a city, or set his sights on Ayodhya. "And how will Ravana return so quickly?" I asked. The journey from Lanka to Janasthana took moons, not weeks.

"He has a flying chariot," my mother said. "It sounds fantastical, but the man is nothing if not brilliant, and he has somehow managed it."

"I knew he would." I couldn't help but smile slightly. He had needed inspiration when we last talked about it, a lifetime ago. Perhaps his grief had fueled him toward this greatness.

We sat in silence for a moment. "Stay with us until he returns. I insist." My mother took my hand in hers, and I marveled at my near-healed skin. "I have a husband, and a daughter and son."

So, she had replaced Yudhajit and me. My other brothers had not been as old, or as affected by her departure, but we had struggled in her absence. I remembered Manthara's admonishment that my mother had no choice in the matter, that she could not have come back to us. But this news hurt much more deeply than logic could repair.

I pulled my hand away, and my mother added, "They would love to meet you. Of course they have heard of you."

"Of me?" I asked.

"Tales of your work in Ayodhya have reached us. You are greatly admired here. My daughter Meena looks up to you." She spoke earnestly, happily, words that cut sharp as knives. The could-have-beens and what-ifs swelled up inside me.

"I am very proud of everything you have accomplished. You have become an incredible woman, despite me. I never thought I would see you again." Her voice shook. "I have not stopped thanking the gods since you appeared. They granted me a wish I did not deserve."

The gods had nothing to do with this. I swallowed. "I am thankful to see you again as well, Ma."

She gave me a small smile and took my hand again. I let her.

Then Lakshmana came rushing into the room, and the moment was broken.

I have had ample time to turn those weeks with my mother over and over in my head. The temptation to put some of the fault on my mother for the debacle of my life has remained strong over the years, but the chain of responsibility has to stop somewhere.

Besides, though I could not help but search for it, I never found an instance of devious behavior from my mother during our time together. She had remade herself remarkably well, away from the shadow of my father. She put me in a room overlooking her gardens, with a window made out of glass instead of paper. I had never fathomed such a thing before—up north, glass was fashioned into beads and trinkets, but never such large, clear panels.

"Ravana's invention," she told me when I stopped to marvel at it. "He has put his mind to advancement. The salve used to soothe your burns is also of his invention—he has devoted much time to the study of healing."

I pressed my face up against the window, hardly believing that I could see right through it. Our paper windows back home let in light—but this was something else entirely.

"You know him," my mother said. She did not phrase it like a question.

I turned to face her. "Yes. Our paths have crossed on several occasions."

The corners of her mouth turned up, but tears pooled in her eyes. "He gave me the first news I had of you in years. A precious gift. He told me you were strong and smart and determined." A teardrop rolled down her face.

"When was this?" I asked. After our last meeting, I could imagine him saying nothing of the sort.

"Seven or eight years ago, it must have been. He passed through Janasthana on his return from a pilgrimage. He lost his daughter, you know, and I had lost a daughter in a way, and we were able to speak openly to each other. He said if his daughter were still alive, he would be hungry for any word of her, so he was happy to do that for me."

I hardly knew how to take her words. Had Ravana been spying on me for my mother that first trip? And yet, he had not even mentioned her to me—a cruelty I thought him incapable of.

The question must have been evident on my face, for my mother said immediately, "He did not know when he met you that you were my daughter. I had not told anyone outside of my family—my family here, that is—of my past, or that my daughter was a radnyi of Ayodhya. But when he came here, he guessed that you were my blood. He said there was a strong resemblance."

I looked at my mother and then down at myself. My mother was taller than I was, with a full figure and clear bronze eyes. I was of middling height, broad-shouldered but flat-chested, with eyes that were often described as obsidian.

My mother laughed. "A resemblance in *personality*."

As she spoke, she reached out a hand to cup my face. I instinctively shied away from the touch, then took a deep breath and allowed it. She caressed my cheek.

"I know I have said this already, but I am so very proud of

you. You have exceeded my wildest dreams for you. Even Ravana has been influenced by you."

I made a skeptical sound.

"I mean it. He said he was inspired by your example and wished to include women on his own Mantri Parishad. That is how I became Minister of Finance."

"I did not know that," I admitted. It was certainly meaningful that Ravana would place her not only on the Mantri Parishad, but within his inner council.

"I am sure he will be glad to see you again," she said, patting my cheek.

After scrubbing the dust of the road and battle from my skin, I went looking for Lakshmana. I did not search long. He was lying on his bed, dressed in a cream-colored dhoti embellished with navy embroidery that reminded me of my mother's robes. Perhaps it was a family color. Despite the unfamiliar attire, though, Lakshmana looked relaxed and comfortable.

"Enjoying yourself?" I asked, tousling his hair.

"Very much." He rolled out of reach and onto the floor. This seemed hilariously funny to me, and I sat on the edge of his bed, laughing until I gasped for breath.

His head peeked out over the top of the bed. "Ma, are you all right? Have you hurt yourself again?"

I put my hands on my knees and took a few deep breaths. "No, no, I'm fine. I am just very happy to see you."

"Are you sure? We don't have to go to dinner. I could have a relapse of fever, and you could stay here with me."

"What? Why would you say that?"

"This must be difficult for you. All of this, all so sudden." He came around to me and rested his head in my lap. My eyes burned, happy yet wistful. "If it makes you sad, we don't have to go."

I stroked his hair. "It does make me sad. But being here also makes me happy. I will take the good with the bad."

We sat for a few moments longer, watching the sun descend as I massaged his scalp just as Manthara used to do for me.

When he got to his feet, he offered me his arm. "I know you don't want to worry your mother about your own health, but I meant what I said. I can have a relapse of fever whenever you need me to."

"My little boy, protecting me!" I pressed a hand to my heart, then pretended to wipe tears from my eyes, and he grinned.

But the sincerity of Lakshmana's words comforted me, and as we walked toward the hall, I felt none of the dread that had consumed me as we first approached the house.

A servant directed us toward a side room, and just as we were about to enter, a young woman appeared.

"Radnyi Kaikeyi!" She pressed her hands together and dropped into a bow, before throwing her arms around me.

Unsure how to respond, I released Lakshmana's arm and awkwardly patted her back.

"I'm...so sorry, I am afraid I don't know who you are," I said, pitching my voice low so as not to embarrass her.

She released me and held me at arm's length, eyes traveling up and down my face. "I'm Meena, your sister. Well, half sister. It's an honor to meet you."

"Meena, let her breathe." My mother emerged from the dining room.

"It is nice to meet you," I offered after a moment. "Forgive my confusion."

"I suppose this is all very new for you," Meena said. An understatement, to be sure. Lakshmana stepped up behind me, and her eyes lit up. She began chattering to him, quickly forgetting me.

My mother smiled kindly. "Meena is very enthusiastic, but

she means well. She has a promising career ahead of her in healing."

"Healing? Really?" She was the exact opposite of the stolid healers I knew. Even quiet Ashvin was a bit too exuberant for the mold. And of course, she was a woman.

My mother nodded. "She has a great talent for the discipline. She and Lakshmana have been talking of it."

Sure enough, a glance over at the pair showed Meena miming what must have been some sort of bandaging technique as Lakshmana looked on with a serious expression.

"Ashvin is an excellent healer," I said. I had not yet decided if my mother deserved to know about my brothers, but this small morsel was a kindness in return for hospitality.

Her face lit up. "Is he? That's wonderful."

"Yes. He had a painful illness as a child that made other pursuits difficult for him, so I arranged to have him apprenticed with the court healers," I explained, watching as grief shaded her initial joy.

"Is he still in pain?" she asked. The vindictive part of me wanted to respond, *Would you care?*

But Manthara had counseled compassion when we spoke of my mother all those years ago, and her advice had not led me astray yet.

"No. He eventually recovered. He is the tallest of all—my brothers now." Somehow, the words *your sons* would not move past my throat.

"That is good. Good." She gestured me through an archway and indicated we should sit on the array of cushions placed on the ground. "And how is Yudhajit?"

"Fine," I said. "He rules Kekaya now."

Her face was inscrutable. "Ashwapati is dead?" she asked.

"He is alive. But he passed the throne to my brother and went away to the mountains. I have not seen him in seventeen years."

Lakshmana and Meena came to join us, and the food was laid out on a low table.

"My husband and my son are traveling to Matanga for business. But do not let his absence fool you. He is a far better husband than Ashwapati ever was."

"That is a low standard to hold a husband to," I said.

My mother paused in the midst of a bite, straightening up to give me a shocked look.

"Did someone tell you what happened?"

"Manthara told me that Father sent you away. She defended you, when I grew angry with your abandonment."

My mother's cheeks flushed. "I would like to tell you my side of it. If you wish to hear it."

We were speaking quietly, and Meena and Lakshmana were still absorbed in their own conversation. I had no desire for my son to hear about this sordid affair, but I could not say honestly that I would be upset if he heard. My burning curiosity was too strong. I had convinced myself over the years that I did not need to know exactly what had happened, or that I already knew the truth of it, but now, given the opportunity—I needed to know.

"Your father…never liked me," she began, a bit haltingly. "Our marriage was arranged when I was born, and I became his bride at sixteen. I had you and Yudhajit only a year later. Ashwapati was ten years older than I was and found me at the same time frivolous and withholding. He looked down on me."

I could not help but nod. I had been enormously lucky to have Dasharath as my partner, but I could still understand well the loneliness she was describing.

"We had eight children—seven pregnancies in all for me. He did not like me, but neither did he hate me. We remained indifferent to each other, each managing our own spheres. And then I became pregnant for the eighth time, and I lost the child soon after. Such things happen. I had been extraordinarily lucky to have seven healthy pregnancies. But he did not think so. I still do not know how he got the notion in his head, but he became convinced that I had been unfaithful to him, and then purposely lost the baby in order to hide it."

"*What?*" I interrupted her. "Why would he think that?"

"Because around that time, a childhood friend had arrived at court and we spent a great deal of time together. I enjoyed hearing stories from home, and I suppose I must have seemed more open around him, happier. Ashwapati had not allowed me to visit my ancestral palace or my parents, and so I sought to spend as much time with this man as possible. But there was nothing between us.

"After the death of the baby, Ashwapati became consumed by jealousy. He sent the man away from court. One day, he told me to walk with him in the gardens. He had shown no interest in my company for many weeks, but I thought at last we were putting this behind us. He instructed me to sit beside him near the stream where the swans would play.

"All of a sudden, as he was gazing at me, he burst into laughter. I thought perhaps he had thought of an interesting anecdote to tell me, or that there was something humorous about my appearance. He had kept his eyes on me the whole time, so I had no reason to believe..." She shook herself and looked up at me. "It must seem so stupid to you, that I am trying to justify myself, when he was the one who erred."

Her story had won some sympathy from me. "Not at all."

"So I asked him, 'Why do you laugh?' and he jumped to his feet and towered over me. I could see the real rage that he had been hiding, and I was very, very afraid. 'I was right! You are trying to kill me!' he shouted. I immediately fell to my knees at his feet and said, 'I do not know of what you speak. Please, forgive me. I am sorry.'

"I said this over and over again, pleading with him as he

seethed, until he grabbed me by the wrist and pulled me to my feet. 'You will be exiled for this,' he said. 'I will not kill you only because you are the mother of my children. If only you would extend the same courtesy to me.' I began crying out of sheer bewilderment and the vain hope that my tears might move him. They did not, but he spoke again. 'You know if I ever disclose what I hear, I will die. Did you think you could trick me?'

"And finally, I understood. He had trapped me. He was so convinced that I was evil, scheming against him, that he gave me an impossible test just to convince himself he was right. I will never know if he was looking for a reason to exile me, or if this really was some twisted 'proof.' But he wanted me gone, and no amount of pleading or begging or promising would change his mind. So, I left."

I had never liked my father, but hearing of his explicit maliciousness disturbed me deeply. I put down the bite I held in my hand, nauseated.

"I thought about all of you every day," she added. "But I knew he would take care of you. My staying would have only stained you by proximity."

"I am so sorry," I said at last. For what else could I say? There had been no other option for my mother, as I well knew. She had been without support in my father's court, without friends to rely on. How lonely that must have been.

"Why would you be sorry?" My mother folded her hands and looked right at me. "None of this was your fault, or Yudhajit's, or the rest of your brothers'. Do you understand? The fault is with your father for sending me away and myself for not fighting for you. I have learned my lesson, and the gods have brought you back to me."

"Yes, they have." I pushed my plate away from me, signaling to the servants that I was done.

My mother ran her hand over my shoulder and down my

arm to my hand. To say I did not enjoy it would have been a lie, but I felt ashamed of my enjoyment all the same. In a strange way, it felt like a betrayal of Manthara, who had filled my mother's role all these years.

"Thank you," my mother whispered. "Thank you for coming here. Thank you for listening to my story. That is all I have wished for these past years. For my children to listen, and to understand."

CHAPTER
TWENTY-EIGHT

RAVANA ARRIVED IN THE city without pomp or ceremony, and we presented ourselves to him the next day. We had
no time to waste on formal invitations.

"Kaikeyi, it is good to see you," he said, bowing his head.
"I hoped you would come. I wish to apologize for my behavior
when last we met."

"It is I who should apologize. I should not have invaded
your rooms in that way."

"You acted as a friend should, and I turned on you. That was
inappropriate. Please, let us not argue anymore." He indicated
a divan set before an open glass window overlooking a verdant
garden. "Sit. We have more pressing matters to discuss."

"The asura." I had ventured through the city the day before
and heard the whispers of Janasthana's people. They spoke of
swarms of imps, unnatural and vicious animals. They spoke of
fields burned overnight. The women spoke of a demonic presence that invaded their minds even inside the city, insidious
and whispering. It was like tales of the asuras of long ago, who
scorched the earth with their campaigns against the gods.

"So you believe him an asura too. The truth is, we know

very little. When I was traveling to the swayamvara, I stopped in Janasthana, for I was curious about the city. I have long admired the people of this area and thought to meet with the king and convince him we might achieve greatness together. But instead, the residents were fearful, talking of bad omens and portents, and Raja Danda was refusing all visitors.

"I passed through the city again on my return, hoping its fortunes might have changed. But when I arrived, I found the city under siege. Creatures made of flame and snarling wolves were terrorizing the people. Commanding them was an asura with the head of a bull and fire running over his limbs. I had soldiers with me, soldiers who were not tired out by days of fighting, and they were able to cut their way through the hordes. They built the walls while I met with the city's leaders. I felt I had a duty to help them. I asked if they wished for my protection."

"But what does an asura want with a city?" Asuras were the enemies of the gods. They rarely bothered themselves with human constructions, with mortal concerns.

Ravana looked away. "You will not like it—but he wishes to go to Ayodhya. I have to believe it is because he wishes to challenge Rama. In that, at least, I might sympathize."

He spoke softly, placatingly, but it did not dull the offense of his words. "What do you have against Rama?" I asked sharply. "Are you still upset about the swayamvara?"

"No, not at—"

I rose to my feet, annoyed at the whims of men. "Then explain why I should not take my son and leave. I thought you were better than this."

"Your son came with you?" he asked. "Which son?"

I turned toward the door, not bothering to answer.

"Wait, Kaikeyi!" he cried. "Sita is my daughter."

That stilled me. I could not have possibly heard right. "What?"

"Sita. She is my daughter. I did not realize it until I saw her that day, at the swayamvara. If I had known, well—the moment I recognized her, I dropped the bow."

There was truly nothing I could say. I stood there, staring blankly at him, my mind failing to comprehend his words.

"Please," he said. "You have to believe me."

"Your daughter died," I said, my voice cold. It felt as though I were speaking from a distance. How dare he lie to me this way. Was he simply mad? Had the loss of his daughter and then his wife driven him to this outlandish story? "You told me this yourself."

He hung his head. "I thought so too, I swear it. But then I saw her, and—she was unmistakable. She was born with the silver hair, the flower-shaped birthmark."

Slowly, I was starting to come back to myself. I was aware of my heart beat returning to normal. "You could not have seen that from such a distance," I protested.

"You know I am not fully human," he said. "It is a blessing and a curse."

His earnestness was making me believe him—but no. This had to be a falsehood. "You said your daughter died," I repeated.

Ravana tipped his face up toward the window. The light cast strange shadows over his face. "We took her to the gardens because she liked being among the roses. I had taken her out of her carrier so she could better look at everything, and Mandodari called me to observe a strange pattern of birds. Sita could not walk or even crawl, so I laid her on the ground. The moment I did so, an almighty cracking sound issued from the dirt, and the earth split in two. I lunged for her, but she had already fallen in. I tried to throw myself in after her, but Mandodari wrapped her arms around me and pulled me back from the abyss. When I took a step away from the fault, it knit itself back together."

"But you...but...How could such a thing happen?" I whispered.

"We thought it a punishment from the gods," he said dully. "At first, we believed that if we repented fully, they would give her back to us. But then moons passed, and years, and we realized she was gone. No matter what we did, no matter how many pilgrimages I made, the gods would not look favorably on us again."

I slipped into the Binding Plane, though he clearly believed in this story so deeply that our bond would show no evidence of deceit.

On the other hand, evidence existed that Ravana spoke truly. Sita was unmistakable, to be sure, but worse than that, I knew she had been discovered inside the earth itself. Sita had told me she and her father guarded that secret jealously. I did not see how Ravana could have uncovered that.

"Swear it to me, that you speak truly."

"I swear to Lord Shiva that Sita is my daughter. If I lie, may he cut me with a thousand knives and feed me to beasts."

I sank back onto the divan and closed my eyes, trying to force my mind into some semblance of order. For a moment, it had felt like the world was tilting beneath me. "Why are you telling me this now?"

Ravana sighed and passed a hand over his face. "Tell me, did Rama accompany you?" he asked.

"No. Lakshmana made the journey with me."

"Good, good," he said, almost to himself.

"I will not tell Lakshmana—or anyone else—what we have spoken of." Ravana had once given me the gift of secrecy and protection. Now I would repay that debt.

He leaned forward and clasped my hand. "Thank you, Kaikeyi. I knew I could trust you. But there is something I must know. Is it true that Rama mistreats Sita?"

That was the second time he had dismissed Rama's character.

I tried not to be too angry. "Of course not. Where did you hear such a thing?"

"I hope you will not be offended if I say I have a few people in Ayodhya's court keeping watch over Sita. But I cannot fully trust their accounts. After all, they are biased enough against Ayodhya to be willing to serve as spies."

"Their marriage is young," I said, giving him a diplomatic smile, even though the thought of spies in my palace unsettled me. "And so are they. She is not always happy, but it is not mistreatment, it is poor communication. They care for each other and are learning to be married. And he is yuvraja, not some asura. If you are worried for her, know that she trusts me, and she will come to me if she ever has real concerns. If need be, I will protect her, as I protect any and all women of my city."

Ravana got to his feet and paced before me. "Your son is more than he seems. I saw that too, at the swayamvara. This asura—he wishes to burn a path to Ayodhya to prove his dominance. I am sure it is because of your son." It sounded absurd, and yet—gods were reborn into this world in order to rid it of evil, and the gods and the asuras were eternal enemies. "I went back to Lanka to see if I could find anything more about this asura. I thought surely there would be something in Lanka's great library. But I found nothing."

"And I'm assuming Janasthana's library was destroyed in the fire?" I asked.

Ravana looked up at me, startled. "No, they keep their books in cellars, and we rebuilt over them."

"This asura is from their forest. Why wouldn't—"

"Stupidity," Ravana said immediately, rising to his feet. "Sheer stupidity."

Of all things, that was easily forgiven.

I went home to collect Lakshmana, for his memory would be of great aid in this task. It turned out Raja Danda had an extensive collection of scrolls and no particular method of organizing them.

On the fourth day of our searching, I found Lakshmana, usually very industrious, sound asleep against a shelf. I shook him several times, but he would not wake. Just when I was beginning to fear some illness had taken him, his eyes snapped open.

"I know where it is, Ma."

"What?" I reached for his forehead, but he ducked under my arm and moved briskly toward the farthest end of the chamber, weaving in and out of the labyrinth of papers. He paused near a hanging shelf, then began shuffling through the scrolls there. He was working through the mess with great determination, so I decided to let him be.

At last he offered me a thin, rather unremarkable-looking scroll. My eye immediately caught on an illustration halfway down the page.

It was the asura from the forest.

"How did you find this?" I demanded.

Lakshmana shrugged. "I dreamed of it, of this shelf and scroll. When I woke, I knew where it would be."

I set aside that odd proclamation for a moment to read. The scroll was dated more than a hundred years prior and spoke of an asura called Bhandasura, born of a forest fire that had nearly razed Janasthana to the ground.

I realized, with mounting dread, that the story had uncanny parallels with what what was occurring here and now. At first, people in the city had dismissed the stories of women as mere nightmares. And had I not done just the same, when the trader had told me her tale? The city's old council had heard the claims that strange beings walked the forest, but when nothing more came of it, they took no action.

It was only when the fires began that people took note. Women would wake up in their own beds, covered in agonizing burns, and describe a demon with the head of a bull and the body of a man, who had kidnapped them. Not all survived.

Now deeply afraid, the people of the city prayed to the gods. But the gods did not come to their aid. Instead, the gods told them the asura was not as powerful as his more ancient counterparts, and a mortal could bring him low—a spearman was fated to strike him down.

So the soldiers of the city armed themselves with spears and marched on the asura. Only five returned.

I could not imagine such devastation, an army breaking against a single being. Was this the fate awaiting Janasthana? Awaiting Ayodhya?

The destruction continued for years, until at last, one of the holy men of Janasthana completed several acts of penance to Sarasvati and was granted a boon. He asked for her to defeat the asura, but the goddess could not kill an asura on earth in her immortal form. Instead, she trapped him in the deepest recesses of the forest, where nobody dared venture for years until a sage became lost and came upon Bhandasura. The asura let him live in exchange for writing down his legend.

"If he was confined to a grove, how has he broken free?" Lakshmana asked, reading over my shoulder.

"I don't know. And I'm not sure how this helps us either. If an army could not defeat him, what can we do?" I scanned the paper again, then shook my head, confused. "We should show this to Ravana. Can you go and ask a messenger to fetch him?"

But when Ravana arrived, he read the scroll and gave a slow smile. "I think it's obvious, then, isn't it?"

"What is?"

"Why he hates women traversing his forest so much."

"Because of Sarasvati?" Lakshmana asked.

"No, because he fears his mortality."

"What is that to do with the traders? Any spearman can kill him," I reminded him.

Ravana looked puzzled for a moment before understanding smoothed his features. "Not quite. This dialect is unfamiliar to you."

In my heart I knew, before he said the words.

"It does not say spearman. Bhandasura can only be slain by a spear*woman*."

CHAPTER
TWENTY-NINE

WE DECIDED TO ENTER the forest at noon, so the asura would have trouble hiding in the dark. As soon as we stepped outside the gate, I regretted it. The sun's heat was scalding, and sweat dripped down my back. We had wrapped our faces in scarves so that he could not recognize us, and I struggled to breathe through the fabric.

In a way, though, I was glad to focus for a moment on minor discomforts. It distracted me from the bone-crushing fear that filled me with every step. When Dasharath and I had fought Sambarasura, I had been frightened, but there was a sharp difference between mortal and immortal danger. How could we be so arrogant as to think that we would succeed where whole armies had failed? I thought of my sons, wondered what would become of them if I never returned from this battle. I imagined Lakshmana in particular, waiting in my mother's house, trapped in the city as flames slowly overtook—

"Radnyi Kaikeyi," said Bhandasura, and I screamed as his hand touched my arm.

Never take your eyes off the enemy.

Heat seeped into my shoulder, and I smelled smoke rising from my plain cotton clothing. "Good to see you again." His voice was high and light, as if greeting me in the halls of a palace, not threatening me on a dirt road.

"Bhandasura," I acknowledged, trying to keep my composure.

His red eyes widened, and when he exhaled, smoke poured from his bull's snout. I tried to force the thoughts of what this asura liked to do to women from my head. Instead, I gripped the staff tight, ignoring the burning pain in my shoulder. Ravana had fashioned me a cunning staff with a hidden point, and now I moved my thumb lightly over the catch that released the spear tip.

"Now, none of that," he said, and the spear was suddenly alight in flames.

I screamed at the sudden pain, the spear falling from my slack fingers. My hand was red and raw, already beginning to blister. His grip burned into my shoulder, and I fought to break free, twisting my body this way and that. His dark hand looked almost human, but his hold on me was anything but.

"What do you want?" I asked. My mouth tasted bitter, and I could no longer feel my legs. My heart was a wild beast in my chest, throwing itself against my rib cage as though trying to escape this place. I felt light-headed with fear.

Bhandasura smiled and gestured widely around him, releasing his hold on me. "Everything." I stumbled, colliding with Ravana, who was watching the proceedings as though paralyzed, unable to do anything to help.

A cry stuck in my throat. Without my spear, we were not going to make it out alive.

And yet, I could not accept it. "There is nothing for you in Janasthana," I said, stalling for precious minutes of life.

He snorted, bull-like. "You really do not understand? I had heard you were intelligent."

"You heard I...How have you heard of me?" I asked. Ravana's sword tapped against my leg, hot from the flames. I kept my eyes on the asura even as I slowly moved my unburned hand behind my back. Warm sweat trickled down my spine.

"My master wished to draw you here," Bhandasura hissed. "And I have done his bidding."

"You have a master? You are less powerful than I thought." I was scrambling, but perhaps I could goad him into a mistake.

"My master is all-powerful!" Bhandasura declared, and angry gouts of flame encircled us in unbearable heat. Ravana stepped closer to me to avoid the flames, and a weight pressed into my hand. I had little faith that this could work, but we had no other choice. "He will create a new empire of this world. He freed me from the prison that meddling goddess placed me into."

"Tell me who your master is, and perhaps I will spare you," I said. The smoke burrowed into my lungs and my words came out weak, punctuated by coughs.

Bhandasura laughed, and his eyes closed. I saw my opening. "Even if I had seen his face, I would never—"

Ravana's long, thin, remarkably spear-like sword embedded itself in his chest. I had thrown it with my nondominant hand, but from this distance I could hardly miss.

Bhandasura looked down, his mouth open in surprise. "This will not—" And then he staggered. He fell to his knees.

"You. Whore," he ground out, one hand pressed to his chest. "You will never leave here alive."

The flames sputtered. Beyond them stood a grotesque assembly of creatures howling and baying. Some of them were familiar animals—wolves, skeletal and starved, their fur matted and torn—while others were imps, horns sprouting from their head and large red eyes bulging.

Ravana stepped forward, throwing a small object over the flames at the center of the pack. It exploded with such force when it hit the ground that I could feel the reverberation across the fire. Many of the animals were torn apart by whatever strange invention Ravana had brought with him, but the rest stayed in place.

If Bhandasura's hold on them did not break with his death, there was no way we could withstand this.

The asura gasped for breath on the ground, and I drew my sword with my left hand. "Can you keep them away?" I said to Ravana. "I have an idea."

He moved to stand in front of me, dropping into a defensive stance. "I will do so for as long as I can."

I entered the Binding Plane. I had never tried to use my magic to control a nonhuman entity, and I did not want to try now, with my life on the line. I tried not to imagine what it might feel like to be killed by these animals. It would be slow, for they were small—an endless onslaught of teeth and claws until we succumbed.

The world wavered before me as Bhandasura's breath grew shallow. The shadows of the forest danced, closing in on me despite the bright sunlight. I ignored them. Pain throbbed in my burns, and I harnessed it, sharpening my focus farther than it had ever gone. All other bonds seemed to fade, and at last, I found them. Faint black wisps rising off Bhandasura, pulling the horde of wildlife like puppets. Once I found them, they shone, lustrous against the deadening veil that covered the world in the Binding Plane.

Distantly, I heard Bhandasura breathe his last. The flames died. I watched, hoping that the threads would die with them. But they did not even flicker.

And then, the animals were upon us.

Ravana fought with the strength of ten men, hacking and carving until the soil was matted and slick with blood. The air was smoky and coppery and utterly soaked with the scent of death. My eyes watered and stung, but I pressed on. Ravana protected me as I grasped at the black filaments that still tied the animals and cut one and then another with desperate intensity. The animals fled the moment they were freed from their magical tethers. But it was slow. I was too slow. I swayed on my feet as the magic sapped my strength.

"What are you doing?" Ravana shouted.

"Trying to save us," I replied through clenched teeth. I pulled at my power, shaping it into a blade. My shoulders heaved, vision tunneling as I pictured a sword of such strength and sharpness that it could cut through this tangle before me in one strike. And with a cry, I swung it into the heart of the knot.

A wave of threads in the Binding Plane snapped. I staggered forward as the tide of animals receded.

"It's working," Ravana called. "Do that again." He was bleeding profusely from a wound in his arm. A set of teeth tore into my legs and I swung my true sword on instinct, clumsily batting away what appeared to be a rabbit with horns. My legs barely had strength left to stand, and my resolve faltered, but I thought of Lakshmana, waiting alone in Janasthana. I would not leave him.

I entered the Binding Plane once more. A bird clawed at my forehead. Sweat and blood stung my eyes and obscured my vision. I could barely see what I was doing. Next to me, Ravana cried out. I felt him stumble back.

Terror turned my blood to ice. And our salvation came to me in a flash of instinct.

I took a deep breath and imagined the fire that I had started in Shishir's forest. In my mind, I set the flame against the tangle, summoning a ball of heat to immolate the bonds. The locus of the puppet strings shuddered, and some of the animals shrieked.

I fell to my knees, pouring all my energy and all my will into the imagined flame. The knot trembled, and there was a moment of terrible stillness before it exploded into thousands of wisps of black, like ash falling from the gray sky.

And then I knew no more.

Ravana came to visit me the day I woke. "Thank you. I cannot thank you enough for your help."

I glared up at him. "Did you hear nothing of what Bhanda-sura said? We played exactly into his master's hands."

"You cannot believe everything an asura says. Perhaps he wished to keep himself alive by bargaining information." Ravana was surprisingly calm. But then, he'd had more time to ruminate on it while I'd been unconscious.

"He thought he was victorious," I whispered. "I need to go back to Ayodhya. At once."

"Wait one week until you have recovered," Ravana said. "I will fly you to the edge of Kosala myself."

"You can fly me now," I said. But my voice was weak. My limbs had no strength. I was powerless.

"One week," Ravana said. "The asura is gone, and Janas-thana is mine. Your kingdom will keep too."

I groaned, knowing there was little I could do to argue. Instead, at my instruction, Lakshmana sent a message to Hirav instructing him to meet us in Sripura and telling him the danger had passed. There was not much more I could do until I recovered.

In the mornings, I spent time with my mother. She helped me to stand and take small steps about the room, as though I were a child. I had no memory of her ministrations when I was so young, but it warmed me now to be cared for, to be loved.

In the afternoons, Ravana visited and taught me a game of his own invention entitled chaturanga. It was delightfully complex, played on a wooden board engraved with sixty-four squares. Each of us started with two rows of beautifully carved players, one painted a creamy yellow and the other a dark forest green. The front row held eight foot soldiers, but the back row had a variety of pieces, most notably a raja and a saciva.

"Why is the saciva a woman?" I asked when we first started playing.

Ravana lifted his own piece to examine it. "The saciva is the most powerful piece on the board. She can move diagonally, horizontally, and vertically. Without her, the raja is nothing." He looked at me, amusement in his features. "Does that seem familiar?"

I resolved then and there to master the game. I even conscripted Lakshmana and Meena into learning the rules and practicing with me. The day before our imminent departure, I finally managed to place Ravana in a lethal stranglehold.

With a rueful smile, he tipped over his king. "You win, Radnyi," he said. "I should have known it would take you no time at all to defeat me."

I smiled in return, delighted by my victory. "Perhaps, once I leave, we can start a game by correspondence."

"I would like that," he said. "By hawk would be simplest. And I can even offer you a hawk of your own to take with you. In exchange, I would ask you a favor."

"Anything," I agreed easily.

"It feels like an eternity has passed since we spoke of it, but Sita is still my daughter. And her husband—I can't trust him. She is young and adjusting, I know, but you can at least make sure her unhappiness does not grow. That her husband never takes advantage of her. You are a powerful woman. Please swear it."

"Of c—" I began, but he continued on.

"This is what I ask of you. Swear to me on the gods that you will take care of her." He spoke formally, as though he had rehearsed this pledge beforehand.

I knew I would do everything I could to help Sita should

something happen to her, regardless of her status as Ravana's daughter. And if a pledge to the gods would set Ravana's mind at ease, so be it. "I swear to the gods that I will look out for Sita and offer her any help that I can provide. And I would have sworn this even without the agreement we made."

I would like to believe that is the moment when I sealed my fate, and his fate, and Rama's and Sita's fate, and all the rest. But I know that even without my promise to him, I would not have done anything differently.

The next morning, we said our goodbyes. My mother came to my room early and hugged me close. "I can never thank you enough for saving the city," she said. "Even when the gods would not come for us, you did."

"You told me once that I would grow up to become strong," I said, the ache of unshed tears in my throat. "You left me a story."

My mother stepped back in surprise. "I thought perhaps you had never found it," she said. "That in my caution, I had hidden it too well. You never mentioned it."

"It took me years to find it," I confessed. "But once I did, I kept it close. Even still it is a reminder. The gods would help themselves but not an innocent woman. I swore I would never suffer such injustice."

"Oh, Kaikeyi," my mother said, her voice sad. "That isn't the lesson I was hoping for you to learn. The gods do what they will. That tale was a reminder to be careful of men. I was drawn to it because I could not believe such an old, unassuming man was capable of such powerful cruelty. He came to the palace, you know, a few years before you were born."

"Who are you talking about?" I asked, mystified. "Someone from the story came to Kekaya?"

"Yes, the man who turned Ahalya to stone. Sage Vamadeva Gautama."

It was as though my mother had ripped the rug out from

below me and set the room spinning. *Vamadeva Gautama.
Vamadeva.*

No. How could it be? There were many Vamadevas in the
world. "You...met him?"

"Yes. He was old then, his hair all white. He seemed quite
ordinary. But when I caught his eyes, I knew he had done it.
They were unnatural, gray and cold. Like a storm." She trailed
off, her gaze fixed somewhere in the past. Then she blinked
and came back to herself. "Anyway, it doesn't matter now. You
should not worry about old stories, Kaikeyi. It is time for you
to go."

She pressed a kiss to my forehead and left before I could say
anything more.

I sank onto my bed, trembling. There was no mistake. She
had described him perfectly. What cruel coincidence would
have placed that man on my path, would have had my sons
learning from him? For the sage who had trained Rama, who
had spent two years in a secluded ashram with my impres-
sionable son, was a monster. A man who would curse his own
wife, who had not seen fit to free her—such a man held hate in
his heart.

And despite my efforts to keep him from Ayodhya, he had
found Rama again. The damage had been done, and to the
yuvraja besides. Why had I let Rama out of my sight for two
whole years? I had been complacent, arrogant that I was the
master of my world and that all would be how I wished it to
be. Sage Vamadeva would hate me too, I was sure, for sending
him away. Had he told Rama I was evil, contemptible?

I knew then, in my bones, that I had not yet seen the extent
of the damage. I needed to be back in Ayodhya, as soon as
possible.

There was no other way to describe it: Before us was a long
and narrow wooden boat on wheels.

From this contraption's side extended a magnificent set of wings, intricately crafted from thousands of feathers the likes of which could not be found on any single living creature.

But more impressive than that were the reins that extended from the front of the boat toward a pair of giant swans. They were as large as Ravana himself, and the graceful arch of their necks appeared sculpted from pure white marble. As we approached, they squawked a greeting so loud I felt slightly deafened.

"What is this?" Lakshmana stared in awe. Even I forgot for a moment the fear that had made itself at home within me.

Ravana ushered us toward the boat. "Pushpaka Vimana," he said, voice filled with pride. "A flying chariot. This is how I will take you to Sripura."

We climbed inside, and I ran my hands along the edges of the vehicle. "How does this fly?"

"The swans were a gift to me from Shiva for my devotion. He would not give my kingdom the reprieve I asked for, but these turned out to be a mighty consolation indeed. I asked the swans for their permission to use them in this manner, and they readily agreed. But they could not sustain the flight of just any vessel. The difficulty was in creating this boat's shape. It had to be just so." He took the reins in his hands. "Then I added the wings, to help sustain our motion in the air. Are you ready?"

Lakshmana looked at me, apprehension clear on his features, but I turned to Ravana. "No time to waste."

He snapped the reins, and the swans' powerful wings immediately beat in tandem. We did not move at all, and I wondered if the Pushpaka Vimana had broken. But after the moment of stillness, the boat rolled forward, slowly at first and gathering speed with every second until I thought the vehicle might break apart with the effort.

At that exact instant, the swans pulled upward and we rose

into the air. The boat steadied, and Lakshmana gave a shout, of fear or pleasure I knew not. I peeked over the side of the boat and saw Janasthana fading into the distance. From here, I could make out the palace, and my mother's house, and the walls and gates that surrounded the city. I turned to Ravana. "This is incredible!" I cried.

"Thank you!" he shouted back, and the wind instantly snatched away his words. "It is my life's work!"

"We should have one of these, Ma," Lakshmana whooped. "I can hardly believe this is real!"

"I do not know if anyone else is ready for this," I laughed. I thought suddenly of the horses of Kekaya and their ancestors who had flown in the heavens. Is this how they had once lived?

"Rama would be so jealous," Lakshmana said with a grin, and for a moment I saw a glimpse of the teasing relationship all brothers should have.

We did not speak much for the rest of the trip, so absorbed were we in the flight itself. I did not want to miss a single sensation. I barely blinked. Forests and rivers passed below us, as small as children's toys. Up here, far above the rest of the world, mountains that had seemed so daunting to cross now looked like they would fit into the palm of my hand. The trees were fibers of a green rug, the rivers twisting hair ribbons.

All too soon, we were lowering down on the outskirts of Sripura. Lakshmana grabbed my hand as the earth hurtled toward us, but I trusted Ravana and his invention.

We landed with a bone-shuddering thump and a jolt, and the wheels rattled against the grassy plains. But we all remained inside the Pushpaka Vimana, in one piece.

"Apologies," Ravana said, turning toward us. "There is no cleared strip for the Vimana out here."

"That was the most amazing thing I have ever experienced in my life," Lakshmana told him. His cheeks were flushed from the wind, and his hair in total disarray, but my son looked happier than I had ever seen him. "Thank you."

"You do not need to thank me," Ravana said. "It was a pleasure. I owe your mother more than I could possibly repay in a lifetime. But now I must go, before I attract any attention."

"Goodbye," I said, embracing him.

"Thank you," he whispered, and climbed aboard his chariot. In a few seconds, he was only a spot in the distance.

Lakshmana and I turned toward Sripura. It was time to return home.

PART FOUR

CHAPTER
THIRTY

A LETTER FROM DASHARATH waited for me with the Chief of Sripura, reassuring me that I had made the right decision in going on to Janasthana and filled with platitudes about how much he had missed me and how eagerly he looked to my return. For the remainder of the journey, I tried and failed to put my finger on exactly what about the missive raised alarm, but I could not decipher it. Perhaps my fear at my mother's revelation was clouding all else, for I should have been happy that Dasharath bore me no ill will for my flagrant disobedience of his orders, and that Bhandasura's supposed master had failed to take Ayodhya in my absence. Instead, I pushed us ever harder through the Riksha Mountains and barely waited for the feast they threw us in Kasi to conclude before moving on once again.

"Why the great rush?" Lakshmana asked me near Kusavati, when we were almost through the plains. I did not answer, signaling to him that we would take the right fork to circumvent the city. I intended to reach Ayodhya by nightfall. In this we were successful, and riders were sent off at Ayodhya's city gate to alert the palace to our arrival.

Dasharath met us at the stables looking as though he had aged in reverse by five or ten years. The persistent lines on his forehead had smoothed, and the invisible weight that pulled down his shoulders appeared to have eased. And still, dread sat heavy on my heart.

"You look well," I said, allowing him to help me off my horse. He did not release me, and instead pulled me closer, embracing me tightly right in front of Lakshmana, who blushed slightly and turned away.

I slipped into the Binding Plane, and my stomach turned leaden. My bond with my husband, that vibrant golden cord, had decreased to half its former size. Foreboding, already itching under my skin, expanded until my limbs felt swollen with it. We had spun that thread over a throne room and a battlefield, over trust and years of friendship. Our connection had been the core of my life in Ayodhya for so long. It should not have melted so easily.

Something had happened, something I was not aware of yet. It was the only explanation. "Is everything all right?" I asked, pulling back from his embrace slightly so that I could look at him. I was afraid of what his answer would be.

"I have decided to abdicate," he said. "I already informed Kaushalya and Sumitra, and the court." Dasharath spoke a bit like a drunk man, his words almost slurred with happiness—or something else.

"Rama is to be king?" Lakshmana asked, and only then did the words sink in. There had been nothing of Dasharath's jesting manner in his words, or I might have thought them a trick.

"Yes," Dasharath said, just as I cried, "Abdicate?"

"Yes, Kaikeyi. While you were gone, I realized that I did not want the throne anymore. And Rama is ready."

"Why?" I asked, unable to stop myself. After what I had learned, after seeing our bond, I knew no good could come of this. I felt ill.

"It just seemed like the right time," he said. "I knew it in my soul."

"You knew it in your soul," I repeated blankly. "Did you consult anyone at all about this?"

"Rama. We discussed it in great depth. He will make a great leader; do you not think so?"

Lakshmana squeezed my arm, and I stopped myself from pointing out that it was in Rama's self-interest to encourage this transfer of power.

"We can talk about this later," I said at last. "It has been a long journey, and I am sure that Lakshmana would like to rest."

"Yes, of course." Dasharath led the way back toward the palace. "I was so excited by this decision that I needed to tell you at once."

"And I am glad you did," I said. "You must be eager to hear of our trip to Janasthana as well."

He blinked, as though this had only just occurred to him. "Oh, yes. Yes. I trust your journey was pleasant?"

"Pleasant?" I repeated, and Dasharath beamed.

"Wonderful! I will leave you both to bathe and rest."

The moment I was out of his sight, I all but ran, Lakshmana on my heels.

"Why would Rama do such a thing?" he asked.

I shook my head. "Not Rama. It is not Rama."

Manthara sat on the edge of my bed, waiting for me. "Welcome home, Radnyi. You have been gone a long time."

"How could this have happened?" I asked without preamble, shedding my dirty riding attire. I was speaking of the abdication, but in the back of my mind the memory of my bond with Dasharath lingered. I was unmoored, my anchor weakened and frayed.

Manthara set a tub of water on the floor of my bedroom,

and I gratefully sank into it, glad to shed the dust and grime of our long journey from my skin. Normally, I would not bathe here in my rooms, but I wanted to speak freely with her.

In the Plane, our bond shone, still thick and proud. The relief of it almost sent me slipping under the water. It seemed Rama's powers had not touched her, nor Asha, who had gone to fetch me some tea. Perhaps his subconscious had realized that they were lost causes, too loyal to me. Or perhaps Manthara's natural suspicion and stubbornness had warded him off. Her unwavering presence beside me was a gift, one that I did not deserve.

"It happened so quickly," she said. "Perhaps two moons after you left."

I brought two wet hands up to cover my eyes. "Why is he doing this now? Why does he need to take the throne? He is so young, and he has so much time ahead of him."

"It was smart." She took the soap from the edge of the tub and, despite her years, knelt down and scrubbed my back. "To consolidate power while you were away."

A knock from the outer door interrupted our conversation, and I gestured for Manthara to answer it while I hastily rinsed my body and donned a robe.

"Sita!" Manthara exclaimed loudly.

I entered the main room, knowing Sita would not be offended by my attire. "Sita, it is good to see you. Apologies for my appearance. I was in the middle of a bath."

"No need to apologize, I am the one who is out of turn." If possible, she looked lovelier than ever, her delicate features luminous even in the dim room. And yet, when she twisted her ghagra, her fingers trembled faintly. "You have heard the news?"

"Yes. Congratulations are in order. You will soon be radnyi."

She turned away from me and toward the window. It felt

peculiar, after my time spent in Janasthana, to see paper windows again. "I am not ready," she whispered.

A pang went through me at the sadness in her voice. "Sita, what is it?"

She rotated slowly back toward me. "I tried my hardest to be like you. I took your place on the Women's Council in your absence, and I had ideas for projects that I took to Raja Dasharath. I even helped a female servant obtain a new home in the city. I know that Rama cares about his people, so I thought by helping them he might be proud of me. But his attitude toward me has not changed."

"Sita, I—"

"And when Rama is on the throne, I doubt he will care more for me. Even now he does not confide in me, so how can I fulfill my duties as radnyi? How can I fulfill my purpose?" She finally paused, and I took my chance.

"Sita, I am sure Rama cares for you." I could not imagine Rama not caring about any member of his family or his city. "But when it comes to matters of the heart—"

"I am not asking for you to make him love me," Sita interrupted. "It is painful, to be sure, that I might feel more for him than he feels for me. But I would at least like to be a part of his life. If I am not the radnyi he needs, he will hate me. I am sure of it."

"No," I protested. "He will not hate you, Sita."

"Rama is a god, and a powerful one. If one day I did not meet his standards, I know he could easily punish me."

"But he would not," I said.

Sita looked at me. "And what if I were to tell you that at night, he talks to me about how easily he can convince people to do his bidding? That he knows exactly what to say to someone to convince them to be a part of his work and sees how to weave people together?"

She was describing my own powers quite well.

"Sita, I know that may seem scary. But think. Rama has not actually done anything to hurt anyone. What he does, he does for the good of others." Even as I spoke, I thought about Dasharath. Was his decision not likely a result of manipulation, even if unconscious? "Has he done something to worry you?"

"He wishes to rule, and now his perfectly healthy father is abdicating. I do not believe that was Raja Dasharath's decision." It was as though she had seen my fears and given them voice.

"Rama loves his father," I said, maternal instinct pushing me to defend my son. But I doubted. For I knew much less about Rama than I thought. He had hidden Sage Vamadeva from me, despite knowing the man's beliefs. I wanted to blame another man for everything, but Rama was his own person. An adult. I believed his actions were unconscious, but could I really know that about him?

"I know that he does, but..." She sighed. "I do not know how to explain it better than this. You are always so wise, and I thought perhaps you would have an answer."

"What would you have me do?" I asked.

"Do you not see? You are the only person who can stand up to him. He has no power over you, but he still cares for you and your opinion, does he not?"

Maybe that had once been true. I did not know any longer.

A wave of exhaustion swept over me. This was all too much. "I need to think. Thank you for coming to me with your concerns," I said to Sita. "Let us talk further tomorrow."

Her face fell, but she bowed her head and left.

Manthara had departed on some errand while we spoke, leaving me alone with my thoughts. The walls felt unfamiliar after moons away, just another piece of my home that was now foreign to me. I shivered under my robe. I was exposed, vulnerable, in a way I had not been for many years. This Ayodhya wasn't quite mine anymore.

CHAPTER
THIRTY-ONE

THE NEXT MORNING, WHEN I arrived at the Mantri Parishad, I was surprised to find several new faces. I recognized the children of some older ministers, young men who were not much older than Rama. They looked at him as though he was already wearing the crown. Until now, I had imagined Rama perhaps wreaking this havoc without understanding his own actions. But this was real and deliberate, not unconscious magic.

I stepped into the Binding Plane. To my shock, I was greeted not by a riot of color, but the sight of thin, sickly strings that nearly blended into the gray of the world around me. My connection to almost every advisor was failing. And the moment I was seated, bright blue threads flared into existence, connected not to me, but to my son. The weakness of my bond to Dasharath still lay heavy in my heart, and seeing this, my life's work, gone in mere months…I felt empty. The absence, in a way, was worse than pain. I could not bring myself to even try to reinvigorate those threads. And every time Rama spoke during the meeting, his bonds shone as if set aflame.

After the council, Rama sought me out. "Ma, it is good

to see you again." His smile was sincere, his warm manner unchanged. This was no incomprehensible stranger, no conniving disciple. He was my son—my son.

"You as well," I said, finding a smile of my own. Even so, my voice sounded uncertain to my ears, and his face fell a fraction. I responded as his mother, on instinct, my arms reaching out and hugging him, rubbing his back to soothe away his sadness. He relaxed against me, as he always had. But between my body and my mind lay a gap of suspicions, the distance between us clear.

"How was your journey?" he asked. "What did you learn of the asura?"

His words unsettled me in the same way Dasharath's missive had. But why? "Janasthana is safe for our traders now," I said slowly.

"I imagine you had something to do with that," Rama said, still smiling. "And I—"

"How did you know there was an asura?" I asked, realization flooding me.

Rama took a step back from me, brow furrowing. "Father told me."

"I have not yet had the chance to tell him what I encountered." Every rumor had named the evil a rakshasa. My heart beat so loudly I thought he might hear it. *He knew. He knew. How did he know?*

Rama pressed his lips together. "Perhaps I—"

"Don't lie to me."

He sighed, and we stared at each other in charged silence. "I do not want you to be angry with me, Ma. You must understand, I only wanted to show you the frightening truth of this world."

"No," I whispered. The stone walls of the room were closing in on me. "You... You sent Shishir and Bhandasura. To frighten me? They could have killed me." I wanted to turn away so I could not see his face. My fingers clenched into fists, nails digging into my palms. He had betrayed me. Betrayed his brother. "They could have killed us," I said again.

"I did not intend for you to ever learn this," Rama said, his voice sorrowful. His sadness was meaningless. He had done the unthinkable. And for what? "But you have a way of finding the truth. I did ask Lord Shishir to assist me by showing you the seriousness of the situation. The asura was already there. His kind have become a plague in the south, and I needed you to see it."

"Lord Shishir injured your brother quite badly. And I almost died." My words came out quietly. I felt nearly dizzy with anger.

At this, Rama's expression flitted first to shock, then to concern. He glanced over me. "Are you all right now? Do you need to sit? How has Lakshmana recovered? That was never—never supposed to happen. I am so sorry, Ma."

His sincerity shone through in his torrent of words, but I was still furious. "An apology is not enough for putting us in such danger!"

"I know." He ran a hand through his hair, then lowered himself to his knees before me. "Please, Ma. Please. I promise that was not my intention." His voice trembled, and at this, I felt some of my own anger loosen. His contrition, at least, was honest.

"I know you did not mean to hurt me," I said, and he looked up at me, hope in his eyes. "But even if that wasn't the intention, how could you risk such a thing?"

Rama rose slowly but lowered his gaze to my feet. "This will sound foolish now. But a wise friend pointed out to me that you only believe what you see directly. And I have watched you. I know that is true. You focus on your own goals, on what is in front of you that needs fixing. I hoped that once you saw the true threat facing this world, you might be able to better understand my purpose."

In the revelation that Rama had thrown me into danger, I had almost forgotten about Rama's erstwhile tutor.

"I knew you would be fine," he continued. "I trusted you, because you are strong, and I want you to be my ally in this. You have always asked what my path is, and now I will tell you. It is my divine duty to rid this earth of the asuras and rakshasas that threaten to overtake it, that creep northward toward civilization day by day. And to do so, I will need the armies and men of Kosala beside me. But that does not mean there is no place for you."

"Oh, Rama," I said, swallowing past a lump in my throat. "I was just as threatened by the god that you sent as by any rakshasa or asura. That does not mean we should wage war against the gods. So why do you wish to do so for the asuras?"

"What of your supposed friend, Ravana?" Rama asked, frustration creeping into his tone. "Do you not find it most convenient that the asura appeared just in time for Ravana to come save Janasthana? He himself is an asura!"

If I had not been so filled with sadness and anger, I might have gasped. It was clear to me Rama was not lying about this, and yet the idea that Ravana had been Bhandasura's master was laughable. "Think about it. He expands his kingdom every day, through trickery and fear. His ancestral lands lie far to the south in Lanka, and yet he prowls toward us."

"Ravana *saved* that city. The people welcomed him as their savior, regardless of his identity."

Rama blew out a breath. "He was right! You only see what you wish to see."

"*He*? You're talking about Sage Vamadeva, are you not?" I demanded. "Your 'wise friend.' You would listen to him over the testimony of your own mother?"

"No, of course not! He is not infallible—nobody is. For all his wise counsel on the matter of gods and demons, he also dislikes you for dismissing him. He advised that I should keep you in the dark. But I know you. You rode out to battle with our father without fear, and you have helped lead this kingdom. I need your aid to wage this war. *Please*."

Once again, my instinct as a mother told me to reach out, to aid him. But this time I held back, for he was asking me to help him do something that I did not believe in, and that had never been my way. "Who told you that your purpose is to fight these demons?" I asked instead.

Rama paused, his mouth twisting for a moment. "He did," he said at last, before adding in a rush, "but it makes sense. Why else would I be sent here? There is a coming tide of darkness that I must stem. I can feel the truth of it deep inside of me. At night I see it—the wars they will start, their fires consuming cities. The women and children who will flee the destruction, only to be overtaken. I have to stop it. Only I can."

"And I suppose your sage has nothing to gain from you becoming king to wage this war. He wants you and your power, Rama, for his own ends."

"Sage Vamadeva stayed at the ashram. I offered him a place on my Mantri Parishad and he refused. He said that it was an honor to teach me, to help me determine my divine path, and hearing of my success one day was all he wished for. But enough about him, Ma. This isn't about him. I need *your* help."

I shook my head. "I love you, Rama, and I always wish for your success. But I cannot help you wage unnecessary war. Already you have put me and your brother in harm's way—even if unknowingly. The cost of further warfare is too high."

Rama made a frustrated noise in the back of his throat. "I have apologized for that. And thankfully, you have both returned alive and well. You have to look beyond that, to the bigger picture."

"Rama, you have said you value my counsel. So please consider what I am telling you."

"You have had a long journey, Ma," Rama said slowly.

"One filled with more pain than I intended. Perhaps, when you are better rested, we might speak of this again?"

I could recognize a dismissal when I heard one.

I had not talked to Kaushalya or Sumitra since my arrival, but I could imagine how they would feel about the proceedings: At the very least, Kaushalya would be excited to see Rama ascend and Sumitra would be looking forward to the celebrations with her usual eagerness. And if Rama was somehow manipulating his own father, he had likely done the same to his mothers.

Still, Kaushalya greeted me warmly, embracing me and inquiring after Southern Kosala. Her rich purple sari was draped perfectly, the kohl around her eyes flawlessly tapered, and I was acutely aware of how disheveled I must have looked. When I gave her a few vague responses, she pulled away and held me at arm's length. "What's the matter, Kaikeyi?" she asked.

"I'm just tired," I said, giving her a small smile. "There has been so much to catch up on since my arrival."

"Yes, the coronation." Kaushalya's voice remained remarkably unemotional even as her eyes bore into me. She was clearly studying me for any sign of discontent.

"Oh, ignore her," Sumitra said, stepping out from behind Kaushalya to greet me. Her smile lines were in full view as she beamed at me, and I found myself returning it without thought. "She has been lying awake at night worrying about preparations for the ceremonies. But now that you have returned to assist us, we can more than manage!"

Kaushalya nodded, gave me a stunning smile, and turned away to take a seat at the table. I entered the Binding Plane and was relieved to see that my bond with her remained strong. My bond with Sumitra, on the other hand, showed some signs of atrophy. Still, both of them were quite sincere in their affection for me.

"Do you not think it quite sudden?" I asked, busying myself with my tea.

"It is happening quickly," Kaushalya agreed. "But Dasharath believes he is ready."

"Dasharath is wise," Sumitra added. "He would not make such a decision lightly. Rama is brave and kind and beloved by his people. I see no reason to delay."

I took a sip of tea, my eyes flicking to Kaushalya from behind the cup.

"Why do you ask?" Kaushalya set her cup down and leaned forward. I did not even bother checking the Plane for I knew what I would find—simply my questioning of the timing had triggered her connection with Rama.

I shrugged. "No reason. I suppose it is all bewildering me because I have been absent so long."

Kaushalya reclined in her seat. I detected a hint of displeasure in her eyes. "What else have I missed in the palace?" I asked quickly, nearly tripping over my words in my eagerness to change the topic.

"So much!" Sumitra angled her body toward me conspiratorially. "Has anyone told you what happened at the wedding of Arya Ravi's daughter?"

When I got to my room, Asha was waiting for me.

"You received a message." She waved the scroll in the air, her other hand on her hip.

I tried to grab the paper, but she pulled it out of reach. "I am your radnyi!" I said, but my reluctant laughter gave me away. It was a balm to joke with Asha, after everything that had happened.

"It has been months since you last saw me."

"I have been busy," I protested. "Much has happened in my absence."

At this, she sobered. "Yes. It has." She stepped toward me and extended the letter.

"And what do you think of it all?" I asked without looking up, opening the scroll.

She must have responded. But I did not hear her over the roar that filled my ears at Ravana's words.

Radnyi Kaikeyi,

I have sent this to correspond with your arrival in Ayodhya, which as you may know does not come a moment too soon. I hope that you are able to put a stop to the nonsense I have heard, but I have hope—not certainty. How is Rama to become king? He is too young, and he will not deal with the pressure well.

My limbs tingled with apprehension. What if someone had intercepted this? It would have certainly bolstered Rama's claim that Ravana's asura blood made him dangerous, for his letter made little sense. Who was Ravana to question the decisions of Ayodhya?

But I recognized in him a parent's concern and took a deep breath, pushing away my nerves. Surely I would react similarly to anything to do with my children.

I know there is no proof, but I have an unshakable belief that Rama mistreats my daughter. Kaikeyi, if you fail to help her, nothing will stand in my way. So far you have experienced only my kindness, but my wrath is not inconsiderable. You will not be around forever, Kaikeyi. When you are gone, will she not have more to fear?

Ravana

I nearly crumpled the letter in frustration. I did not have time for Ravana's nonsense, nor was I inclined to indulge him after learning he had lied long ago about his heritage—in my reply, I would need to make clear that I could not change matters of governance simply because he requested so. And despite his strange belief, Sita was not being mistreated by Rama, only vying for his affection. Ravana's grief over losing her was clouding his mind.

"Did you hear what I said?" Asha asked. "What is this?"

"It's too much," I muttered.

"What is? Are you listening?" She came to stand in front of me and waved her hands before my face. "Rama may be unready, but he can grow into the role. You will be his saciva, like you were his father's, and show him the right path. It is all very sudden, yes, but you have done more difficult things."

"Yes," I said softly, but I was uncertain. In truth, I did not know what I could do.

I rubbed my eyes. The warmth of the room was pressing down on me. Without warning, I was standing before a holy fire, Agni's words closing around me like a trap. *It is what you will do.*

At the next meeting of the Mantri Parishad, Rama and I found ourselves at odds. At our eastern border with Videha, a village had happened upon a seam of gold while digging the foundation of a new temple. Some had been sent to Ayodhya, and Dasharath wished for suggestions on what to do with the unexpected windfall. I immediately suggested we build another granary, remembering what had happened just this past season. We would not have had the funds for such a construction otherwise, and it was the prudent thing to do.

But as soon as I was done speaking, one of the new advisors cleared his throat. "That is an excellent suggestion, Radnyi, but it seems to me that the past season's problems were due to a rakshasa. If we wish to prevent such occurrences again, perhaps this gift would be better spent on new weapons for the army."

This was such a silly idea that I almost felt bad for the boy. Demons outside our borders cared little about the strength of Kosala's armies. But before I could explain the folly of such a plan, Rama said, "The gods gifted this gold to us, in exchange for our kingdom's piety in building a new temple. It would be fitting, then, to use it to strengthen our army on their behalf, and to defend ourselves from their enemies. We may find ourselves at war sooner than we expect."

I saw Rama's bonds brighten around the advisors. "We haven't been to war in years," I protested. "Most of you haven't seen a battlefield. But some of us have, and we know the pain of it. It is not something to aspire to. A granary will help our people, and it will do so without stealing our kingdom's children." I looked around, hoping one of the senior ministers, those who had been around when Kosala faced border skirmishes year after year, might agree. But nobody else spoke. When Dasharath asked for a vote, only a third of the council was with me.

"I will consider both proposals," Dasharath said.

Could I think of the last time he had expressly contradicted the will of the Mantri Parishad? My heart sank.

I waited until after the meeting was over to approach my husband. "Kaikeyi, I must allow Rama to start making decisions," he said, already knowing why I sought to speak to him.

"But do you agree?" I pressed him. "You have always worked for peace. Stability. The granary will help on both counts."

"I see the merits of both ideas," he said. In the Binding Plane, the blue cord lay steady above his shoulders. "So in this instance, I will follow Rama's will."

"And the will of the Mantri Parishad," I reminded him.

"Yes, of course."

"You truly wish to see Kosala's armies strengthened for war?"

"Rama has told me of his travels, of the dangers he has

seen." Dasharath's expression was earnest, but I wondered how much of this was truly what he felt, and how much was what Rama had impressed upon him. "If he believes this to be the right path, then I trust him."

I could not remember the last time my counsel had been so deftly set aside by Dasharath. I had worked so hard for his respect, for the respect of the Mantri Parishad, and now—

Rama needed to be told what power he held, so he could keep it in check. I had to speak to him directly, not get wrapped up in my own emotions. I pushed aside the hurt and caught up to Rama in the hallway.

"Are you upset?" he asked immediately. "Your idea was a good one, but the necessity of preparation—"

I raised a hand to stop the flow of words. "Do you realize why the rest of the Mantri Parishad agrees with you so readily?" I asked.

He frowned. "Because my ideas are sound, and they respect me."

"That may be true," I said, thinking back to what Sita had told me about Rama's sway over others. "But you also try to move them, do you not? With some innate part of you?"

Rama considered these words, one finger on his cheek in such a boyish gesture that for a moment I had the urge to send him to his room. "I have always been able to see people's souls," he said finally. "And perhaps I have used that knowledge, but who wouldn't? That does not mean I am forcing them into anything."

"Aren't you?" I asked. "You are extremely powerful. When you seek to sway someone, have you not considered you might be controlling them instead?"

"I—I don't know." Rama turned to face a tapestry spun from dark, shadowy hues. Vishnu's third avatar, Varaha, stood in the cosmic ocean, his blue-black body half-submerged in the water. On his tusks sat the earth, woven in delicate floss of emerald and sapphire. Varaha had rescued the earth after she had been captured by an asura bent on destroying her. "I suppose...I have never been able to see your soul, and I have always had a hard time persuading you. And the same is true of Sita."

I considered what to say next. Revealing my true nature to Rama might be the best way to prove to him what he was doing, but I wondered what he would think if he knew what I was. Would he look upon me with suspicion?

No. I was his mother. He loved me, just as I loved him—despite all my other doubts, I was sure of this. "You cannot see my soul because I am different. Because I too can see some of people's souls. And when I look at them, I can see your influence. Your control. You may not have realized it, but it is there."

Rama swallowed. The colors of the tapestry devoured the light, leaving shadows on his face. He reached out a hand to touch the flank of the boar, almost reverently. Did he think himself Vishnu, rescuing the earth? "I do not like to know I did such a thing unwittingly, Ma. But—it's not bad, right? This influence? People want to obey the gods. It must be my gift, this ability to reach people."

I wanted to shake him. "You are forcing people to do your bidding!" I said. "I am the only one speaking to you clearly, without influence."

"Or," Rama said slowly, turning back to me, "whatever places you outside my influence makes it harder for you to see the good in what I'm doing."

He was right, in a way, and I hated it. Being gods-touched, and godsforsaken, had made me far more skeptical of the gods. And now, my own child. "Your father is not choosing to abdicate," I said instead. "It is far too soon for him to be stepping down. He has many years left to rule, and yet, you are making him give up the throne. Does that not disturb you? The kingdom is strong, prosperous—"

"Which is why it must be now, before Kosala weakens, before the asuras' power spreads." He threw up his hands in frustration. "Why do you mistrust me so? I respect my father, and I always heed his counsel. With his blessing, I am doing what is best for the kingdom."

"How do you know?" I asked him. "How do you know what is best for the kingdom?"

"Because I am a god!" he said. I could see it again, that great shadow he cast, and hear the ringing in his voice.

But it did not frighten me anymore. Instead, I was filled with a deep sorrow. He was convincing himself of his righteousness with every word he spoke, blinded to the truth. "You are still so young," I told him. "And you have grown used to getting your way. But that does not make your way right. Wait to take the throne. *I promise* it can wait." In my voice was a plea I hoped he would hear. This was as close as I could get to begging my son for something.

Instead, Rama shook his head and began striding toward the end of the corridor. "I do not have time to keep talking in circles with you, Ma. I wish you would just listen to me."

"And I wish you would listen to me," I said softly. But he did not hear. He stepped through the door and was gone.

Although Rama and I were still in our uneasy truce, he trying to recruit me while I tried to talk him down, I knew there were others in the court—the young men who would become advisors or those who had simply never liked me—who saw our split in the council and Rama's impending coronation as an opportunity. In small ways, they began their work, spreading rumors about the Women's Council or snubbing me during court events and social gatherings. I tried to pay them no mind. But one moon after my return to Ayodhya, they became impossible to ignore.

"Did you hear about the incident with the serving maids?"

Sumitra asked me as we walked arm in arm through the gardens—a routine that remained a sanctuary for me.

"No, I did not. What happened?" Today, petals of flowers carpeted the path. They released a fragrant odor as we crushed them underfoot, but beneath that was the faintest scent of rot.

"How did you not hear of this?" Kaushalya chimed in, a strange note in her voice. I glanced at her and saw that her elegant brows were drawn together.

"Kaushalya feels sorry for the girls," Sumitra confided. "But I would not. They made their own beds." She gave a little giggle as though making some joke.

Kaushalya pursed her lips in disapproval. "I do feel sorry for them. Several of the women in our employ, it seems, were rumored to also be working in a brothel. The accusation was made anonymously, and the head of staff immediately dismissed them, despite not knowing whether the gossip was even true."

"*What?*" I asked, struggling to catch up. "Were they new?"

"No. Some of them have worked here for years. They're quite old for the brothel too. You might remember Saralaa or Mugdha—they were the first to seek audience with us, back when we had only a women's circle."

I felt hot and cold at the same time. "Yes, I remember them," I whispered. "The accusation was anonymous?"

"I do not think you should worry overmuch about that," Sumitra said. "After all, those beyond reproach would never have such things said about them in the first place."

"Of course," I muttered, for there was nothing I could do now, after the fact. Kaushalya gave me an odd look, lips downturned, and I glanced away.

Rama's head might have been preoccupied with demons, but those who saw him as an opportunity to gain power had much more material concerns. If the goal was to purge my influence from the palace even at the lowest levels, they were succeeding. I was relieved that Riddhi had left to care for her aging mother and had been spared such an indignity.

The more I thought about it, though, the more I wondered whether perhaps this was what I could bring to Rama to show him the dangers of his influence, of his disrupting the balance of power in Kosala before he was ready. Surely he would not wish for innocent women to be dismissed from the palace?

But that evening, before I could make my way to my son, I received a summons to Dasharath's chambers.

The moment I saw my husband's drawn and weary face, all thoughts of Rama vanished.

I went to his side immediately. "What is it?" I asked.

"I do not know, but I cannot imagine it is pleasant news. A messenger just arrived from your brother, nearly dead on his feet, with an urgent missive for you."

"Yudhajit?" I took the still-sealed papers from Dasharath and tore them open.

Kaikeyi, Father has returned, and he is dying. The healers give him one more moon, maybe less. He is asking for you, and your son. And there are matters we must discuss. Hurry back, sister.

"Kaikeyi? What does it say?" Dasharath's face looked lined with worry, the peace of abdication gone in his concern for me. I might have been touched, relieved that he still cared so for me, had the news not been so dire.

"My father is close to death," I whispered. My voice shook, not out of any emotion for him, but because I could not fathom having to leave Ayodhya now. "He wishes to see me, and to see Bharata, before it happens."

Dasharath took my free hand in his, mistaking my nerves for sorrow. "I am so sorry. We will make preparations for you to leave at once."

CHAPTER THIRTY-TWO

"DO YOU THINK WE will make it in time?" Bharata asked as we made camp the first evening of our journey. It was the most time I had spent with him in some time, for I had only seen him at meals or passed him in the halls in the tumult since my arrival. "Before Grandfather dies?"

The uncertainty in his voice pierced through my fog of thoughts. I realized with my mind on Rama I had hardly comprehended the fact that Ashwapati—that my father was near death, or how much this might hurt Bharata.

"I do not know," I said honestly. Bharata's face reminded me of Yudhajit's when we had been young, with his narrow nose and dark eyes.

"Uncle Yudhajit said that Grandfather was getting better."

"When did he say that?"

"In his letter, a few months ago. He tells me how all our family in the kingdom is."

I imagined Yudhajit painstakingly writing out the status of each of our brothers and their wives for Bharata, and I almost laughed. Even I did not want all that information if nothing was amiss. "That is very kind of him," I said. Bharata leaned his head on my shoulder and I gently stroked his hair. "Do you remember when we first visited? My father was very sick then, and that is why he was away. He recovered enough to live a few more years. But now his turn has come, as every person's must."

"I don't know him, and yet I feel sad."

Bharata had never experienced death before, I realized. None of my sons had. Not on the battlefield, not in the loss of the oldest generation of family. They had been blessed in many ways. "It is always sad when any life is lost. And especially because, even if you have never met him, he is your grandfather."

"You and Uncle Yudhajit will be sad," Bharata said in a small voice. "I do not want that. I could not imagine how I would feel if Father died."

"My father has been sick for a long time. Yours is healthy, vital. And you are strong. When that time comes, many years from now, you will be prepared." I longed to embrace him, but something stayed my limbs.

"Are you prepared?" he asked.

It had been so long since I had seen my father, and longer still since I liked him. And now that I had met my mother, and learned how he had driven her away, I found it difficult to muster up any strong emotion. I was prepared—by virtue of not caring very much. But that is not the answer I wanted to offer my son. "Yes," I said. "I have not lived there for some time. And you are much closer to your father than I ever was to mine."

"But it will be very hard for Uncle." Bharata's voice was thoughtful. "He has told me so many stories about your childhood."

"He has?" I asked.

"Oh, yes. We send letters all the time, you know. He has a lot of interesting stories about you. But...I suppose you're not in the ones with Grandfather that much. You must have been busy with your other duties."

That was a tactful way of framing his shrewd observation. "That is probably what happened," I agreed.

Before I knew it, we were crossing the Sarasvati River.

"Do you remember what happened here, with Rama?" he asked as we passed by. "I always knew he was special, but I had never realized that he was blessed until that moment."

"I remember," I said quietly.

Bharata seemed content to continue rambling. "I hope we return in time for coronation. It will be a splendid occasion."

"What do you want to do, when Rama becomes the king?" I asked.

Bharata shrugged. "Whatever duties he feels I'll be best suited for. I suppose I could become an advisor on his Mantri Parishad. But he will not have much need for help."

"I suppose not," I murmured. I could not tell if this was a manipulation or Bharata's true feelings. Either way, it saddened me to hear that Bharata had given up on that ambition he had confessed to me on a different trip to Kekaya, of being best at something, of being a good raja. Bharata too had become unfamiliar to me, more Rama's brother and less my child.

With every passing day, my heart drummed a stronger rhythm against my ribs. *Time is running out. Time is running out.* Above us, the moon grew fatter and fatter, until only a sliver remained darkened, and the next morning the city of Kekaya came into view.

A breathless Yudhajit met us at the gates.

"Not a moment too soon," he said. He grabbed my hand and pulled me through the palace as though we were children. Bharata followed.

"Is he truly that poorly?" I gasped out, tripping on legs gone numb. He strode on without answering, guiding us through twisting corridors until we arrived at a plain wooden door.

Raja Ashwapati lay in a small bedchamber, propped up on several pillows. His face was ashen, his whole frame diminished. Ashvin stood at his bedside. He looked up at our appearance and gave me a tiny smile.

"Kaikeyi is here, Father," he said in a low voice.

"Kaikeyi?" My father's lips barely moved when he spoke. His voice was a whisper, a mere remnant of his grand courtroom manner. I almost pitied him.

"I am here, Father." I stepped into the dim room and approached his bedside, my son and Yudhajit close behind. "It has been a long time."

"Yes, yes." His hand lifted and he limply motioned me closer. I leaned in to hear him.

"You were a good daughter," he rasped out. "You performed your duty to your kingdom well, and soon our blood will sit on the throne of Kosala. I am proud of you, Kaikeyi."

"Thank you, Father." His praise confused me. Although I did not want it, although I told myself I did not care what he thought, his words also warmed me. Instinct brought me to the Binding Plane, where I discovered a thicker-than-expected lustrous white bond connecting us, somehow bright against the dull surroundings. I felt ashamed at the bloom of joy under my skin. "How are you?" I asked foolishly, wishing to change the subject.

"Dying." He produced a coughing laugh. "Soon, I hope."

I bowed my head.

"It is my time and I am ready. Do not be alarmed. But, Kaikeyi, I need to tell you something." His hand found my arm, and he gripped it with all his feeble strength.

I looked up at Yudhajit, but he appeared equally bewildered.

"Your mother," he whispered, and I pulled back in alarm. How did he know? I would not apologize for seeing her, not even to comfort a dying man. He mouthed something else, but from my distance I could not hear it. I sat on the edge of his bed and gingerly put my ear next to his mouth. "It was my fault."

I must have misheard. But no: "My fault," he repeated.

I studied his face, the way the skin appeared paper-thin and worn dry. His eyes were damp. I had never seen him cry—could barely even conceive of it—but here I was. Guilt had done this. For a moment I remained there, paralyzed. But perhaps I could ease his pain. I lowered my lips to his ear. "She is alive, and happy. I have seen her."

He turned his head slightly toward me. "You have?"

"Yes." I pushed the hint of happiness through our bond, then looked up at the others. My eyes alighted on Bharata. "This is your grandson," I said, beckoning him forward. "My son."

Bharata brought his hands together and bowed his head. "It is an honor to meet you."

Ashwapati's eyes lit up, a faint gleam of what he had once been briefly visible. "He is a fine boy."

"Yes, he is." Pride and grief squeezed my chest.

"Take my hand, child," my father instructed Bharata. Bharata took the wizened hand in both of his own.

My father sighed and went limp against his bed. Alarmed, I looked around, but Ashvin shook his head. "He has lapsed into sleep again. This happens more and more frequently." He stepped around me and placed two fingers under my father's chin. "His pulse grows weaker."

Yudhajit put an arm around my shoulders, and we stood together in silence. Even Bharata managed to stay still as we kept vigil. Raja Ashwapati's breaths rattled in his throat, so slowly they encompassed five or six of mine at a time, until at last, his chest rose no more.

Ashvin checked once again for the beat of his blood but found none.

Yudhajit placed his hand over our father's eyes and said a short prayer, and so my father died.

I am not ashamed to say that my father's death had little impact on me. He was old, and there was no love between us. But watching him die took a toll on all of us, dimming our lives by a fraction. Our little party ate a subdued meal in Yudhajit's private rooms, and afterward I went straight to bed, changing into a shift and lying down alone. I stared at the ceiling for over an hour, unable even to close my eyes, lest strange and frightening nightmares carry me away.

Then a knock sounded on my door. Not just any knock, but a pattern. Three beats, with an emphasis on the third.

He rapped it again, a bit louder this time, probably intending to wake me. I slipped out of bed and tapped out my corresponding signal. A soft laugh came from beyond, and I opened the door, letting Yudhajit in.

"What is it?" I asked.

He reached out to hug me, holding me tight. "Nothing. I missed you."

"You came to my room because you missed me?" I led him back to the bed and sat on it, cross-legged. After a moment of hesitation, he joined me there.

"Obviously not."

"Then? Out with it." I poked him in the side.

He scratched the back of his neck and looked past me toward the wall, and our blue bond jumped. I braced myself for bad news. "I wrote in my letter that we had much to discuss," he said at last.

"Yes," I agreed. "And we do have much to discuss. I have news for you as well." I wanted to tell him about our mother. It might anger him to know that she had a new family, a new life without us, but he deserved the chance to go see her, or send for her.

"Well, let me tell you what I wish to discuss first. Do you

remember Dasharath's promise? The one you extracted before you agreed to marry him?"

I nodded. "Of course. I made him swear that my son, were I to have one, would be heir to the throne. But things changed. I released him from that oath."

"It was not yours to release," Yudhajit said gently. "Raja Dasharath swore that oath to our father, not you, for our father was the one to give you away in marriage."

His words came to me as if from a great distance, and I struggled to understand them.

If I could have believed that the gods took a special interest in my life, I would have thought they were the reason for my misfortune. What other reason could there be that over and over again my family brought me this strife? How could he be saying this to me now, after all that had happened?

"Father is dead," I said carefully, "so that no longer matters."

"News reached us of Rama's impending coronation." Yudhajit looked down at his lap, oblivious to my pain. "Father heard of it and grew very angry. He made me promise that I would ensure Bharata took the throne. I made a vow. To the gods."

And it seemed once again, my wishes held no weight. It was almost incomprehensible that my desires should matter so little, and yet I was ashamed at my surprise. Had I really believed that things had changed? Years and years of work, to have a voice, to be respected, but my brother would still honor the words of men over my will.

"*Why* would you promise such a thing?" I asked, tugging at the sheets in agitation.

"It makes a mockery of our kingdom to let such an important oath be broken so publicly and easily. I cannot let that stand."

"Look at me," I instructed him. He slowly raised his eyes to meet mine. "Kosala is not your kingdom. *This has nothing to do with you.*"

"Kaikeyi, the appropriate response for such flagrant oath breaking is war." An overwhelming sorrow permeated our bond. Was it from Ashwapati's death, I wondered, or the fact that he was threatening his sister's kingdom?

"I can try to ensure that Dasharath holds the throne for several more years," I offered instead. "I have his ear and his confidence. Would that give you the time you needed to calm the court?" I had not tried approaching Dasharath directly, because Rama's hold over him was so strong and I had not wished to compromise our own bond. But it was worth the risk to try to stop this madness, and such a delay would be good for Kosala too.

Yudhajit gave me an incredulous look. "We have diplomats in your court, and they have sent word of Dasharath's firm intention to step down. And even if he didn't, it would merely be a delay of the inevitable. His choice of heir is clear, and so is the insult."

"What are you saying?" I demanded.

"I swore an oath," Yudhajit said. "I am sorry to hurt you, but I have a duty to listen to my advisors and ensure my kingdom is respected. If Bharata does not take the throne, there will be war."

I could not believe what he was saying. *War,* so that a young man who did not want the throne of a kingdom could fulfill the wishes of another. "The promise Dasharath made was to *me*. It was extracted by *me*." But even as I spoke up in protest, I knew it would not matter. If my father and the kingdom wanted Yudhajit to do this, and if he himself agreed with them, there was nothing I could say to stop it.

"I will not have Kekaya be seen as weak."

"You could change people's minds," I insisted.

"Kaikeyi, how can you find it acceptable for your husband

to break the first promise he ever made you? You, of all people!"

"Yudhajit, he did not break his promise. I agreed to release him from it, after careful consideration. It was not done on a whim. Please, I am begging you. Think of the toll to our kingdoms if you do this."

"Protecting our line is more important," Yudhajit retorted.

I stared at him in shock for a moment as our bond thrummed with his conviction.

I had once felt that way. But I had inserted myself deeply into the lives of Kosala's people and, in doing so, had long left that view behind. Perhaps Yudhajit had never experienced such a thing, as aloof a raja from his people as our father had been. But he was still a king, bound to his subjects, and he should have been better than this. "Our people matter. How could you say such a thing?"

"Kaikeyi, there is a difference between you and some person on the street. Of course every person has value to me, but you are my sister. I will always love you more and seek to protect you first."

I groped for a response, any response that might move him, but we were at an impasse. Once our passions had caused a storm, but it seemed that his dispassion would be what truly destroyed us. *"Please,* Yudhajit. Hear me when I say you are not protecting me." I looked into my brother's eyes and willed him to understand.

"I'm sorry," he said again, and perhaps he truly was. "But there is no other choice. Even if you cannot see it is right, I know what I must do."

"So that's it, then? Bharata takes the throne, or we go to war?"

"Yes," he said, clearly so there was no mistaking him. "That's it."

CHAPTER
THIRTY-THREE

I MADE THE RIDE back to Ayodhya in a daze. Once, I awoke in the night and turned over to look at my son, his face so peaceful and open in sleep that I nearly wept. I opened my mouth to ask him, *Do you want to be the raja, instead of your brother?* but came to my senses and instead just ran my fingers through his hair. His face, already childlike, melted into a sleepy smile. For a moment, the wall that I was trying to erect around my heart shook dangerously, but then I turned away and the feeling passed.

We arrived in the city only two days before the coronation, but I hardly cared. If I succeeded in changing Dasharath's mind, I would become the most hated woman in the kingdom. Bharata would hate me too, and the people would hate him for taking the throne. And then there was the matter of convincing Dasharath at all. I knew that it was very possible that I would snap our bond, destroy our relationship, and still fail to put Bharata on the throne.

But there was one person who could change Dasharath's mind, one person who might be able to stop this catastrophe.

I found Rama, in a rare moment, in his rooms. They were

spare and clean, containing only the furniture he needed to live. As soon as he saw me, he came to embrace me. "I am so sorry," he said. "So very sorry about your father. How is Bharata?"

His question gave me hope. "He is unhappy, of course. But he was not close with my father, and his grief will fade with time."

"You seem very sad indeed," Rama said. "Do you want anything? Water? It must have been a long journey."

I shook my head. "Rama, I need to speak with you about something. About the throne."

It was as if I had thrown a spark onto oil. His entire demeanor shifted, hardening. "You have scarcely returned from the death of your father and already you are talking about this?"

"*Listen* to me," I said, pushing every bit of fire I had left in me into the words. Rama stilled, then nodded for me to continue. "Long ago, your father made my father a promise. That any son I bore would become king."

Rama opened his mouth at that, but I pressed on. "I relinquished that promise years ago. I was happy for you, my son, to become king. What I did not know was that my father remembered this promise, and that he intended to hold your father to it." My voice wavered as I spoke, and Rama put a hand on my shoulder. This small act warmed me. I covered his hand with my own.

"Before his death, my father forced my brother, the raja of Kekaya, to make a vow. A promise to the gods that he would see your father's promise fulfilled. See Bharata become king." Rama's hand tightened on me, but he did not let go. I looked him in the eyes. "If Dasharath does not follow through on his promise, Kekaya will march to war against us. Rama, I would rather it be any other way than this. But you must let Bharata take the throne."

Rama bent his head. It was a heavy thing to ask, and I could see the pain of it in the set of his jaw. I let myself imagine what might happen next. We would go to Dasharath together. He would surely be shocked, and dismayed, but he would accept it if it came from Rama. And then—

"No." His eyes met mine, blazing. His hand dropped away. "I am sorry, Ma, but I cannot do that."

My stomach plummeted, the fragile hope I had built crumbling away. He had barely even considered it. "Rama, we are talking of war. Not with rakshasas or asuras, but with other people. Innocent people, who worship the same gods we do."

I could hear my heartbeat in my ears as I waited for his response. "It would not be right," Rama said after a long moment. "The people of Kosala want me to become king. I cannot bow to the whims of another kingdom. We are not so weak."

"It is not weak to avoid war," I said, and my voice broke. Tears pricked at my eyes, and I let them. "It is the strongest thing you could do, to avoid unnecessary bloodshed."

"Please do not cry, Ma," Rama said softly. But now he did not move to comfort me. He took a step back, as if to avoid getting caught in my emotion. "I do not do this to hurt you. Perhaps it will be useful for Ayodhya to clash with another kingdom first. To learn its own strength. You have to understand, there is a divine purpose at work. Nothing can compromise it."

"What could be more divine than preventing death and destruction?" I asked him, a pleading note in my voice. I clasped my hands together in front of me, stretching them out like a supplicant. "I have breathed the stench of the battlefield, Rama. I have watched men die. I have taken lives. It has convinced me that saving them is the better course."

"War may cause destruction, but it is also glorious. You know that," Rama said, shaking his head slightly. He was calm, aloof, as though this did not affect him. Seeing it was more painful than standing in the searing heat of Bhandasura's flames. I had believed him immature, unready, but this willingness to jeopardize his entire kingdom for his own ascension was something new. It was a failure—my failure. And for it, both the kingdoms I loved would go to war.

The destruction that two large kingdoms might bring to each other was immense. If he had seen what I had on the battlefield, watched his father nearly die, perhaps he would not be so eager—

And then it came to me in a flash. On that day so many years ago, I had saved Dasharath's life.

In return he had granted me two boons.

Rama was continuing to talk, to try to convince me of the glory of battle. But there was no time to dwell on it, this unholy ambition of my son. I held up my hand, and the torrent of words stopped. "I am sorry I asked you," I said. "I see that you cannot be swayed. Forgive me." I left him without a backward glance.

Manthara waited for me in my rooms, and when I saw her familiar form, clad in her usual soft cotton sari and smelling faintly of mint, I crumbled. The story of what had happened with Yudhajit came pouring out of me, as did my conversation with Rama.

"But I can use a boon to put Bharata on the throne. I will not let this war come to pass," I finished. Even as I said it, I felt the rightness of the decision. I still had some power.

Manthara considered what I had said for several long moments. "This is a good plan," she said at last. "But you must ask for your second boon from Dasharath immediately after your first. Ask for Bharata's crowning, and then ask that Dasharath keep the reason secret from all others. Nobody will know, so nobody will blame you." Manthara's allegiance had always been to me and not to Kosala, and normally I drew great comfort from that. But doing what was best for me would hurt my husband too deeply.

"It would pain Dasharath to not say why he snubs Rama in this way," I protested. "I could not."

"You can and you will," Manthara said. "If you want to maintain any power in this kingdom. If you want your son to take the throne smoothly."

"I do not wish to—" I began. But the words I might've said remained lodged in my throat. *I do not wish to hurt my husband.* I loved Dasharath. He was a dear friend, and I would never wish to cause him pain. But if I used my boon to ask this of him, it would hurt him regardless. Now that Manthara had pointed out the need for secrecy, I could imagine what might happen if it became known that I had forced Dasharath to place Bharata on the throne. I would become a pariah, and the Women's Council would fall by association. Those opportunists who circled Rama would swoop in at the crumbling of my reputation.

And so, as relieved as I was to know that I could avoid this war, I also knew claiming my boon would tear apart my family. I worried about Dasharath, but I worried too about Rama. I could not tell him in advance, for he would try to stop me. A part of me felt guilty for taking this away from him.

That night, I slipped through the corridors of the palace until I reached Sita's chambers.

Her rooms were quiet, a breeze flowing in through the open veranda door. I found her sitting there, her back to me. Before her was a glow so bright I had to shut my eyes against it. Even through my eyelids the brightness burned, and I knew I was standing before divinity. I had felt this inscrutable force before.

After a few moments, the weight of the presence lifted. I opened my eyes, blinking against spots of darkness in my vision, to find only Sita. She had rotated on her stool to face me. "I was sorry to hear about your father," she said.

"Thank you." I took a step toward her. "I hope I did not interrupt."

"I asked them to stay," Sita said. "I suggested that they might speak to you, but...they refused."

"Well, that is nothing new." I tried to smile, but I could barely manage a quirk of my lips. Sita was gods-touched too, and yet they openly spoke to her.

"It is not like that." Sita rose to her feet, her eyes beseeching. "They are merely trying to help me."

"So am I," I said. "You do not have to pretend. They have never wanted anything to do with me."

She looked away. "It is not that they dislike you. They say there is no point in them talking to you because you will not listen to them. That you are concerned with only that which is before you, and that you cannot change what is to come."

It was true that I cared little for the gods, yet I still smarted at the idea that they would both ignore and insult me. But I had come here for a reason, and it was not to hear the goddesses' belittling remarks. "How have you fared in my absence?" I asked instead.

Now Sita looked away. "I wish to be a good wife," she said at last. "But I think I will never be enough for Rama. I was crying, just now—that's why they came to me. They really are kinder than they might seem."

My heart fell. Trying to put Bharata on the throne would upend Sita's life too, and if things had not yet improved between her and Rama..."What happened?"

Sita's mouth twisted. "He has become consumed with preparing to fight the asuras, to the exclusion of all other affairs of the kingdom. Sometimes at night I find him pacing, unable to sleep for his dreams are filled with demons. I told him that there are no asuras or rakshasas here and he said to me, 'Other men do not ask for the support of their wives, they simply command it. Perhaps it is time I learn how.' I thought it in jest.

But he said a wise man taught him that disagreement with the gods was sympathy for evil, and that he would not allow such a thing among those closest to him." The words came pouring out of her. "I want to help him rid this world of evil if I can. But I worry he does not see that."

At any other time, the thought that my sweet, gentle son had grown into a man who would treat his wife so would have driven me to distraction. But I had a war to avert, and I could not give in to the weight of my emotions. "Do you think it would be better if he waited to take the throne? Until he was more ready?" I asked at last. "Perhaps I could find a way to ensure that."

This was the wrong thing to say. Her mouth pressed in a line. "Radnyi Kaikeyi, I appreciate what you are trying to do for me. But I do not wish to anger him further. It is up to me to convince him, to love him enough for him to listen to me. The goddesses are right in this at least. You cannot help me."

Early the next morning, as I stretched my body to prepare for the day to come, a knock sounded on the door.

I found Sita on the other side, her eyes bright with tears.

"What is it?" I asked, ushering her in. The moment the door slid shut behind her, the tears began slipping down her cheeks.

"He was angry," she said, her voice steadying as she spoke. "He was explaining to me how you had come to see him asking him to give up the throne two days before his coronation. I told him that you must have been tired, that perhaps you misspoke and . . . and he could not believe I had seen you, that I was defending you." She stood up, twisting the end of her braid in her fingers. "He said a *friend* had told him that if he did not use a firm hand with me, I would never listen to him. That he hadn't thought it good advice at that time, but perhaps he had been mistaken."

This was a nightmare. It had to be. Rama was single-minded,

and perhaps gullible, but he had never once shown himself to be this kind of man. *A firm hand.* It did not take much imagination to uncover what this might mean. I wanted to cry, even though it had happened to Sita. "What can I do?" My voice trembled. I did not want to believe that any man would consider hitting a woman, let alone a god. But perhaps she was just a mortal to Rama, someone who was getting in his way. And perhaps he was more man than god in some ways. How had so much changed in the span of one night?

Sita took my hand in hers. "You seemed...I mean...last night." She kept trailing off and restarting, and I squeezed her fingers.

"You can say anything you want to me, Sita."

"Can you really do something to help him? Stop him from actually doing this?"

I could not imagine how putting Bharata on the throne would help Sita. No. I would have to do something more. A thought sprang into my mind—I could send Rama away, far away from the pressures that had consumed him. That had turned him from a kind boy into a person willing to sacrifice his subjects in order to take the throne. It was difficult to imagine doing it, forcing him away for years, and yet perhaps there he could safely pursue his divine war without harming anyone else. And when he had worn himself out on this fool's quest, he could return as the man Kosala needed him to be.

"I will see what I can do," I told her.

She left with a small, hopeful smile, but when she did I let myself sink to the floor and give in to heartbreak. I had raised a son who would threaten a woman. Who would insinuate violence toward her. It was a grief beyond tears to contemplate, the totality of my failure. I sat crouched against the door until my thighs cramped and went numb. Only when Asha came through the door and nearly hit me did I rise on unsteady feet and set out to try to mend what I still could.

*　　*　　*

Some instinct directed me to the training fields.

Rama stood alone, his back to me and a bow in his hands, loosing arrow after arrow at a target.

"Ma," he said without turning. "Would you love me if I did something terrible?"

"Of course," I said, knowing where this was going. "But I might still be angry with you."

He turned around. His eyes were red, as though he had been crying, and despite everything, I wanted to gather him in my arms. But the moment passed, for he was not the baby I had sung to sleep nor the child I had chased around the yard, as much as I wanted him to be. "You know, then. What I said to Sita."

"Yes." I wanted to comfort him, but he did not deserve it. I clasped my hands behind my back. "I am disappointed in you, Rama."

"I wasn't thinking," he whispered. "I don't know what came over me. I just—I feel so burdened. The pressure of my purpose is unbearable. And I wanted your help, so after we talked, and I realized you did not believe in me, I just... snapped. I am so sorry for what I did. For what I said."

He hung his head in shame, the picture of contriteness, but it was too little, and it came too late. For I saw it then, the pattern. Under stress, Rama lashed out. He put people in danger. He had done it to me, to his brother, and now to Sita.

"Please, Ma," Rama was saying. "You have to believe me." But he was speaking from a distance. I had heard husbands speak like this before. I had heard it for years, since the inception of the Women's Council.

"I believe that you are sorry, Rama," I said. "But you have been sorry many times, and yet this is not the first time you have behaved this way. You threaten people because you feel a lack of control. It's not right."

"I know." We stood there in silence for a few moments, and then he raised his head. "It will be better when I am raja. When I can actually carry out my purpose."

"No." His expression became confused, but I shook my head. "Your responsibilities will only intensify when you are king. You cannot treat your family this way, not for any purpose. Do you not see that?"

His brows drew together, and I could sense his annoyance building. "I understand what I did was wrong. Of course I do. But you are overreacting. *This* is more important. And I do not understand why you move so quickly to defend Sita, but not to defend the entire world, which I am telling you will suffer under the coming onslaught. Why do you not care for those countless others?"

"You are wrong, Rama. And I am sad you cannot see it."

"Are you?" Rama demanded. "Or are you only seeing what you wish to see, so that you can keep your life comfortable? I feel as though you are abandoning me, Ma." His voice cracked ever so slightly on that word, and I had to remind myself to harden my heart.

"Don't turn this on me," I said. "You committed the sin, not I." As I said it, though, I remembered slapping him long ago. Had I been the one to teach him to use violence? *No.* It was not my fault alone.

"And what sin is it to turn your back on your son? My tutor told me you were blinded, that you cared not for the will of the gods, but I've never had reason to believe it until now."

"This again?" I demanded. "Did you know Sage Vamadeva cursed his innocent wife? Consigned her to a life as a stone statue?"

"What are you talking about? Sage Vamadeva's wife betrayed him with another man. She lied to him. He showed mercy not striking her dead."

"How can you believe that?" I demanded. I had thought

that perhaps when Rama heard the truth, he would reconsider. But even here, Vamadeva had reached Rama before me. "Do you think a woman should be killed for infidelity?"

"You might be different, Ma. But surely you know that most women introduce weakness into the world." It was as though I had been hit in the chest by a horse, a blow that hurt so badly my fingers and toes tingled with the pain. It was finished. Rama was beyond my reach.

His quest had been given to him by a madman. I had to protect him from himself, protect others from him. I needed to take this responsibility from him and give him space to realize the error of his ways. And he needed to do this somewhere he could not harm anyone else.

I had to exile Rama.

As the sun began its descent, I found Dasharath in his suite of rooms, at his desk composing letters. The sight of him was a dagger. I knew this was what I must do, but even so the loss of Dasharath's friendship would be an enormous blow. He had been a steadfast presence in my life for years, able to lighten my heart despite the heavy crown he wore. And now I would crush him. I knew when I did this, I would never again hear his laugh, experience his delightful mirth, or be wrapped in his comforting arms—and yet I would see him every day, and live with what I had done.

"Kaikeyi, I am so sorry," he said the moment I entered. In this moment, his kindness was a curse. "I have been so busy today, I meant to send for you. Our entire kingdom grieves for your family."

"Thank you." I held myself stiff as he embraced me. I could not let myself have even this small pleasure, or I might have lost my nerve.

"Is something the matter?" he asked. Genuine concern thrummed across our diminished bond, and for a moment grief at what I had to do overwhelmed me. I took a deep breath and found my resolve.

"I have come to claim my boons."

Dasharath's brow furrowed in confusion then cleared. "Oh, yes, your boons. I granted you two for your service in the battle against Sambarasura."

"Yes, my raja."

"Well there is no need to use those," he told me. "Whatever you wish I will give. Surely you know this by now, Kaikeyi."

"I do," I said. "But not this."

He studied my face for a moment, then stepped back. "What is this about?"

I swallowed. "It is about Rama. He is not ready to take the throne."

Horror etched itself in the planes of Dasharath's face, and the thickest blue chain I had ever seen choked him in the Binding Plane. "No, Kaikeyi. He is ready, and he will receive the crown tomorrow."

"Somebody who treats his citizens as though they are expendable should not become king." I wished, not for the first time, that I could tell him of everything else, of Rama's magic and my own, and of Ravana's confession besides. I wonder, if I had never kept it from Dasharath, might things have been different? But I had no reason to tell him now, for I had seen firsthand what happened if I tried to insinuate anything at all about Rama's control. Rama's influence on Dasharath superseded mine.

"Please, I beg of you, postpone the ceremony." I poured everything I had into our bond.

"I will not." He held himself like a soldier, although he had not been to battle in over ten years. His body hardened into sharp lines, and he stared at me as though I was the enemy.

"Then, Raja Dasharath, I ask these two boons of you. First, you must exile Rama beyond our borders for ten years."

He stared at me blankly as though he could not believe my words. I felt as though I stood outside of my body, watching the hurt begin to creep over his face as he realized this was truly happening. Bleakly, I thought about taking it back, about pretending I had jested. But I said nothing, and we tumbled together over the precipice.

"No, no, I cannot, no," Dasharath said, repeating these words over and over like a prayer.

"And second, you must place Bharata on the throne for these years. These boons I ask of you."

"No!" he shouted, and I startled. But even then I was not afraid of him. I trusted him. I loved him. Even if I had managed to burn that all away, the impression of all we had shared would not be so easily erased.

He grabbed the collar of my blouse and hung his head. "Please, Kaikeyi. You are wrong. Please do not ask this of me." His body shook with the force of his weeping, and still he clutched me.

Tears came to my eyes as well. "Dasharath, understand. He is unready. I would not ask this otherwise. When he has spent some time alone, improving himself, then he can come back and rule." I kept my voice admirably steady as I tore out my husband's heart.

"Kaikeyi, you do not know what you ask. I cannot go through with this." He gasped out each word as though it physically pained him.

"Give me one reason why Rama must become raja now," I said. "A single legitimate reason, and I will gladly withdraw my request."

Dasharath at last lifted his red-rimmed eyes to my own, and I saw the despair there. "I have a feeling, deep in my chest, that it is the right thing to do. You would not ask me to contradict my sincerest beliefs, would you?" I could see that feeling, wrapped around him, controlling his every moment.

"I would," I whispered. "You have already broken one such promise to me. Kekaya remembers. My brother remembers. He threatens war upon you for it, unless you make things right. Surely you would not bring war upon your people for breaking your sworn oath?"

Dasharath shook his head as though he had not heard my words, and any hope I had that my husband, at least, might see reason, was extinguished. "Please," he begged, and I felt the tears slipping silently down my face. But I could not back down now.

"Dasharath, I am talking of war. You made an oath to my family. You made oaths to the gods. Your word cannot be broken."

A knock sounded on the door, but Dasharath, nearly insensible, merely cradled his head in his hands. I opened my mouth to speak, but no sound came out. On the second attempt, I managed to croak, "Who is it?"

"Kaikeyi?" came Kaushalya's voice. She appeared in the doorway, and as she took in my tears and Dasharath's posture, she swept forward and grasped my hands. "What is happening?" she asked. "Kaikeyi, is this about your father?"

I shook my head, unable to tell her what I had just done. Dasharath glanced at Kaushalya. "Long ago, I promised this treacherous woman that I would grant her two boons at any time. And now she has come to redeem them."

Treacherous? Kaushalya mouthed at me, baffled and even a bit amused.

"She has demanded as her first boon that Rama be exiled for ten years. And as her second that Bharata become king in Rama's stead."

However I thought Kaushalya would react, this was not it: head tipped back in laughter, howls of mirth, tears of hilarity spilling from her eyes.

"It is true," I said quietly.

Her laughter died as she took in my face. "What?"

I merely nodded my head.

"Kaikeyi. *No*. Why?"

"I am so sorry, Kaushalya." I reached out a hand, but she backed away from me until she had pressed herself against the wall.

"*Why?*" she repeated. "Have you been so jealous of me all this time? This is your way of taking revenge?"

"It has nothing to do with jealousy." I managed to keep my voice steady, despite the sharp sting of pain. Deep in my heart, in a place I could hardly admit to myself, I had imagined that Dasharath and Kaushalya might still come around. Imagined that our bonds were strong and true, and could resist the divine influence of our son. "He is not ready."

"You are a faithless woman," Dasharath proclaimed, rising to his feet. "Your oaths to the gods are meaningless. They forsook you long ago. I cannot believe you so fooled me, that I took you into my confidence. Rama was right. I never should have given a woman so much power."

"What?" Kaushalya asked, but we paid her no mind.

"You swore to me and to the gods," I said, my voice shaking slightly. "Now say it in front of Kaushalya as your witness. Will you fulfill your boons to me, Raja Dasharath?" I lifted my chin and composed my face into as haughty an image as I could muster. If they wished me to be a jealous, faithless, prideful woman, I would give them what they wanted. That was what it would take to see this task through. I gave the golden string a final push.

Our bond, that great construction that had carried us through my father's hall to the palace of Ayodhya, from the battlefield to the council room to the building of a revolutionary kingdom—that golden thread that had been so vital, so precious—snapped in two.

Dasharath fell to his knees, and the impact ricocheted

through my body. It felt as though if I were to exit the Binding Plane, the world would remain grayed. Fragments of gold fell to the shrouded floor and vanished like the last fragments of a dream.

A piece of my soul dissolved with them.

And Dasharath, broken and tired and suddenly much older than his years, whispered, "I will."

CHAPTER
THIRTY-FOUR

MY HUSBAND COLLAPSED.

You did this, Kaushalya's expression seemed to say as she rushed to his side and tried to rouse him. Or perhaps that was simply my own mind. I thought my heart would burst from the agony of it.

Dasharath did not wake.

Undeterred, Kaushalya hooked her arms under his, trying to move him.

At last, my limbs loosened, and I helped her to lift him onto his great bed. We did not speak as we went about our task, and each time our hands brushed, one of us jerked away.

At last, she broke the silence. "Should we call a healer?"

I pressed my fingers under his chin. "Yes. But his heart holds steady." I turned away so I would not have to see her expression.

"Kaikeyi," she said. I did not turn around. "Kaikeyi," she repeated, and placed a hand on my shoulder. I shrugged it off, unable to face her.

"I will say my piece. I am incredibly angry at you. I am so very angry, I could slap you, claw at your eyes."

"I know." I hung my head, unable to face her disappointment.

She sighed. "You know nothing, you monumental idiot. I am furious because you did not tell me of any of this. You never mentioned a thing. I want Rama to take the throne, and one day he will be a great ruler. But *I agree with you*. He is unready. I could not do anything about it, I can barely open my mouth in his presence, but you have always been stronger—and for that I am grateful."

I spun around. "*What?*"

"I trust you more than anyone in the palace, and yet you do not seem to trust me."

"You said you thought I was jealous," I blurted out. I could not allow myself to think that Kaushalya spoke honestly.

I forced myself to reenter the Binding Plane, though my heart resisted it, after what had just transpired with Dasharath. I had to recite the mantra in my mind, for the first time in nearly a decade, for the Plane would not come easily.

In the faded world, I saw no evidence of deception, and only the faintest of blue bonds around her neck.

"I did not know what to think. I was hurt, and I lashed out," she said. "That, I think, should be understandable. I am Rama's mother. You think I do not know the way he holds forth before other men, trying to impress them? The way he obsesses over war at the cost of all else? A king needs to be grounded, secure in himself. But Bharata is none of those things either. So what was I to believe? It seemed like you cared not for the kingdom's welfare but for your own blood son's power." She gave me a slight smile there. "Yet in all the time I have known you, all you have done is helped others. You saved Dasharath's life less than a year after marrying him. Therefore, logic says you must have had a reason for making Bharata raja."

I cradled my head in my hands. "Dasharath swore my father an oath many years ago. He said that any son of mine would be heir to the throne. My brother has heard of Rama's impending coronation and threatened to wage war on Kosala unless Bharata was crowned. But when I tried to tell Dasharath, he... he hardly listened."

Kaushalya considered this, eyes wide. After a moment, she reached out, gently maneuvering me so that my forehead rested against her shoulder. Only then did I realize that I had begun crying again. "Shh. You must stay strong now. Would you like me to speak for you?"

Before I could answer, Dasharath stirred. "Kaikeyi? Kaushalya? What happened?" He lifted himself up. "Why am I in this bed?"

Seeing Dasharath, I felt within me the throb of emptiness where our bond should have been. "No." I stepped away, wiped my face dry, and set my shoulders. "No, he will need someone."

She nodded. "I am furious with you," she said at a normal volume, and I knew that too was true, even if she spoke for Dasharath's benefit.

"Furious?" Dasharath echoed weakly. "Why—oh no, no, no."

"You fainted. We have sent for a healer." I kept my tone cold and tried to bring some distance back to the proceedings. My aloofness had all but disappeared as I bore witness to his pain, but now it was time to be unyielding. For Kosala's sake, and my family's.

"You're crying," he said, gaze searching my face. "Please tell me you have changed your mind. You have realized the error of your ways."

"I have not changed my mind. Please, though, I beg of you, do not tell the rest of the kingdom why you have arrived at such a decision. If they know it came from me, they may not respect it." He would not do it, and I had no leverage over him, no bond to rely on—but I asked it nonetheless.

His face was pale as he said, "The whole kingdom will know who is responsible for this crime. The whole kingdom will hate you and hate what you have done to them."

It hurt me more than I wanted to admit. But in the pain of this moment, of the loss of what I had once shared with Dasharath, I could hardly comprehend what loss was to come next. When I tried to think about it, my mind protested, as though it was too much to even contemplate.

"I told you that I acted in the best interests of the kingdom. Even if you disagree with me, you should not wish this fate upon me. I am your wife."

Dasharath bared his teeth at me. "You are no wife of mine. I will honor the boons I granted you. But you are already dead to me."

At this, Kaushalya stepped forward, anger clear on her features. I shook my head at her, but she opened her mouth anyway.

"I do not care," I said, speaking over whatever she intended to say. I would not let Kaushalya lose everything too. "I will leave you with your *real* wife." And I swept out of the room before anyone could say another word.

I sat in my room and cried. Asha and Manthara stood watch over me. My stomach heaved with the force of each breath, and I thought my insides might spill out of me. I waited every moment for my heart to fail. They offered me food, water, but I could not bring myself to accept any part of it. Part of me wished for death.

Sometime after my confrontation with Dasharath—I wasn't sure how many hours had passed—a messenger came and spoke with Manthara. She relayed to me that Dasharath had called a special meeting of court and requested my presence.

He wanted me there when he denounced me.

Asha gave me a cool cloth to press to my red eyes as she

wrapped me in a simple silver sari, although in the low light it appeared gray and dull. She applied color to my face, the red powder quite stark, for my skin was pale and drawn. She fastened a simple gold chain around my neck, placed a kiss on my brow, and then left me alone with Manthara.

"You did the right thing," Manthara told me. "No matter what is said about you, Kaikeyi, remember that you did the right thing. You are not wicked."

"Then why do I feel wicked?" I whispered.

"Because those who are good question themselves. Because those who are good always wonder if there was a better way, a way that could have helped more and hurt less. That feeling is why you are good." She too pressed a kiss to my forehead. "This will be terrible, but you are so strong. You can make it through."

I leaned into her and wrapped my arms around her waist. "I love you," I said. "I could not do this without you."

"You silly girl. I love you too. Now you must go."

With each step I took toward the throne room, my heart steadied. I was strong, and I was in the right. I took measured paces, fortifying myself in icy reserve, and as such was one of the last to reach the throne room.

Dasharath was there on his throne looking old, older than his years. Kaushalya and Sumitra sat stiffly in their formal seats on his left. On his right, all four of my sons appeared equally confused, which meant that I would get the privilege of watching their reactions in person.

When I took my seat, Dasharath stood, and a hush fell over the court. He spoke without preamble. "As some of you may know, long ago, Radnyi Kaikeyi accompanied me to the field of battle and saved my life. In return, I granted her two boons. Generous, to be sure, but I thought her deserving."

I pasted an indifferent expression onto my face. Whatever the court would think of me now, they would not find me weak, or uncertain.

"She has claimed those two boons today," Dasharath continued.

Whatever happened, I would not waver.

"Her first request is that Rama be exiled to the forest for ten years."

Gasps echoed throughout the room. Sumitra's hand rose to her mouth in shock. Rama sprang to his feet and looked right at me. I could see the surprise in his eyes, the hurt—and behind that, the rage. All around the room, the blue loops of control Rama had created flared into brilliant existence.

"Her second wish is for Bharata to take the throne during that time. I am powerless to repel her wickedness, for I swore an oath to the gods." The crowd broke out into murmurs and shouts, and Dasharath faltered. Rama caught his arm. "Rama, my son. I am so sorry."

Rama looked once more to me, his expression one of naked betrayal. Then he helped Dasharath back to his throne. I struggled to maintain my cool demeanor as I watched my son stand with his back to the crowd for a moment, watched him force his expression into a more neutral gaze, watched him take a deep breath, before turning back around.

"A boon is an oath that cannot be ignored. An oath witnessed by the gods. If this is what my father orders, then of course I will obey," Rama said, lifting his arms. He paused. "Sita and I will depart Ayodhya tomorrow."

My gaze shot to hers, and I saw her still. We all knew that she would have no choice but to go along with it. The whole court had heard Rama's proclamation, and they were under his thrall besides.

"I too will go with them," Lakshmana proclaimed, rising to his feet. "My brother will not be without protection." At this, my mouth dropped, my entire mask falling away. Of course Lakshmana would do this. And sacrifice ten years of his life in the process.

I heard Sumitra whisper *No*, felt her hand clutch my arm. She must have not fully comprehended that all of this was my doing, or she would not be touching me now.

"Thank you, brother." Rama embraced Lakshmana, and over Rama's shoulder, Lakshmana mouthed a single word at me. I shook my head, uncomprehending, and he mouthed it again.

Panchavati, it looked like he was saying. Panchavati? I searched myself for any reference to that name, but none came to mind. Lakshmana's memory was too good, how was I to know what he meant—

And then I knew. Panchavati was a forest to the south of the Vindhya range. At its eastern border lay Janasthana.

I raised my chin. "Lakshmana, you are so good to accompany your brother and his wife to Panchavati Forest." I projected my voice over the hubbub in a slow, unhurried manner.

"Panchavati Forest?" Rama turned to me now, his expression unreadable.

"Yes. That is the place I have selected for you to pass your exile," I said.

"How dare you?" somebody shouted from the amassed audience. Threads in the Binding Plane frayed and snapped, but I paid them no mind even as their loss ricocheted in my stomach. *I do not need the court to like me any longer*, I told myself, but the strange blankness of the Binding Plane without connections turned my stomach. It was exactly the same as the real world but leached of color. Hollow.

"How dare I?" I asked, turning my head toward the crowd with practiced slowness. Even if they were under Rama's influence, I could still command their attention for this moment. "My boons were earned, and mine to do with as I wished."

"Traitor!" someone else called. Others shouted far less kind words.

Rama lifted a hand for silence. "My mother speaks truly,"

he said. "We cannot fault her for what we perceive to be failures in judgment. Please, do not act too harshly toward her."

"They are not harsh enough," a voice interjected.

My heart stuttered. It was Bharata.

I stood. "Bharata," I began, all affectations dropping away. "Bharata, please do not be angry with me." My plans to claim my boons had been formed in a rush, all at once, and I had not stopped to consult Bharata. But this was about him too, and it had been wrong of me not to at least warn him. I bowed my head.

"How could you, Ma?" he demanded. "I thought you loved us. All of us."

"I do. And I love this kingdom. That is why I did this," I said, and I broke my vow to never influence him. I pushed everything I dared into our fragile, pulsating bond, every bit of love I had for him.

"You do not love us, or this kingdom." Bharata spoke softly, but everyone quieted to hear him. "You love only power."

"Bharata, that is not true." I spared a glance for Dasharath, but he sat quiet in his throne, oblivious to all around him.

Shatrugna placed a hand on Bharata's shoulder. "You cannot reason with her," Shatrugna said, throwing me a look of undisguised loathing.

"Please—" I tried one last time.

The bond between Bharata and me shattered quietly.

As the pieces fell around me in a dreadful rain, Bharata turned away from me and said to the court at large, "You are no mother of mine."

CHAPTER
THIRTY-FIVE

"MY LADY?" CAME A muffled voice from the front room.

You are no mother of mine.

I was lying in my bed, repeating Bharata's words over and over again to myself. How had anybody gotten into my rooms? Manthara and Asha had left, or so I thought.

Then Asha walked into my bedroom, and I realized she must have only pretended to leave, in order to keep watch over me. I did not deserve friends like this. "Urmila and Lakshmana have come to say goodbye."

I waved a hand at her, and Asha interpreted it according to her own will. She walked away and returned a moment later, Urmila and Lakshmana in tow. I did not get up.

"Ma," Lakshmana murmured, kneeling beside my bed. "Ma, I am so sorry."

I wanted to turn away from him but could not muster the energy to do so.

"I brought him here," Urmila said. "He did not wish to disturb you, but he should not leave without saying goodbye."

"I did not wish to be disturbed," I whispered, my lips barely moving.

Lakshmana's hand found my own. "I am so sorry, Ma. You truly are the best of us."

"Ha." The sound came straight from my belly. I made it again, because I could. "Ha."

He remained undeterred. "I promise I will not let you down. I will not let Sita leave my sight."

"When you sleep, Rama can do as he pleases," I said. "It matters not. Stay in Ayodhya if you wish."

"You cannot possibly want that." He rose to his feet. "I will not sleep if that is what it requires."

"Lakshmana," Urmila said fiercely, "do not kill yourself for Sita's sake. I will not lose both my sister and my husband to this idiocy."

"I can do it," he insisted. With great determination, I focused my eyes on him and caught an intense glint in his expression. "I swear it. I will protect Sita with my life, I swear this to the gods."

"The gods are not listening," I said. Even though I knew that much of Rama's sins lay at the feet of a man, not the gods, they had done nothing to stop him, just as they had done nothing to help me. But Lakshmana and Urmila were paying me no mind—they had turned away from me. Of course, I had summoned all my remaining vigor for words nobody would listen to.

I pushed myself up onto my elbows, just as Lakshmana dropped to his knees. *What in the world?* I blinked a few times, watching as the shadow in the corner of my bedroom moved, coalescing into the shape of a woman, swathed in a cloak of deep, glimmering black.

The shadow woman approached me, but my eyes had difficulty grasping onto anything but her face. Her form remained shrouded in slippery darkness.

"I am Nidra," she said, and each word reverberated within the walls, within the cage of my ribs.

I tipped my head back and laughed. I felt halfway out of my body, uncontrolled, hysterical. Nidra had been my favorite goddess to pray to as a child. Every night, when dreams eluded me in my stone room in Kekaya, I sent a prayer to the goddess of sleep. And every night, I learned anew that the goodwill of the gods did not extend to me.

"I hope you do not expect me to bow, my lady."

Sorrow passed over her features. "I heard every one of your prayers," she said. "And each time, I hoped to respond."

"Hope is useless," I bit out. "I was a child."

"It is, is it not? You achieved greatness without us. Imagine what you might have done with us."

"I would rather not." This conversation stung like thousands of grains of salt pressed into a hundred bleeding wounds. Of course, now the gods would choose to talk to me, to approve of my worst actions.

"Oh, Kaikeyi," Nidra breathed, and she passed a hand over the top of my head. As she did, tension and exhaustion melted out of me. The pain and the despair remained, but I felt calmer, like a ship that had just weathered river rapids to arrive bruised and beaten at a dock.

Then my mind caught up. "I thought you gods could do nothing for me. Gods-touched, forsaken."

She gave a slight smile. "I suppose, but I have found my way around the rules before. Your dreams have not been wholly barren. And I awoke your son when Bhandasura first attacked you. I sent him the location of a scroll in a dream."

Lakshmana gaped at her, but I simply said, "I do not want your influence in me. My mind is my own, and that is all I have left." Even as I spoke it, I wondered what she had already done to me.

"Your mind is still your own. My magic—it is not in your Binding Plane. It simply soothes your body into sleep, or into wakefulness." She now looked less than divine, as though she had taken on my own fatigue. My experience with gods was admittedly limited, but I did not expect Nidra to seem so... mortal. "But I did not come here for you."

"Of course not," I said, but there was no heat in my voice.

Nidra turned away. "Lakshmana, you are a virtuous man. I have been in your mind before this, and I know you are steadfast. Is it your intention to guard Sita every moment of the day for the next ten years?"

"It is," Lakshmana said from his position on the ground.

"Even the gods must sleep," Nidra said. "But as the goddess of sleep, I will make an exception for you."

"Thank you, Devi."

"Do not thank me yet. As with all things, there is a price. Someone else must take on the burden of sleep for you. For these ten years, they will sleep for nearly the whole day and spend only a few waking hours each evening. If you can find someone willing to shoulder this responsibility, I will grant you this allowance."

"I will do it," Urmila said at once. "I will take this burden if it means that Lakshmana can protect my sister and stay alive."

"No, you cannot," Lakshmana said, quiet desperation in his tone. I did not need the Binding Plane to see there was a deep affection between my son and his wife. "I will not ask you to do such a thing."

"You do not have to ask me," Urmila said. "I have already made this decision. I am not as bold as Sita or as brave as Radnyi Kaikeyi. I will have nothing to contribute to Ayodhya, but I can do this. And in ten years, I will have my life back once more. I will have you and my sister back. It is not a death sentence."

I had never truly gotten to know Urmila, something that I now regretted. Clearly, she was an extraordinary young woman. I knew I would not have been willing to make such a sacrifice at her age.

"Very well," Nidra proclaimed. "It is done. From the first night that Lakshmana stays awake until he returns to Ayodhya or loses his life, you, Urmila, will pay the cost of his sleeplessness." She turned toward me. "If you have need of my powers, you may pray to me. We minor goddesses cannot do much, but I promise that from now on, I will answer. And perhaps I will not be the only one."

A gust of wind blew through the fully enclosed room. I blinked, and when I opened my eyes, the goddess was gone.

Urmila and Lakshmana rose to their feet, rubbing their knees. "I had never heard of the goddess of sleep before," Urmila said.

I turned to look at her. "I would bet anything that your sister has heard of her. But it matters not."

"It matters a great deal," Urmila said. "She has just blessed us. Or cursed us."

"It is all right," Lakshmana said softly. He came to me, first touching my feet and then embracing me. "Goodbye, Ma. Do not worry. I will do my best."

Somehow I managed to wrap my arms around him. "I know," I said. "Please be safe."

And then, in another moment, they were gone. I sank back on my bed, my eyelids suddenly heavy as iron. I watched Lakshmana's back vanish as my eyes dragged closed.

For the first time in my life, after the worst day of my life, sleep came easily.

I awoke with total lucidity, just as the sun's rays brushed the edge of the horizon. And with that clarity of thought came the realization that I needed to speak to Rama one more time.

I knew without much reflection where I would find him. And sure enough, he stood with Shatrugna on the palace's training field, conversing in low tones.

"I did not expect to see you, Ma," Rama said without turning.

Shatrugna, however, spun to face me. His usually sweet face filled with hatred. "What are *you* doing here? How dare you—"

"Shatrugna. Please leave us," Rama said. Shatrugna looked back at Rama, and then pushed past me without another word.

"This whole time I thought I could convince you," Rama said softly. "This whole time, I thought you were on my side. But it turns out you were deceiving me. Deceiving everyone. Everyone else was right about you, and I was a fool."

"No, Rama. I was never deceiving you. I am your mother, and I love you still."

He turned around. "Don't lie. You were never a friend to me. How could you be, when you have forsaken the gods? I should have listened, should have taken away your power when I had the chance."

"Listen to yourself," I said. "What has happened to you?"

"I was betrayed by my own mother," he said.

"Betrayed?" I demanded. "I *love* you. I gave you everything I could. When you cried, I sang to you. I handed you the moon. I played with you, took you to my homeland. And in return, you turned your back on me. You spurned my teachings and put me in danger."

"Then why are you sending me away?" He looked away, a thick curl falling into his eyes as he blinked rapidly. There was real hurt in his voice, and the knowledge that I was responsible for it stung.

"I am helping you," I said, my voice thick. "Removing the responsibility that you said burdened you. I asked that you only be sent away for ten years. I believe you can change. You need not spend every hour being crushed by this divine responsibility you feel you are called to carry out. When you were a child and unhappy, I could hold you. Make you feel safe, tell you everything would be all right. I cannot do that anymore. But I can do this."

"You think I don't want the responsibility, but I do. It is my duty. And you are attempting to thwart it." He shook his head. "You think people only agree with me because I have forced them to. But there are so many people in the city whom you have ignored or pushed aside. You asked I be sent away for ten years because you knew you could not get away with exiling me for my whole life."

"You are a child. Just a child. You do not know what you speak of," I told him. "Do you not remember how it used to be? Our family was happy."

Perhaps I imagined it, but I thought for a moment his eyes grew distant, watery. "We were," he said softly. I wondered which memory he saw playing out before him.

I could remember clearly watching my sons running in the bright Kosala sun, chasing one another, getting stuck in barrels and teasing their father. I remembered too that sense of foreboding that we would be torn apart. How I wished I had been wrong. "We can be happy again," I said at last, for I had to believe it was true.

We stood there, heads bowed in the early morning light. Mother and son, both wishing for something different than we had. Then he straightened. "I doubt it," he said.

I stepped back, pushing away the hurt, for this was not a surprise. The pause had given me a moment to think, consider the other person bound up in this besides us two. "At least do not bring Sita with you."

Rama shook his head. "I see. Even now you did not come for me, your supposed son. You came for Sita."

I had come to see Rama, to speak to my beloved son before he left, but he would not believe me if I said so now. "How can I convince you to let her stay?" I asked instead. "Surely there must be something."

"I did not come here to bargain, and yet you insist upon it. Fine. Repent everything, Ma. Support me, and you may keep your seat on the Mantri Parishad. You get to keep your power."

Maybe once that had been what mattered to me, but now it wasn't even a choice. I took a deep breath to collect myself, and when I spoke it was with a steady voice. "I am sorry, Rama. I have failed you as a mother. I raised a cruel, callous child. This hurts me too. But I deserve this pain."

His eyes widened almost imperceptibly, and I could tell I had shocked him. But it was too late. This was not enough.

"I hope your time in the forest serves you well," I said at last. I turned from him and walked back through the door.

Sita came to see me before she left.

"I am so sorry," I told her over and over, but she ignored me. Our connection in the Binding Plane still appeared strong, stark against the dearth of bonds. But I wanted to remember her face as it was, not as it looked in the world adjacent, and so I let go of my magic and simply sat by her side. Against her pale and drawn face, her silver strip of hair looked luminescent.

At last, an attendant came to my room to tell Sita it was time to leave. Before she left, the woman gave me a glance filled with pure disgust.

When she was gone, Sita turned to me. "Do you remember our first conversation?" she asked.

"Yes." How could I forget. I had met a funny, sharp girl and reassured her that her marriage would work out, and that she would be happy. One did not easily forget such sins.

"I asked you what your purpose was, and you said you did not know. I asked you what my purpose was, and you told me that I would know it when it happened." Sita sat with her back straight as an arrow, arms at her side. There was no inflection in her voice.

"I am so sorry," I repeated uselessly. "Please know that had I known how things would turn out—"

"I am not interested in your apologies," she said. "I think your purpose is clear. Helping the women of this kingdom is noble indeed. But I have not yet found mine. If you have any idea what it might be..."

Her purpose, I believed, was to spark all that had already happened. But she could not know that, because she did not know about Ravana—

Ravana. In all of this, I had forgotten about him.

Lakshmana had asked me to pick Panchavati because it was far away from Ayodhya and near to a friendly city that could harbor Sita, if needed. I had gone along with it, swept up in the moment.

But Janasthana held more than a safe haven. The moment Rama left, I needed to send Ravana a missive. I had kept his hawk for that purpose, after all. Because for Ravana, this outcome was the best possible one. He would be close enough to watch over Sita and take matters into his own hands if need be, without ever harming Kosala or Ayodhya.

"So you do know," Sita said, and I quickly set my expression to something less obvious. Not fast enough, though.

"No, I do not, but..." Sita needed to know at least a bit of the truth. I was tired, so tired, of secrets. "I am sure that with Lakshmana's presence, you will be well taken care of in Panchavati Forest. But if anything should ever happen, the nearest city is Janasthana. The ruler of that city will give you anything your heart desires, and you can trust him absolutely."

"You have spoken with him?" she asked, confused. "Did you know Rama would take me along? Is that why you made such an arrangement?"

"No! No. I had no idea. And I have not yet spoken to him, but I will. The ruler of Janasthana and I are old friends. You have met him once. Ravana, raja of Lanka."

Sita wrinkled her nose. "I remember. But I do not think that an old jealous suitor will help me much."

"Trust me. He is not a jealous suitor, and he bears you no ill will. He will protect you. So do not hesitate. There is no need to be a martyr."

"I am already a martyr," she said. "But thank you. I will go to him, should I have need." She stood up in a single fluid motion.

"I am sorry," I repeated, unable to rise to my feet. "I hope that one day you can forgive me for what I have done."

"There is nothing to forgive." Sita opened the door slowly, and as she stepped into the hall, she squared her shoulders and lifted her head. I watched each piece of armor settle into place until no weakness could be found, and then she disappeared from view.

CHAPTER THIRTY-SIX

THEY SAY THAT DASHARATH'S cries could be heard from the palace to the city gates. They say he pleaded with the gods and cursed my name and made absurd promises if only Rama would remain in Ayodhya. They say he ripped at his clothes and beat the ground and wailed, a sound so primal and intimate that people turned away from their broken king.

The departure, Manthara told me, was like a funeral procession. Crowds lined the streets that Rama would take, and he rode out at a snail's pace, Sita behind him, Lakshmana at his side, allowing everyone a chance to observe the cheated prince of Ayodhya. He wore an ascetic's robes and carried only a small pack on the back of his horse. Rama had an excellent sense of drama, if nothing else.

I myself sat in the gardens alone, straining to hear the faint hubbub of the city.

It felt like hours had passed until Kaushalya came and found me. "You must come. It is Dasharath," she said.

"Is he executing me?" I asked dully, not getting up. "I would like to die here. It is beautiful, and peaceful. He should come to me."

"What are you talking about?" Kaushalya demanded, grabbing my wrist and dragging me to my feet.

I rolled my eyes. "You said I needed to come and see the raja. I was wondering when he has set the date for my execution."

Kaushalya slapped me across my left cheek. I reeled back with an audible gasp. "Dasharath had a fit. He collapsed, and the healers do not know if he will wake up. I am bringing you to his room. Not everything is about you."

I resisted the strong urge to tell her that I had almost definitely caused the fit, and therefore this was about me. Instead, I let her lead me away. But as we navigated the deserted hallways, dread burrowed into its ancestral home in my stomach. By the time we reached the door to Dasharath's rooms, it was all I could do to bite back the sob building in my throat.

The door swung open to reveal Sumitra, tears running down her face and dripping from her chin.

"Kaushalya! He is—" She broke off when she spotted me. "Why have you brought *her* here?" The venom in her voice cut straight through me. "Don't you dare cry now about what you have done," Sumitra hissed. "How dare you?"

"Peace, Sumitra," Kaushalya said. "She is still his wife. She loves him just as we do."

"She is nothing like us." Sumitra looked me up and down. "She is a rakshasa in the clothes of a radnyi. I never thought I would need to tell you to be more cautious and less forgiving, Kaushalya."

The sob escaped me. "Sumitra, I beg of you—"

"Do not speak to me," she said, leaning away as though I was diseased.

That particular act of cruelty brought me back to reality. The events in the throne room had given me hope that perhaps she did not hate me, but sometime between yesterday and now our bond had dissolved into nothingness. She blamed me for Lakshmana's departure, a near-unforgivable loss, and perhaps I could appeal to that. "Do you not think I grieve to see our sons leave? Please, you have to understand why—"

"You grieve for nothing," she snapped. "Your son is still here."

I could tell I would not get another word of explanation, and my heart sank. Was Sumitra to be lost to me forever?

"He is in his room," Sumitra said to Kaushalya, gesturing her in. I stepped inside after them, although Sumitra scowled at me. "The healers are with him, but they say we should not go in, as it might disturb his rest. He had another fit a few minutes ago, and though it was shorter, they say it may have caused further damage to his mind."

"Oh, gods." Kaushalya pressed a hand to her forehead. "Do they know what caused it?"

"Stress, they say. Though they have yet to rule out other-worldly causes—demonic influence, perhaps?" She glared at me pointedly.

"Kaikeyi is not a rakshasa, and she had nothing to do with this," Kaushalya said firmly. "You might be upset at her, but please, do not push so far. And as you well know, we do not have time for this foolishness. Kaikeyi, do you wish to see him briefly? I am sure we can go in for a moment."

I nodded, thankful for Kaushalya's steady presence beside me. How many people would I lose when this was all over?

We slipped off our shoes and tiptoed into the room. Four healers stood around the bed, one at Dasharath's head checking his temperature and color, one examining Dasharath's arm, one gently pressing on Dasharath's stomach, and one at Dasharath's feet, mixing together some plants with a small mortar and pestle. It reminded me of the scene around his battlefield bedside all those years ago—I felt the same panic, the same guilt. But this time I was not his savior. I was his ruin.

"Radnyi," the healer at Dasharath's stomach whispered. "You should not be here."

I thought he had addressed me, for I was so used to my role as the radnyi that people consulted with. I began speaking, but Kaushalya cut me off. "We just wished to see him."

I received a look of skepticism from the healer, and he responded to Kaushalya only. "His hold on this life is tenuous. Any disturbance might break that. We need to work."

"I understand," she whispered, but did not move, studying our husband. I watched her for a moment before transferring my attention to him as well. There was a yellow stain at the corner of his mouth, and his whole face was so pale it looked nearly white, except for the high spots of red on his cheeks. He was still, far stiller than in sleep, and yet his limbs appeared strangely rigid.

"Please, Radnyi. Give us time to work," the healer said.

This time we followed his orders and left the room. Sumitra was still waiting when we shut the door.

"How is he?" she asked Kaushalya desperately.

"Unchanged. I am sure if we all pray, he will recover."

I pressed my lips into a line, for I knew prayer would not help. If at all, the gods might further punish Dasharath for acquiescing to my demands. Sumitra, it seemed, noticed my expression. "I cannot be in a room with *her* anymore," Sumitra said. "She spent years gaining our confidence only to destroy the kingdom. She is the reason Lakshmana is gone."

"Your son decided to go of his own free will," I said, because Lakshmana would not have wanted Sumitra thinking such things. "I will not blame him for wanting to do what is right, even if his mother cannot see it."

"Kaikeyi," Kaushalya said in warning.

My shoulders sagged. "I'm leaving. Call me if he awakens."

I did not wait for her to respond, but slipped out the door. Each step I took toward my room felt like a severing of sisterhood.

Sumitra, sweet and loving Sumitra, hated me. Would the hatred fade, I wondered, as Rama's influence seeped out of Ayodhya? Or would his control linger even as his physical presence left?

I left my room only thrice while I waited for news of Dasharath, each time to seek Bharata, clinging to the fragile hope that he might hear me out.

It was not to be.

The first time, I waited for him in his rooms. He physically recoiled when he saw me, then ignored my presence and went about his business. Despite this, I started speaking.

"Your father made a promise to me once, that my son would take the throne. Your uncle told me that if this promise was not upheld, it would be an offense to Kekaya and he would wage war on us. Surely you would not want that? I know it is hard, that what I did made you angry, but please, Bharata, you have to understand."

I thought perhaps he was listening, because he stood still when I mentioned Yudhajit and the possibility of war. "Thousands of lives will be spared when you take the throne. Please, do it for your uncle at least."

He remained still for a moment longer, then shook his head as if to clear it and walked toward the door. I entered the Binding Plane, anxiety high in the back of my throat, and in the empty gray saw quite clearly the blue tether around Bharata's neck. He left the room, and I wondered if he could even hear my pleas.

The second time, I caught him in the hallway outside of a council meeting, hoping that the presence of others would force him to show me some respect. It was a stupid plan, for all the citizens of Ayodhya despised me, but I tried it regardless. I put my hand on his arm and asked for an audience, but he shrugged me off and gave me a light push away from him. An advisor rushed between us and his men bustled him away, leaving me in his wake.

The third time I wrote him a letter explaining everything and left it in his room on his bed after the servants had finished their morning cleaning. Bharata—or one of his servants—burned the letter and left the ashes in a bowl outside of my room, only a scrap still remaining so I could recognize my own hand.

Six days after Dasharath's collapse, a messenger came to my room. I answered the door myself, and he blanched. He had clearly not expected to meet me face-to-face. After a moment, he delivered his message in stammers and halts: The raja had awoken and Radnyi Kaushalya had sent for me.

I flew to Dasharath's rooms and found his antechamber deserted. Before I could second-guess myself, I crept into the hall outside his bedroom and found Kaushalya.

"He does not want to see you," she whispered sadly. "But you can listen, if you wish."

"Kaushalya," came Dasharath's voice. He sounded awful, his voice rasping and a shadow of what it had been not so long ago. It reminded me, despairingly, of my father's death only last month.

"My raja," she said, slipping into the room. "How are you?"

"I must confess something to you," he whispered, and I strained to hear. "When I was a boy—"

"No, no, there will be time for that later."

"No!" I imagined him grasping her hand, a sharp glint in his eyes. "No. When I was a boy, I went hunting, alone, in the forests just outside of the city. For some reason, I could not find

428

any game, but I knew I could not return to Ayodhya empty-handed; such a thing would bring great shame to me. I went to the lake, hoping I could find some animals there who had come for water. After a few moments, I heard a rustling. In an instant, I had nocked an arrow and shot it, and was rewarded with a high-pitched cry. I ran to the bushes on the opposite bank to claim my kill, but when I reached them, I found only a boy, a few years younger than myself. In his stomach was my arrow."

"You did not know. Accidents happen," Kaushalya murmured.

He ignored her. "As soon as the boy saw me, he started speaking. His name was Shravan and his parents were hermits, he said. They wanted to go to a pilgrimage site nearby. But they could not walk the long distance themselves, and their family was quite poor. So, he had fashioned a device with a pole and two baskets, and he had placed a parent in each basket and carried the pole on his shoulders. Shravan had borne their weight for the entire journey.

"His parents had grown thirsty, he said, and so he put them down and came to bring them water. He had leaned down to fill his pot when an arrow pierced him.

"I cradled the boy in my lap and told him it had been my arrow. Shravan immediately told me he forgave me this honest mistake. In his last breaths, he told me where I could find his parents and begged me to bring them some water.

"When I explained what had happened to his parents, they began wailing and beating their chests. Every breath they took became more labored, and I quickly realized that they too were going to die. I offered them water, but they poured it onto the ground instead of drinking it. And then—" Dasharath cut off, taking deep shuddering breaths that were audible even through the door.

"Peace," Kaushalya said. "You need not continue. I am

sure they too forgave you an honest mistake. Such things happen."

I personally did not think such things simply *happened* or were so easily forgivable, but I no longer had any standing to judge others.

"No, they do not," Dasharath told her, and longing ran through me for our years of partnership, of perfect coordination. "His parents, with their dying strength, cursed me. They said that just as they had lost the light of their life, their beautiful and generous Shravan, I too would one day experience that same grief. I too would lose the son I cherished most. And they hoped it would kill me.

"When Kaikeyi opened her mouth and demanded those boons, I could see it was not her, but the curse itself coming for me. I am being punished for my sins."

"You are hardly being punished in the same way. Rama will return in ten years, and you simply have to live to greet him again at the gates," Kaushalya said. "Your son is alive and well."

"I am being punished," Dasharath insisted, and he gave a great rasping cough. It was too painful for me to hear, and I peeled myself from the door to lean against the wall instead, studying the tiled floor with bleary eyes.

After what seemed like an eternity, Kaushalya emerged from the room. "He is unconscious," she said. "You can go see him."

Unsteady and heartsick, I went up to his bed and brushed my hand against his forehead. His face radiated heat, and my fingers felt as though they had been burned. I had witnessed a fever this intense only once before, with Lakshmana.

It seemed as though he pushed up into my touch, but perhaps it was only my imagination. I rested my whole palm against his forehead, hoping the coolness would provide some relief. Too soon, too soon, Kaushalya rested a hand on my shoulder. "It is time for us to go," she said. "Say farewell."

I brushed my lips against his cheek.

"Goodbye," I murmured in his ear. "I am so sorry, and I love you. May you suffer no longer." I knew there was no point in hoping anymore that he might wake up again to forgive me. I had heard his deathbed confession and recognized it for what it was.

CHAPTER
THIRTY-SEVEN

DASHARATH OF AYODHYA, THE greatest ruler Kosala had known, died the next night. I heard the cries before a messenger reached me with the news, and by the time he arrived at my door I was already on my knees, tearing at my clothes and beating my chest in pure grief. However difficult our last week together might have been, he had been a dear friend to me. He had given me everything. I had lost a confidante, an ally, a partner.

I stood silent, wrapped in a thin white sari that made me feel like a ghost, while they burned him. As the flames leapt up to claim my husband's body, I considered joining him on the pyre.

It was not unheard of for women in the depths of grief to fling themselves into the fire after their husbands, though it rarely happened in such civilized and progressive societies as our own. And yet, I thought about it. The release of death might be preferable to the life that stretched before me now.

I spared a glance for Bharata and Shatrugna, standing with their backs stiff at the edges of their father's bier, and I knew that if I were to die, they would immediately reverse their father's last judgment. As I watched, Shatrugna placed an arm around Bharata's shoulders. I wished desperately I could have done that myself, and this longing kept me planted where I stood.

That night, Kaushalya came by my rooms, to inform me that Bharata had ridden out, postponing his coronation by a month so that he could find Rama on the road and beg him to return home. She would be ruling Ayodhya in Bharata's absence. Despite my fear that Yudhajit might hear of this, and march to war, the news brought me a small smile. In previous eras, Shatrugna would have taken the throne, or one of the senior members of the Mantri Parishad. But times had changed, actually changed, and this was proof. This is what I had fought to preserve, and for a sweet moment it was worth it.

Bharata returned to the palace alone.

Kaushalya came to find me soon after, her elegant features twisted in confusion. "Bharata said that he arrived in their camp in the middle of the night and found Lakshmana standing awake by the horses. He spoke with Lakshmana for an hour, he claims, and in the end, his brother convinced him that his first act as raja could not be to undo his father's last."

"Smart boy," I said, and Kaushalya ignored me.

"Lakshmana said it was shameful for Bharata to be there, and that Rama would feel the same way if he knew about this midnight conversation. He said that Rama wanted to honor his father's wishes and would gladly spend his years in the forest to do so. He said that Rama would be angry to learn that Bharata had visited at all. Bharata did not want to offend Rama, so he asked for Rama's chapals."

"His chapals?" I repeated, confused.

She sighed. "I do not understand either. Lakshmana slipped Rama's sandals off his sleeping form and gave them to Bharata. Bharata departed immediately and brought the shoes here, to Ayodhya. And he says his coronation will be tomorrow, with no fanfare. He has told me he feels this is a tragedy, not a celebration."

The next morning, I armored myself in my finest sari, a blue and gold heavy silk embroidered so finely that it shimmered like water, and made my way to court. I ignored the whispers of the nobles around me as I made my way across the hall, focused only on my son.

Bharata sat on the ground near the throne, cross-legged. The low pressure of murmurs built, no longer just about me. *Has he gone mad?* I am sure they wondered. The tension swelled, filling the entire chamber, until Bharata rose to his feet.

"People of Ayodhya," he proclaimed, his voice stronger than I'd ever heard it, ringing out across the room. "We have lost in a short time our great raja and our beloved yuvraja. I mourn them just as you do. My father and my brother were meant to rule this kingdom, and they were torn from us. I am not worthy of taking this throne in their stead. So, while Rama is in exile, I will not."

He lifted his hands, and I realized he held a pair of shoes. "These are my brother's chapals. They will remain on the throne for these ten years, to remind us that he will return to his rightful place in time. I will spend these years in penance, praying and atoning for the sins of the woman who bore me."

No, I thought. *No, this cannot be happening.* The heat rose in my cheeks as all eyes turned to me. I wanted to cry, to scream, to run up to Bharata and shake him, but instead I stood paralyzed, stomach churning. Bharata's gaze found me, and he walked toward me with slow, deliberate steps. Sumitra and Kaushalya each took a rustling step back, so that he and I faced each other alone on the dais.

"Hear me now," he said, as though sentencing a common criminal. "I curse you for your sins."

Curse me? My own son? "Bharata, *please*." My voice shook despite my best efforts. "I have tried to tell you, you know not what you are doing. You would risk the whole kingdom for this?" I took a step toward him, but Shatrugna was there, blocking my path, forcing me away from my other son, my blood.

"I heard everything you told me," Bharata said, and at this, the last shred of hope I carried in my heart vanished. If he had truly listened, then he knew what his actions would unleash. And to look at him, he did not care. "You have been a plague on this kingdom, an awful, godsforsaken woman. But it shall stop with you. You, Kaikeyi of Kekaya, will be the last of your name." Each word rang as he spoke it, and I felt the sentence come down with finality. It would have hurt to hear anybody say such a thing, but coming from my own son, I knew it in my very bones: I was cursed.

How appropriate, that I should be the first of my name and the last. How fitting, that now, at last, I knew what that threat meant.

CHAPTER
THIRTY-EIGHT

I CALCULATED THE TIME out. Ten days for the news to reach my brother. Another two weeks for him to gather his forces, provided he was already making preparations for war, and then two weeks for him to move his army to Kosala's border. They would plunge straight into our lands rather than deigning to meet at an appointed place, for that was not the Kekayan way. He would slash and burn his way toward our capital, hoping that such devastation would force us to accede to his demands.

In the face of Bharata's abdication of responsibility and Shatrugna's apathy about ruling, Kaushalya had stepped up to make important decisions for the kingdom. Sumitra sat by Kaushalya's side, assisting her in managing the responsibilities of both radnyi and regent, and so in many ways the Women's Council had become the court itself. My life's work had come to better fruition than I could have ever expected. But all I could think about was that I had no part in it. The entire city hated me. Besides, what did my counsel matter? I had pushed two of my sons into exile, one into penance, and the one remaining would not acknowledge me. I had broken my husband and hastened his death. I had brought war upon the two kingdoms I loved most.

So while Kaushalya prepared, I stayed secluded in my chambers. In the Binding Plane my few strong connections stood in bleak contrast to the gossamer webs that were all I had left. It was an empty, colorless place. I had once been lord of the Binding Plane, but now I merely floated through it, unmoored.

It became harder to get out of bed. In the mornings, Manthara would try to cajole me to get dressed as though I was a small child. But the idea of lifting my limbs out of the soft nest of blankets, of having to hold up my own body and my own head, was overwhelming. Only when the need to eat or relieve myself became too strong would I emerge. Asha and Manthara tried to coax me into taking short walks in the garden, but I let their words drift over me just as Kaushalya's did when she visited me in the evenings, for speech was just air.

One evening, she brought me a letter addressed to her. I recognized the hand immediately.

Yudhajit was giving Kaushalya one week to fulfill the promise made to Kekaya.

"Has anyone else seen it?" I asked her. My voice was hoarse with disuse. "People may no longer believe such a promise was ever made. They will be even angrier that it concerns me."

Kaushalya sat beside me, weariness in every angle of her body. "I will tell them I have heard from a spy that Kekaya intends to strike us while we are weak. Your home will come off poorly for it, but at least there will be no equivocation."

"You should ask Bharata one more—"

"I already showed him the letter," Kaushalya said, shaking her head. "He did not seem bothered by the prospect of war on his behalf. He told me it is what Rama would have wanted." The sorrow in her expression was evident, and I took her hand. We sat there for some time, mourning what was to come.

Perhaps this is why the mood in the capital over the next

few days struck me as so odd. While people had been solemn and despondent with Rama's departure, they turned practically ebullient with the tidings of war. I could hear the enthusiasm from my balcony, and Manthara and Asha told me stories from the marketplace. The last time Dasharath had ridden to war, an eerie shroud of quiet had fallen over the city, for people knew many sons would not return. Yet now men answered the call to arms with enthusiasm, talking of glory and righteousness.

Kaushalya had asked me not to attend meetings of the Women's Council, and I obeyed her as my radnyi. But the day before her departure to the border, she told me of their last meeting. A group of women had begged Kaushalya to sue for peace, and Shatrugna had stepped up to dismiss them, accusing them of disloyalty. In the face of his fervor and Sumitra's silence, Kaushalya had been unable to do anything.

"He will be leading the men into battle, and he seems almost gleeful about it," she confessed. "But maybe he is trying to hide his nervousness."

Kaushalya knew nothing of magic, or Rama's true nature, and I did not have the time to explain it to her now. I simply agreed with her, glad that she was accompanying Shatrugna at least as far as the last camp and could perhaps temper any reckless tendencies. But on the morning Kosala's soldiers were to march out, I forced myself out of bed, curiosity overpowering the shroud in my mind. I dressed myself in coarse cotton and made my way through the city streets until I slipped into the camp at the outskirts of the city to witness the strangeness for myself. The men laughed and joked as they made preparations to leave for the border, swinging their weaponry with something approaching delight, and only then did I fully comprehend Kaushalya's meaning.

Entering the Binding Plane filled me with dread, but I did it all the same and found myself in a sea of blue strings. Rama's blue.

His influence had not waned in the two months he had been gone. Was it Rama's influence causing these boys to run headlong into war? He had wanted to take the men of the kingdom to war against evil, but perhaps the seeds of belligerence he had planted were flowering in this way instead. I could not know.

Worst of all, I was powerless to diminish his sway at all.

I returned to my rooms and watched from the palace as Kosala's army left and wished with everything in me that I had the strength to intervene in some way. But my presence among the soldiers would only incite them to further violence, of that I was sure.

And then, that evening, a bird from Ravana arrived.

My dear Kaikeyi,

You have my sincerest apologies for my failure to respond. At first, I was enraged at what you had done and did not wish to write you a letter for fear I might declare war on your kingdom within its pages. How dare you send my daughter into exile?

My hands shook slightly. Had Ravana always been so passionate and foolhardy? He talked so casually of declaring war on a kingdom months of travel from his own, as though that was the natural reaction to displeasing him. Matters of children were different, and yet—

I see now an opportunity, one the gods denied to me. I intend to introduce myself to Sita. I am no longer angry at you and am relieved I did not act against you in haste. Instead, I offer you my sincerest thanks for this great gift you have given me.

Ravana

Ravana was running headlong into Rama's path. He was no longer the man I knew, who I had trusted to be calm and logical. This plan would end only in another conflict, and I was too far to stop him. The seeds of this destruction might have already been sown in the days it took his letter to reach me.

I needed help. But neither Manthara nor Asha nor Kaushalya could give it.

I staggered toward my bed, collapsing on the edge of it and clasping my hands together, searching for the words of the prayers I had once known by heart, when I had been desperate for the blessings of the gods. For the first time in years, I truly and sincerely prayed, whispering supplication to the goddess Nidra. I only half believed it would work, but still I closed my eyes and bowed my head and murmured the ancient words.

When I opened my eyes, unexpectant, she stood before me in that same cloak of shadows. Her bright eyes glimmered, and I felt a strange sense of happiness, of triumph, before remembering myself.

"Sri Nidra. All around me I see nothing but pain, stretching far into the future. Can you stop it?"

She stared at me for a moment. I felt myself growing tired and forced my eyes away from her divine form. "No, I cannot," she said, her voice like a soft night breeze, and my heart clenched. "But do not despair. A man walks among you with human follies and the powers of Lord Vishnu himself, and you manage to stand firm with nothing of your own. You are stronger than you think."

Vishnu? Through these years, I had continued to believe it was Agni whose divinity resided within my son. I had never even considered it could be anyone else, let alone Vishnu. I was glad I was seated, for the more I thought about it, the more my head spun. Vishnu was the protector, one of the strongest gods. He returned to earth, age after age, to save us from demonkind. Rama himself had said something similar—and I had missed it. What if he had not been misguided? What if our world truly did need cleansing, and I had stood in his way?

It could not be. I had traveled far and seen no possible reason for the kinds of all-consuming war Vishnu always brought. "Please. Surely you can do something to help me. You answered my prayer, after all."

"I answered because I made a promise to you." She reached out a hand to cup my face. "Of all the godsforsaken I have known in my immortal life, you drew the worst lot. Your fate was written out thus: that you had to exile your own son, and thereby ignite the great battle between good and evil."

I drew away. "The great battle between good and evil?"

"Yes, between your son, Rama, and the forces of darkness amassing in Bharat," she said.

"*What* forces of darkness?" I demanded.

"Rama was sent to your world for a great and glorious purpose. Your fight with him was of his choosing, and I will offer no wisdom on who was right, for it matters little to us. He may not have known it, but he always had to depart Ayodhya, no matter the cost."

I shook my head, parsing her words to find only terrible answers. "Are you saying that whatever I did had no consequence, because it was destined that Rama needed to depart Ayodhya at a particular time?"

"What you did had a tremendous influence," Nidra said, but she turned away as she spoke.

"You cannot leave me now," I insisted, briefly forgetting that I spoke to a goddess. I remembered now Rama's calm acceptance of his exile. Had he wanted this all along? No. He had been sincere in his desire to militarize Kosala, true in his belief that such might was needed for the war to come. "Please, you must tell me what Rama intends to do."

"There is a great asura whose influence stretches across the south of this land," Nidra said. "He does not bow to the power of the gods but instead brings unnatural creations into this world, usurping our authority. It is Rama's duty to bring the gods' rule back to this earth. His preparations here have been extreme, but I have no doubt they will prove useful."

I gaped openly at her. Perhaps Rama had been right all along. An asura threatened our world, and when he had tried to show me, I had accused him of madness.

It struck me then, with the force of a Pushpaka Vimana to the chest.

Rama had told me all along who he thought the threat was, and I had failed to understand. But Ravana was not evil, could not be evil. He had saved Janasthana—or perhaps had manipulated its takeover. He cared deeply for his daughter—or perhaps he looked for a reason to make war on Kosala.

No. Ravana had helped me, done me a great service, and asked for nothing in return, while Rama had turned on me at the first sign of disagreement. And now Rama would carry a fight to his doorstep. I had read stories about what happened when the gods waged open war in the mortal realm. The world burned.

"What Rama intends to do, tell me—can I stop it?"

She shook her head. "You have both done what you had to do, for your kingdom and for the world. What is left now is for the good of all, can you not see that?" She passed a hand over my head, and my eyes began to close. "You do not have to worry anymore, Kaikeyi. Be at peace."

I stood in the forests of Panchavati, outside a small house. Morning sun filtered down into the clearing. Lakshmana and Rama walked out of the house, laughing to each other as they plunged into the trees. Intrigued, I followed them for a few minutes or maybe a few hours as they half-heartedly hunted and played. I could not help but smile as they roughhoused and threw leaves at each other. They seemed happy, like the children they still were. Though I was standing right next to them, their words came to me unintelligibly, as if through a ring of cotton around my head, but I longed to hear their laughter just once.

Time bled past, blurring my surroundings. The sun was directly overhead when Rama suddenly grew still, his face grim as he held up a hand and wordlessly led Lakshmana back toward the house. They were tiptoeing now, truly silent, until they reached a conveniently hidden gap in the trees and peered through.

There, on the steps of the forest house, stood Ravana.

He was dressed in the robes of a traveling monk, but his bearing was unmistakable. Sita leaned in the doorway, a smile on her face but wariness in her eyes. I didn't know how I could tell from this distance, but her expression was sharp and clear as her gaze scanned the tree line.

"There," Rama whispered to Lakshmana. I could hear his every word now as though he was speaking in my ear. "Already he thinks to steal from me."

"Rama, there is only a monk talking to Sita."

"No." Rama's eyes blazed. "He is an asura, here to continue his conquest."

A ring of light spilled forth from him, consuming everything in its path until the woods faded and only my son remained. "I will cleanse the world of his kind."

After speaking to Nidra, it was obvious, painfully so, that Rama's detour into mortal politics had been a product of his mortal form from the start. He would not need the men or armies of Kosala for his campaign—he had only believed that to be the case.

The ground gave way beneath me. I closed my eyes to brace for the inevitable impact and opened them to find myself in a camp of war. I knew immediately it was Kosala's.

"What is your plan?" I heard Kaushalya ask, the words ringing in my head, and I entered the large tent in front of me.

"We will attack them in the night," Shatrugna said. "Burn

their tents to the ground. Slaughter them before they have the chance to fight back." I could see sparks of Rama's light reflected in his eyes.

Kaushalya stared at him in horror. "That is against the laws of the gods! Surely you know that."

"Perhaps if we were fighting against equal opponents. But the kingdom we fight is ungodly. They have done us a great dishonor and we must crush them."

"They are not ungodly," Kaushalya protested. "Their men have done nothing wrong." She turned toward Bharata, who stood with his arms crossed and a small frown on his face. His eyes flicked up to her, then back to the ground.

"I am the leader of these warriors. Not you. I will not allow further dissent." Shatrugna raised his voice, but Kaushalya did not flinch.

"I am your mother and your radnyi," Kaushalya insisted.

Shatrugna shook his head. "Maybe so. But these men answer to me."

I fought to come awake.

My body was bathed in sweat. I tasted blood in my mouth, and the inside of my cheek stung fiercely. Half of me wanted to move, to take action and do something to stop this carnage. But the other half of me, the one that had kept me lying in my bed unmoving until noon, paralyzed me. What use was action? My actions had been meaningless. All I had done was hasten Rama toward his destiny. I had failed to protect Sita and consigned Lakshmana to ten years of sleeplessness, and Urmila to ten years of dreams. Ravana's fate was sealed. I had destroyed my relationships with my brother and my sons, and now they were about to go to war.

I thought of what Yudhajit might feel in his last moments, murdered by his nephew's army. I wondered whether he would be surprised when death came to him, or whether he would have a chance to fight his way clear.

Bharata loved his uncle. How would he live with himself when this deed was done?

It was clear that I had no power to help them. And yet, how could I live with myself if I did not try?

Sitting up seemed an insurmountable task. I lay there for another minute and imagined what Bharata might say when he returned. *You forced me to do this*, he would probably tell me. Or, *How could I have done something like this? I will never be whole again.*

That final thought was what stirred my cold limbs to movement. This would be my final attempt to set things right. After this, I promised myself, I would never interfere again. I would live out the rest of my days in seclusion. But I could not sit back now.

I wrapped myself in my warmest cloak and began to fill my traveling bag, my mind shaking off the weeks of cobwebs as my hands worked. Riding fast and alone, I could outpace our army's daylong head start even if I kept off the road. I could sleep in the forest and arrive in time to warn Yudhajit. Our bond had frayed, but I was still his sister, and well respected in Kekaya besides. My years of practice in cajoling men into listening to me would serve me well now. I would convince him of Shatrugna's plan. It was a betrayal of my son, but it was an act of loyalty for my people in both kingdoms—I was saving my sons from their worst impulses and from Kekaya's inevitable revenge. This war would not be a slaughter. I could do at least that much.

"Do you need something?" Asha asked as I entered the main room. I had not realized she was sleeping in my room this night, but a single candle was still lit, and from her position on the floor it appeared as though I had woken her. Asha had taken to occasionally sleeping in my chambers, when she was particularly worried about me. Manthara might have too, if her old age had not made it difficult for her to sleep on the floor.

"No, Asha. Please go back to sleep. I am sorry for disturbing you."

Her eyes darted to my attire as she rose to her feet. "Where are you going?"

"Where do you think?"

Asha smiled slightly, her face looking young in the flickering candlelight. With her hair in two thick braids, I could remember clearly our first meeting—another lifetime ago, on the eve of another battle. She bent and passed me a large bundle from next to her pallet. "There is food enough for a week-long journey in here. Manthara helped me pack it." Next, she removed a scabbard. "And here is your sword." She hesitated, then threw her arms around me. I returned her embrace, and we parted with shining eyes.

"Godspeed, Radnyi."

I laughed then, and the rough sound of it startled me. "The gods will have nothing to do with it."

CHAPTER THIRTY-NINE

I ARRIVED NEAR THE outskirts of Yudhajit's camp just as the sun set on the sixth day. Listening to the faint clamor, I decided to sleep and approach my brother in the morning, better rested to make my case. I had set a punishing pace, and my body ached from the abuse. I considered praying to Nidra to help me—but somehow, after the dream she had given me, I could not bring myself to ask for her aid.

In the sleepy hours before dawn, I tied my horse to a nearby tree and snuck past the bleary-eyed guards without much difficulty. While I had no bonds with them to manipulate, if one seemed close to spotting me, I simply tugged on their bond with another soldier, causing them to turn away.

Yudhajit's tent was not particularly opulent, but it stood out at the center of camp. I slipped in through the back to find my brother alone and asleep. He had entered my tent the same way once, a lifetime ago, seeking adventure in the forests.

For a moment, I just watched him, his chest rising and falling, and the kernel of love I always kept for him expanded in my chest. We had been so happy. He had been carefree, quick to laugh and play. But now he looked tired and worried, even in his sleep, and my failure was responsible for that in no small part.

It took me several minutes to move from my position, for I wanted to preserve this moment, where we could both simply be together. When I woke him, I knew, I would have to face his anger. I stepped toward him, and the soft sound of my footfall startled him awake. He sat half up on his pallet, his hand reaching for his sword. When he realized it was me, he relaxed slightly, then stiffened again. "Kaikeyi. Have you come to kill me?"

Of all the possibilities I had envisioned, this reaction was not one of them. "Kill you?" I echoed blankly. He studied my face in the dim light, then dropped his sword and stood.

"Why are you here, then?"

"To warn you," I said. "You and your men are in danger."

Yudhajit raised one eyebrow. "What is this, Kaikeyi? What game are you playing?"

"I'm not playing any game. Shatrugna and Bharata—"

"You sat next to me and convinced me that you would ensure Bharata became king. And then to discover your own son hates you so much that he renounced the throne?" Yudhajit shook his head, unseeing or uncaring that every one of his words was a thorn in my heart. "So have you come here hoping to regain favor in Kekaya? It will not happen."

"No," I said firmly, trying not to let my growing frustration show. I took a step forward and grabbed his arm, tugging him around to look at me. "I am trying to keep you alive."

Yudhajit met my eyes, his expression growing serious as he scanned my face. I thought, for a second, he might actually hear me out, but then he laughed slightly and extricated himself from my grasp. "So you think I am such a weak and feeble warrior that your soft people will defeat me?"

"It's not going to be a battle," I said, and I was about to explain the rest when a soldier burst into the tent. He stopped

448

short at the sight of me, his glance darting from me to Yudhajit, and I realized this young man had no idea who I was. He probably thought Yudhajit and I were—

"Radnyi Kaikeyi of Kosala." Yudhajit's words tumbled out of him like we were children again, caught doing something mischievous. "What is it?"

The soldier seemed to remember his purpose then, because he straightened and yelped, "A messenger came from your brother, Prince Rahul. He said it was urgent and he needs a response right away."

"All right." Yudhajit was already dressing himself, strapping on his sword, and I knew my opportunity was slipping away.

"Yudhajit, please—" I began, but he cut me off with a sharp nod.

"Stay here. I am going to have one of my men guard you so you cannot cause any trouble. We can discuss this later." And with that he was gone.

I gave him several minutes' lead, then attempted to sneak out the back way. I was greeted by a guard who immediately stood in my path. So Yudhajit had been thorough. "Where are you going?" he asked.

I thought quickly. "I tied my horse not far from here, and I need to tend to him." I could see the conflict play out on the guard's face, for we would never allow our horses to suffer in Kekaya.

At last he said, "Very well, let's go." It was the only reasonable thing for him to do, but still I was disappointed. As we walked to the clearing, I tried to make small talk with him, attempting to create a bond between us. By the time we reached my horse and belongings, I had succeeded in spinning only the smallest thread, nowhere near what I needed to successfully manipulate my release—if I was even able to stomach using the Plane.

As I untied my horse, I considered whether I should make an escape. But what use was that? If I injured this man, Yudhajit would never listen to me. And if I ran, then I could not warn him. Resigned, I returned to the camp. The guard brought me food and water, and I sat in Yudhajit's tent cross-legged, waiting.

My thoughts drifted to Sita. I wondered how she fared, what the exile had brought her. She was strong, but I worried about her now knowing she would be trapped between Ravana and Rama, caught in their great war. But I was also tired, weary to my bones. I closed my eyes with Sita on my mind—

And opened them at a familiar river.

"Sri Sarasvati," I whispered. I looked down to find my feet submerged in the earth, and almost smiled at the sight. This, at least, felt familiar. "I have need of your divine wisdom."

Ask. The voice came from the river, from the cool mist and the dark trees and the damp soil. It came from inside my head.

"How fares Sita?"

We will protect her, the voice said. It was not quite a response, and yet it revealed everything. I had been right to worry. The goddess thought she needed protection.

"You admit it," I said. "That Rama was wrong in the way he acted toward her."

Yes. It was a matter-of-fact statement, spoken in her thousand voices. But how else would she speak? The divine could not understand doubt or embarrassment or shame.

A strangled chuckle rang in the dream clearing, and it took me a moment to realize it was coming from my mouth. I wanted to weep, I wanted to attack the river with my bare hands, I wanted to scream for an eternity. But the gods were untouchable. I could not make them understand, for cruelty was human and they were not.

Still, my anger spilled out of me. "He was a child. He still is, even now. Pulled in too many directions." My voice increased in volume, until I was shouting, letting myself rage. "You put a child in this world without guidance, but with the knowledge he was divine. What else would he do but listen to those around him? You made a young man believe he needed to be powerful and righteous. Is it not only natural he sought glory through war? He fell into the care of someone who seemed to have a ready explanation for what was happening to him, for aren't the sages the interpreters of your word? Why wouldn't he revere such a man? Why wouldn't he make himself in that image?" I was not trying to excuse Rama, for he had made his choices. But none of this would have happened without the influence of the gods.

I stood there, panting, feeling drained. The river remained quiet, but neither did she send me away. I did not know what else I had expected. I wanted to ask her, *Did I do the right thing?* But I knew better now. Another question, a curiosity, sprang to my mind. "In the end, Rama said that what I had done disrespected the gods. That you believed women brought weakness to the world. Is it true?"

No.

It was a simple word, and yet... "If our sages were wrong, why did you remain silent?" I demanded. "You could have told him. It might have changed everything!"

We are not concerned with the rise and fall of mortals. What you want would not bring change. It is something you have never understood.

If I had not known better, I would have said she sounded almost sad. And then the river dissolved into blue wisps of mist, and I was alone in a tent in my mere mortal world.

Only when the sun had begun its descent across the sky did Yudhajit return, weariness wrapped around him like a cloak.

"What is it you came here to do?" he asked.

"Are you all right?" I asked instead. "Is everything in order in Kekaya?"

"It was a missive from Rahul," he said, rolling his shoulders.

"But I cannot further discuss such matters of state with you. Our kingdoms are at war."

"They didn't have to be," I said, but before we could begin arguing about whose fault this was, I pressed on. "Shatrugna leads the Kosalan army, and Bharata is with him. They do not intend to fight you."

"Suing for peace is useless. Even if Bharata were to accept the throne right now..." He trailed off. "I'm sorry. I don't think the people would accept it."

"They haven't come to make peace. They intend to sneak into your camp at night and burn it all to the ground. It will be a massacre."

Yudhajit stared at me for a moment, then started laughing. "The Kosala army would never do anything of the kind, with all their rules about noble warfare," he said when he had caught his breath. "They must have been joking with you, knowing that you would not understand the ways of war."

"*You* trained me in the ways of war." I rose to my feet, trying to inflect my words with steel. "We fought together, I rode into battle with my husband, and even years later I can still wield a weapon as well as any soldier."

Yudhajit held up his hands in mock surrender. "Yes, you're quite experienced." The *for a woman* hung heavy in the air between us.

"Please, Yudhajit. What is the harm in taking me seriously?"

"It sounds like you want me to keep my men awake all night, or even move the camp. And I have no way of knowing that what you say is true. What if you are trying to make my army tired and weak so that tomorrow morning we are ripe for your sons to cut down?"

"I am your *sister*," I said. Once, I knew such accusations from Yudhajit would have caused me to cry, but now I felt empty. My own son did not recognize me as his mother. What did it matter if my brother thought this of me?

"And you are their mother," he said. "I appreciate you coming here, but it is clear that you are not in control of these situations."

"At least post a few scouts," I argued. I had expected some level of disbelief, and now I used my prepared compromise. "You know where the Kosalan soldiers are. Send some riders with fast horses. A few men will not change the outcome of a battle tomorrow. You are a good commander, you know you should at least be cautious. You told me to never take my eyes off the enemy. Surely you will take your own advice."

He pressed his lips together. I entered the Binding Plane and found only a small thread of blue between us, a sad remnant of the brilliant bond we had once shared.

My words would have to be enough.

After some interminable minutes, Yudhajit nodded. "Very well. You will stay here tonight. And if this was some sort of ruse, I will not be pleased."

I recognized in his words a threat, and for the first time I wondered whether perhaps Kaushalya had successfully persuaded Shatrugna away from this plan. When the morning came…no. Any punishment for being wrong, any humiliation or pain would be more than worth it so long as there was no massacre. I gave a sharp nod. Against my protests, Yudhajit had me escorted to a small tent at the edge of camp and posted a guard outside.

With nothing else to do, I sat on the cold ground and began my wait.

CHAPTER FORTY

THE HOURS AFTER THE sun set felt like an eternity. I shifted uncomfortably as my body froze, and rose to stretch periodically, massaging out the aches. The camp slowly fell silent, and when I could bear it no longer, I poked my head out of my tent flap. The guard next to my tent had fallen asleep.

The wind pricked gooseflesh along my arms, and a chill of foreboding wormed its way down my spine. I was at the very outskirts of camp, near the forest, and farthest from where Kosala's armies would attack. The moon was a small sliver in the sky, and I could see barely twenty paces in front of me.

I took a few hesitant steps toward the center of camp, and this time, when the wind blew, it carried the scent of smoke.

No.

I broke into a run, and it seemed that at the same time the camp erupted. Screams and clangs rang out, and then a gout of flame leapt up toward the horizon.

How many eyes had Yudhajit put on the enemy? Men came running out of their tents, and in the confusion, I managed to grab a large discarded spear. It hampered me, making my gait uneven, but I needed something with which to protect my brother.

The flames roared toward me, even as I ran toward them, and my mind took me back to the forest, to Bhandasura. I stumbled a step and then fell, my free hand breaking my fall. I pushed myself back up as men rushed past me, the swarm sweeping me along to the center of camp, where fighting had already broken out. I could not make out who was winning, because smoke billowed around me, stinging my eyes. But I had a sinking feeling that not many of Kosala's men would be here, actually fighting. Shatrugna had contrived a horrifying plan, but he at least cared for Kosalans, and where there was a fire there was great risk. There were likely only a small number of our Kosalan soldiers here, ones who had volunteered to keep Yudhajit's men distracted.

I made my way toward my brother's tent. The guards posted there were gone.

"Yudhajit," I shouted, coughing against the char of the smoke. "Yudhajit!" I crashed through the flap and stopped short, struggling to catch my breath as I took in the horrifying scene before me.

Shatrugna stood over Yudhajit with a sword in hand. My brother had fallen back on the floor, his own blade just out of reach.

When he saw me, my son's lips twisted into a snarl. "What are you doing here?" he demanded.

"I—"

"What are you doing here?" He took a threatening step toward me.

"I wanted to—"

"Did someone tell you of our plan?" he shouted. "Did you come here to *warn* them?"

"I came here to convince Yudhajit to return home!" I lied, slipping into the Binding Plane. As I did, my bond with

Yudhajit grew slightly. "To sue for peace. And then I heard screams, and—"

"So you're a traitor, then." Shatrugna took another step, and I backed up until I was flush with the tent edge.

"What?" I asked. "I came on behalf of Kosala."

"You had no right to do that!" Shatrugna said. I recognized the intent in his eyes just as he moved, and I lunged awkwardly out of the way, bracing for the impact of his blade. Instead, there was a muffled thump as Yudhajit tackled him down.

"Run, Kaikeyi," he shouted, but I could not. I remained rooted to the spot as Shatrugna and Yudhajit grappled. I tried to raise my spear, to prepare a strike, but my arm was leaden, unable to move. How could I strike my own son? Even if I had never known him as well as the others, he was still my child.

Shatrugna rolled on top of Yudhajit, who shouted once again, "Kaikeyi! Run, now!"

Under the dim light, everything looked gray, and in the Binding Plane, our bright blue bond was sparkling. He knew now that I was telling the truth, and he had just saved my life. We were in it together, he and I, once again.

"Get off of him," I cried to Shatrugna. "He is your uncle. This is not the way you want to fight."

He ignored me and reached for his sword, but in a swift step I kicked it out of the way.

"Shatrugna, look at me. *Shatrugna!*" I shouted, and at last his eyes locked with mine. I found the blue cord tying him to Rama and tried desperately to loosen it, but it was like chipping away at rock with my bare hands. "This is your uncle. Think about what you're doing." I held his gaze, trying to convince him. He seemed to relax back slightly just as the tent flap opened.

"Shatrugna, have you persuaded him? We need to—no!" Bharata shouted.

Time seemed to slow. I had looked toward Bharata when

he entered. And when I turned back, the hilt of a dagger protruded from Yudhajit's chest.

Bharata, without even acknowledging me, leapt forward to push Shatrugna off Yudhajit. I dropped to my knees beside my brother as he coughed once, twice, his hands pressed around the dagger as his life seeped away.

"You're going to be fine," I whispered, and he gave me a smile. I put my hands over his own, applying pressure, knowing that if I pulled the dagger out, he would bleed faster.

It did not matter. He was going to die.

"You really came for me," he said, his smile never slipping. Beside us, someone was whimpering in pain, but I did not look over.

"Of course. I never—I didn't—" Time was not on my side. "I'm so sorry."

"Come here," Yudhajit gasped. I bent my face down to him, and he kissed my cheek. I pressed my forehead to his, counting his breaths. One, two, three—

And then, like that, he was gone. I sat bent over him, unable to move. I could barely breathe, even though the smoke was less dense down by my brother's body. His *body*.

A hand touched my shoulder. I grabbed the hand and twisted, pulling the person down as I rose, prepared to strike them. Then the haze around my vision cleared. "Bharata?" I whispered.

"He's dead?" Tears had already left streak marks on Bharata's face. How long had it been? I turned back toward Yudhajit and saw Shatrugna's crumpled form next to him. He appeared unconscious, a bruise already forming on his temple.

I lent a bloody hand to Bharata and pulled him up. He shuddered, a low keening emerging from his mouth, and without thought I closed my arms around him and held him tight. I knew he probably still hated me, and that he was under Rama's thrall, but he was my son, my beloved son, and I could not help but comfort him.

I wondered blankly why he seemed more grief-stricken than I did, but could not summon any further emotion. I was holding my son, and he was *letting* me, and my mind was too exhausted to feel anything more.

After a few moments, I realized Bharata was speaking. "I'm sorry," he whispered over and over again. "I'm sorry, I'm sorry, I'm sorry." He coughed, and I felt a sympathetic stinging in my throat. No. The tent was filling with smoke. Suddenly Bharata was pulling away from me. "We have to go," he said. "Come on, Ma."

The name, *Ma*, startled me out of my daze. *You are no mother of mine*, he had said, and now—

"We have to move!" Bharata shouted, and I looked down at my bloody, empty hands. Bharata grabbed Shatrugna's arms and began dragging him toward the back of the tent. "Shatrugna was supposed to come and take Raja Yudhajit away. He promised not to harm him. He promised. I never thought—never—how could he. *I didn't want this.*"

I tried to pull Yudhajit's body with me, but my hands were slippery, and he was heavy. "Help me," I said.

"Ma, we have to move quickly," Bharata said. His voice sounded thick once more, but whether it was the smoke or emotion I could not tell. "The gods will understand. They have to."

For a brief moment, I contemplated telling him to drop Shatrugna and take Yudhajit, before I snapped to my senses. My son had done a horrible thing, maybe an unforgivable thing, but he was still alive. I brushed my hands over Yudhajit's eyes, closing them, pressed a kiss to his brow, and then followed my son out of the tent.

The air was thick with smoke and screams, but Bharata seemed to know the way. He heaved Shatrugna onto his back with a strength I did not know he possessed, and cut through the tents, glancing back every few seconds to make sure I was following him.

Yudhajit's camp was encircled by fire as far as I could see, except for a narrow opening by the forest. Only when we approached the gap did a row of men materialize. Kosalan soldiers. It chilled me how well my sons had engineered this massacre.

And how well it had worked. We passed through the Kosalan line, and it finally hit me. My knees gave out as Bharata passed Shatrugna on to a healer's care.

Yudhajit was dead. The Kekayan army had been massacred.

I screamed then, a sound that had been building inside me for hours, days, weeks. I had not allowed myself to feel it, this all-consuming rage and grief, but now I was overwhelmed with it. This was all I was.

I could vaguely tell that the soldiers were surrounding me, shouting orders, but I did not care. I screamed until the breath in me was gone and I was empty.

CHAPTER
FORTY-ONE

I AWOKE THE NEXT morning in a spacious tent, the air fresh and sweet, to see Kaushalya sitting at my bedside.

"I am so sorry," she said the moment my eyes opened. "Kaikeyi. I am so very sorry."

I opened my mouth but only a croak came out, and Kaushalya brought me a steel cup filled with water.

"Yudhajit still loved me," I said, for that was my first thought upon waking. He had tried to save me. "I tried to save him."

"You could not have done anything more." She took my cold hand with her warm one. "I should have stopped them. I tried—"

"You did your best," I told her. "I know you did." I let the shroud of gray fall over the world so I could reassure her in the Binding Plane too, then tumbled out of it when the memory of the washed-out tent resurfaced. The night before was coming back in flashes, along with the raw edges of the grief-pain. "Did the whole camp burn down? Or did Bharata send someone back for the...for the...?" I couldn't force the word *body* out of my mouth.

460

Kaushalya shook her head. "You'll have to ask him, but I don't think so. I'm so sorry."

My mind repeated the facts to me, numb. Yudhajit was dead. The Kekayan army was slaughtered. Bharata had watched his uncle die, and in the harsh reality of the morning probably blamed my presence there for what had happened.

I recalled my promise that I would never interfere again and wished I had taken such a vow sooner.

"Thank you for sitting with me," I whispered. "But I would like to be alone."

Kaushalya smoothed my hair back with her fingers. "All right. There are some clothes in the corner when you are ready to rise," she said. "If you need something, ask any of the guards. I will see you soon."

My eyes pricked with tears at this kindness, for I did not deserve it. Did she not understand that I was the architect of all this misery? I watched her leave and then let my body go limp in the pallet, imagining Yudhajit's final moments. He had seemed at peace, but it was a brutal, early, unnecessary end. And even when I had known what was coming, I failed to stop it. I wondered, when the story reached whichever brother of mine was set to assume the throne, whether any survivor would mention my name. *Radnyi Kaikeyi was there*, they might say. *An omen of death and destruction.*

Or perhaps they would just blame Bharata. After all, it was his unwillingness to assume the throne that had led to this pain. Now he was truly without family. His father was dead, two of his brothers gone, and his third brother had murdered his beloved uncle.

I realized, with a sudden panic, that here in this tent Bharata could find me. I could not face him, not after everything that had happened. I could not receive his condemnation again, for it would break what little was left of me. This fear gave me the energy I needed to lift myself up and change my clothes. There was likely a guard posted at the front of my tent, so I slipped out through the back.

I had not thought through my next steps, only that I could not face my child, but now my path seemed evident. I crept along the woods that bordered the tent, searching for what I needed, until finally I spotted a horse tied to a tree. It was unbelievably good luck, but I did not stop to question it. A bit of fortune after an eternity of poor luck left little impression. A stupid soldier had evidently left his mount unattended, and that was all. I untied it and slowly led it several steps into the trees so that no one could startle at my sudden movements.

Then I mounted the animal and began to ride. I would go home, where Asha and Manthara would draw me a bath and I could lie in bed undisturbed for the rest of my days. Only secluded was I no longer a danger to everyone I loved.

But even riding could not erase the images from my head.

Yudhajit, eyes staring at the top of the tent, unmoving.

Shatrugna, knocked to the floor by his own brother.

Bharata, tears streaking down his face.

Lakshmana, pale with fever.

Sita, sleepless shadows under her eyes.

Rama, just after I had slapped him all those years ago.

Everyone I cared for, I hurt. Every time I tried to help, I made things worse. Why had I bothered to seek out Yudhajit? There had been a moment, lying in bed, when I had thought to stay in Ayodhya. By going, all I had done was to make his final moments more worried, more frenzied. Perhaps without the distraction of my presence, Yudhajit would have been able to fight back more effectively. He was the better, more experienced warrior. It must have been me who killed him.

After only a few hours of riding, my body was close to giving out. My limbs ached, my throat burned with every breath, and I struggled to keep my eyes open. But out here on the road, if I stopped, I might never start going again. That was too easy for me. I needed to suffer for what I had done. I stayed slumped over on my horse, but it kept moving, until I saw through my half-closed eyes a collection of dilapidated huts that looked the way I felt.

The horse halted in the dusty center of the group, and I sat there, my fingers still clutching the reins. I did not move, even as several women came to see who I was. They murmured among themselves, and I expected them to leave me or drive me away. Instead, one reached up and pried my fingers off the reins, then helped me down. My knees buckled when my feet met the ground, and I felt an arm wrap around my waist, holding me up.

"What are you doing?" I asked, my words coming out slurred.

"She needs water," someone said. "And a meal."

Hands guided me to a stone seat, and someone pressed a ladle of water into my hand. I drank it, the coolness jolting me awake, as another woman handed me a bowl of rice.

"I cannot pay," I explained, ashamed, and the woman laughed.

"Radnyi Kaikeyi, it is an honor." I wondered how they knew who I was, but did not care enough to ask.

"Thank you," I mumbled.

"I came to the Women's Council once," the woman who had helped me from my horse said as I ate. "My husband was dead, and I had no family, and the men of the village thought I brought misfortune. The other women managed to send me to the city to see you, and you gave me several chickens to make my own living with. You wrote me a letter saying my work and person should be respected. It changed my life."

"I am glad to hear it," I said, although her words were barely reaching me. I shoveled the rice and lentils into my mouth, the food giving me new energy. "This is delicious, thank you."

"The men are all gone to war," another woman said. "We have room, so surely you can stay a night?"

"Yes, Radnyi, it would be no trouble to give you a place to stay before you ride for the city."

I shook my head. "I must keep going. I need to reach Ayodhya as soon as possible." The women all nodded, solemn, as though they believed I had some greater purpose. I could have laughed at the irony—for once in my life, I was trying to escape to dullness—but I could not muster the will.

"Take this," one of the women said, handing me several mangoes.

Another woman gave me some hard biscuits, and a third passed me dried sweets. Soon I had enough food to last me several days' travels. "You need this more than I," I argued. A bit of my old passion rose up in me. "Please, do not be offended, but I could not possibly do this to you."

An older woman shook her head. "It would be an honor to know that we helped you. It is the least we can do," she said. "Safe travels."

As I rode away, I pondered the strange reception. They had given me what little they had, knowing full well what I had done to the kingdom. The story of Rama's exile would have reached them some time ago. Perhaps they had not realized how disfavored I was and feared for their lives if they did not show deference. Yes, that was it.

By nightfall, any concerns over their treatment of me had faded as I stared up at the sky. I did not deserve Nidra's blessing and the peace of mind that came with it. Instead, I fought to keep my eyes open, and when they closed, I watched Yudhajit die behind my lids again and again. This was my legacy.

At last I reached Ayodhya.

I left the horse at the stable door and took the familiar route up to my rooms. As I climbed the steps to the women's quarters, something dripped onto my hands. I looked up, bemused. Was it raining?

Only then did I feel the coolness against my cheeks and realize that I was crying. By the time I reached my rooms I was weeping, the first true tears I had cried for my brother. I did not understand what had sparked this, only that in my chest I could feel the deep hole his presence had left.

Somehow, word of my arrival at the stables must have gotten to Manthara before I did, because she was already pouring water into a tub for a warm bath. I kept weeping as I stepped into it, and she scrubbed my hair as though I was a small child. The story came out of me in fits and starts, and she murmured soft reassurances to me. "It is not your fault. Hush. It is not your fault."

But I knew better.

I spent the next day entirely in my bed. Asha brought me warm broth, and I drank it to make her feel better, for her worry was rolling off her in waves. Being back in Ayodhya reminded me only of my greater failures. I had failed the people of my kingdom, failed the women who would no longer be protected and the men who would die in pointless wars. I slept lightly on and off, my dreams the same as my waking thoughts, before slipping into a longer tortured rest.

The next morning, I awoke to rough hands pulling me out of bed. I did not struggle—perhaps they were soldiers, coming to execute me—but when I pried open my eyes it was just Manthara. She handed me a rough cotton sari, which I put on to avoid further argument. I had a strange sense that this had happened before, but could not place it. Once I had worn it, she grabbed me by the wrist and dragged me through the palace, out the servants' gate, and into the streets of Ayodhya. She should not have had enough vigor in her aged body to pull me, but I could not bring myself to resist.

I kept my eyes on the ground, focusing on putting one foot

in front of the other. When Manthara at last stopped, I fell into her, then righted myself, eyes still downcast. She placed two fingers under my chin and tipped my face up, forcing me to look at—

Ayodhya's marketplace. I had not set foot here in over a year. At first, I could hardly take in the intensity of the sights, my eyes unfocused and watering in the bright sunlight.

But after a moment, my gaze fixed on one thing: a woman nearby, selling pots, haggling with a buyer.

"Watch, Kaikeyi," Manthara whispered. "Just watch."

And so I watched, even though the sight was a familiar one on the streets of Ayodhya. Something about it touched my heart, dampening the unshakable pain.

But then the relief passed, and I tore myself from Manthara's grip, shuffling back to the palace in shame.

That night I lay awake in bed, unable to get the pot seller out of my mind. Her firm posture, her smile—she was not unhappy or angry because her yuvraja was gone and the soldiers had marched out. She was earning her livelihood, and glad of it.

The next morning, Manthara, without asking, took me back to the market. Part of me felt like I did not deserve to see such things, but a larger part of me longed for that singular moment of peace again.

This time, my eyes were drawn to a group of girls, thick black braids down their backs, sitting alongside boys in the open-air market school under the shrine. An elderly man stood before them, pointing at one then the other to recite sums. One of the girls mouthed the answer to every question, confident in her abilities. Instead of averting my eyes, I watched greedily. They switched from sums to religious studies, something that women had once been forbidden from practicing. But still the girls sat there, learning the lessons.

Part of me expected one of Rama's men to come running,

to stop them, to shout that I was a monster and so was all I touched. Nobody seemed to care. Rama had said that my influence on Ayodhya was poison, and after all that transpired, I had believed it. But this was not poison. It was a child, freer than her mother had been.

Each day for the next week, as Kosala's army made its slow march back to Ayodhya, I went out and watched the women. On one memorable occasion, I saw a man slouch toward a woman shopkeeper's stall and ask her something. She drew herself up, angry, and I approached them to better hear.

"You spent that money already?" she demanded. "I will not give you more."

"I allow you to work here because I am generous," the man said. "You owe me what you have earned." My heart immediately jumped to my throat. What would this husband do to a wife who disobeyed him?

But the woman was not afraid. "I work here because you are lazy," the woman shouted back. Other women were drifting toward the scene.

"Give me just a few coins," the man said, and I realized he was begging her.

"Why?" the woman asked. "Where do you keep spending my hard-earned money?"

"Reena said she saw your husband enter one of the night-houses," one of the watching women called out.

The woman gaped at her husband. "Is this true?"

He spun around and glared at the other woman. "What was Reena doing there?" he demanded.

"So it's true, you do not deny it!" his wife shouted. "You ought to pay me back, you useless man. Do not think I will ever let you touch me again!" I could not help the smile that broke out across my face, although I tried to hide it behind a hand.

"You are my wife," the man said, but I could tell the fight was going out of him. "You will do as I say."

"You are a lazy good-for-nothing," one of the women watching heckled. "Stop bothering her."

One by one, the other women joined in, until the whole marketplace was giving this man his due. Even men were raising their voices.

The fact that the sages, that Sage Vamadeva, and therefore Rama, had cared at all about moments such as this seemed suddenly so absurd, I could not contain myself. I laughed so hard I felt I could not breathe. And the other women were laughing too. I was just one voice in the chorus.

This was a changed Kosala. I had not prevented Yudhajit's death. I had caused my family great pain. But there were others besides the gods and the godsforsaken. Their paths were not set. And it seemed possible—no, with each passing day it seemed certain—that perhaps I had been able to change something after all.

I returned, day after day. I lurked near lessons, wandered among stalls, and even snuck my way into the treasury, watching young women my sisters and I had sent there sorting coins. I drank in every sight greedily. I was a desert wanderer who had happened at last upon an oasis.

I could not help these women anymore, but I did not need to. Now they helped me.

"Has this one caught your eye?" one woman asked me when I stared at the small clay horse displayed among her various dolls.

"My son had one like this," I said. "When he was young."

She gave me a smile. "My husband made my children toys like this when they were young too. When they got older, we decided to make them for others."

"Do you like the work?" I asked, hungry to hear more of her story.

"Yes. He is a skilled craftsman, but if he tried to sell them, we would never sell a single ware. I love talking to people, and now our daughter has an excellent dowry."

My heart was so full I thought I might cry, an absurd reaction to some children's toys. Instead, I bought the horse. I walked slowly back up the path to the palace, feeling for the first time in a long time that moving forward was not an impossible effort.

The door was open when I reached my room, and I entered warily, wondering if some servant had left it open or something worse was afoot.

"Ma," Bharata said from inside. I startled. I had not thought to hear my son's voice again. He sounded choked. "I'm glad you are here. I worried when we couldn't find you, but eventually we received word from the palace and I came as fast as I—" He took a deep breath, slowing the torrent of confusing words. "Can I speak with you?"

I stepped inside and closed the door. Bharata stood differently, his shoulders back and his posture confident. There was something in his bearing of his father, and of his uncle, even though the two men had looked nothing alike. I did not know what to say, and the lump in my throat grew painful.

"I am going to take the throne, Ma," Bharata said after several moments of silence. "I know it may sound sudden after my insistence I would not, but I've realized the folly in what I did. Kosala needs peace, and stability. It needs what Father brought to the kingdom, with you by his side. I am so sorry it took this... Uncle's... this tragedy for me to realize that." He took another steadying breath. "But I am here, and I will listen to you now."

I could not understand his words. I took two unsteady steps to a stool and sat down, the toy dangling from my numb fingers. Bharata's eyes alighted on the little horse. "I had something like that, didn't I? When I was young?" I nodded numbly. The reminder of who he had once been forced me to confront that this was real. I was not imagining this, and he was not making some terrible joke. He was standing before me saying these words with purpose.

I had assumed Rama's control would be with him forever. But now, in the colorless world of the Plane, I found no trace of that bright blue. *Could it be?*

"Rama had one of these too," I said. But no blue bond appeared. Bharata had somehow freed himself, all on his own. My heart stretched, beating fast, bursting with pride. But my head ached too, for if Bharata had only decided this a fortnight ago, my brother would still be alive. And yet it had taken my brother's death for Bharata to realize his folly.

My thoughts circled in this way, until Bharata asked, uncertainly, "Ma?"

I shook myself from my stupor and found myself smiling, despite everything. The women of Kosala were strong. I could be too. "Do you really mean that?" I asked.

Bharata ducked his head. Gone was my mischievous, troublemaking child, and in his place was a young man who stood on his own. "I have said some horrible things to you. Things you did not deserve. I am ashamed, and I hope that one day you can forgive me. It was like I was a different person. But watching Uncle Yudhajit die, something in me just snapped."

I remembered then what he had done. "Is Shatrugna—"

"The healers say Shatrugna will recover, but I hurt him badly."

I wanted to tell him, *You did the right thing*, but what I really meant was that half of me wanted Shatrugna to pay the ultimate price for what he had done and part of me couldn't bear to see him hurt at all, and in the end, Bharata's punishment seemed just. "And all of a sudden you have realized the error of your ways?" I asked, trying to infuse some kindness into the harsh words.

"Yes. I am so sorry." The Binding Plane pulsed with the sincerity of his words.

By never using the Binding Plane around my sons, I had missed the signs of Rama's godhood. That mistake had cost me Rama. Lakshmana had been taken from me too. In every step, trying to protect my children, I had failed them. But now, in the Binding Plane, I had one son back. My throat swelled with the knowledge that Bharata was really here, talking to me. He loved me. "I regret what I did. I know you may never forgive me, but—"

"Of course I forgive you," I interrupted.

"How—"

"I am your mother," I said simply. "All I ever want is what is best for you and the kingdom. It seemed that you were the one unwilling to forgive me for what I had done. But I did it to protect you, to protect us all."

"You wanted to avoid this," Bharata said softly.

"Yes."

"I know I can't fix what has happened. But I want to be the ruler you meant for me to be. I have been up all night thinking, preparing. In a few days' time, we will perform the rites to bless my reign, for I want to take all the correct steps. The gods have not smiled on Kosala for some time now."

I did not dispute that at all. Kosala had become a pawn of the gods. But now, I thought the gods might leave us alone, busy following Rama's adventures instead. And that would be far better than their blessing. "That is a good idea," I said. "I did not think anything would change your mind."

"I should have listened to you," Bharata said again. "It was a mistake not to before, but I am going to fix that. I am going to fix the rift in our kingdom. And I cannot do it without you. Will you help me?"

In front of me stretched the years of Bharata's reign. The people of Kosala, standing together, powerful and safe. Their paths forever altered, stretching toward a future of peace. I could even advise Bharata, but that power mattered little to me. Kaushalya could do it just as well. What truly warmed my heart was the idea that if I spoke, Bharata would listen to me.

I would have my people back. I could not help Rama, I could not even stop him, but I could do this. I could have this. "Of course," I said. "Whatever you need."

Bharata smiled then, tired but genuine, and leaned in to embrace me. Everything else faded away as I held my child in my arms. "Everything will be better now," he said in my ear, and I believed him. "I promise I will make you proud."

EPILOGUE

SOME YEARS LATER, I stand alone at the banks of the Sarasvati River.

I am returning to Ayodhya after nearly three moons in Kekaya. Bharata and I traveled here together, but he departed before me to attend to his duties, while I lingered with my living brothers.

On our journey to Kekaya, he and I crossed the river without fanfare. But now, alone, something compels me to stop several paces downstream of the bridge. I remove my shoes and roll up my comfortable riding breeches to wade into the shallows. The current washes over my feet, a pleasant change from hours of riding. A refreshing breeze blows across the river, almost welcoming. Perhaps Sarasvati is watching me.

"I suppose you are right," I say. "In the end, I have always been concerned with mortal affairs. But the fact that they were mortal did not make them small. Nor did it make me wrong."

Behind me, birds chirp in the forest. The river continues down its course, unceasing.

Have I ever been happy here before? I felt alone, abandoned when I came as a child. When I crossed it for the first time as a new bride, I was devastated at the loss of my brother's friendship. But I had been hopeful then too. I stood on the banks with Rama, fear penetrating my core so deeply that I could hardly breathe. And when Bharata and I made our desperate dash to my father's bedside, my thoughts were consumed with what I left behind in Ayodhya. Even when I knew I was forsaken, even when the gods helped to tear my family apart, I wanted the comfort of her approval, and she had always disappointed.

But now I stand at the banks of the Sarasvati River, at peace without her. The years have blunted the loss of Yudhajit and Dasharath, so that it is no longer all-consuming. Yudhajit made his choices. I played a hand in his death, but it was not my fault. If not for his pride, he might have convinced his people that war was not necessary. He might have showed his sister more trust and respect.

Rama too made his own choices, to trust the voices of strangers, of a poisonous madman, over that of his mother. He sought my counsel, then discarded it when I did not say what he wished to hear. No words of mine would have made a difference.

I have heard he stands just across the ocean from Lanka, preparing for war with Ravana, Lakshmana at his side. I cannot pretend to know every detail of what has transpired between them. Ravana's missives ended shortly after he took Sita with him to Lanka. I hope she has been happy there, but I cannot honestly know—Ravana's final letters were not those of the kind man I first met, but that of a man—an asura—readying for unnecessary war.

Rama's march to the sea has taken years, and I have heard he has cleansed the world of evil in his path, has deposed false kings and installed the righteous back to power. He has, to hear it told, befriended giant vultures and won the allegiance of the monkey people. I know too how this will end: Rama will defeat Ravana and will return home victorious. His path has taken him longer than he might have wished; I doubt he will return at the end of his ten years, only a few months from now. But when he takes the throne, three or four years hence, he will be even more beloved than when he left.

And perhaps it will not be so bad. Even with Rama, change is possible. The boons have, in their own way, worked magic. For I have heard from several people that Rama on his travels found a woman made of stone, and with his divine touch freed her. The letters say this woman took Rama into her home, overgrown with plants and time, and washed his feet. That he asked her questions of her life, of how she came to be stone, and he listened to her answers. That he blessed her before he left and wished her a long and happy life.

Maybe the passage of the years has done its work, and that free of the influence of others Rama has matured into the man I always wished him to be. I must hope for it, because I have read enough scrolls to know that one day these events will be Rama's alone. The sages will tell of a righteous prince who cleansed the world of asuras, and perhaps deign to mention his heartless mother who exiled him.

A small part of me wonders if I should pray, perhaps for knowledge of Sita or Lakshmana or Rama, or perhaps simply for a blessing. Instead, I watch the sunlight reflect off the running water, bright diamonds of light that glint and fall and glint again. A brilliant blue-green fish jumps, creating small ripples in the current. No goddess emerges from the depths.

I give a slight laugh, then, for what else had I expected?

"I suppose some things never change," I say to the water.

Then I walk away, toward my horse, and my son, and my kingdom. I am at peace, for I know the truth.

Before this story was Rama's, it was mine.

ACKNOWLEDGMENTS

Kaikeyi would not exist without the work and kindness of many extraordinary people. To my rockstar agent Lucienne Diver—I cannot possibly thank you enough. I have benefitted in so many ways from your vision and guidance, and I am so grateful to have you in my corner. You are truly a constant font of wisdom. Thank you also to the team at the Knight Agency. The work you do to make things run smoothly for authors is so very appreciated.

Thank you to Priyanka Krishnan, my inimitable editor. From day one, you saw exactly what I hoped *Kaikeyi* could become and held me accountable to that vision. Because of you, *Kaikeyi* is the book I always dreamed of writing, and I am a better writer. I am also indebted to the amazing team at Redhook, including Alex Lencicki, Alexia Mazis, Angela Man, Ellen Wright, Lisa Marie Pompilio, Paola Crespo, Rachel Goldstein, SallyAnne McCartin, Stephanie Hess, and Tim Holman. I still can't believe I am going to be one of your authors.

Beyond my publishing team, there are so many others I want to thank who helped me bring *Kaikeyi* into the world. First, my Pitch Wars mentor Sarah Remy, who believed in this book before anyone else did and helped me bring the idea of *Kaikeyi* to life. Meeting you changed the entire trajectory of my writing career. And to my Pitch Wars community—Amanda,

Chandra, Emily, Gigi, Kate, Sami, Sarah, Tanvi, Victor, and so many others whom I do not have space to name—thank you for your constant support, humor, and advice. Team NDZ forever!

I am forever grateful to all my friends who allowed me to be insufferable, provided a listening ear, and read *Kaikeyi* before it was fit for human consumption. In particular, thank you to Sanika, Juveria, Jamie, and Dan. Thank you also to my law school pod—it's because of you I made it through the trial that was the 2020–21 school year.

Lastly, I owe a huge thank you to my family. I would be nowhere without their unwavering support. My mom, who has been my sounding board from the start and has been endlessly patient as I embarked on this journey. My dad, who sent me encouraging texts to wake up to when I was overwhelmed. My grandmother, whose incredible storytelling ability and dedication to passing down these myths inspired *Kaikeyi*. Aditya and Sona Mavshi, for your constant love and encouragement. Rucha, for the notebook and creativity that started me writing all those years ago. James, there are no words to describe the impact you have had, but suffice to say *Kaikeyi* would not exist without your kindness and selflessness.

And Ananya, the best sister a girl could ask for. I owe you much more than a few lines in the acknowledgments. I am a published author because of you. Your loyalty and generosity have not gone unnoticed. You have made me a better person. I love you.

MEET THE AUTHOR

Vaishnavi Patel is a lawyer specializing in civil rights. She likes to write at the intersection of Indian myth, feminism, and anti-colonialism. She grew up in and around Chicago and, in her spare time, enjoys activities that are almost stereotypically Midwestern: knitting, ice-skating, drinking hot chocolate, and making hotdish. *Kaikeyi* is her debut novel.

READING GROUP GUIDE

1. *Kaikeyi* is a reimagining based on the epic the *Ramayana*. Were you familiar with the original story before reading? If so, how did that impact your response to Kaikeyi's character and journey in this book? If not, did *Kaikeyi* spark your interest in learning more about the *Ramayana*?

2. In the original epic, Kaikeyi is often considered a villainous character. Does this version of the story make it clear why? Is she to blame for the way certain tragic events unfold?

3. The original epic also vilifies Manthara as a poisonous servant, because it is only at her urging that Kaikeyi chooses to use her boons as she does. What did you think of the way the author portrayed the relationship between Kaikeyi and Manthara here?

4. How did Kaikeyi's relationship with the gods impact her relationship with her son Rama? Was she correct in her judgment of what was best for the kingdom and in the actions she took to try to stay the course?

5. While Kaikeyi has many strong and loving relationships, she does not experience romantic love or sexual attraction in the story. Does this impact Kaikeyi's decisions—and the way she views the decisions of others around her—in any way?

6. Kaikeyi's access to the Binding Plane is more personal—and potentially more manipulative—than many other forms of power in this book. What does Kaikeyi's use of this power say about her? About other characters who wield similar abilities?

7. Kaikeyi is constantly aware of the power imbalances between women and men but doesn't often question the imbalances where she may be in command (for example, the imbalance between nobility and commoners). What does this say about Kaikeyi's character? Does it put any of her actions in a new light?

8. Every character in *Kaikeyi* has their own view on the role of women in society—and in fact, some of the most powerful men are the most egalitarian. And yet the society itself remains divided by rigid gender rules. Why might this be?

9. One of Kaikeyi's goals is to push back against patriarchy (even if she doesn't name it as such). What are the different ways in which patriarchal ideals are shared and adopted in the story?

10. The gods in the story seem to have very different concerns and views from those that the humans believe them to have. What does this difference say about humanity?

11. The book portrays several different types of female friendships and relationships—among mothers and daughters,

friends, and sister-wives. Do these ring true to the times of the book? How do they subvert or conform to stereotypes about women?

12. How does the novel comment on the role of women in mythology and folklore? Do you think asking "what if" about the characters who exist in the margins is a useful means by which to interrogate and expand our understanding of how stories impact and shape our lives (and vice versa)?

13. Were you satisfied with the way Kaikeyi's story ended?

A Q&A WITH VAISHNAVI PATEL

Kaikeyi *was inspired by the* **Ramayana.** *Can you tell readers unfamiliar with the* **Ramayana** *a little of what it's about?*

The *Ramayana* is an ancient epic. It tells the story of Rama, who is the Hindu god Vishnu reincarnated as the prince of a great kingdom. Just as he is about to be crowned king, Rama is banished from his home by his stepmother and sets off on a fourteen-year exile, accompanied by his wife, Sita, and his brother Lakshmana. From there, the *Ramayana* follows the kidnapping of Sita by a demon king, Ravana, and the war Rama wages to save her. Ultimately, he defeats Ravana in a great battle and returns to his kingdom, triumphant, to take his place on the throne.

In the epic, Kaikeyi has a small role. She's the stepmother who exiles Rama, sparking the entire journey that follows.

How does **Kaikeyi** *reimagine the events of the epic?*

There are three major plot points in the *Ramayana* that concern Kaikeyi: First, upon her marriage to Dasharath, Dasharath promises her father that Kaikeyi's son will become king. Then after her marriage, she saves her husband's life in battle and is granted two boons by him. And many years later, she exiles Rama using those same boons so that her own son will be king.

All these plot points from the *Ramayana* appear in *Kaikeyi*, but the novel takes these and expands on her story, filling in the gaps and giving Kaikeyi an inner life—motivations and desires and relationships—so we can understand why she takes the extreme actions that she does. There are also events in the novel that are inspired by stories from the *Ramayana* but modified for *Kaikeyi*—for example, the story of Ahalya is in both the *Ramayana* and *Kaikeyi*, but it plays a very different role in my novel.

Of course, there are some plot elements that are changed from the *Ramayana*, but the arc of the epic remains the same. *Kaikeyi* ends before Sita's kidnapping, so it doesn't cover much of what would usually be considered the major parts of the *Ramayana*. But I have tried to include important elements from later in the *Ramayana* in *Kaikeyi*, either by reference or by using the characters in other roles, so I hope the story will still be satisfying to readers who know the *Ramayana*!

Is Kaikeyi *a standalone novel or the first book in a series?*

Kaikeyi is a standalone. I wanted to tell Kaikeyi's story from childhood until her major actions in the *Ramayana*. The *Ramayana* itself is a sprawling epic with thousands and thousands of verses, and I didn't want to retread its ground. By focusing on one person and one specific set of events within that person's life, I've kept *Kaikeyi* more cabined. I almost think of it as hearkening back to oral tradition, where you might hear a tale that fits into a larger epic tapestry but is also complete in itself.

Is *there anything that people interested in* Kaikeyi *should know about the story or the character?*

This answer isn't necessarily for every single reader. But for South Asian or Hindu readers who are doubtful about picking up this book because of who it focuses on, I want to reassure you that I love the original *Ramayana* and am not trying to disrespect it. While *Kaikeyi* feels different from the *Ramayana*, the critiques in it are meant to make us think about what messages these religious stories are sending so that we can more consciously consume these myths. *Kaikeyi* comes from a place of love for this story and for my culture.

People who've read Kaikeyi *have compared it to Madeline Miller's* Circe, *a retelling of the* Odyssey; *Jennifer Saint's* Ariadne, *which reworks the myth of Theseus and the Minotaur; and Genevieve Gornichec's* The Witch's Heart, *a reimagining of the life of Angrboda from Norse mythology. How do you feel* Kaikeyi *compares to them?*

First, I love all three of these books and I'm still so excited that *Kaikeyi* is being compared to them! *Kaikeyi* has similarities to these novels in that they all take a mythic woman who has not always been looked upon kindly and retell the story from her perspective. I am honored every time somebody compares my book to *Circe* or *Ariadne* or *The Witch's Heart* because I think they're all fantastic. If I can be half the writer that any of those authors are, then I'll have succeeded with *Kaikeyi*.

But I do also think that *Kaikeyi* is different from other popular retellings in some ways, because it is reinterpreting a story from a religion that's still very widely practiced and has great modern weight. The *Ramayana* is an important part of Hinduism, so *Kaikeyi* is set in what many people believe to be our past. As a Hindu, I'm not sure that I can definitively say that these events occurred—certainly I don't think they happened exactly the way they are told in the verses of the *Ramayana*—but I do think the stories are based at least in part on historical figures and kingdoms. And the critiques that the book touches on are grounded in present-day interpretation and belief and trying to navigate current religious waters.

What writers and stories do you think had a big influence on Kaikeyi (in addition to the Ramayana)?

I was influenced by all the Hindu myths I grew up with, because that cultural environment shaped my approach to this story. I read all the Amar Chitra Katha comics (a series that offers abridged versions of mythic tales and folklore) as a kid, and I watched some animated *Ramayana* shows, so I'm sure that's swimming around in my subconscious. Adaptations of the *Ramayana* in live and animated screen media are almost ubiquitous in India!

Also, I have to give thanks to the modern fantasy authors Roshani Chokshi and Tasha Suri, who inspired me to write unapologetically South Asian stories and proved that there was a desire and market for that.

if you enjoyed
KAIKEYI

look out for

ITHACA

by

Claire North

From the multi-award-winning author Claire North comes a daring reimagining that breathes new life into ancient myth. Beyond Ithaca's shores, the whims of gods dictate the wars of men. But on the isle, it is the choices of the abandoned women—and their goddesses—that will change the course of the world.

Seventeen years ago, King Odysseus sailed to war with Troy, taking with him every man of fighting age from the island of Ithaca. None of them has returned, and the women of Ithaca have been left behind to run the kingdom.

Penelope was barely into womanhood when she wed Odysseus. While he lived, her position was secure. But now, years on, speculation is mounting that her husband is dead, and suitors are beginning to knock at her door.

No one man is strong enough to claim Odysseus's empty throne—not yet. But as everyone waits for the balance of power to tip, Penelope knows that any choice she makes could plunge Ithaca into bloody civil war. Only through cunning, wit, and her trusted circle of maids can she maintain the tenuous peace needed for the kingdom to survive.

CHAPTER 1

TEODORA IS NOT THE first to see the raiders, but she is the first to run.

They come from the north, by the light of the full moon. They do not burn any lanterns on their decks, but skim across the ocean like tears down a mirror. There are three ships, carrying some thirty men apiece, coils of rope set by the prow to bind their slaves; oars barely tugging the sea as the wind carries them to shore. They give no cries of war, beat no drums nor blow trumpets of brass or bone. Their sails are plain and patched, and had I power over the stars I would have willed them shine a little brighter, that the heavens might be eclipsed by the darkness of the ships as they obstructed the horizon. But the stars are not my domain, nor do I usually pay much attention to the dealings of little people in their sleepy villages by the sea, save when there is some great matter afoot that might be turned by a wily hand – or when my husband has strayed too far from home.

It is therefore without celestial intervention that Teodora, lips inclining towards those of her may-be lover, thinks she catches sight of something strange upon the sea. The few fisherwomen who ride the night are all known to her and their prows are nothing like the shapes she glimpses in the corner of her eye. Then Dares – a young fool, certainly more foolish than she – catches her by her chin and pulls her deeper into his embrace, hand fumbling somewhat impertinently for her breast, and she has other things on her mind.

Above the village, a torch gutters upon the cliffs. It has been only briefly raised, a guide in the night to show these raiders where to go. Now its work is done, and the figure who has held it retreats down the hard stone path towards the inland slumber of the isle, feeling no compunction to stay and witness his work. It would be fair of this fellow to think himself unseen, save by his allies – the hour is late and the hot day had faded to a cool, slumbering dark, suitable for vast snoring and dreamless sleep. How little he knows.

In a cave above the shore, a queen in rags and dirt looks out onto the night, the blood still sticky on her hands, and sees the raiders come, but does not think they come for her. So she does not call out to the village below, but cries for her lover, who is dead.

In the east, a king rolls restlessly in the arms of Calypso, who hushes him and says, it is just a dream, my love. Everything beyond these shores is just a dream.

To the south, another fleet with black sails sits becalmed, the rowers asleep beneath the patient sky, while a princess caresses her brother's sweating brow.

And on the beach, Teodora is beginning to suspect that Dares may not be entirely pure in his attentions, and that they should really start talking of marriage if this is the way things are going to go. She pushes him away with both her palms, but he holds her tight. In the brief shuffling of their feet on bony white sand, his eyes turn up and he at last sees the ships, sees their course for this little cove, and with a sluggish wit he declares: "Uh . . . ?"

Dares' mother owns a grove of olive trees, two slaves and a cow. In the eyes of the sages of the island, these things are in fact owned by Dares' father – but he never came home from Troy, and as the years ticked down and Dares grew from whelp to man, even the most pedantic elders stopped labouring the point. One day, shortly after his fifteenth birthday, Dares turned to his mother and mused: "It's a good thing for you I let you hang around," and in that moment her hope died, though he was a monster of her own making. He can fish, not well, dreams of turning pirate, and has not yet tasted hunger in the winter.

Teodora's father was sixteen when he wed her mother; seventeen when he went to Troy. He left behind his bow, being a weapon for cowards, a few pots and a shawl his mother made. Last winter Teodora killed a lynx that was as hungry as her, the knife with which she would otherwise gut fish driven into its snapping jaw, and has few qualms about making snap decisions when death is on the line.

"Raiders!" she shouts, first to Dares, who hasn't yet released her from his embrace, and when he finally does, to the village above and the slumbering night, running towards the low mud of hut and home as if she could catch the echo of her own voice. "Raiders! Raiders are coming!"

It is well known that when a grieving wife looks to the sea for the ship of her husband and glimpses a sail threaded with gold, time will slow its pounding chariot to a crawl, and every minute of the ship's return is an hour pricked out in sweating agony. Yet when pirates come to your shore, it is as if their vessels grow Hermes' wings and leap, leap across the water, now rounding the hard pillars of stone where the crabs scuttle sideways, black-eyed and orange-backed, now driven by the relentless oars prow-first up the soft lip of the sand. Now men leap from the decks of the beaching ships; now they have axes in hand and carry crude shields of battered bronze and animal hide, their faces painted in pigment and ash. Now they charge from the water's edge, not as soldiers do, but as wolves, splitting and circling their prey, howling, teeth bared silver in the moon's gentle light.

Teodora has reached the village before them. Phenera is a place of little square houses set above the thin stream that carves its passage between two cliffs of blackened stone to run giddy into the cove. When it rains too hard in winter, the mud walls slop and flop away, and the roofs are constantly a-mending. Here they dry fish and pick at mussels, tend to goats and gossip about their neighbours. Their shrine is to Poseidon, who protects the thin-hulled boats they push into the bay and who, if I know anything about the old fart, doesn't care a whelp for the meagre offerings of grain and wine they spill upon his altar.

That at least is the picture that Phenera wishes the eye to behold; but look a little closer and you may find trinkets that shine beneath the rough wooden floors, and many a finger that is skilled at more than just fixing a net to catch fish in.

"Raiders! Raiders!" Teodora howls, and slowly a few dusty cloths are pulled back from the crooked doors, a few eyes blink into the shallow dark and shouts begin to rise in alarm. Then voices older and a little more respected sound as other eyes behold the men rushing upon their shores, and hands reach to gather their most precious goods, and like ants from the boiling nest, the people flee.

Too late.

Too late, for so many – too late.

Their only blessing is that these men of snarling lip and beating shield do not want to kill the youngest and the strongest. It is enough to scare them into cowering submission, to beat them and bind them with rope to take to some place to sell. The two slaves kept in Dares' house look upon their new captors with weary eyes, for they have been through all this before, when they were first taken by the bold men of Ithaca. Their wretched despair at finding themselves encircled by blade and shield is a bit of a let-down for their attackers, who expected at the least some abject grovelling, but the whole atmosphere is somewhat redeemed when the masters and mistresses of Phenera wail and weep. They are reduced now to the level of those they had mastered, and their former slaves tut and say just do as we do, just say what we say, you will learn – you will learn.

Teodora stops to gather only one precious thing – the bow she keeps for killing rabbits. Nothing more. She has nothing so precious as her life, and so she runs, runs, runs for the hills, runs like Atalanta reborn, grabbing the branch of the thin-trunked dying tree that juts out from a promontory to pull herself up; climbing over stone and under leaf to the chittering black while below her home starts to burn. She hears footsteps behind her, the drumming of heavy weight upon the scrubby path, glances over her shoulder, sees torchlight and shadow, near stumbles on a treacherous root in her path, and is caught before she can fall. Hands grasp, old eyes stare, blink, a finger to the lips. Teodora is pulled quickly from her path into darkness, into thicket-leaf shadow, where hunkers a woman with hair like autumn clouds, skin like summer sand, an axe in her hand, a hunting knife on her belt. She could with such implements perhaps fight back; perhaps slam her blade into the throat of the man who pursues them, but what use would that be? None, tonight. None at all. So instead they hide, wrapped in each other's eyes, their gazes screaming *quiet, quiet, quiet!* Until at last the footsteps of their pursuer fade away.

The old woman who holds Teodora in safety is called Semele, and she prays to Artemis, who does not deserve her devotions.

In the village below, Dares is less sensible. He was raised on stories of the warrior men of Odysseus, and like all boys has learnt something of the spear and the blade. As the straw rooftops begin to burn, he retrieves his sword from beneath the cot of his mother's house, steps four paces from his smoking door, gripping the hilt with both hands, sees an Illyrian dressed in flame and blood approach, takes up his stance, and actually manages to parry the first blow that comes for him. This surprises everyone, including Dares, and at the next thrust he turns his body and manages to smack his blade down so hard on the end of the short stabbing spear that the wood cracks and splinters. However, his delight at this development doesn't last long, for his killer draws a short sword from his belt, turns in the direction of Dares' next attack, comes under his guard, and splits him clean across the belly.

I will say this for the pirate – he had the courtesy to drive his blade through Dares' heart, rather than simply leave him to die. The boy hadn't earned such a clean death, but neither, I suppose, had he lived long enough to deserve the one that came for him.

CHAPTER 2

ROSY-FINGERED DAWN CRAWLED ITS way across Ithaca's back like an awkward lover fumbling at long skirts. The
light of day should have been as crimson as the blood in the sea
below Phenera; it should have circled the island like the sharks.
Look towards the horizon, and even the eyes of the gods strain
a little to see three sails disappearing into the east, with their
stolen cargo of animals, grains and slaves. They will be gone,
long gone, before the ships of Ithaca raise their sails.

Let us speak briefly of Ithaca.

It is a thoroughly backwards, wretched place. The golden
touch of my footstep upon its meagre soil; the caress of my
voice in the ears of its salt-scarred mothers – Ithaca does not
deserve such divine attentions. But then again, its barren misery leads the other gods to rarely look upon it either, and so
it is a miserable truth that I, Hera, mother of Olympus, who
drove Heracles mad and struck vain royalty into stone – why
here at least I may sometimes work without the censure of my
kin.

Forget the songs of Apollo, or the proud declarations of
haughty Athena. Their poems only glorify themselves. Listen
to my voice: I who have been stripped of honour, of power and
of that fire that should be mine, I who have nothing to lose

that the poets have not already taken from me, only I will tell you the truth. I, who part the veil of time, will tell those stories that only the women tell. So follow me to the western isles, to the halls of Odysseus, and listen.

The island of Ithaca guards the watery mouth of Greece like an old cracked tooth, barely a scratch upon the ocean. A stout pair of even human legs might walk it in a day, if they could bear to spend so much time staggering through grubby forest of skulking trees that seem to grow only so far as the laziest necessity for grim survival, or over scrambling rocks of jutting stone that protrude from the earth like the fingers of the dead. Indeed, the island is remarkable only in that some fool thought it an apt locale upon which to attempt to build what the uncouth locals consider a "city" – if a scraggy hillside of crooked houses clinging to the harsh sea may be considered worthy of the name – and above this city, a so-called "palace".

From this termite hall the kings of Ithaca send forth their commands across the western isles, all of which are far more pleasant than this wretched rock. Yet though the people of Hyrie, Paxi, Lefkada, Kephalonia, Kythira and Zakynthos who live beneath Ithaca's dominion may grow olives and grapes upon their shores, may eat rich barley and even rear the occasional cow, all the peoples of this little dominion are as ultimately uncouth as each other, varying only in their flawed pretensions. Neither the great princes of Mycenae or Sparta, Athens or Corinth, nor the poets who travel door to door have much cause to speak of Ithaca and her isles save as the butt of a joke about goats – until recently, that is. Until Odysseus.

Let us therefore to Ithaca go, in that warm late summer when the leaves begin to crinkle and the ocean clouds tumble in too mighty to be bothered by the little land below. It is the morning after full moon, and in the city beneath the palace of Odysseus, some few hours away by bare foot on hard soil, the first prayers are being sung in the temple of Athena.

It is a crooked wooden thing, squat as if frightened of being blown apart in the storm, but with some notable pieces of pillaged gold and silver that only rustics would find magnificent. I avoid passing even a place so dull, lest my stepdaughter show her smug, preening face, or worse, whisper to my husband that she saw me afoot in the world of men. Athena is a priggish little madam; let us move by her shrine in haste.

There is a market that runs from the docks all the way to the gates of the palace. Here you may trade timber, stone, hides, goats, sheep, pigs, ducks – even the occasional horse or cow – beads, bronze, brass, amber, silver, tin, rope, clay, flax, dye and pigment, hides of animals both common and rare, fruit, vegetables and of course – fish. So much fish. The western isles, every one of them, stink of fish. When I return to Olympus, I will have to bathe in ambrosia to wash the stench away, before some gossipy little nymph catches the whiff of me.

There are many houses, ranging from the humble homes of the craftsmen who can barely keep a slave to the grander courtyard sprawls of the great men who would rather be across the water in Kephalonia, where the hunting is better and, if you go inland, you might lose the smell of fish for a few minutes to catch instead the whiff of dung – change being a relief of its kind. There are two smiths, who after many years of rivalry finally realised they were better fixing prices together than competing apart. There is a tannery, and a place that was once a brothel but which was forced to take up the weaving and dyeing of clothes when a large part of its clientele set sail for war, and as no ships have returned from Troy carrying victorious Ithacans, they continue weaving and dyeing to this day.

It has been nearly eighteen years since the manhood of Ithaca sailed to Troy, and even the many ships passing through port since that city fell have not been enough for whoring to be better economics than mastery of a nice bit of dye.

Above it all: the palace of Odysseus. It was the palace of

Laertes for a while, and I have no doubt the old man wanted it to remain known by that glorious name, his legacy carved into stone – an Argonaut, no less, a man who once sailed, under my banner, to fetch the golden fleece, before that little shit Jason betrayed me. But Laertes grew old before all the men of Greece were summoned to Troy. Thus the son eclipsed the father, new daubs of black and red smeared across the corridors, wide-eyed and ochre-tinged. Odysseus and his bow. Odysseus in battle. Odysseus winning the armour of fallen Achilles. Odysseus with calves of an ox and Atlas's shoulders. In the eighteen years since the king of Ithaca was last sighted on this isle, his somewhat short, unimpressive and far too hairy form has grown in stature and personal hygiene, if only in the poet's eye.

The poets will tell you a lot about the heroes of Troy. Some details they have correct; in others, as with all things, they lie. They lie to please their masters. They lie without knowing what they do, for it is the poet's art to make every ear that hears the ancient songs think they have been sung for them alone, the old made new. Whereas I sing for no creature's pleasure but my own, and can attest that what you think you know of the last heroes of Greece, you do not know at all.

Follow me through the halls of the palace of Odysseus; follow to hear the stories that the men-poets of the greedy kings do not tell.